FREEDOM'S CHALLENGE

"Another rousing episode . . . The action is fast paced and riveting, and the characters are well limned and exhibit great individuality. McCaffrey continues to amaze with her ability to create disparate, well-realized worlds and to portray believable humans, convincing aliens of varied sorts, and credible interactions between them all. A very satisfying tale."

—*Booklist*

"Rip-roaring adventure no science fiction fan could possibly resist."

—*Romantic Times*

FREEDOM'S CHOICE

"A fun adventure . . . delightfully audacious."

—*Locus*

"This episode of the Freedom saga is as exciting and convincing as the first."

—*Booklist*

"The setting is crisp and expertly detailed and the plot spins out smoothly, with more than enough hints of future developments to keep readers eager for the next installment in the series."

—*Publishers Weekly*

"McCaffrey helpfully recaps the previous book's events; overall, series fans will be delighted."

—*Kirkus Reviews*

"Ms. McCaffrey's marvelously absorbing tale features sharp, vivid characterization and a tremendously appealing plot."

—*Romantic Times*

FREEDOM'S LANDING

"Exciting and totally convincing . . . There can only be more action in the sequels McCaffrey presumably plans."
—*Booklist*

"McCaffrey has created another set of winning protagonists and a carefully detailed, exotic background."
—*Publishers Weekly*

"A brand-new series that has 'classic' written all over it."
—*Romantic Times*

"Not for nothing do her fans call the author 'the Dragon-Lady' . . . along the way she crafts a sci-fi adventure that will please followers of the genre, and of the author."
—*Dayton Daily News*

"There are enough problems and mysteries involved in establishing a colony to keep things interesting and to promise intriguing developments to come in this new series."
—*Locus*

"The narrative hits an admirable groove."
—*Kirkus Reviews*

not science fiction—fantasy

FREEDOM'S CHALLENGE

ANNE MCCAFFREY

ACE BOOKS, NEW YORK

FREEDOM'S CHALLENGE

An Ace Book / published by arrangement with
the author

PRINTING HISTORY
Ace/Putnam hardcover edition / 1998
Ace mass-market edition / June 1999

The Penguin Putnam Inc. World Wide Web site address is
http://www.penguinputnam.com

ISBN: 0-441-00625-6

ACE®
Ace Books are published
by The Berkley Publishing Group,
a division of Penguin Putnam Inc.,
375 Hudson Street, New York, New York 10014.
ACE and the "A" design are trademarks
belonging to Penguin Putnam Inc.

PRINTED IN THE UNITED STATES OF AMERICA

10 9 8 7 6 5

Don't look back in anger, I hear you say.

No longer mourn for me when I am dead
Than you shall hear the sullen surly bell
Give warning to the world that I am fled. . . .

SHAKESPEARE

Acknowledgments

I HAVE, AS USUAL, ACKNOWLEDGMENTS TO make for some of the material used in *Freedom's Challenge*.

Especially helpful was Dr. Susan Edwards, Ph.D., social cognitive psychologist, author of *Men Who Believe in Love*, who helped me with the social and trauma techniques, which have been used so successfully to help the victims of catastrophes, both personal and public (such as hostage situations), in recovering their personalities and self-confidence.

Margaret Ball, bless her heart, had all the Swahili and hunted down information about the customs and traditions of the Maasai tribes of East Africa. Fortunately, she also speaks Swahili, though I didn't have to use that much, since so many of the tribal chiefs are fluent enough in English.

I also wish to thank Georgeanne Kennedy for her careful copyediting and invaluable suggestions of what she wanted to know "more about" in this story.

What errors a spell-check, even the most advanced ones, do not catch, the sharp eye of the intelligent reader does. And I give my spell-check a lot of hard names to cope with. Thank goodness it can't complain . . . ALOUD!

Freedom's Challenge

Preface

WHEN THE CATTENI, MERCENARIES FOR A RACE called Eosi, invaded Earth, they used their standard tactic of domination by landing in fifty cities across the planet and removing entire urban populations. These they distributed through the Catteni worlds and sold them as slaves along with other conquered species.

A group rounded up from Barevi, the hub of the slave trade, were dumped on an M-type planet of unknown quality, given rations and tools and allowed to survive or not. A former marine sergeant, Chuck Mitford, took charge of the mixed group, which included sullen Turs, spider-like Deski, hairy Rugarians, vague Ilginish, gaunt Morphins, with humans in the majority. There was also one Catteni who had been shanghaied onto the prison ship. Though there were those who wanted to kill him immediately, Kris Bjornsen, lately of Denver, suggested that he might know enough about the planet to help them.

He remembered sufficient from a casual glance at the initial exploration report to suggest they move under cover, and preferably rock, to prevent being eaten by night crawlers, which oozed from the ground to ingest anything edible.

Installed in a rocky site, with cliffs and caves to give them some protection, Mitford quickly organized a camp, utilizing the specific qualities of the aliens and assigning tasks to every one in this unusual community. However, the planet was soon discovered to be inhabited—by machines, which automatically tended the crops and the six-legged bovine types. After being caught by the Mechs, Zainal, the Catteni, with his scout party, not only escape but rescue other humans trapped by the Mechs in what proves to be an abattoir.

However, human ingenuity being rampant among the mixed group, they soon learned how to dismantle the machines and design useful equipment.

Zainal, in a conversation with one of the Drassi drop captains, gets not only a supply of the drug which will keep the Deski contingent from dying of malnutrition, but also aerial maps of the planet. And discovers a command post, presumably built by the real owners of the planet. While it has obviously not been used, a mechanically inclined member of their scouting party launches a homing device.

Both the Eosi overlords looking for Zainal and the genuine owners of the planet note the release of the homing device.

The search to bring Zainal back to face the consequences of his delinquency continues. But Zainal manages to lure the searchers into the maws of the night crawlers and acquires their scout vehicle.

Meanwhile, six more drops of dissidents from Earth and a few other aliens have swelled the population of Botany, as the planet is now called, to nearly ten thousand folk: some of them with skills that benefit the colony and improve conditions. Zainal, now with a constant companion in Kris Bjornsen, and others explore this new world.

What Kris slowly discovers from her "buddy" is that Zainal wants to implement a three-phase plan: one that will end the domination of his people by the Eosi and, incidentally, bring about the liberation of Earth.

Following this agenda, Zainal explains to Mitford and other ex-naval, air force, and army personnel how he means to proceed: by capturing the next ship which drops more slaves on Botany. This plan necessitates some alteration when the next ship turns up in such poor condition that only quick action saves it from blowing up. But the captain has sent out an emergency message and looks forward to being rescued from the planet. By a clever plot, the rescue ship, which is a new one, is captured by Zainal and "other Catteni" staff, thus giving them two operational ships, plus the bridge equipment of the one they have now cannibalized for parts.

Because Zainal was dropped on Botany, his brother Lenvec has had to take his place, becoming subsumed as a host for an Eosi. The Eosi is somewhat amused by his host body's violent hatred of his brother. And soon becomes obsessed with finding the runaway.

An immense ship does a flypast of Botany and replaces the machines, which the colonists have salvaged to provide themselves with useful vehicles and equipment. At this reminder that they live on Botany on sufferance, the entire colony decides that they should show goodwill to their unknown landlords by leaving the farmed continent on which they were dropped and moving to a smaller, unused continent across a small strait. They are in the process of moving when the Mentat Ix, hosted in Lenvec's body, does a search of the planet to find the missing Catteni. Without success.

No sooner does this inspection tour end than the real owners of the planet, who accept the appellation of Farmers, arrive in unusual form. They seem able to give personal messages to all they meet: the important news is permission for the colony to remain. They also protect it with a most incredible device, a Bubble, which surrounds the entire planet while still permitting the sun's rays to filter through even as it impedes the exit of the Eosi ship. Once free of the obstacle, the Mentat orders its ship to fire on the Bubble, which has no effect on it. The impenetrable protection of this planet infuriates the Mentat who decides that the shield must be broken and the recalcitrant colony disciplined. To this end, the Mentat retires to its home world to accumulate an armada. And also to probe the minds of human specialists to see what knowledge they must possess.

The two ships owned by the colony are able to leave the protection of the Bubble, while the two Eosi satellites are on the other side of the world, and succeed in raiding Barevi for much needed fuel, supplies, and more plursaw for the Deski's diet. Kris, who had already learned enough Barevi to deal with merchants, and others accompany Zainal. While there, they learn of the plight of Humans whose minds have been wiped by the Eosian device with which they had enhanced the basic intelligence of the Catteni race. From Barevi, Zainal makes contact with dissident Emassi who are also pledged to end Eosi domination. Having found slave pens full of the mind-wiped Victims of the Eosi, the Botanists are unable to leave their compatriots to sure death in slave camps. So they contrive to take over yet another ship. Between the two, they are able to rescue several thousand Victims, irrespective of the problems this might cause the colony.

Zainal's first two phases have been successful: the planet is safe and they have ships with which to seize additional supplies. But will he be able to talk the colony into supporting his third-phase plans? And liberate not only Earth but also the Catteni from Eosi domination?

Chapter One

WHEN ZAINAL HAD ORGANIZED THE DATA
he wanted to send to the Farmers via the homing capsule,
he let Boris Slavinkovin and Dick Aarens fly it down to
the Command Post for dispatch.

"You have a nasty sense of humor, Zainal," Kris said
when the hatch of the scout vessel Baby closed behind
the messengers. She had been surprised by his choice of
Aarens, considering the man's behavior on their first visit
to the Command Post.

"Well," and Zainal gave a shrug of one shoulder and an
unrepentant grin, "Aarens has had experience sending
one off. Let him do it official this time. As a reward for
his improvement."

"What improvement?" Kris still had little time for the
self-styled mechanical genius who had deliberately
launched a homing capsule without authorization on their
first trip to the Command Post.

They both stepped back from the takeoff area, as much
to avoid the fumes as the wind, although Boris lifted the
little craft slowly and cautiously. They watched as it

made an almost soundless vertical ascent before it slanted forward and sped off, disappearing quickly in the dusk of what had been a very long and momentous day.

The wide landing field that stretched out level with the immense, Farmer-constructed hangar could accommodate a half dozen of the K-class ships that had arrived today. They now were out of sight, within the vast hangar. At the far end of the landing area grew small copses of the lodge-pole trees: young ones in terms of the age of the mature groves above and beyond the hangar. In the nearest of those groves the cabins of the colonists were being constructed, out of brick or wood, in separate clearings to allow the privacy that everyone preferred. Further up the slope were the infirmary, which today was crowded, and the huge mess hall, which served food all day long and well into the long Botany night. The largest building that faced Retreat Bay was the administration, where Judge Iri Bempechat held court when necessary, with the stocks just outside as a reminder that offenses against the community would be publicly punished. The building also held the living quarters for the judge and other members of the body known as the Council, which included those with experience in management and administration to run the affairs of the colony. In the earliest days, when Master Sergeant Charles Mitford had taken charge of the dazed and frightened First Drop colonists, he'd kept records on pieces of slate with chalk. Now the admin building posted weekly work rosters and the community services that all were required to perform. (It still shocked Kris to see Judge Iri washing dishes, and he did it more cheerfully than many.)

Ex-Admiral Ray Scott had elected to live in a small room behind his office in the hangar complex. It was he, disguised as a Catteni Drassi, who had insisted that the Victims be rescued from the fate to which the Eosi had condemned them: working until they died as mindless slaves in the appalling conditions that existed in the mines, quarries, and fields. There had been no way that those of his crew who had been among the first dropped on Botany would have allowed those battered people to be transported to their deaths.

Considering the excitements of the day, the unloading of the victims of the Eosian mind-wipe experiment, which had occupied a good third of Botany's settlers, the field was now abnormally quiet, peaceful. Kris sighed and Zainal gave her a fond look.

"ZAINAL? KRIS?" Chuck Mitford's parade ground voice reached their ears over the muted sounds that Baby was making. They looked back to the hangar and saw Chuck urgently waving to them. He was talking to someone who had just pulled up in a runabout.

"Oh, now what?" The testy demand left Kris' mouth before she could suppress it. She was tired and she earnestly desired a shower and a long sleep. She'd even arranged with the crèche to keep Zane overnight since she knew herself to be stretched to the limit after the tense voyage home and the stress of landing all the pitiful mind-wiped people.

"We'd better see," Zainal said, taking her hand in his big one and pressing it encouragingly.

"Don't you ever get tired and just . . . have too much, Zainal?" This was one of those moments when his equanimity bordered on the unforgivable.

"Yes, but it passes," he said, leading her to where Chuck Mitford waited for them with the passenger of the runabout.

It wasn't a long walk but long enough for Kris to get her irritation and impatience under control. If Zainal could hack it, so could she. But *when* would she get a shower? She stank! Well, maybe her body odor would encourage whoever this was to shorten their errand.

"What's up, sarge?" she asked, noticing that he was

talking to a woman she vaguely recognized from the Fourth Drop: as much because she managed to look elegant in the basic Catteni coverall. Kris wondered if she'd taken it in at crucial spots to make it look so fashionable. She was fleetingly envious of such expertise.

"Dorothy Dwardie who's heading the psychology team needs some of your time, and right now," Chuck said and had the grace to add, "though I'd guess another meeting's the last thing you two need right now."

"It is," Kris said without thinking but she smiled at the psychologist to take the sting out of her candor.

"It is important?" And Zainal's question was more statement than query.

"Yes, it is, quite urgent," Dorothy said with an apologetic smile. "We need to know more about that mind-probe before we can proceed with any sort of effective or therapeutic treatment."

"Why'n't you use the small office?" Chuck said, gesturing to that end of the immense hangar.

Zainal squeezed Kris' hand and murmured: "This won't take long. I know very little about the probe."

"I was hoping you'd know something, if only the history of its use among your people," Dorothy said ruefully and then looked about for a place to park the runabout.

"I'll take care of it for you," Chuck said so helpfully that Kris smothered a grin.

Dorothy Dwardie gave him a warm smile for his offer.

"We've had a bit of outrageous luck," she said as they walked to the right-hand side of the enormous hangar where other small offices had been constructed.

"We could use some," Kris agreed, struggling for amiability.

"Indeed we could, though I must say that hijacking all those poor people out from under Eosi domination is certainly *their* good luck. And you deserve a lot of credit for that act of kindness."

What she didn't say rang loud and clear to Kris. There were some who weren't sure she and Zainal deserved any credit? As well for them that Ray Scott had loudly declared that he took full responsibility for the decision to save the damaged Humans so no one could blame that on Zainal or her. Actually the guilty were the Eosi but too many people failed to make a distinction between overlord and underling. Kris' mood swung back to negative again.

"But until we . . ." and Dorothy's hand on her chest meant all the psychologists and psychiatrists on Botany who would now take charge of the mind-wiped, "understand as much as possible about the mechanism . . . ah, here we are . . ." and she opened the door to the small office and automatically fumbled for a light switch on the wall.

Kris had seen the cord and pulled it.

"Oh . . . I suppose I'll get used to it in time," Dorothy said with an apologetic grin.

"You're Fourth Drop, aren't you?" Kris replied as neutrally as possible while Zainal closed the door behind them. There were several desks against the long stone wall but a table and chairs made an appropriate conference spot by the wide window. There was nothing but darkness outside, since the hangar faced south and there were no habitations yet beyond the field. "You said you had a bit of outrageous luck. . . . ?" Kris asked when they were seated.

"Yes, not everyone in the group you brought *had* been mind-wiped."

"Certainly the Deskis, Rugs, and Turs weren't," Kris said.

"Nor all the Humans," Dorothy said, smiling over such a minor triumph.

"They weren't?" Kris asked, exchanging surprised glances with Zainal.

"Yes, some faked the vacuity of the mindless . . ."

"Faked it?"

Dorothy smiled more brightly. "Clever of them, actually, and they got away with it because those in charge weren't keeping track of who had been . . . done."

Kris let out a long whistle. "All us Human look alike to Eosi? Proves, though, doesn't it, that the Eosi aren't all that smart after all. Clever of us Humans to run the scam."

"They're also able to give us names for many of the people who no longer remember who they are." Dorothy gave a little shudder. "I've dealt with amnesia patients before, of course, and accident shock trauma, but this is on so much larger a scale . . . and complicated by not only emotional but also physical shock and injury. We have established—thanks to Leon Dane's work with injured Catteni—that there are more points of similarity than differences between our two species since both are bipedal, pentadactyl, and share many of the same external features, like eyes, ears, noses. We can't of course cross-fertilize," and to Kris' surprise, Dorothy ducked her head to hide a flush.

"As well," Kris said dryly.

Dorothy flashed her an apology and continued. "Internally, though the Catteni have larger hearts, lungs, and intestinal arrangements, Leon says that the main difference is the density of the brain matter. It's also larger though similarly organized as ours are, as far as the position of the four major lobes is concerned. Leon was amazed at what damage a Catteni skull could take without permanent injury. I think," and she paused, frowning slightly at what she did not voice, "that the initial injuries to the prisoners were attempts to recalibrate the instrument to human brains."

"Initial injuries?" Kris asked.

"Yes," and Dorothy seemed to wish to get over this

topic very quickly, "though they would have been dead before their nervous systems could register much."

"Oh?"

"Yes, and leave it at that, Kris," Dorothy went on briskly. "Will Seissmann should not dwell on the details although he seems to want to . . . a part of his trauma."

"Will Seissmann?" Kris asked.

"Yes, he and Dr. Ansible . . ."

"Dr. Ansible?" Kris shot bolt upright. "But he's—was, rather—at the observatory. Only I think he was away on some sort of a conference when the Catteni took Denver."

"Yes, he was and took refuge at Stamford," Dorothy replied, nodding. "He tried to argue others he knew to follow Will's example. I don't know whether or not the dogmatic scientist has an innate martyr complex but only a few would resort to the trick to save themselves." She broke off with a sigh. "At any rate, we are able to put names to most of the Victims. But I need to know whatever details you may have, Zainal. They will be so helpful in correcting the trauma . . . if, indeed, we can."

Zainal shook his head. "I know little about such Eosi devices." Then his expression changed into what Kris privately termed his "Catteni look," cold, impassive, shuttered. "I do know—it is part of the Catteni history—that they have a device that increases and measures intelligence."

"Oh?" Dorothy leaned forward across the table in her eagerness. "Then it could possibly extract information, too?"

Zainal blinked and his expression altered to a less forbidding one. He gave a slight smile. "It would seem likely since I only know of the one device. The Eosi used it on the primitive Catteni to make them useful as hosts."

"Really?" Dorothy's expression was intensely eager as she leaned forward, encouraging Zainal to elaborate.

"Yes, really. Roughly two thousand years ago, the Eosi discovered Catten and its inhabitants. We were little more than animals, a fact the Eosi never let us forget. About a thousand years ago, my family started keeping its records for our ancestor was one of the first hundred to have . . . his brains stimulated by the device. Each family keeps its own records—how many males it has delivered to the Eosi as hosts and details of children and matings."

"A thousand, two thousand years to develop into a space-going race? That's impressive," Dorothy said.

"Humans did it without such assistance and *that* impresses me," Zainal said with an odd laugh. "But that's how the Emassi were developed. To serve the Eosi."

"They didn't use the mind thingummy on the Drassi?" Kris asked.

"To a lesser degree," Zainal replied and turned to Dorothy. "There are three levels of Catteni now . . . Emassi," and he touched his chest, "Drassi who are good at following orders but have little initiative or ambition: some were rejected for the Emassi ranks, but are able to be more than Drassi—ship captains and troop leaders. Then there're the Rassi, who were left as they are."

"Rassi?" Kris echoed in surprise. "Never heard of them."

"They do not leave Catten and are as we all were when the Eosi found us."

"So you, as a species, did not evolve by yourselves? But had your intelligence stimulated?" Dorothy asked. She turned to Kris. "The Eosi evidently never heard of the Prime Directive."

Kris giggled. A psychologist who was a Trekkie?

"The Prime Directive means an advanced culture is not supposed to interfere with the natural evolution of another species or culture," Kris explained to Zainal.

"The anthropologists will have a field day with this," Dorothy added, jotting down another note. "Was one . . .

application sufficient to sustain the higher level of intelligence?" she asked Zainal.

He shrugged. "I do not know that." Abruptly his expression again changed to his "Catteni look," impassive, expressionless, shuttered. "When I had my full growth, I had to be presented to the Eosi, to see if I was acceptable as a host. And what training I should be given."

"And?" Dorothy prompted him when he paused.

"I was passed, and I was to be trained to pilot spaceships." Then his grin became devilish and his "Catteni look" completely disappeared. "My father and uncles had worried that Eosi would find me too curious and unacceptable."

"Too curious? Why would that make you unacceptable?" Dorothy asked.

"Eosi tell Emassi what they need to know. That is all they are supposed to know."

"Before you start training? Surely you had basic schooling?" Dorothy asked, surprised.

Zainal gave a snort. "Emassi are trained, not schooled."

"But didn't you learn to read, write, and figure before you were fourteen?" Dorothy was having difficulty with this concept. "Surely you've had to learn mathematics to pilot spaceships?"

Zainal nodded. "Emassi males are taught that much by their fathers . . ." He grimaced.

"The hard way?" Kris said, miming the use of a force whip.

"Yes, the hard way. One tends to pay strict attention to such lessons."

"And yet you were curious enough to want to know more?" Dorothy asked.

"Because it was forbidden," Zainal said, again with the twinkle in his eye. He must have been a handful as a youngster. Kris was also immensely relieved that his intelligence, which she suspected was a lot higher than hers, was natural, rather than artificially stimulated.

"So the device assessed you. Can you give me any description of it?"

Zainal looked down at his clasped hands as he organized his response. "I was taken into a very large white room with a big chair in the center and two Eosi, one at a control desk. I was strapped into the chair and then the device came down out of the ceiling to cover my head."

"Could you see what it looked like?" Dorothy asked, and Kris realized how eagerly she awaited details.

Zainal shrugged. "A large shape," and he made a bell form with both hands, "with many wires attached to it and dials."

"It covered your head or just your face?"

"My head down to my shoulders. It was heavy."

"Did you see any blue lights?" Dorothy asked, scribbling again.

"I saw nothing."

"And the sensations? What were they like?" She turned to Kris as Zainal once again considered his answer. "We're trying to establish if any invasive probe is used: Needles or possibly electrical shock. We need to know whether the brain itself has been entered and damaged: whether or not there has been physical damage—rather than just memory, emotional, and fact erasures."

"There aren't any scars on the Victims?" Kris asked, and Dorothy shook her head.

"Not visible ones, certainly. Which is why Zainal's recollection is so vital to us."

"Like electricity," Zainal said, putting his hands to his temples and moving them up to the top of his broad skull. "And here," and he touched the base of his cranium. "But no blood. No scar."

"Oh, yes, that's interesting, very interesting," and

Dorothy wrote hastily for a minute. "No pain in the temples?"

"Where?" Zainal asked.

"Here," and Kris touched the points.

"Oh. Not pain, pressure."

"Isn't that where lobotomies are done?" Kris apprehensively asked Dorothy.

She nodded. "Anywhere else? Pressure or pain or odd sensations? I'm trying to discover just which areas might have been . . . touched by this device. If they coincide with what factual, emotional, and memory centers humans have," she added as an aside to Kris. "There are more parallels than you might guess."

"A sort of stabbing, very quick, to the . . ." and Zainal put his hand to the top of his head, "inside of my head."

"Quite possibly a general stimulation," Dorothy murmured. Then, with a kind smile, went on. "So you were assessed and passed. Then what happened?"

"I was told who to report to for training." Then he grinned. "I know that my uncles were disappointed that I was acceptable. My father was relieved. More glory for our branch of the family."

"How old are you now?" Dorothy asked, a question which Kris had never bothered to ask.

Zainal hesitated and then with a grin and a shrug, "Thirty-five. I have been exploring this galaxy for sixteen years."

"Sixteen?" Kris was surprised.

"That would make only four years of formal training? Of any sort?" Dorothy asked, surprised.

"Three. I have been here two years now. Two Catteni years." And he grinned at Kris.

"Pilot training is all you had?"

"I learned what I needed to know to do the job which the Eosi ordered for me. I worked hard and learned well," Zainal said with a touch of pride.

"Amazing," Dorothy murmured as she made more notes.

"But you know a lot about a lot of things," Kris protested.

Zainal shrugged. "Once I am officially a pilot," and he gave Kris a mischievous look out of the corner of his eye, "it was no longer wrong for me to learn what I wish so long as I pilot well. The Eosi," and his face slid briefly into Catteni impassivity again, "require their hosts to have been many places and seen many things."

"Then you don't have any knowledge about your own body? No biology?" Dorothy asked.

"Bi-o-lo-gy?" Zainal repeated.

Dorothy explained, and he laughed.

"As long as my body does what I need it to do, I do not ask how it does it."

Both Dorothy and Kris smiled.

"When I compare what our astronauts went through to qualify as space pilots . . ." and Dorothy raised one hand in amazement.

"The earliest aviators flew by the seat of their pants," Kris remarked.

"Seat of their pants?" Zainal asked, frowning so Dorothy and Kris took turns explaining the meaning.

"I did that, too, when training did not cover all I needed to know. So I made those who build the space-craft show me how everything worked," Zainal said.

"And those . . . engineers . . . were also trained by families who were engineers?" Dorothy asked, and Zainal nodded. "Very restrictive educational system. Only a need to know. However did they manage?"

"The Eosi do the manage part," Zainal said in a caustic tone. "Emassi follow orders just like Drassi and even the Rassi."

"It's amazing even the Emassi can do what they do," Kris remarked, regarding Zainal with even more respect.

"Yes, it is," Dorothy agreed, "and we tend to rely on the educational process . . . or the genetic heritage," and she gave Kris a look. "Depending on which school of thought you adhere to." She gave another sigh and then said more briskly, including Kris, "Are there any special aptitudes which Catteni have which Humans do not? For example, the way the Deski can climb vertically and have extraordinary hearing?"

"Night vision," Zainal said promptly. "Our hearing is more acute but not as good as the Deski. We can last longer eating poor food . . . or is that body difference, not brain?"

"Metabolic differences certainly," Dorothy said, having written "eye" and "ear" on her pad. Kris could read such short words backwards. Then the psychologist spent a moment doodling. "Could you possibly draw me a sketch of the device used on you?" She turned to Kris in explanation. "Those that got a good look at it can't talk, and those who can talk didn't see it."

"Zainal's very good at drawing devices," Kris said, with a touch of pride.

"Yes," and Zainal complied, using the pen with the quick, deft strokes that Kris had seen him use in delineating the mechanicals. "There!"

Dorothy regarded the neat sketch and hmmmed under her breath. "Hmmm, yes, well it looks like something an evil scientist would create." She sighed. "Considering who the Eosi chose to brain-scan, they seem to have been on an information hunt. But why? Their level of technology is so much more sophisticated than ours. Or were they just trying to strip minds that could possibly help foment riot and rebellion? Or maybe reduce humans to the level of your Rassi?"

Zainal made a guttural noise and his smile, while it did not touch his eyes, was evil. "Ray Scott said that he recognized some of the people as scientists. So the Eosi are looking for information. If they were wiping minds to make you like Drassi, they would start with children and block learning." He grinned. "The Eosi look for ideas. They have had very few new ones over the past hundred or so years."

"Really?" Dorothy remarked encouragingly.

"Maybe they need to stimulate their own brains," Kris said. "Or would it work on them?"

Zainal shrugged.

"Will Seissmann and Dr. Ansible felt that the Eosi were taking a vicious revenge on humans by destroying minds in a wholesale fashion," Dorothy said in an expressionless voice. "There seemed to be no reason to include some of the individuals—TV reporters and anchor men . . . and women . . ."

"Really? Who?" Kris asked in astonishment.

"Who? *Anchor men and women*?" Zainal didn't understand the term.

"Oh," he said, when Kris explained, and added, "information would be the first thing Eosi want to control. All your satellites and communication networks were destroyed in the initial phase of the invasion."

"Did you know they were choosing Earth?" Dorothy asked.

Zainal shook his head with a rueful grin. "I am exploring on the far side of this galaxy. I had stopped at Barevi for supplies and fuel when . . ." And then he shrugged as if both women knew his history from then on.

"Zainal picked a fight," Kris said, answering the querying look on Dorothy's mobile face, "killed a Drassi and went on the lam. I saw his flitter crash and went to see whom the Catteni were after this time. I had no idea what I was rescuing. If I had," and she gave Zainal a mock dirty look, "I might have thrown him to the wolves. Then I decided I'd better get him back to Barevi. Only we both got caught in one of those gassings the

Catteni spray to quell rebellion." Kris knew that Dorothy would be familiar with that tactic which was often used on Earth. "And ended up here on Botany."

"For which many of us are exceedingly grateful," Dorothy said sincerely. "Will, Dr. Ansible, and a former TV reporter, Jane O'Hanlon, were able to bring us up to date with the situation on Earth, by the way. Which I can give you without benefit of sponsors or commercials," Dorothy said in a droll tone of voice. "I think there was probably more than one reason for the Eosi to resort to extracting information from human beings. Not only have we here on Botany produced a new wrench in the works with the Bubble but resistance is increasing on Earth despite their attempts to control or contain it.

"I gather that there will be an effort made to support activities on Earth now that there're three spaceships at our disposal?" And she looked at Zainal for comment.

"We haven't heard of any," Kris said and added "yet." Zainal had been so busy getting pictorial proof to send the Farmers that they hadn't discussed any future plans.

He shrugged. "Three ships are too few against as many as the Eosi have."

"Not even for a teensy-weensy hit," and Dorothy left a very tiny space between her forefinger and thumb by way of illustration, "just to serve notice on the Eosi?"

"I think we've just done that," Kris said with a droll grin.

"They will try to penetrate the Bubble," Zainal said. "They will have to figure out what it is and how it is maintained. That will annoy them seriously." And he was patently delighted. "We must hope that it remains. The Eosi have other weapons that destroy planets."

"Do they?" And Kris felt a twinge of fear under her bravado.

"If they cannot possess, they do not leave it for others to have."

"Oh!" Kris had no flippant reply for that.

"Does the Council know?" Dorothy asked, concerned.

"I will tell them," Zainal said, nodding solemnly.

"Well, then, that's all I can bother you with," Dorothy said, beginning to gather up her notes. Then she paused, tilting her head at Zainal. "You don't have any idea where the Eosi came from, do you?" When Zainal shook his head, she managed a self-conscious laugh. "From a galaxy far, far away?"

Kris chuckled, delighted that Dorothy was not only *Trek* oriented, but could also quote from *Star Wars*.

"Thank you, Zainal. You've given me valuable information."

"I have?"

Dorothy smiled. "More than you might think. I do apologize for besieging you after what has been a very difficult day but we needed this input." She held up the notes. "We can design appropriate treatment now. In so far as our resources permit, that is."

Zainal opened the door, and they stepped into a moon-lit night.

"Over here, Dorothy," Chuck said, flipping on the runabout's light.

"Oh, thank you, and thank you again, Zainal, Kris." She hurried over to the little vehicle, murmuring her thanks to Mitford before she turned it northward.

"I've one of the flatbeds and there's room on the boxes for you two to ride back to your place," Chuck said. "Don't want any night crawlers grabbing you."

"Thanks, Chuck," Kris said, only too grateful for both the offer and the sentiment. She was really dragging with weariness right now. Sitting down for a spell had not been as good an idea as it had seemed. It only emphasized her fatigue.

"Over here," and Chuck reached the flatbed and turned on its light to guide them.

Kris was already climbing on the cargo before she realized that the boxes didn't resemble anything she had purchased on Barevi.

"What's all this, sarge?" She couldn't see the printed labels in the dim light.

"It's the books we found," Zainal astonished her by saying.

"Books?"

"Yes, books," Zainal repeated calmly. "Ray saw them. As trading captain of the KDI, I thought such paper stuff would be good for packing material." He grinned. "The Drassi did not argue, glad to be rid of the stuff."

"But there must be fifty boxes here? They're not *all* the same book, are they?"

"Nope," Chuck said. "Catteni looted libraries, too. We've got some former librarians just drooling to catalog what we managed to 'liberate.' This is only part of what we unloaded. Our kids won't grow up ignorant, though they might have some rather interesting gaps in their education."

"Books," Kris said and suddenly realized that she had missed books . . . certainly the availability of books. "Wow! That was a real coup."

"Books?" Zainal asked. "Schoolbooks?" His tone was sly though Kris could not see his expression in the dim light. "Bi-ol-o-gy?"

"Don't know yet," Chuck said, "though that's a possibility. Why?"

"Zainal has just acquired a need to know," Kris replied drolly. Oh, well, she'd had good grades in biology, though just how much human biology would expand Zainal's understanding of how his body worked was a moot point. And she was too tired to inquire.

All three were silent for the rest of the journey.

Once Zainal closed the door behind them, Kris gave up the notion of a shower as being too much work and a ruse to keep her from getting horizontal, and asleep, as soon as she could make it to the bed. She did take her boots off, as Zainal was doing, but that was all she managed.

THE K-CLASS SHIP, WHICH ARRIVED AT BAY forty-five to collect a shipment of slaves for an ice planet's mining operation, was furious to discover that someone else had taken them. The Drassi lodged a protest about that, and then another one that he had been forced to wait eight days before sufficient slaves could be assembled. So insignificant a report went unread.

The costs submitted against a ship with a KDI identification code were duly registered although it was later noted that this ship had supposedly been listed as "lost." The charges were paid and the anomaly forgotten.

Chapter Two

IT SHOULDN'T HAVE SURPRISED KRIS THAT
by the next afternoon many people were aware of the
substance of their discussion with Dorothy Dwardie.
Rumor circulated the settlement as fast as a Farmer or-
biter. Fortunately, it worked more in favor of Zainal than
against him. The Catteni were, however briefly, also seen
as Victims of Eosian tactics, more to be pitied than
feared.

A quintet of anthropologists, while loudly deploring
the forced evolution of the Catteni, requested most politely for Zainal to take some tests to evaluate his "stimulated" intelligence. Kris was furious and Zainal amused.
In fact, Kris was so incensed that she was even mad at
him for agreeing.

"They cannot do me any harm," Zainal said in his attempt to placate her.

"It's the whole idea of the thing . . . as if you were no
better than a laboratory mouse or rat or monkey," she
said, pacing about the house while her mate and her son
regarded her with surprise.

"They are also testing the Deski and the Rugarians." He grinned at her. "I would like to know how I rate."

"How can they possibly evaluate you fairly? In the first place," she said, waving her arms about as she paced, "lots of the questions require a similar cultural background . . . and history and things you've never had a chance to study."

"So?" Zainal reached out and stopped her mid-stride as she was going past him. "You are annoyed for me? Or with me?" he asked at his gentlest, a gleam in his yellow eyes.

"With *them*! The nerve, the consummate gall," and she tried to struggle out of his embrace.

"Sometimes, Kristin Bjornsen, you protect me when I do not need it," he said, smoothing her hair back from her face. "As you would Zane."

"Nonsense," Kris snapped, trying to push him away. "You don't know when to be insulted. I am insulted. For you."

Zainal laughed and easily resisted her attempts to break free.

"It is difficult to insult an Emassi," he said. "I think it is better for them to find out that I am very, very smart. It will solve other problems."

That mild remark stopped her struggling.

"What problems?" she demanded, suspicious.

"The ones I must solve."

"Which are?"

"How to free us . . ." and he gestured himself and then to her, "and your people from the Eosi."

"But we need the Farmers' help for that and we have no idea when we'll have a response—if any—to that report you sent them. What are you planning, Zainal?"

"This time you, too, must wait and see," he said, giving her a final squeeze before he released her. And she got no more out of him.

He went off to the session with the anthropologists while she fumed and fretted as she did the household chores. She was not due for her shift until late afternoon. She couldn't even find satisfaction in taking care of Zane, which she usually enjoyed thoroughly. She all but pounced on Zainal when he returned a few hours later.

"Well?" she demanded as soon as he entered the cabin.

His grin was a partial reassurance but she insisted on details. "They say I am very smart. At the top."

"How could they figure that out? What did they ask? How did you reply?"

"Carefully," he said, pouring himself a cup of water. "Thirsty work."

Kris let out an explosive "oh" of total frustration. "You'd drive a saint to drink."

"Saint? More of that God stuff?"

"What sort of questions?" She would not be diverted.

"Logic ones which I am well able to answer. Sorrell told me that they used some of the Mensa tests? That you would know what those are?"

Kris nodded, obliquely reassured. "And?"

"I passed," he said and then bent to lift the lid on the pot over the fire. "We eat here tonight?"

"Yes, it's the stew you like. How high did you pass?"

Zainal's grin was malicious. "Very high. They were surprised and . . ." he paused to let his grin broaden, "they were respectful."

"Well, it's about time."

He turned and put his arms about her, drawing her close to him so that he could look her in the eyes. "One earns respect. It is not just given."

"But you've earned it twenty times over, Zainal," she said, not quite willing to be totally placated by his proximity but letting her arms creep around his neck. "When I think of how lucky we were that you got dropped . . ."

"I was very lucky," he said, burrowing his head in her hair. "Very lucky."

They remained in that embrace, enjoying the simple pleasure of touching and being together until Zane, waking from his afternoon nap, disturbed their communion.

"So, what have you been planning in that devious stimulated Catteni mind of yours?" Kris asked.

"I think we have to go to Earth," he said so casually that she nearly dropped her son.

"Just like that? Go to Earth? How? Why? Can you? Will they agree?"

"It is safer right now than it will be . . ." he began, taking Zane from her to dandle on his knee, which had the boy chortling with delight, while she tasted the stew.

"Oh?" The stew needed a pinch more salt, which she added.

"Yes, because it will take time for the Eosi to discover that the Victims did not get to the intended destination. They will also be thinking of a way to break through the Bubble. They do not like such defenses."

"So? What good would a trip to Earth do?"

"Now I think there may be other Catteni, who have had enough Eosi," and he grinned at her. "I am not the only one who thinks for himself. Who is smarter than the Eosi want us to be. I know of five who are like me. I need to know where they now are. I need to know if there are more now."

"Five? Against how many Eosi?"

Zainal considered as he tickled Zane's toes while the little boy giggled, withdrawing his feet and then presenting them again.

"I think there are no more than one hundred."

"Because that's all the Catteni they upgraded? Don't they reproduce or something?"

Zainal shook his head. "Not that we know of."

"We?"

"The others of like mind I told you about. We have met, in small groups, from time to time, to exchange knowledge."

"You mean, you've been plotting against the Eosi for a long time? What would have happened if you had to be subsumed?"

"A risk all Emassi take," he said with a shrug. "Yes, I do believe that we have been looking for some way to shake Eosian domination. Your people have shown a resistance no other species has. That's good."

"As far as it goes and look what happens to Humans who resist . . ." and Kris's gesture included the planet. "How many worlds *do* the Eosi dominate? I mean, there're the Deski, the Rugarians, the Turs, the Morphins, and the Ilginish . . . How many others?"

"The Eosi control fifteen star systems that have at least one intelligent race: another ten where they take metals and materials."

Kris laughed. "You honestly believe a rebellion has a chance against such a setup?"

"If we have the Farmers' help . . ."

"Boy, oh boy, oh boy, are you an optimist!"

"It is a start. It is more than we have ever had."

"With two spaceships and a scout, we can go up against that sort of opposition?"

"It is a start."

"I've got to hand it to you, Zainal. God loves a trier," Kris said, shaking her head at the impossible task he had proposed. And yet . . . "Have you mentioned any of this to any one else yet?"

"I talked to Chuck. I will speak to others. We need to go to Earth as soon as possible. Earth needs to know that Botany is!"

"Let's eat first, shall we?" Kris said as brightly as

she could, trying to assimilate the magnitude of his vision.

DOROTHY DWARDIE'S TEAM SPENT THE FIRST week assessing the condition of the mind-wiped and divided them into various arbitrary groupings, according to the perceived severity.

As she said in her initial discussion with her aides, there were two levels of healing: one, the physical trauma of assault on the tissue and/or function of the brain, and two, the psychological trauma of assault on the psyche or self. She expected that some trauma would be time-limited.

"The mind has gone into functional frostbite," she said, "and when it thaws after the trauma, returns to normal function without help. Since most of these people were trained scientists, it's possible that many will simply reestablish old neural pathways. There may be some loss of factual memory; maybe even a great deal. Even then much may return over a period of time.

"Right now, they need reassurance, interaction: music, smells, kindness, encouragement, gentle exercise. As normal a routine as we can manage. Talk to them, about anything and everything: help them reestablish themselves. Where we know the name, repeat it often. When we know something of their background, refer to that as frequently as possible. Help them reacquaint themselves with themselves."

Kris had three women, all in their late fifties: two had been research physicians in a drug company—Peggy Ihde and Marjorie Flax; the third they called Sophie because Sarah McDouall said she thought she looked like a Sophie. Kris was to supervise their meals. Just putting a spoon or a fork in their hands stimulated self-feeding. She read to them from Jane Austen's *Pride and Prejudice,* which they might even have read in their younger days. She took them on quiet walks in the lodge-pole copse, or sat with them above the bay where benches had been placed for meditation.

"Pleasant surroundings are extremely important after the holding pens they've been in," Dorothy said. "Soft, kind voices, gentle handling will reassure even the most damaged."

There were a few whose condition was clearly catatonic but Dorothy was serenely confident that, in time, even these would recover.

"There's something about this place," she said, spreading both arms out to include the entire subcontinent, "that will generate healing. The smells are good, the food is fresh and tasty, and the vibes . . ." she smiled at using the vernacular description, "are good because we've made them so. Beauty is a natural stress-absorber, you know. It reassures on a nonverbal level that they are now safe.

"You see," she went on in her soft voice, "we've decided to use a multi-modal treatment of this stress. The right hemisphere—which thinks in pictures—can't tell time: therefore it needs pictures to counteract the negative images of the trauma. The left hemisphere stores rational thought processes in thought and ideas. The two hemispheres interact and each approach can help the other side. We need to maximize good input and involve as much as possible in terms of brain resource utilization. Many of our friends here may never recall exactly what happened. That would truly be a blessing."

"But won't we have to explain something of how they got here?" Sarah McDouall asked.

"Oh, yes," Dorothy said with a smile, "and by then we'll probably have a coherent answer for them. They are, to all intents and purposes, on a holiday from their own minds right now."

"We could always tell them they're in Oz," someone at the back of the room quipped.

"And no red slippers in sight," someone added.

Dorothy's expression was droll. "We're all in Oz."

"The Eosi are the wicked witches . . ."

"Let's leave the analogy there, shall we?" Dorothy said in the firm tone of she-who-must-be-obeyed.

Kris felt her shoulder muscles relax. She had been readying herself to protect Zainal. Really, she had to stop doing that. He had made his own position here on Botany and was firmly entrenched. She didn't need to fret over possible snide remarks and animosity. She devoutly hoped!

THAT EVENING WHEN ZAINAL CAME HOME from the construction site of the new units for the Victims, he very carefully put a book down on the table.

"That's for kindergartners," she said in surprise, recognizing the title.

"Kindergartners? It is for learning to read," Zainal said and gave it a little shove with one large and very dirty thumb.

"Please wash up, dinner's nearly ready," she said, because she really couldn't tell Zainal not to handle the book—which might be the only one of its kind—with his dirty hands.

"I learn to read," he said and gave it another, almost angry push.

"You?"

Zainal scowled and Zane, who was seated in the high-seated chair his adoptive father had made for him, began to whimper in apprehension. He was very quick to sense moods. Immediately Zainal turned a smiling face and diverted the child by tickling his feet until he was hilarious with tickle laughter.

"I need to read to use computers."

Kris blinked in surprise, having forgotten for the moment that Botany now possessed working computers . . .

which were being put to all kinds of good use. There had been several uninterrupted sessions to develop adapters for the units to run on solar power.

"Oh, yes, of course you would," Kris said. "Dead easy for a man with your smarts."

Zainal turned his smiling face from Zane and gave the little book a dark scowl. "Not when all those . . . squiggles . . . make no sense at all."

"Are there many—" and Kris thought swiftly for a less insulting description than "kids' books"—"primer books in what we got?" She hadn't had occasion to look in that section of the hastily assembled "library."

"This was given me. I wash my hands . . . and Zane's feet . . ." he added pointing to the oily smears now marking the child's bare feet.

ONCE ZANE WAS IN BED, SHE TOOK, NOT THE book, but a pad and pencil and wrote out the alphabet in upper and lower case, as large as she could lengthwise across the page.

"But I brought the book to read . . ." he said, pulling it toward him with now clean hands.

"First you must know the . . . squiggles that spell the words we use. Too bad we didn't have a book on English for second-language speakers . . . although come to think of it, that wouldn't do *you* much good. Now, this is the first letter of the alphabet . . . 'ay.' Which can also be pronounced 'ah' . . . just to confuse you. It is a vowel. B, which is usually just 'bee' is the second letter and a consonant."

He had repeated "vowel" and now spoke "consonant." Zainal had no trouble committing the sequence of the alphabet to memory—nor of naming any of them when Kris drilled him. His concentration was incredible. He kept her going until even such words as "Spot" and "Jane" were blurring her eyes. He had also read through the book nine times and had it memorized.

"No Spot and Jane on the computers," he said.

"We'll work on computer language tomorrow," she said, rising stiffly from the chair in which his need to learn had pinned her for hours. She yawned.

"I work more now," he said, looking at her expectantly.

"Okay, see how many words you already know that rhyme with Spot . . . like dot, and tot, and Scott . . . or with Jane, like mane . . . no not drain . . . ah, try run, fun, gun, stun . . ."

"Oh," he said, delighted at such an exercise.

She went to bed. When Zane woke her in false dark, hungry, Zainal had filed pages of similarly sounding words, not all of which were spelled properly but she had to give him an A for effort. Spelling would come later. What did astonish her as she fed Zane by candlelight was the computer manual she found under a pile of his laboriously hand-printed sheets. He had underlined all the un-words . . . ctrl, del, esc, Pgdn, Pgup, num, menu.

"He can't have read the manual," she murmured and smothered a laugh. "He may be one of the few who ever did before they turned on a computer."

She and Zane had gone back to sleep again before full daylight and, by then, Zainal had gone off to work. In a neat pile on the mantel he had left all but the primer. Doubtless that had gone back to the library shelves for something more challenging. The manual was still there but then, there had been plenty of those in the packing cases they'd brought back from the marketplace at Barevi. But why this sudden need to understand computers . . . ah, yes. It probably had something to do with Zainal's master plan. Maybe it was plans since he intended not only to free Earth but destroy the Eosi *and* release Catten from slavery. Did he also plan to use the mind stimulator on everyone? To equalize the Catten race? Ooops, she sort of thought that might be a bad idea.

Zainal was a most unusual Catteni. Still, there might well be similarly motivated Emassi among those whom he was going to enlist to help. But the Drassi . . . and the Rassi . . . though she despised herself for generalizing . . . were different: especially since they were such big people with lots of muscles and not much common sense.

She had an early shift this morning so she and Zane started off in the fresh morning air to the day care center. He was crawling around everywhere, even trying to climb, and spent more time falling down. But she let him fall . . . and let him get up. He rarely hurt himself. On the advice of other mothers, she had put extra padding on the knees of his trousers, saving him scratches if not bruises. Actually, Kris thought, Botany's new generation was generally sturdy and few mothers had the time to pamper their children. With the notable exception of Janet and Anna Bollinger. Their kids, however, had enough rough and tumble at the day care center to have developed allergies to maternal fussiness.

No television, no Coke, or chocolate—though sometimes Kris' craving for a chocolate bar was almost overwhelming—was all to the good. She did miss caffeine and, while the experiments with beer and other spiritous liquors had been successful, there was as yet no tobacco substitute. As soon as the children were able, they were put to little tasks and chores that would make them as self-sufficient as their parents had learned to be.

Raisha Simonova was checking in the children at the day care center this morning. Zane toddled firmly off to the room that catered to his age group. One of the Deski children, Fil, was on its way (gender in Deskis developed later) so he waited for Fil. Another plus for Botany—no racism. Well, not to fret over, because the few who had trouble assimilating with the Rugarians and Deskis were gradually losing their sense of Human superiority: difficult to maintain when a Deski walked *up* a wall to carry slates to the roof. Or a Rugarian easily hefted weights that took two or three Humans to manage. Both races were also becoming more and more fluent in English, though they had trouble with past tenses of verbs. Who didn't? And a good couple of dozen Humans were attempting to master their languages.

Almost, Kris thought, as she stopped by the library to pick up the day's reading, it would be a shame to have to open Botany up. It could easily ruin the harmony that had been achieved. And yet . . .

All three of her charges were sitting in their bedside chairs, an aura of anticipation about them.

"They know to the minute when you're due, Kris," Mavis Belton said.

"That's good, isn't it?"

"You don't know *how* good," Mavis said with a deep sigh, slightly turning her head toward one of the "difficult wards" where the worst of the Victims were kept.

"Good morning, Marjorie," Kris began, initiating her morning routine by touching the arm of each in turn, "Good morning, Peggy. Good morning, Sophie."

"Why do you call me Sophie? That's my middle name. My *Christian* name is Norma," the woman said with a hint of petulance. "Norma Sophie Barrow. Miss Barrow."

"I do apologize, Miss Barrow," Kris said sincerely, holding her hand now for the woman to shake. "I'm Kris Bjornsen, the nurse's aide."

"Of course, you are. We've been expecting you," Miss Barrow said almost tartly. "Aren't we?"

Marjorie and Peggy nodded.

"In that case, let us walk up to the dining hall," Kris said.

Behind the newly restored Miss Barrow, Mavis was almost in tears with joy at the breakthrough. It was a very mixed blessing. Miss Barrow was stunned to find herself in such rural, primitive surroundings.

"Rustic, I should say," she remarked as they entered the log-built main hall. "I would certainly never take my vacation in such a setting." She wanted coffee and refused to drink the herbal tea which was all that was served. She wanted white bread toast and butter and did not like the berry preserve, which did service as a spread. Nor would she eat the hot oatmeal. Porridge was for children or invalids. She wanted an egg, boiled, three minutes.

Although Marjorie and Peggy were hungry enough to eat what Kris served them, they began to falter as Miss Barrow's complaints jarred their own memories of breakfasts or homes or what they had once been accustomed to.

Just as Kris was beginning to think she wouldn't be able to cope with this sort of insurrection, Dorothy Dwardie slid in beside Miss Barrow.

"I am so glad to see you looking so well, today, Miss Barrow."

Miss Barrow recoiled from Dorothy, a hint of fear contorting her features.

"Surely, you remember me, Doctor Dwardie?"

"Doctor?" Miss Barrow was only slightly reassured while Kris admired the friendly but not intimate tone Dorothy used.

"Yes, Doctor Dwardie, I'm in charge of your case."

"I've not been well?" As Miss Barrow's fragile hand went to her chest and her expression became even more confused, Dorothy nodded, still smiling with great reassurance.

"Yes, but nothing life-threatening, I'm happy to report. The tests have all come back negative. You may not remember things in the detail you used to but we're positive that you will make a complete recovery."

"I *was* working very hard," Miss Barrow said, running one nervous finger along the edge of the table and watching its progress, "the merger, you know."

"Yes, exactly, the merger. One of the elements of your convalescence has actually been a change of diet to a very bland one. A change to flush the toxins of fatigue out of your system. If you just look at Marjorie and Peggy, you'll see how healthy and fine they are. And you're very much improved."

"Toxins . . . yes, there were toxins," Miss Barrow said. "Some of them . . ." She closed her lips and gave a weak smile. "I'm not allowed to talk about my work, you understand."

"Yes, yes, Miss Barrow, we do. Miss Bjornsen is the soul of discretion but as I have a top security clearance, perhaps if we had a quiet little chat in my office, I could relieve your mind, and we can figure out just what other therapy will speed your recovery."

Gently Dorothy got Miss Barrow to her feet and led her out of the dining room and toward her putative office.

"She'll be all right, won't she?" Marjorie said, her eyes wide with fright. It was also the first time Marjorie had said more than yes, no, and maybe. Peggy stared from one to another and then back to Kris for reassurance.

"She'll be fine," Kris said firmly, smiling and nodding her head. "But I think we'd better finish our breakfasts. Then we'll find a quiet spot for me to finish reading *Pride and Prejudice.*"

"I read that once," Peggy said in a vague tone, frowning slightly.

"I like Kris reading," Marjorie said.

"Why, thank you, Marjorie."

"You know you don't have to be so formal, Kris. I don't mind if you call me Marge like everyone else."

Then she grimaced, looking down at the table and, with furtive glances, gradually looked around the room. Peggy, however, held up her cup for more tea, which Kris instantly supplied.

"Some of your friends aren't here with you, Marge," Kris said, thinking some explanation should be offered before Marjorie's returning awareness caused her dismay.

"They aren't?"

"More tea?" Kris offered and Marge shook her head.

"Doesn't really taste like tea to me."

"It's part of the bland diet to reduce the dose of toxicity you had," Kris said.

"But you're drinking it, too. Did you get a dose?"

"No," Kris replied, "but we aides thought it wasn't fair for us to drink something you aren't yet allowed."

"Oh!" Marge accepted that.

Kris tried not to wonder what else would happen today or who would have a breakthrough but the rest of her eight-hour shift went without any further incident, other than Marge making comments about beautiful scenery and the lovely fresh air. Peggy said nothing more and seemed to be deep in her own thoughts. And Kris certainly hoped she was having some. She got her two charges back for their afternoon nap and, for once, they lay down in their beds immediately and were asleep in moments.

Mavis beckoned her into the nurse's office.

"That Miss Barrow's a pisswhistler," she murmured in rather unprofessional language. "And that's exactly what brought her around."

"How so?"

"She ran a huge lab for Erkind Pharmaceuticals and everything, but everything had to be precisely in place and exactly done."

"Oh! And suddenly her neurones meshed and nothing here was as it should be in her neat little mind?"

"Exactly."

"Has she realized where she is now?"

Mavis cocked her. "She's fighting it but with every twitch of disagreement, she's remembering more. She's more than halfway back to sanity."

Kris grimaced. "If precision and order are her sort of sanity, she could be a real pain in the arse."

Mavis shook her head this time. "No, we'll let her manage our lab when she's fully recovered. It'll be the envy of . . ." Then Mavis giggled. "We couldn't actually ask for someone with a better background."

Kris thought of Leon Dane, of Thor Mayock's hooch, and the easy, if effective, way the hospital facilities had been run, and wondered.

"You'll see," Mavis said. "How're the other two?"

"Some speech from Marge . . . she prefers that . . . and one sentence from Peggy but that one's been thinking hard all day long."

"Good," and Mavis made notes on the day pad. "We'll see if we can improve on your start. You're mid-shift tomorrow?"

Kris nodded and then another group returned to the dormitory and Mavis went to help settle them for their rest.

ON HER WAY TO COLLECT ZANE, SHE WON-dered just how the prim and proper Miss Barrow would view the Deski and Rugarians with whom they shared the planet. And how she could react to Zainal's presence when she saw him. Once the Victims started being people again, they would have to see, and become accustomed to, the one Catteni since he was the one who had organized their rescue.

Zane was having a late nap and Kris looked rather enviously at all the small bodies, all curled up under their blankets on the mats that had been woven for the purpose.

"Go grab some zzz's yourself," murmured Sheila, who was in charge. She was also working on a detailed map of the eastern coast of this continent, from measurements Kris's exploratory team had brought back. "I'll *never* get used to the long days here. Not to mention the long nights. I'll wake you when Zane's up. I allus say, leave sleeping dogs and chilluns lie."

There were bunks for the nighttime staff, two of which were already occupied, so Kris climbed as quietly as possible into an upper one and very shortly fell asleep.

A SLOPPY WET KISS WOKE HER: THE DONOR being her dearly beloved son, who had managed to clamber up the ladder at the head of the bunk. He giggled, delighted with his accomplishment, though Kris was only too relieved he had escaped unscathed. She'd take ladders away the next time she slept here.

"Hey, love, you don't know how to climb ladders yet," she said, alternating between being frightened at the risk he had taken and proud that he had tried.

"Ahh, Mummy."

Kris threw back the blanket, jumped lightly to the ground and held up her hands for him. Quick as could be and without a moment's hesitation, he flung himself down at her, giggling when she caught him neatly. Ssssh-ing him, they left the sleeping room. Two beds were still occupied.

Zane was in great form and, as it was snack time, they went hand in hand to the dining room, which was crowded with others. With such long days, four or five meals were frequently offered. A hearty breakfast, a mid-morning sandwich, a three-course dinner midday, a mid-afternoon fruit and sandwich, and then a good supper. Late-night snacks were leftovers of bread, cake, and sandwiches, whatever needed to be eaten up and usually was. The herbal tea and, with spring now leading into summer, fruit juices were available all day long. Caterers worked in several short shifts but nevertheless worked a twelve-hour day. Food preparation was as often as not a punishment detail for minor infractions of colony laws, but everyone took a turn at those chores. The big difference here on the new land was that the food didn't also have to be picked, dug, fished, or gutted: other working groups had already processed it for cooking.

On the northern wall of the dining room were the listings of jobs and rotas so that there was no excuse for anyone to miss assignments. Diners customarily checked before or after they ate to see what their duties were for the next day or the next week.

Zainal was listed as working with ex-Admiral Ray Scott, Bull Fetterman, Bert Put, John Beverly, Chuck Mitford, Jim Rastancil, Salvinato, Gino Marrucci, Raisha Simonova, Boris Slavinkovin, Hassan Moussa, Laughrey, Ayckburn, Peter Easley, and Worrell. These week-long meetings were scheduled at the hangar. Considering that most of these men were ex-service of one country or another, Kris had no problem figuring out that Zainal was probably talking up his master plan. Whether the others would go for it or not was debatable. Certainly there were significant absences from that list, such as the odious Geoffrey Ainger, the Brit naval commander, Beggs, who had been Scott's gopher, and Sev Balenquah, who had so nearly blown their disguises on their sneak trip back to Barevi to obtain the supplies which were making all the difference in the efficiency and productivity of the colony.

And if all those with experience in flying the Catteni craft, including Raisha, were there, she wondered just what escapade was being planned. And why wasn't she included?

SHE AND ZANE HAD THEIR SNACK, A HOT rolled sandwich with a sort of sausagey filling, the constituents of which she did not wish to know but the result tasted good. Zane licked his fingers so hungrily that she found a small extra one to give him.

"We've our garden to tend now, love," she said, and he hopped and skipped alongside her as they returned to their cabin. She got out the hoe and his little weeder prong and they finished that chore by the time they saw Zainal being dropped off from the flatbed, still occupied by those living farther up the way to the main administrative area.

"Daddy, daddy!" And Zane made a wobbly beeline to his father who heaved him up so high that Kris caught her breath, even though she knew perfectly well that Zainal would never drop the boy.

"And what might I ask are you and all the high, low, and middle brass doing at the hangar these days?"

"Heard one of your old girls remembered who she is," he replied.

"Ah, how good the gossip system is here," she said drolly. "First, please, the answer to *my* question?"

"Those who played . . . doggo?" and Zainal's yellow eyes twinkled as he looked for confirmation on his use of the slang, "knew a lot more than they thought they did."

"That's good. About what did they know more?"

"I believe Scott calls it 'the state of the nation.' "

"And?"

"We're mounting an expedition." He did not meet her gaze, but threw the delightedly squealing Zane up in the air again.

"Soon?"

"Quite likely."

"Who all's going?"

"That's what's taking so long to decide," and Zainal gave a heavy sigh.

"Just think how much more time that gives you, my dear, to learn how to operate computers."

"That is the only reason you find me in such good fettle."

Kris burst out laughing. Zainal knew just how to get her into a good mood . . . proving that he'd mastered yet another Terran expression.

"Can we eat here tonight? Kurt Langsa—well, however you pronounce the rest of his long name—said he would come?"

"I'm not good enough?"

He had Zane safely ensconced on his shoulders now and pulled her against him, kissing her cheek. "I read nine books during the talking," and he wrinkled his nose. "I need someone who uses computers all the time to show me what the manual says. It uses words I know but not the same way."

"I know exactly what you mean, Zainal. I'll go get some food from the Hall."

"No, Kurt brings. I would like you to go over the words I have learned so that I pronounce them correctly. The spelling is always different and yet the words sound alike." He sighed now in exasperation.

"I don't imagine it's any consolation to you, Zay, but we had to learn, too, as kids."

"In Catteni, the sound is always the same . . ."

"If you're accustomed to gargling, yes, they would be," Kris agreed affably, remembering how hoarse she had been when she'd had to talk to the Catteni scout ship before they captured it. "I do speak some Catteni," she added, slyly glancing at him. "More Barevi."

He gave her a sideways look, so that she couldn't really see the expression in his eyes.

"That is known," he said at his blandest. "But you must learn to understand more."

"When do the classes start?" she asked in an equally bland tone, determined to find out.

"Soon."

"Ah, then let us continue teaching you antonyms."

Zane was busy in his play corner with the blocks and the miniature vehicles that Zainal had fashioned for him. He was mimicking the solar panel hum as he played, oblivious now to the adults.

She had no sooner reached for the list than there was a knock on the door, and Zainal called out "Enter!"

Kurt Langsteiner peered cautiously around the door, a thin-faced man with an expression of perpetual anxiety. He smiled, which altered his face considerably to a pleasant appearance, and stepped inside, carefully closing the door with one foot as both hands were full.

"Name plates would help," he said. "This is the third house I've tried in your neck of the woods."

"Let me help," Kris said, rising to take the basket from one hand. She immediately exclaimed with real pleasure at the three long loaves of bread that stuck out around the stew pot. "Rocksquat . . ."

"What else?" Kurt said with a droll laugh, "but they put some salad in as well and something for young Zane." He stepped up to the table now and placed on its surface the six large bottles of beer that had been tied at the neck and clanked against each other.

"Remnant of my student days when I found that beer made the studying go more easily." He put the bottles down, and he shook his creased fingers to circulate blood to them.

First Kris brought three glasses to the table. They were still sort of odd shaped, with uneven blemishes from the not-quite-expert glass blowers. In fact, some said that the glasses, with their slightly skewed sides, looked half-drunk. A new guideline had been formulated: if a drinker was asked if his glass was straight and he answered "yes," you had proof he had had more than enough to drink. She was setting out plates and utensils as Kurt started pulling out notepads and books from the various pockets of his ship suit. It still looked new, by which Kris figured he must have been in the Sixth Drop. She didn't know that group of arrivals as well as she did those from the other five.

"What is the worst trouble you're having, Zainal?" Kurt asked as he made an orderly pile of his materials.

"It is the words that sound the same that are not the same," Zainal said with considerable asperity.

"Quite understandably. They're bitches to get right at any age." Then he turned to Kris. "I used to teach computer in junior high school before I got rounded up so Mitford thought I'd be the best candidate to do both jobs on Zainal," Kurt said to her as he organized his teaching materials on the table. "And Zainal here," and Kurt nodded at him, "said he'd teach me how to read and write Catteni."

Now Zainal grinned at Kris and pointed to the third chair. "You will learn, too."

Obediently Kris settled down. Leave it to Zainal to throw her a real curve ball. Oh, well, she had only herself to blame.

"You learn a lot better on an full stomach . . . and it gives you a base for the beer. Zane, please wash your hands for dinner," she said, using hot pads to lift the stew kettle to the table.

The three males obediently went to wash their hands as she finished setting the table. Kurt must be well liked by the caterers for a whole cake had been carefully tied between two baking tins to keep it from being damaged by the hot stew pot. And so had a good portion of salad greens, though the heat from the stew had wilted some of them.

THEY MADE A GOOD MEAL, WITH ZAINAL BEginning his part of the teaching bargain by using the Catteni words for everything on the table. Even Zane tried to repeat them, giggling as easily at his own mistakes as at his mother's but had the good sense to cover his mouth when Kurt had trouble. Though Langsteiner certainly seemed to get the guttural sounds more easily.

"German was my first language," he said in an aside to Kris.

"You'd never know it to hear you speak English," she replied.

"My parents spoke both," he explained.

"We really should make Zane learn Catteni, too," Kris said, leaning toward Zainal.

"And Rugarian and Deski," Zainal said at his blandest.

"Them, as well, of course," was her quick, equally bland response, and Kurt laughed.

"And what a hodgepodge they'll all be speaking," he said.

"It will be helpful," Zainal said, "when we free Rugar and Deski, too."

Kurt's eyes bulged at that, and he looked quickly at Kris to see her reaction.

"Why settle for freeing just ours?" she said with a diffident shrug though this was the first she'd known of *that* facet of Zainal's master plans. "Besides, Zane already speaks some Rugarian and Deski at day care."

"Really?" Kurt was startled.

"Gets a bit like the Tower of Babel in there some days," Kris said, dipping the ladle into the stew pot to offer second helpings. The pot had been graciously full.

They all had two pieces of the excellent nutty-flavored cake that had a topping of thick sweet blue-colored berries that did not at all taste like blueberries, or have similar seeds.

As was often the case with young Zane, he was ready to go to sleep with his stomach nicely full so Kris prepared him for bed while the two men cleared the table. When she returned, she rather thought the humorous glint in Kurt's eyes was for the accustomed manner in which the Catteni had performed the KP duties.

The beer helped a great deal as the two Humans struggled with the guttural, harsh Catteni words, first jotting them down phonetically and then in the Catteni script. This was a cross between runes, Kurt's definition, and glyphs, which was Kris' notion. By the time the beer had run out, the two of them knew how to count to five hundred in Catteni, and Zainal could now spell all the words that had bothered him as well as understand all the computer abbreviations which had so baffled him. They set a time for the next lesson, and then Kurt got into the runabout and made a slow but competent turn to head back to the main settlement.

SINCE THE MIND-PROBE HAD DISCOVERED very little useful information—apart from some shady dealings among the former administrators and administrations of the planet's political divisions—the Ix had abandoned the project: bored even by the occasional scientific theories that had yet to be proven. Most of these were already in use by the Eosi: and far more sophisticated usage than the silly Humans had ever thought to employ.

Unfortunately the obsession to destroy those protected by the Bubble had become so entrenched in the Ix Mentat's mind that it thought of nothing but the means to do so. Where the Bubble had come from and what comprised the amazingly invulnerable material was almost a secondary consideration. The Juniors—which was not how they were called in Catteni but the translation was close enough to their actual position and authority within the Eosi context—had repeatedly tried to divert the Ix with other matters. Lest the Ix be provoked by their counter-arguments into another seizure, they had no choice but to proceed with the Mentat's latest plans: to organize the greatest force the Eosi had ever assembled, even larger than the one with which they had assaulted a planet that many High Emassi wished they'd left strictly alone. But it had seemed such a useful place: with a population density that would provide other, less desirable locations with an endless supply of workers needed to produce and refine the raw materials that kept Catteni ships in space. There was also the added fact that the Eosi were committed to extending their control of this arm of the galaxy as far as they could—and as fast as they could.

So the orders were sent out to the naval shipyards and the plants and planets that produced the materials needed to build more AA-ships, and devise heavier, more devastating missiles to launch at this mysterious Bubble.

The Ix Mentat was approached by one of its peers and tactfully asked why one small, insignificant world was its target.

"Because it's there," the Ix replied, glowering and seething with rage. "Because it defies us!"

"Defiance is not permitted," the Le Mentat agreed and that was the end of that.

Chapter Three

MARGE BECAME MORE VOCAL BUT STRUG-
gled painfully for sentences or words and would often
burst into tears. Peggy would watch her, lean over, and
pat her shoulder or her hand, then immediately go into
what Kris called her "meditative" state.

When discussing her charges with Dorothy, the psychologist advised her to suggest words, if she could, to
Marge or show pictures. Peggy was obviously aware of
what was happening about her, and that was a very good
sign.

"Miss Barrow," and Dorothy gave the mischievous
smile that made her seem much younger, "wants to take
charge of our laboratory. She is naturally appalled at its
primitive facilities and amazed that we aren't all down
with something fatal. Leon, Thor, and the others need her
skills so much that they're willing to put up with her . . .
disorientation." Dorothy sighed. "Miss Barrow will not
be pleased when she accepts that she's on another planet
entirely and will never get more than the equipment we
have."

"I wouldn't bet on that, Dorothy," Kris said with a grin.

"What do you know that they haven't told me?" Dorothy asked, eyeing Kris with mock annoyance.

"I'm not sure they've told me any more than you will have heard, too. Like they *are* going to try to get back to Earth."

"They couldn't bring my shopping list with them, could they?" the psychologist asked in a wistful tone, then added more briskly, "I am encouraged, though. We're getting almost daily breakthroughs now. Though how we'll fit some of these people into Botany I haven't a clue. I mean, an astrophysicist who was on the Hubble team and a meteorologist when the weather here is already controlled—Do we even have a clue how that's done?"

"Zainal thinks that huge square block we discovered on the seashore has something to do with it. There are four others in sort of a pattern."

"Any idea of *when* the Earth trip will take place?"

"We've a lot of studying to do first," Kris said and rose, not wanting to spread more gossip, even to someone as discreet as Dorothy was, professionally or personally.

KRIS FOUND HER NAME UP ON THE ROSTER board for a late afternoon meeting with the Central Council. She checked in with the day care to be sure that the day's manager knew that she wouldn't be in to collect Zane at the usual hour. Sarah McDouall had already been informed. Zane did not notice his mother, since he was involved in some complicated game with Fek's child and two Rugarians whom Kris didn't know. The Rugarian babies were born with as much body fur as their parents, and it really was difficult for humans to tell them apart without going through the list of names until the yaya (which was Rugarian for the unadult) answered to the right one. A Deski young one was called a slib. Some of them were easier to identify since their skin had different tones.

Zainal caught up with her in the dining hall where they were both eating a quick meal.

"What's this all about then?" she asked him.

"Plans have been made. Discussion now."

She knew him well enough to know that she would get no more out of him. Then she noticed Miss Barrow threading her way to an empty table. She wore a look of disdain, as if wrapping herself carefully away from the reality of an ambience she could not escape. Unlike everyone else garbed in the ubiquitous ship suit, she wore a dress, severely cut, in one of the dark greens, which Kris had brought back from her excursion to the markets of Barevi. The dress was long-sleeved and buttoned up to a high collar, with a hemline at calf-length. To Kris' astonishment, Miss Barrow did incline her head graciously as she registered Kris' presence, but she straightened into consummate distaste as she recognized that Kris was seated with a Catteni. She turned her face haughtily away.

"Poor woman," Kris said, shaking her head.

"Why? She was saved the mines."

"One day, she'll find out. I hope," Kris added as an afterthought, "the notion that she is beholden to you doesn't throw her."

"She is good in lab, they say," Zainal remarked.

"So she is. We'd better go."

Kris saw the biggest of the flatbed vehicles draw up to the dining hall and heard it toot its horn. Half the diners immediately made their way to the door and climbed on the transport.

THEY WERE DELIVERED TO THE IMMENSE main hangar where the scout ship and the two transports lurked in the shadows cast by the one work light left on in their area. Not for the first time, Kris wondered what the Farmers had used this vast area for, so neatly carved from the mountainside.

In the center of some of the unused space, chairs and benches had been set up, facing five large mounted slates that were still the best Botany solution for large displays. She could see that one held the diagram of this system and another of Earth. The other two were probably the systems in which the Barevi planet and the home planet of the Catteni were situated. The fifth held lists and names.

So, thought Kris with a surge of anticipation, we are moving outside again.

There was a table to one side of the slates with chairs crowding around it. Judge Iri Bempechat was seated in the center and was obviously the moderator for the meeting. Kris liked the old man enormously for his wit, his humor, and his vast store of judicial wisdom. So far no one had contested any of his decisions and she hoped the situation would remain that way. On his right was Ray Scott, on his left two men who were vaguely familiar to her: they also had the gaunt look of Victims despite two weeks of restorative treatment and therapy. Even those who had played "doggo" showed the effects of their incarceration in the brutal open pens where the Eosi had contained them. Dorothy Dwardie sat beyond those two men. The rest of the Council, from Chuck Mitford to Leon Dane, occupied the other spaces. Raisha and Gino sat together, trying to look unconcerned and anonymous at the end of the right side.

Two seats were still unoccupied and, as Kris and Zainal entered, he gave his head a slight tilt toward the table, indicating those chairs were for them. Kris was quite glad to join him there. That gave her a chance to see who else had been invited. Mostly those who were technically skilled in one way or another, including Dick Aarens, and a great many of those who had been in the Fifth and Sixth Drops.

Well, she thought, we won't have to contend with Anna Bollinger and Janet.

Ray stood up and whatever private conversations had been going ceased.

"Zainal has proposed several plans of action since we cannot be sure that the Farmers will answer our latest message to them, nor when. We've been fortunate enough to have the latest information of Earth from those we rescued from the Barevi slave pens. Zainal?" Ray sat down and Zainal stood, going to the slates.

"First, we need to know who or what is watching Botany outside the Bubble," he said. "This is the point where the Eosi tried to ram their way in." Someone had drawn in cartoons of the debris. "They left enough behind so that I believe the scout ship can poke her nose outside the Bubble and have a look."

"What about the geo-synchronous satellite up there?" Aarens asked, jumping to his feet to forestall the others who more politely raised their hands to signify that they had a query.

"It may or may not be able to see the scout's nose among the rubble," Zainal said, "but by the time the report is sent back, Baby will no longer be there. The records will show only what has been seen before. Unless the film is sent to a very high-ranking Eosi, it will be considered what you call a glitch. In order to get out of the Bubble, we need to calculate the speed and direction of the new satellite that the Eosi have put in place. We can then figure out where to leave the Bubble without being detected."

"Yeah," Aarens said in a dubious tone of voice, "but that sat would see the scout's ion trail, wouldn't it?"

"Not if the speed of the scout is sufficient to get it behind one of the moons. Its direction would be unknown."

"What about if there's a fast ship just waiting for us to try something like that?"

"There are ways," Zainal said with a grin. "That scout is much faster than anything but another scout. Such ships are never used as watchers."

Aarens shrugged and sat down.

"That is the first step," Zainal said.

"If you're going back to Barevi, I've a long shopping list," someone said and received a chuckle.

"No, Barevi would be too hot for us right now," Zainal said. "We go to Earth and we use two ships; the scout and the KDM which will be renamed and altered to look as if it had been hit by space . . . stuff."

"That metal'll be hard to dent," Gino said, shaking his head. "You Catteni make a good hull."

"It'll be camouflaged," Hassan Moussa said and grinned. "I'm a past master at that."

"But going back to Earth?" Aarens asked, stunned.

"Last place they will expect us." And Zainal turned to one of the Victims who nodded agreement. "Ricky Farmer here was senior air controller for O'Hare airport while there was still Human air traffic. When all your planes were grounded and he was victimized, he took notes on Catteni routes and procedures. He has code words—though his Catteni is about what my English once was," and that rated some chuckles from the audience, "and these will help us get into some of the landing places now used by Catteni transport ships. I understand from Jeff Fawcett," and he gestured to the other Victim, "that large amusement areas have been built around the landing sites for the crews. These would be useful places for us to find out more information."

"You mean, that cool as a cucumber, we're going to reinvade Earth?" Lenny Doyle said.

"We also intend to . . ." and Zainal had the merest smile on his lips, "invade Catten."

That provoked a widespread eruption from the audience, more an elated one than fearful, although quite a few faces bore skeptical expressions.

"Hey, ain't that pushing our luck?" Lenny Doyle asked, raising his voice to be heard above the babel.

"Only volunteers," Zainal said with a sly grin. "And mostly to learn what would be impossible to learn on your planet. More codes are needed and Catten is the only place to go for that."

Kris waited for someone to ask what was so obvious to her: if Zainal was going to contact Catteni dissidents. She didn't know how many people on Botany—besides Chuck Mitford—knew anything about that facet of his grand scheme. Surely Zainal would have confided in Ray his hopes that he could muster assistance on his home planet to help overthrow the Eosi.

"We got to have information we can't get any other way," Ray Scott put in. Kris heaved a small sigh of relief. Ray did know and seemingly approved. "We're also going to ask for volunteers to remain on Earth and contact the resistance groups."

"I don't know all of them," Jeff Fawcett said in a voice still hoarse from his recent ordeal. "But enough for us to get the word spread."

"Jeff's also going to need a volunteer to go with him," Scott said, "preferably from the First or Second Drops . . ."

The number of hands that shot into the air gave Kris a thrill of pride. The most eager had jumped to their feet, to establish their willingness: Joe Latore, both the Doyle brothers, Mack Dargle, Bart Lincoln, Matt Su, and Sandy Areson were those she recognized first in the show of hands.

"Thank you very much," Zainal said.

"Gratifying, most gratifying," Ray said, holding up his hand, too, as did all the other military men seated at the table. "More than the ships can hold."

"Some must speak and understand Catten," Zainal said.

"We're learning," quipped someone.

"You will learn harder," Zainal said with a wry expression.

"What about the Farmers?" Jay Greene asked when the laughter at that threat died. "Shouldn't we wait for their response? And their advice?"

"No, the time to move is now," Scott said.

Zainal stood. "The Eosi will try very hard to break through the Bubble. That is their way. Run shod roughly over any opposition with the force of their weapons. We must leave before they reinforce their warships. They have many."

"But they haven't been able to penetrate the Bubble, and we know they've tried," Jay said.

"They will keep trying until they have," Zainal said. "That is why they tried to discover new information in the minds of your specialists."

Dick Aarens jumped to his feet, his expression angry and obstinate. "And what happens to those of us left here when they do break through the Bubble? Have you contingency plans for that—if you're taking all three ships away with you?"

"We move quickly and not where they expect us to go and learn what they plan and how to . . ." Zainal looked down at Kris for the word he needed.

"Counteract," she murmured.

"Counteract their plans."

"We're still fleas on a dog's back," Jay said, "with all the ships you said they have. I was talking to Rick Farmer, and he says they've got hundreds in their navy. What if they use all of them against the Bubble?"

Judge Iri Bempechat raised his hand and was given precedence over others who wanted to add their comments.

"Zainal, such a fleet is widely dispersed, is it not?" And when Zainal nodded, the Judge went on, still looking at Zainal, "and it would take weeks, even months, to direct them all here. So we have some leeway if we make our moves quickly. Admiral Scott believes that they would try to install a battery on the moons that are outside the Bubble. To do so, they must bring in machinery, material—and life support systems for whichever unfortunate species is drafted for such an undertaking. I am also of the opinion, with which our military and naval representatives concur," and, with one hand on his chest, he bowed his head to the right and left, "that the Farmers must have placed some sort of sentinel to monitor our protective Bubble. They made it clear, in that one regrettably short interview with various groups of us, that they intend to preserve us. I believed in their sincerity as well as their interest in us . . . even if it should be the interest of a scientist watching ants to see how they contrive—"

"Now, wait a bloody minute . . ." and Geoffrey Ainger jumped to his feet. Kris had not noticed him, seated at the back, and wasn't happy at his presence. "What is all this going to do for us? Except put the colony in more danger? Simply because one . . ." and his pause was pregnant with his distrust and animosity toward Zainal, ". . . person wants to pursue a private revenge?"

"First duty of a captured soldier . . . sir . . ." and it was a stern Mitford whose parade ground voice dominated the shouted reactions from an angry audience, "is to do his best to escape and return to his unit. Mine is on Earth. And if Zainal wants to see his people freed of the Eosian domination, we sure as hell do, too, 'cause it means we'll get out from under 'em. Militarily, a combined assault has many advantages."

That speech set the cat among the pigeons, Kris

thought, struggling to keep from cheering. Or maybe the night crawlers after live meat.

Ray Scott, with help from Peter Easley and Judge Bempechat, finally restored enough order to continue the meeting. Easley had been discreetly seated to one side where Kris had not noticed him. Not too far, as it turned out, from Ainger. Not far either from Beggs, whom she saw sitting by the British ex-naval officer. Had Pete sat there to keep an eye on those dissidents? Quite likely, she thought.

"You gave me the impression, sergeant, that you had no wish to leave Botany now." Ainger could put a wealth of venom in a seemingly casual comment.

"I don't, but I'll do a great deal to preserve what we all have made here. So I can enjoy what I've—we've—worked so hard to achieve." Satisfied with the applause to his answer, Chuck sat down again.

"There are risks," Ray said, once more taking charge of the proceedings. "Most of you can figure them out without much help but, if our people on Earth knew that there was an organized *space* resistance to the Cat—I mean, the Eosian overlords—it would give them heart and purpose against the tremendous odds they've had to deal with. Especially if we can also prove that we've rescued the ones the Eosi were brain-wiping."

"Speaking of tremendous odds, admiral—" And Ainger was again on his feet. "Just how large a fleet exists? That's pertinent even if getting the entire naval arm of the Catteni here would take time." He looked directly at Zainal for the answer.

"Some of the oldest ships in service are slow and their equipment obsolete," Zainal replied. "There are only four of heavy—new in service dreadnoughts, did you call them, Ray—" And when Scott nodded, he went on, "that much information Admiral Scott and I learned on Barevi.

Until just recently spaceship builders have been concentrating on producing ships like the KDL and KDM, to replace those no longer space-worthy, like the first ship we attacked."

"So what sort of ships and weaponry do they have to bombard those of us left behind on Botany?" Ainger asked.

Boy, thought Kris, *that Ainger has a bad negative attitude.*

"Only the four of the dreadnoughts but there are . . . ships of the line . . . which are able to destroy satellites, small moons, and large asteroids. To my knowledge, which is now not up to date, there are thirty of them. They are assault vessels, which supported the kind of large transport that landed on your planet. They are larger than the two K-class we have here."

Ray Scott leaned over the table toward Ainger. "Zainal has given us a list of the types of spacecraft used by the . . . um . . . navy. We've also been able to get a fair translation of the data from the scout ship, so we have useful details about range, crew complement, firepower, and maneuverability of all types, except the dreadnoughts, which are so new. You are certainly welcome to peruse the data at your leisure."

Ainger waved away that offer with a flick of his fingers. "Those of us remaining on Botany are going to be vulnerable . . ."

"Only if the Bubble fails," Ray Scott said in a testy tone, "which seems unlikely, given the advanced technology of the Farmers which is so upsetting the Eosi." Then he deliberately looked away from Ainger. "So we have three expeditions to mount: first, a reconnaissance at the Bubble edge; second, sending off both the scout and one transport to Earth to see what—" he grinned "—trouble we can cause there and how we can help the resistance movements; and third, an information-gathering jaunt to

Catten. I think that has to be under your command, Zainal," and he nodded in his direction, "with your choice of crew but we'll accept volunteers for both expeditions."

"Who gets to peek out of the Bubble?"

Zainal stood. "A full crew." Then he pointed at individuals. "Gino, Raisha, Bert, Laughrey, Boris, and Hassan. Those only who speak good Catteni and are the right size will come with me," and his eyes flickered briefly at Kris.

"We feel we should pack the Earth expedition with as many infiltrators as possible," Ray said and had to raise his hand to finish his sentence when most of his listeners rose and shouted out their names, "to spread the good word."

"What if there're some traitors among us?" Dick Aarens asked.

Ray Scott gave the mechanic a long incredulous look. "How many do you think there could be?"

There were smothered giggles, and Dick Aarens swung about, trying to find the sources.

"Well, there might be," he muttered with sullen aggressiveness. "Particularly on the last drop—and even among the Victims. One of them might have been lying 'doggo' for very *good* reasons. He kept his brains while others got them wiped."

"Now, just a cotton-pickin' minute." Will Seissmann was on his feet, shaking a fist at Aarens across the audience.

"Young man . . ." began Miss Barrow who was puce-faced with indignation.

Dr. Ansible was so apoplectic at the mere suggestion that he had to be restrained from diving across two rows of seats to Aarens.

"I'd retract that, were I you," Peter Easley said.

"I won't because it damned well is a possibility,"

Aarens said, jutting his jaw out as if asking for a punch which would have many willing to oblige him.

Dorothy Dwardie jumped up. "In my professional opinion, Mr. Aarens, there is little possibility of treachery among those who suffered, or even avoided, the Eosi mind-wipe. We have had trauma counseling sessions which would have exposed a quisling."

Which, Kris devoutly hoped, was accurate. But the suspicion had been raised and would hang there, a dark doubt in everyone's mind: even among those who had learned a great deal about each other in the years they had worked together on Botany.

Another of the psychology team, Ben Bovalan, rose. "We may have neither a lie detector nor any sodium pentathol but there are ways of testing responses. That is, if anyone feels such a procedure is at all necessary above and beyond our trauma counseling." He gave Aarens a dire look before he sat down.

"I won't close what has been a very constructive meeting on that kind of sour note," Ray Scott said. He was not the only one scowling in Aarens' direction. "I will summarize what we," and he indicated the others at the table, "have been planning, and why there is some urgency in the scout making a reconnaissance run. We do take Zainal's advice that Earth would be the last place the Eosi would look for us to appear," and he grinned, "and the best place for us to set in motion a coup d'état. If Zainal is willing to risk his life returning to Catten for the information he considers vital to our ultimate goal of freedom from the Eosian domination, then I wish him all the luck he'll need and the support of everyone on this planet. We all have many reasons to be grateful he was on that first drop. Don't we?"

The spontaneous cheering, and the warmth of it, brought tears to Kris' eyes. She never would have expected that sort of public gratitude . . . especially from

Ray Scott who had not always agreed with Zainal. The applause and stamping continued for so long that she gave him a nudge to stand and acknowledge it. He did so, with typical diffidence, but his wave of acceptance took in the entire audience and became a formal salute to Ray Scott.

That was when Kris noticed the very satisfied grin on Iri Bempechat's face. Chuck looked suspiciously bland, one eyebrow twitching while he played with his pencil, slipping it up and down through the fingers of his right hand, a sure sign of complicity. And suddenly Aarens' niggling little suggestion was only Aarens tossing a spanner in works that didn't happen to include his participation.

THE VERY NEXT DAY, THE DESIGNATED PILOTS climbed into Baby, the scout ship, and took off for the peek out of the Bubble's remarkable material. They drew straws for takeoff and landing and the other in-flight duties since this was also a training mission.

The official mission directors took places in Ray Scott's office, grouping around the bridge console, which had been taken from the crash-landed transport that had made the Fifth Drop. So those in Scott's office would have a chance to see what Baby did and saw. Someone had thought to rig speakers outside the hangar so that the many that wouldn't find places in the office could at least hear what was going on.

"On site," Raisha said, her voice ringing with suppressed excitement. "Still the same space flot. Can't see that any of it has moved a centimeter. Gino's easing Baby's nose in between two of the largest of the disks the Eosi vessel left behind." She chuckled.

"Good choice," Ray said, grinning. "The geosynchronous satellite might not even notice we're looking out."

"Hold it right here," and there was such a change in Raisha's tone that everyone tensed. "How big did Zainal say the Catteni fleet arm is?"

Apprehensively, Ray looked toward Zainal. The Catteni immediately leaned over the speaker grill.

"How many do you see?" he asked as calmly as if he was asking how many rock squats were visible.

"Two of those dreadnoughts, I think. We're not entirely outside the Bubble yet but the skin is transparent and we can see out." What she didn't add, "and I hope they can't see in," hovered unsaid but understood.

Kris felt goosebumps rising on her arms and rubbed them away.

"There are also three flotillas of other smaller craft," and Hassan Moussa took over the reporting, "five in each group, beside and above the two big guys you can probably see on the bridge monitor."

"Yes, we see them. Are they the dreadnoughts, Zainal?" Ray asked, beckoning for Zainal to stand beside him.

Zainal nodded. "What else?"

"Wouldn't they be enough?" Jim Rastancil asked facetiously.

Zainal shrugged.

"Hey, we've got other junk in the sky," Hassan continued. "Shall I widen the screen?"

"Yes, please," Zainal said, crossing his arms on his chest, the picture of objective observer.

"It's the dreadnoughts I worry about," Ray said, rubbing his chin nervously.

"What other ships are there, Hassan?" Zainal asked blandly.

"Bulky cargo type carriers and one transport larger than the KDL or KDM. Heading toward the nearer moon."

Ray looked at Zainal. "You were right about the moon

base. What sort of air-to-ground missiles would they have? Something heavy enough to penetrate the Bubble?"

"Stay where you are, Gino," Zainal cautioned. "I do not know, Ray. Eosian weapons are powerful but the Bubble is an unknown quantity."

"Baby has not fully penetrated the Bubble," Gino said. "Hassan's just telling you what we can see through it."

There was a sudden flash of blinding whiteness, which stunned everyone watching, causing them to have retinal flashbacks. It took several seconds before clear vision was restored to those in the office.

"I do believe they're trying to breach the Bubble," said Hassan after a moment, and he sounded highly amused.

"What was that flash?"

"Them," Hassan replied. "Quite likely with every weapon on board."

"I'd say they fired all forward weapons," Laughrey said, "although that flash was so strong, I don't think any of us are seeing more than the damned flash. Baby evidently saved us the worst of it with some sort of instant screen." Zainal nodded.

"Any pain in your eyes? Headache?" Leon Dane asked, present in his capacity as a physician.

"Do you have a clearer idea of what happened down there?" Zainal asked.

"We got the flash right on," Ray said, blinking furiously, "but I'm seeing all right . . ." He looked around for confirmation from the others and everyone nodded.

"Us, too," Laughrey said, "even with lots of retinal echoes, all shaped like Baby's forward screen. Yeah, and hey, nothing got through the Bubble to us."

"All systems functioning perfectly," Raisha said, calm again.

"And whaddaya know?" Gino's tone was jubilant. "There isn't a ship out there—'cept the one heading toward the Moon, which is in the same place they were before they fired."

"Some of the smaller ones are tumbling end over end," said Bert Put. "That was some backlash! Shake 'em up good."

"I don't think they'll try that kind of a broadside again real soon," Boris said in his deep bass voice, rippling with laughter.

"They've lost a whole mess of gear again, too," Gino said. "I doubt they've even reception from the nearer ships."

"Could they have fired because they saw Baby?" Ray asked anxiously.

"No. We put the brakes on the moment Raisha spoke. The fo'ard screen was right against the Bubble film but we hadn't penetrated it," Gino said.

"You might say our timing was serendipitous," Laughrey said, chuckling.

"Can you pick up the newest Eosi orbital satellite?" Ray said, reminding them of the second purpose of their flight.

"On screen," Boris said. "Tracking and recording. It is not as fast as the Farmers' orbital. In fact, it is as slow as a horse-drawn vehicle compared to a Formula One racer."

"Really?" Jim Rastancil said.

Kris made a note to herself to tell Boris what a lovely comparison that was. And very reassuring. She turned to Zainal and saw that he was grinning, even if he couldn't possibly know anything about Formula One racers. She'd told him about horses. But Formula racing had not yet come up in any of their conversations.

Now Zainal was nodding. "As soon as we know its trajectory and timing, the scout and the KDM must leave. They will take a while to get ship-to-ship communications back on-line, and then it will take the Eosi time to calm down at this defeat of their weapons. They will be so angry, they could argue for days before they come to a decision about what to do next."

"What about the moon base?" Ray asked.

Zainal shrugged. "That will take many weeks, months even, before it is finished. They may not even know *we* can get out when we want to."

"But we landed on Barevi and stole a ship," Ray said by way of reminder.

"They do not know that those ships are in here now."

"How stupid are these Eosi?" Bull Fetterman asked, his eyebrows raised high in surprise.

"You might be surprised," Zainal said.

"Then how long will it take to provision and crew the scout and the KDM?" John Beverly asked, speaking for the first time.

"How long is the trip to Earth?" Chuck asked Zainal.

"At top speed, about ten of your days," Zainal said.

"Didn't think it was that close," remarked Beverly.

"From here it is. From Barevi it is longer."

"I'd say we can provision, water, do a quick service in about three days," Chuck said.

"Do it in one and a half," Zainal said. "Sooner is better than later."

"Okay, gang, let's do it," Chuck said, clapping his hands as a signal to move out. He got to the door of Ray's office, stopped, turned, and asked, "So who's going?"

Ray Scott was pulling a file to the center of his desk. "I'll tell you by the end of dinner. All right, now, where's that provisional list we made up?"

DINNER THAT NIGHT WAS MORE OF A FEAST than a normal repast and there were loud calls for the evening's cooks to come out and take a bow. Dowdall stood on his table and announced a call for volunteers to hunt enough rocksquat and catch enough fish to provision the ships with "edible" food, not that Catteni issue.

"Dorothy warned me that there're a lot of scarce items on Earth. The Catteni take almost everything that's produced," he said with a very sober expression.

"Hey, Dow, we still got crates of the Catteni bars," Joe Latore said. "They don't taste like much . . . unless you're real hungry."

"There are so many hungry people," Dr. Ansible said in a sad tone, but loud enough for many to hear.

Sandy Areson leaped atop her chair. "We got lots here we can send along. Botanical care packages. Any volunteers?"

"We can let all the kids sleep in the center tonight," Patti Sue Greene shouted. "They'd love that and I'll volunteer me . . ."

"You'll need more than yourself," Mavis Belton said.

"I will be glad to assist Patti Sue," Anna Bollinger said and prodded Janet beside her who nodded quickly but without much enthusiasm.

Zane! Kris had to cover her mouth with one hand. What if she never came back from Catten? Never saw Zane again . . . Then she felt a hand squeeze her shoulder and looked up into Peter Easley's eyes. He nodded his head once and smiled reassuringly. Kris sniffed, patted his hand, and sniffed again. No, Zane would be fine.

She was going on the Catten mission with Zainal and he had not yet set an established departure time. There had to be dings painted into the KDM: he had to do a little fixing with the recognition beacon, so that it gave only so much of the normal patterning before jamming. That would also verify the damage it had suffered. There were uniforms to be fixed: hair to be dyed gray, and the yellow contact lenses to be fitted so that this group would look more Catteni than what was called the first Botany expedition to Barevi had. Sandy Areson had fixed up cheek pads for Zainal and several rather nasty-looking scars that could be glued on his face—she instructed Kris on the process. These would sufficiently alter his appearance and would also explain the persona he was adopting for the expedition. Sandy gave Kris small cheek pads that gave her more of a rounder, Catteni-shaped face. For Chuck she had yet another wad, in between his gums and teeth. Subtle enough but effective in altering appearances.

They'd spend the longish journey to Catten learning as much of the language as they could cram into their skulls . . . as well as the drills that would mark them as Drassi. Coo and Pess would also be in the crew: Deski and both Rugarians often accompanied transport crews because of their strength. There were always Rugarians on Catten as well. Coo and Pess might even be able to discover as much information from their species as Zainal could.

When dinner—and the accolades to the cooks—was completed, Ray Scott climbed to the top of a cleared table and read out the names of the crews for each ship. At the end there were more cheers than long faces.

"If this first run works," Ray said, "we'll make as many as we can and save as many who may be at risk as possible."

That met with a rousing cheer, foot stamping, and hand clapping.

"Can we handle more?" someone shouted.

"Don't be silly," a woman replied contemptuously. "We've got plenty of space."

"Yeah, but who's to say who's in a real risk situation?"

"We'll find out," Ray said, waving down others who wanted to discuss that issue. "We've got people from quite a few nationalities so we can make good contacts everywhere."

"Any specialist is at risk," Norma Barrow surprised everyone by saying in a firm and unusually loud voice which defied contradiction.

"And no quisling accepted," a man said from somewhere in the dining hall.

Aarens whirled about trying to find who had spoken.

"Cool it, Aarens," Ray Scott said. "It's not as if the Eosi have coerced many humans. At least I hope not."

"I'll find me a lie detector and some sodium pent," Leon Dane said. "We'll process anyone we think might be suspicious. And long before they find out we've got our own transport," he added with a grin. He was going along as mission medic and to see what medical supplies he could acquire. He was hoping that not every one of his dissident friends in Sydney had been rounded up when he was. Joe Marley hoped to find help in Perth. Ricky Farmer had said that Catteni ships flitted from one continent to another, seemingly without orders or on special missions.

"It's got so even the sight of a Catteni transport sends everyone into hiding," Ricky said. He had volunteered to go to Chicago where many were now living in the old underground sewer and transport system, which had been constructed in the 1800s and had been virtually forgotten.

Leila Massuri and Basil Whitby had volunteered to go to London and Paris. The Chunnel had not been finished or opened up but it was completely dug from shore to shore and had provided a means of getting to and from the continent. Boris and Raisha would pilot the scout and see what they could find in their homeland, Russia. Bull Fetterman, Mic Rowland, Lenny Doyle, and Nat Baxter completed the Baby's crew. Bert Put and Laughrey would pilot the KDM, with Lex Kariatin, Will Seissmann, Joe Latore, Vic Yowell, Ole, Sandy Areson, and Matt Su as crew while John Beverly was de facto captain. They hoped to have all four decks full of refugees on the way back. And at least some of the machinery, tools, and equipment on the wish lists.

Zainal, Gino Marrucci as backup pilot, Kris, Chuck Mitford, Coo, Pess, Mack Dargle, Ninety Doyle, and Jim Rastancil were those going on the KDL to Catten.

Chapter Four

IT WAS AS WELL THAT BOTANY DAYS
were so long because every minute was needed as engineering groups under Peter Snyder—with Dick Aarens
working as hard as anyone else despite a sour mood as he
took exception to everything and argued any alterations—checked and provisioned the ships.

"If he comes into the infirmary with a wrench-shaped
wound on his head . . ." Pete muttered to Thor Mayock at
breakfast.

"I won't give him any painkillers when I stitch it up,"
Thor finished for him. "You look ghastly."

"Ha! Speak for yourself."

Worrell was everywhere, living up to his nickname
of Worry, checking lists and trying to supply whatever
he could to take back as care packages. Beth Isbell and
Sally Stoffers were his shadows, discreetly double-checking since every one was working flat out to accomplish the necessary miracles.

To be sure of accuracy in the configurations, five people checked out the trajectory and time of the thirty-hour orbit of the second world-circling Eosian satellite and several windows were discovered: Bert chose the south polar ones that he felt gave both the scout ship and the KDM the longest escape shot. The first propitious window left little time, but both KDM and Baby were ready, so the crews scrambled aboard. Weary but satisfied teams cheered as they took off. Following the example that had worked with the return procedure of the first Barevi raid, they made all possible speed to the Bubble, slowed and pressed prows through at minimum thrust. The scout went first, just in case, and gave the KDM the all-clear. After that they were lost to those watching. Nor could any message be sent back to reassure those on Botany.

Zainal, Ray Scott, Pete Easley, and Judge Iri spent hours trying to work out, from copies of Baby's records, a plausible mission that would explain where Zainal and his ship had been before they returned to Catten. Zainal couldn't remember if any of the earliest of the K class had gone missing, although that was likely enough. They were used for large crew explorations of habitable planets, for mining expeditions and supply runs. But the clever damage to the hull would explain a space collision. Pete Snyder got Aarens challenged by the need for a fault that would appear to have disabled the engine. A small part, actually, which as everyone knew, was the kind that could be easily overlooked in a servicing and yet cause considerable problems when it malfunctioned. A bogus part for the gyro was constructed, using imperfect metals to account for its sudden collapse. Aarens was very pleased with his handiwork and received generous praise. His basic need for constant appreciation was wearing on those who had to work with him. But, as they all said, he produced when the chips were down.

Then Aarens redeemed himself once again, by pointing out that the boards in the bridge helm positions were the same. Everything salvageable from the crashed ship had been saved: just in case some unexpected use could be made of the parts. As it turned out, even the unusable pieces had been stacked at the back of a cave. Zainal went through the worst damaged, scorched boards and chose several which, when they reached Catten, he would substitute for the usable ones, thus confirming the substantial damage which had delayed their return. These and the malfunctioning gyro unit would be sufficient.

"They will not let us dock at the space station with such damage," he said, waving the scorched boards about. "They'll shunt us to the surface, to a small emergency field until they can send technicians to inspect. But we need some sort of cargo. A ship picking up materials from a mining center . . ."

"Duxie's prospectors have mined more gold than we need," was one of Judge Iri's suggestions.

"Platinum, too," Ray put in.

"Those are good," Zainal said. "Any other rare metals? Even a crate or two of raw ore would be useful. Rhenium, any of the platinum group. We'll say we had to leave cargo behind to lift with such a damaged ship. The gyro went first, we were in a meteor shower . . . took us a long time to jury-rig the boards. I think that's a suitable scenario," and he grinned slyly at Kris for that latest addition to his ever-expanding English vocabulary. "Good Drassi bringing home what they can. And I can raise such a fuss over the shoddy manufacture that delayed us that I shall be sent from one office to another with my complaints, and that's how I'll learn what I need to know. Make loud accusations of poor servicing and second-rate materials."

"Is Catten so bureaucratic, too?" asked Ray with a frown.

"Only the Eosi cut corners."

"You're sure you can carry this impersonation off?" Judge Iri was clearly worried.

Zainal shrugged. "Why not? Who but a Catteni ship would go to Catten? It is not a comfortable place to be," and he glanced over at his volunteers, chosen as much because they were all sturdily built and would be able to manage the heavier gravity of Catten. Kris wasn't so sure about her own ability but nothing would have kept her from going along, even if she had to remain in the artificially lower gravity of the ship the entire time. She now had enough Catten to answer any communications the ship might be sent.

"We have been away a long time, whoever we are," Zainal said with a little sly grin, "so it doesn't matter that we have landed and changed the ID. Who will know?"

"How fast does your paint dry?" asked Ninety facetiously.

They still had the uniforms that had been tailored to fit the first Barevi raid but Sandy Areson had some new artifices to contribute. First, she'd an awful-smelling mixture that bleached their hair a dingy gray. One of the recovering Victims was a skilled optician (though he never did explain what he had done on Earth that would have caused him to be victimized by the Eosi). When he realized that gray hair and skin would not entirely present the team as Catteni, he finally managed to produce yellow contact lenses, cursing the need to improvise, since he had not considered his first attempt to be successful. But he managed.

"You'll have to take them out and wash them every day," Riz Kamei said, unhappy with that necessity. "No plastics here at all."

"Yet . . ." one of his helpers said with a grin.

"Whatever," and Riz flicked his long fingers irritably, "but the lenses will do what's necessary." Then he shook his head as if he found even the requirement of yellow as an eye color an offense.

He showed them all how to put them in, how to clean

them in a solution he provided, again muttering about insufficient supplies until everyone really did wonder what his Earth side job had been. He did however allow himself a slight smile of approval when the contacts were in place.

Kris had never considered herself especially vain, but she had had a brief flush of dismay when her hair had not only been clipped very short on her head but bleached such a hideous gray. Now, with the yellow eye lenses, she looked so much like a Catteni, she was almost nauseated.

"You're still much too pretty to be a typical Catten broad," Ninety Doyle remarked. He added a smile that, with his yellowed teeth and dyed skin, made him look all too much like other Drassi they'd seen in the Barevi markets.

She gave a shudder of repulsion. "You look awful, Ninety. Lenny would disown you."

"Lenny's mad enough he couldn't come along," Ninety said, closely examining his gray complected face. Their Botany suntans also helped approximate a Catteni grey skin. Sandy had said both body paint and hair dye would last about two or three weeks, depending on how often they bathed.

"Yeah, but Lenny's closer to a Guinness than I am," Ninety said gloomily.

Looking around, Kris remembered that the Catteni who had crewed Baby hadn't washed at all, remembering the stench in their quarters.

"If there is any Guinness left, Ricky Farmer wasn't so sure about that. But I'm sure he'll bring you back a bottle," Kris said, meaning to console.

"Bottle?" Ninety roared in dismay, as if she had uttered an unforgivable blasphemy.

"Can?"

"What'd you bet he frees the last vat in Dublin?" Mack Dargle said.

"I never bet on sure things," Kris said, grinning.

"They gotta get your teeth yellower, Kris. That smile's a giveaway."

"And not a tube of Colgate to whiten my teeth anywhere on this planet," she said in wistful retort.

"They may bring some back, you know," Mack Dargle said, taking the mirror from Doyle so he could inspect himself and did a good comic double take. "My own mother wouldn't recognize me."

"Just so long as a Catten wife doesn't," Ninety said.

Mack shuddered. "I saw some of those crew-women. No thank you. I'd sooner wrestle with a crocodile."

THE PREPARATIONS FOR THIS FORAY INTO enemy territory were finally complete. The window was a nighttime polar one so Kris hurried into the day care where Zane was sleeping, for one last look.

Zainal came to join her, resting his big hands sympathetically on her arms.

"He's a fine strong lad. He'll do well here," he said into her ear and pressed his face against her cheek in his special display of affection.

A noise made them both turn to the doorway and there was Pete Easley, a slightly droll smile on his face.

"I drew night duty," he said, though all three knew he had probably done so on purpose. "He'll be fine. Don't worry about him."

"We won't," Zainal said with a nod of his head and with one arm still on Kris', led her out of the room. Both stopped at the threshold for one more look at the sleeping child.

Kris tried not to, but she sniffed all the way to the hangar and had to blot her eyes twice. She hadn't thought—in all the fuss and furor of these preparations—that she would experience the same anguish at leaving him as she had on their first expedition to Barevi.

"Zane *will* be all right with Easley," Zainal murmured as he lifted her down from the flatbed that had brought them to the now-battered and space-worn KDL awaiting them outside the hangar.

The Judge, Ray Scott, Worry, Pete Snyder, Jay and Patti Sue Greene, and even Aarens were there to wish them a safe journey. Worry was even bold enough to clasp Kris in a bear hug. The judge kissed her hand and then both cheeks. If Ray Scott only shook her hand hard and warmly, Patti Sue was openly weeping as she hugged Kris tightly, murmuring over and over, "I'll never forget you, buddy, I'll never forget you."

"I'll hold you to that," Kris said, feeling as she might weep like Patti and, ignoring whatever protocol to board there might have been, she scrambled up the steps into the KDL. Everyone else followed, with Chuck Mitford growling how he hated farewells.

ZAINAL INDICATED THAT GINO SHOULD DO THE honors on the takeoff, while he punched the final bits and pieces of their "delayed return story" into the ship's log. He grinned with unusual good humor when the log acknowledged the entries. There were enough computer hackers to have made it a proper job "as long," they teased Zainal, "as his Catteni was okay." They had even coded into the log appropriate star chart coordinates. If, that is, any one would dare question the report of Emassi Venlik, Zainal's new alias.

"He lived once. Died badly, and only I know where" was all Zainal would say of the man whose identity he was assuming.

"Was he a chosen?" Chuck asked.

Zainal gave a quick shake of his head. His next word startled everyone. "Schkelk!"

Chuck was the first one to fall into the stance of an alert Drassi, with Kris a second later before Mack and

Ninety suddenly realized what had been said: "Listen." Even Coo and Pess straightened from their usual languid positions.

Distinctly and slowly enough for them to understand, he gave orders for the ship to take off and the course it was to assume as soon as it had lifted from the ground.

"Emassi!" was the appropriate reply said in crisp unison and then each went to the duty station they had been assigned.

Coo and Pess buckled into the two drops seats that had been placed on the bridge for their use in takeoff and landing.

Zainal never spoke another word of English during the entire eight-day voyage. Neither did they after one of Zainal's thumps, and Kris was no exception—though she didn't think he whacked her as hard as he did Gino, Chuck, Mack, or Ninety. But it sure reminded her to keep in her part.

The yellow lenses irritated Mack's eyes. Riz had mentioned that someone might have trouble and sent along eyewash, with the recommendation to keep the contacts in for short periods, lengthening the time each day to allow the eyeball to adjust. By the time they were orbiting Catten, he could keep them in most of the day.

Seen from outer space, Catten was a lovely planet! Almost as beautiful as the pictures of Earth sent back from space by Russian and American astronauts. There were larger landmasses but inland lakes the size of seas and several enormous rivers to judge by the width of them. It was also remarkably green, which caused a good deal of surprise.

Zainal grinned. And said in Catten: "They have destroyed enough planets so that they are careful about this one. All manufacturing work is done on other worlds."

"You should see Earth," Ninety said proudly.

"Not all of it is as pleasant as . . . ." Mark paused because there was no Catteni word for Ireland, "where you live."

"More unpleasant since Catteni come," added Gino grimly with an apologetic glance at Zainal who merely nodded. "KDM and . . . yaya . . ." which was all Gino could think of as a Catteni description of "Baby," "will not like what is there now."

Everyone paused in reflection on that unhappy observation. Then Gino pointed to a good-sized satellite. "How many moons?"

"Four," Zainal replied, then added as an immense space station spun leisurely into view in its geosynchronous orbit above Catten, "we do not want to dock there."

Everyone gawked at the sight of the monstrous edifice, with gantries and netted supplies far larger than the KDL floating on tethers about it. Ships of all sizes made their way in and out of docking slips. One entire quadrant seemed to be a shipyard, taking advantage of the lack of gravity to push large structural members into position for assembly.

Suddenly the com unit blurted out a harsh barking which was either muffled or distorted so much that only Zainal understood; the others caught maybe one word clearly.

". . . chouma."

Zainal rattled off his assumed name, the fact that his ship was damaged and requested landing at an isolated emergency site on planet.

By listening with intense concentration to the Catteni language, the crew got most of the next exchange, demanding details of the damage. Zainal responded that he could not maneuver into the moon base with currently faulty equipment. Immediately he was bluntly told to sheer off his present course while a landing site could be warned of his imminent arrival. Zainal twitched fingers

Anne McCaffrey

behind his back to indicate to the others how well their scheme was going. Considering the size and complexity of the space station, the Terrans could well appreciate the need for caution, and why ships had to be in maneuverable condition. They were probably as fastidious about unstable cargoes.

The interrogation went on. What was the trouble? Where had the KCX been? Was it contaminated? What cargo did it have on board?

Zainal signaled to Gino to go into his well-rehearsed reply, the pilot scrambling to get his notes out of his pocket in case he needed to refer to them.

"Engineer Tobako speaking," he said. He'd had fun choosing an alias. "Gyro unit, two-three-eight . . ." and he spoke the Catten letters appended to the part, "malfunctioned in meteor swarm, flash-back damaging many boards in control panel and causing helm problems. Maneuvering affected. Suffered hull and interior damages. Landed on largest meteor to repair damage. Gyro part badly made," and Gino infused a lot of contempt in his voice for that failing. "Imperfect metal. Had to reduce cargo to lift from meteor. Only one cargo deck remains. Three crew died."

"Only one part cargo?" The contempt and dismay was clearly audible and nothing at all was said about the loss of lives. "Go to field at . . ." and the Catten rattled off the coordinates so quickly that, while Gino managed to jot down the English equivalents of the first four numbers, that was as far as he had got by the end of the message. He gave Zainal a startled and anxious look. Zainal nodded to assure those on the bridge that he had heard all he needed to obey.

"What is the cargo?"

"Platinum, gold, rhenium, some germanium." Zainal took up the report now.

"Ah . . ." and that drawled exclamation was close to approval. "Is there more where that was found?"

78

"Yes. All can be collected again. I will return to the meteor with a repaired ship, and braver crewmen than the Drassi who died. These were only a step above Rassi . . ." Zainal paused to be sure that his complaint was understood. "It is a cargo I do not wish others to get."

"Ah . . ." and there was more warmth and approval. "A vehicle and mechanical support will meet you on the surface. Klotnik."

"Klotnik," Zainal responded. "Out."

When the com line had been cut, every one reacted, sighing, or whistling or mimicking the wipe of a sweaty brow. In fact, Ninety took out a square of cloth and was about to mop his face when Zainal thumped him. Immediately Ninety used his finger to scrape off the sweat, as a real Drassi would do.

"There is really not that much of a cargo," Kris said dubiously. Would they get in trouble with what they had? It was all that Walter Duxie, the head miner, could find that might be considered valuable by the Catteni in the short time he had to do any prospecting. The germanium had been pure luck. And what little of the platinum groups they had so far discovered. While the gold had seemed a real sacrifice to some people, the metal had little intrinsic value on Botany. The two professional and many amateur jewelers used it as settings for some of the rather magnificent gemstones which had turned up on the planet during the general assessment of mineral and metal deposits.

"It is enough, since they think we go back for what was left," Zainal said and grinned, looking more like the man she knew so well than the very Catteni Emassi who had barked answers over the com. "It has gone well. Now proceed slowly until we are in atmosphere and remember to vent smoke often."

That was an effect that Peter Snyder had been particularly pleased to install. It would dissipate fast enough in space but would certainly be visible from the space station, to enhance the story of a "damaged" ship.

"Much traffic," Gino said, glad enough to be steering away from the space station with so many other vehicles zipping here and there or ponderously moving out.

"There are two dreadnoughts in dock, nine large surface landers," Zainal said, pointing to the stern ends.

They were visible once you knew what to look for, Kris realized. They looked bigger to her than the Empire ship from *Star Wars*.

"I count eighteen H-type ships," and again Zainal indicated where to look. What initially looked just like protrusions of the spaceship were, in fact, spaceships in dock. The H-types were similar to the one Kris remembered landing at Denver. She shuddered. Zainal went on. "Look beyond the station to your right, past the freighters and drones." His big finger now indicated a three o'clock position. "There's a full flotilla there."

"I can spot another one on the screen, farther out," and Gino tapped the screen with the proximity display.

"Wow!" Mack swallowed as he saw the incredible number of ships being handled by the station. He stared at the display as they moved slowly away from a direct view of the massive unit.

"How big a navy did you say the Catteni have?" Ninety asked, looking quite anxious.

"More than you see here," Zainal said.

"Lots of traffic, too," Chuck said.

"That is good. For us." And Zainal smiled.

When they were far enough from the space station for Kris to feel as if there were no eyes on them, she and the others began to relax. Now they could spend the descent watching, as more details of the planet were visible.

"I know the field we've been assigned," Zainal said as their ship slowed for landing. "It has some facilities. Always be Catten there. I pilot now."

• • •

"SMALL?" KRIS MURMURED, REMEMBERING TO speak Catten as she took in the landing site. Nine football fields wide at the very least, and long as a Denver jet runway: almost larger than the landing field at the Farmers' hangar on Botany. Low, large buildings framed one side, and beyond them, across an access road, were separate structures, small enough to be dwellings though they reminded her more of the hovels in a Brazilian barrio.

They came down, venting more of Pete's smoke for effect. Zainal's handling of the ship made them all glad they were well strapped in but the motions certainly imitated a ship that was barely controllable. He also halted at a distance from what looked to be hangar or servicing facilities.

Immediately he and Gino, who seemed to be moving slowly for such a generally deft man, removed the panels of the control positions and substituted the scorched boards, handing the good ones carefully to Ninety and Chuck to wrap and store in a prepared hiding place. Ninety and Chuck grunted and seemed to get out of their seats like old men. Zainal replaced the damaged panels, as Gino couldn't seem to get his hands to work properly.

"What's the matter with me?" Gino demanded, in English, looking at his hands.

Ninety and Chuck were taking forever to walk down the short passage and Kris then realized that she felt awfully heavy. It took a real effort to bring one hand over to release the safety belt.

"Me, too," she said, struggling to stand.

"Hmmm," was Zainal's anxious response. "Catten's gravity is heavier than Earth's. You will adjust—but slowly. Just move slowly and pretend that is how you move."

"Wow!" exclaimed Gino when, with considerable effort, he pushed himself to his feet. "My knees are not going to like this."

"Hurry with the hiding," Zainal called out down the passageway to Ninety and Chuck.

"We try, Emassi. We do," but even Chuck Mitford's heavy baritone voice sounded strained by the heavier gravity.

"They will think me a great pilot," Zainal said, with a toothy Catteni smile, "to bring down a ship in this condition."

"Will they believe that we're Catteni?" Gino muttered.

Zainal gave one of his inimitable shrugs and grinned. "Who else but a Catteni would come here?"

"I can sure believe that," Gino said in English. Zainal thumped him and cocked a warning eyebrow at him. "Kotik," he answered, chagrined at his lapse.

Zainal gave him a gentler pat for the proper response.

A pounding on the door and Zainal leaned forward to flick the release switch on the hatch.

There were Catteni growls of "get out of the way" and the thud of nailed boots on the deck as three men, none of them small, stalked into the cramped bridge compartment. Remembering all the drills, Kris somehow managed to get to her feet and assume the proper attention stance. She thought her arms would lengthen from the weight on her shoulders and it was hard to keep her chin up. Fortunately, she didn't have to say or do anything.

"Kivel," said the lead man who acted as Emassi as Zainal did. Since he neither stated that he was Emassi or saluted, Kris knew he had to be the same rank. His brutish features and small bright yellow eyes were also more typical of the species than Zainal's.

"Venlik," replied Zainal and waved to the scorched, warped panels while Gino, who was supposed to be another Emassi, displayed the carefully manufactured defective gyro part.

"Hmph." Kivel took and examined the gyro and handed it back to the Drassi behind him.

Kris decided she was getting good at differentiating the ranks.

Kivel now gestured for the damaged panel to be opened, and turned slightly so that Kris, being a lowly Drassi, could do it.

"Too many in here," Zainal said irritably, and with an imperious wave at Kris, "open cargo, bay three. You hear me?"

Kris nodded which was a lot harder to do in the heavier gravity than she would have believed. And, by sheer effort of will, passed the other two big Drassi and, when she was out of sight, put both hands on the sides of the companionway to give herself some support. She made it to the cargo deck and was grateful that she knew how to operate it. As soon as the cargo hatch swung open, she saw the vehicle, load bed against the side of the ship, and stepped aside as seven men swarmed aboard. One was Drassi and the other poor wretches were obviously the Rassi, the primitives from which the Eosi had made the two more intelligent groups.

The Drassi shouted his commands, obviously delighting in his ascendance over these dumb creatures. For that was what they were. He had to show them where to place their hands on the crates, shoved them toward the open hatch, and even walked them onto the vehicle and pointed to where the crates must be stacked. He sent them back for another load but paused long enough to pick up one of the gold lumps, scratch the soft surface as if to reassure himself it was gold, before he dropped it with a dull thud back into the crate. Then he walked back and forth, the gravity not affecting him one iota, Kris noticed enviously, as he supervised the unloading.

"Is that all?" he asked, glowering at Kris.

"All on board," Kris replied negligently.

"Humph," was his unimpressed response. She then handed him the receipt that Zainal had prepared.

"Everything must be signed and acknowledged," Zainal had told her, in a discussion of the unloading procedure. "He has to take it up front for my signing and whoever is his leader."

"Sign," she said firmly and held out the Catteni issue clipboard that had been in the KDL's supplies.

"Humph." He scrawled some runes.

She pointed to the companionway for him to take the board to his commander and with another "humph" he stomped off. She hung on to the control panel until she heard him returning before she straightened up against the awful weight. He jabbed the clipboard into her midriff. Fortunately she was leaning against the bulkhead so he didn't quite knock her down. She did remember to check that there were two new rune lines before she nodded and gave him the wave to leave. She was appalled to see him jump off the cargo deck to the ground—but then he was Catteni and had on heavy boots—her ankles ached from even watching him. He strode to the front of the vehicle and she was able to close the hatch and just slide down the bulkhead to sprawl on the deck, exhausted by this battle with Catteni gravity.

She was actually close to tears, thinking that she would be no good to Zainal at all on this mission when she couldn't even stand up for more than a few minutes without collapsing.

When she heard voices and booted steps in the companionway, she started to struggle to her feet but the noises stopped; she heard Zainal request transport for him and his crew for shore leave.

"Not much here," Kivel said. "Try Blizte. Small but adequate."

"I know the place," was Zainal's reply.

"Transport will be dispatched on our return."

"Good."

She didn't hear the hatch close and wondered what she

should do now. Get to her feet or collapse again. She knew which she preferred but did so want not to disappoint Zainal.

Suddenly he was there, hands under her armpits, lifting her, almost effortlessly, from the deck. He managed a quick press of his face against her cheek.

"You and Chuck must stay on board as guards," he said swiftly in English. "When the repair men arrive, you are off watch and asleep. Chuck only has to stand around and look suspicious."

"He does that well," she murmured back.

"You did very well, Kris," Zainal said again, his tone warm and loving. She leaned into him for strength until they heard steps approaching and separated from their close embrace. But Zainal kept one hand under her arm to support her.

"They're gone, and a smaller vehicle is on its way here," Chuck said and moved forward to take Kris' other arm.

If she hadn't needed their support, she would have pushed both away from her to walk on her own two feet, but she didn't have the strength and was far too grateful for their assistance.

They eased her back into the bridge compartment and into the com seat.

"Your Catteni is enough for any messages," Zainal said, keeping one hand on her shoulder. "Anything you don't understand, make them repeat. Tell them com unit is also faulty. Then act stupid Drassi and you will tell the Emassi when he comes back. You don't know where he has gone . . . but then they wouldn't ask you since you wouldn't know."

Kris was glad that gravity was not affecting her ears because she understood every Catteni word Zainal spoke.

"Chuck, you will admit only the service men who will have a proper clipboard you will have to sign as they enter, put in the time—I showed you how—when they leave. Whenever they come, Kris is to be off guard and asleep."

An obnoxious klaxon announced that the transport was awaiting its passengers.

"I gotcha," Chuck murmured in English.

Zainal bent to Kris' ear. "The first few days are the hardest. Move as much as you are able and use hot showers," he said in English. "Walk around the ship if you can. We will not be here long. If I can help it."

Then, with a final squeeze of her shoulder, he nodded for Gino, Ninety, Mack, and the two Rugarians to follow him.

Kris saw the ground transport as it sped diagonally off the field, toward the road, away from the command post and the hovels. It was all too quickly lost as the road took it into the thick forest of tossing greenery. She didn't even have the energy to compare Catteni botany with Botany's vegetation.

While she was sunk in the seat, she heard Chuck moving around. When he reentered the bridge compartment, he carried cups and gave her one. Rather, he put it in her right hand where it lay, almost useless with the gravity, on the armrest.

"Try it, gal, you need the energy. Some of Mayock's special."

"Oh, Gawd," she said. It took two hands to get the cup to her mouth but liquid didn't seem to object, and she was able to get a good swig down her throat. Did the heavier gravity make it go down faster? She took another sip and it did seem to drop into her stomach really fast.

"Any better?" Chuck asked in a conciliatory tone.

"I don't know. It all seems like so much work."

"It's never too much work to drink, Kris," he said and took the other chair, looking out at the scenery. "They don't seem to do much in the way of forestry."

"I saw the Rassi," and despite the gravity she managed a little shudder. "You wouldn't want them as work gangs. They barely managed to carry the crates into the waiting truck. I begin to understand why Drassi have such short tempers . . . if they have to work with that level of unintelligence. Not even room temperature. More like just above freezing."

Even talking was hard because it meant she had to move her jaw.

"Just sit, honey," Chuck said, lightly touching her arm in compassion.

"We'll get used to it?" she asked.

"If Zainal says we will, we will. Look, Kris, finish the drink and then get some sleep. That'll help. We've already had a busy day."

"Would I feel too heavy to sleep?"

"Finish that drink and believe you me, you'll sleep, honey."

She did just that, taking the second half of the drink in one gulp and letting Chuck help her back to the crew quarters. Even the bed, which had never been all that soft, felt harder to her. The blanket hadn't gained any weight but it felt rough, even through her uniform. The pillow was a rock but that didn't prevent her from falling deeply asleep.

ZAINAL COMMUNICATED WITH THEM ONCE THE next morning; his blunt phrases indicated all was well. To expect repair crews the next day. He gave a com contact number. Drassi Chuck would give their Drassi leader the prepared list of resupply items. Zainal was getting the rest.

Kris felt somewhat better by midday, with frequent sips of Mayock's Superior Hooch. In fact, it did make her feel lighter. Not light-headed for her head still felt thick. She insisted on standing a watch while Chuck slept. She answered several com unit calls quite adequately. Four were obviously a check to see if the ship's guard was actually on duty. Another, from a very pompous Emassi, inquired if the ship was still in a dangerous condition. She replied firmly that it was not. When the Emassi wanted to speak to Zainal, she gave him the contact number Zainal had left, grateful that he had since she had absolutely no idea where he was. There had been a lot of noise in the background during Zainal's call, which led her to believe he was in a much larger place than the Blizte place which Kivel had mentioned.

She did make herself leave the ship and managed, with very slow steps, to do a full circuit. She sat on the hatch steps and made herself do a second circuit the other way round. When she reentered the ship, she felt as if she had done a marathon at top speed. More of the Mayock Superior with very little water in it helped relieve the exhaustion. In fact, it helped enough so that she did another walk two hours or so later, bored with doing nothing. This excursion didn't leave her feeling as wrecked afterward.

She managed to make some food for Chuck and herself. By then Chuck had slept a good deal longer than his legendary six hours, but he had needed it. She woke him and they ate together, with more of Mayock's supportive aid.

They decided they had both better be on duty when the repair crews arrived, to give a show of exemplary attention to duty. Chuck made her sleep until just before dawn.

"You've got to see dawn here, Kris. Never seen anything like it in my life," he told her. "Then I'll kip out until you see the service crew arriving."

That sounded fine to her. Food helped nearly as much as Mayock's brew, and she slept again until Chuck woke her and, with a friendly hand supporting her, led her into the bridge compartment so they could watch the dawn together.

There weren't many clouds in a Catteni sky—too heavy an atmosphere, Kris decided, or they'd just drop down. But the sky coloration went from the most delicate aqua into fantastic—almost lightning-like—displays of yellow to orange to red and then back to orange and fading into yellow that turned greenish before the blue-green of a normal Catteni sky settled, and the very bright white sun came up. Instantly the bridge screen darkened.

"Too bright for Emassi and Drassi?" she asked facetiously.

Chuck yawned widely and stood up. At least he seemed to be adapting to the heavier gravity. Maybe she would . . . probably just about the time they could leave.

Chuck went off to sleep, and she fixed herself some breakfast. Her stomach must be adjusting because it felt empty, not merely heavy and unready for any new burdens.

She took just a slight dose of Mayock. She didn't want the repair crew folk to smell any liquor on her breath because it would be very difficult to explain where she'd gotten it. Besides, they'd only brought enough for their personal needs. Even if her personal need for continued potions seemed excessive, considering her generally abstemious habits.

Remembering the state of Baby and the KDL when they had captured them, she did wonder if perhaps this ship was a little too neat and orderly to be a proper Catteni used vessel. She'd ask Chuck if they shouldn't throw a few things about. She did leave dishes on the table and the cooking pan on the heat pad.

She never had a chance to discuss this detail with Mitford because she saw the repair crew vehicles, massive affairs, Catteni-style eighteen wheelers, come careening across the field. She had only enough time to shake him awake before the trucks screeched to a halt by the cargo hatch. Someone banged on it. Chuck gave her a shove forward to the bridge compartment.

"You're on com watch," he muttered and then in fine, annoyed Catteni, yelled that he was coming, he was coming.

He undogged the hatch and was almost mowed down by the Emassi who charged in, scowling and punching Chuck out of his way. But years of army discipline intervened, and Chuck assumed a properly military stance, far more humble than any American soldier would present even if a four star general *or* the president of the United States confronted him. Kris' com unit blurped for her response.

"Crew are there?" was the inimical query.

"Yes, Emassi," she replied meekly.

"Get Emassi Yoltin to speak."

"Yes, Emassi." And Kris actually managed to increase her stride to something approximating "hurry" to the hatch and, with a proper salute, begged Emassi Yoltin to speak to Emassi on com.

Meanwhile, the repair crew, burdened with heavy kits and a variety of portable affairs that resembled the weaponry of a bad science fiction movie, went astern to the gyro unit. Another group waited outside the hatch, carrying more carefully some packaged units that looked like control board replacements. Managing to glance outside, she saw others, led by a second Emassi, examining the "meteor" damage, Pete Snyder's magnificent efforts. Several of the outboard sensors on the port side had also been broken off to add verisimilitude to the supposed crash. Suitable gashes had taken a lot of time to make but the Emassi was nodding, touching the marks and then rattling off orders to his crew. A third group were setting up what looked amazingly like a field kitchen. Kris breathed a little sigh of relief that she wouldn't be expected to feed this lot.

Considering what she saw being prepared and smelled

cooking, she hoped that she and Chuck wouldn't have to eat any of it.

"You," Emassi Yoltin said, returning from the bridge, but he pointed to the group waiting outside, "repair controls." He passed by her as if she didn't exist but Chuck now followed Yoltin astern.

"Emassi Venlik orders me to check replacement unit," he said.

Emassi Yoltin gave Chuck such a look that a snake would have died of the venom in it but Chuck held his ground until Yoltin gave an abrupt nod of his head and allowed Chuck to follow him.

Totally superfluous, Kris decided she needed more Mayock to get through this experience.

When the control panel repairs were finished, she did resume her station at the com unit. And saw the arrival of another vehicle. This time she remembered how to initiate communications with an on-surface vehicle and made contact.

"Cargo, supplies. Open hatch," she was told and dutifully followed such orders, wondering what Zainal had acquired.

It was considerable. Foods, crates with runes she couldn't quite understand, but thought they were spare parts. Certainly a good deal of fuel canisters was onloaded, taking up a full cargo deck and then half of another. Some open slatted crates proved to be fresh foods.

"Good," she said, when the Drassi supervising the loading looked at her for some reaction. She smacked her lips. "Not much fresh to eat for a long time," she added. She recognized some of the fruits she had seen, and bought, in the Barevi markets. She'd thought they were indigenous. Then remembered that Zainal had said the Rassi worked the land and produced great quantities of food for both Eosi and Catteni ships. "We eat well."

"We will. And soon," the Drassi said but he jerked his head to the exterior and the rather unusual smells coming from the outdoor kitchen.

The Drassi had been marking off items on the clipboard as the Rassi came on board with their burdens. These seemed slightly more intelligent than the ones there the other day. Possibly because they had resupplied ships so often.

Then the truck was empty and the Rassi sat on the floor, waiting for whatever would happen to them next.

The Drassi handed her the clipboard, and she wrote down her rune and then took it from him to get Chuck's signature. He was standing in the passenger hatch, watching the repair crews eating. He signed and winked at her.

"We weren't invited," he said, mouthing the words with little sound.

She rolled her eyes in relief, aware out of the corner of her eye the ravenous way in which the meal was being consumed, with much smacking of lips and slurping. Even eating in such company would have been nearly as nauseating as the food they consumed so greedily.

She returned the double-signed records to the Drassi, and he also jumped to the ground and barked an order at the apathetic Rassi. They slowly rose and followed him around the ship to the eating place.

She closed and locked the cargo hatch, three of its decks now full of supplies. Zainal had gone whole-hog here. Would they get away with such bald-faced piracy?

"We can eat," Chuck muttered to her as he pushed her past the open cargo hatch. "Water's pretty good."

They used that to dilute the Mayock with which they washed down the fresh fruit and what passed for bread in the Catteni cuisine. It was so fresh that it was easy to chew and didn't taste half-bad.

"D'you know what they're eating out there?" she asked Chuck.

"You don't want to know," Chuck said and took a long swig from his mug.

That was enough to inform Kris that the Catteni were probably eating Rassi. She ate nothing more despite Chuck pantomiming that she should.

The exterior crew had filled in the gouges, and the main hole, using some sort of mastic. When the interior specialists had finished their job, they drove off but left Emassi Yoltin behind to supervise the rest of the repairs.

A Catteni day was longer than one on Earth but shorter than one on Botany. There was actually more exterior damage, between the "meteoric" gashes and the hole, because the stumps of the broken external units had to be removed and replaced. This required technicians going in and out of the ship, and coming awfully close to where the undamaged control panels had been secreted. Kris thought she might have indulged in the first faint of her life but managed to pinch herself hard enough to retain consciousness. They'd come so far and done so well, she simply could not jeopardize everything with such a reaction.

So they had another day to endure the proximity of sweaty men whose clothing was smeared with the repair compound, which intensified the stench of them.

Chuck did offer the Emassi the captain's quarters but that was curtly refused, and Chuck and Kris were left to themselves. They did, however, close the passenger hatch as night descended on the field. That meant they didn't smell whatever it was the Catteni were eating. Kris was ravenous by now and made a huge meal for them both.

"I'll take first watch," Chuck told Kris, and she could not demur. The day's excesses as well as the gravity had reduced her to total exhaustion.

He woke her six hours later. "We've had a few calls, and one from Yoltin to be sure we're keeping watch. So you've got to stand one."

"I'm fine, Chuck, fine," she assured him. Indeed, she realized that it wasn't quite as difficult to sit up and get out of the bed though she still felt as if all her muscles and flesh were being pulled inexorably groundward.

She got a call from Yoltin shortly after she took the com. Yoltin was a real Catteni bastard. Checking up. She had a sudden notion and put it into action by removing the undamaged control panels from where they had been stashed and putting them quietly behind a huge crate in the cargo deck that was currently available. If they should be discovered, though she doubted that, they were no concern of hers. The Drassi had checked off all the items that were brought on board, and being Drassi herself she could pretend she didn't read well. Not many true Drassi did unless they "needed to know" as Zainal would have put it.

By the time all the repairs had been done, Emassi Yoltin did an onboard inspection of every panel and locker of the main ship. Chuck turned an awful deeper shade of gray until she managed to give him a wink. He leaned briefly against the bulkhead in relief.

Yoltin could find nothing to reprimand them for—apart from unwashed dishes in the kitchen, and he ticked them off soundly and loudly for that, while they looked humble, meek, and repentant.

As Yoltin left, Chuck said very angrily to Kris "that the galley must be spotless when Emassi Venlik returned. You are responsible, you will do it."

"Yes, Drassi Chuck," Kris responded with earnest sub-servience. Both were close to laughing at their little charade and did, when the passenger hatch was closed.

They heard the vehicles revving up and immediately strode to the bridge compartment to see the last of the crew leaving, dust rising at the speed of their passage. They also saw a smaller transport coming out from the field buildings.

"Oh, God, what now?" Chuck demanded. "Go do the galley thing, in case that's what's to be inspected."

They really had not been that untidy but she sloshed water and what went for cleaning liquid about the sink. Her hands were raw, and she checked to make sure that the liquid had not taken off her skin dye. It looked paler but she didn't dare do a touch up—the dye had a very noticeable odor to it—until their latest visitor was gone.

It was Kivel after all, with two Drassi, who inspected the ship as well, spending more time on the exterior to approve a smooth hull.

"You go soon?"

"Emassi Venlik is not back," Chuck replied.

"He must come soon. This field will be needed," Kivel said at his most pompous.

"We have been in space months," Chuck said with a very good imitation of a Zainalian shrug.

"Months? Where?"

The query was innocent enough but there was a gleam in Kivel's eyes that suggested rumors of an abandoned cargo of considerable worth had circulated.

Chuck shrugged again.

"We will talk of this at the evening meal," Kivel said, far too affable to have confused even a Rassi.

Chuck looked slightly eager and then relaxed. "I am on guard. Emassi Venlik is a hard commander."

Kivel inclined his head at Kris. "The little one can stay on guard. We will enjoy ourselves this evening," he went on, his tone an insidious promise.

Chuck allowed himself to consider this and, looking hard at Kris, he finally nodded. "You will say nothing of this to the Emassi."

"No, Drassi Chuck."

"Come, then," and Kivel gestured affably for Chuck to take precedence out of the hatch.

Chuck, bowing politely, insisted that the higher-ranking officer leave first. With Kivel's back turned, Chuck had a chance to throw an inquiring look at Kris, and she winked in encouragement. She'd close the hatch and not open it until Chuck got back. Mitford really didn't have much choice, not since a Drassi more or less ordered his company.

Kris ate by herself at the com, watching the dark creep across the beautiful forest and then the first moon rise, a large orange crescent. Two, one very far away and small, also started their ascent with the first one mid-heaven. She almost wished the com unit would blurt at her so she'd have something to do. She poured herself a respectable tot of Mayock's superior and then wondered how Chuck would be handling the Catteni equivalent. Mitford had often boasted that he could drink anything alcoholic and keep his wits about him. She certainly hoped he could tonight.

The fourth moon was rising, and the level in the bottle of Mayock was only a finger high, when she heard a transport, and loud, off-key singing. Then there was a spirited banging—by more than one fist—on the hatch and she hastened to open it.

Kivel almost threw Chuck inside, waving back to the transport and peremptorily waving the driver to go on.

"You made it," she said, hearing herself slurring her words.

"On . . . ly just," Mitford replied, having far more of a problem than she in enunciating.

"I'll get you to bed," she said, pleased that she was so much soberer. "Whad' he wan'?"

"Cooooo . . . orrrr . . . dinates," Chuck managed, lurching from side to side, even with her trying to keep him upright.

"Thought so."

"Doan . . . know . . . 'em. On . . . ly Drassssssssi," Chuck said and hiccuped. "Stuff . . . was . . . worst . . . thing . . . ever . . . drank. Drunk. Drink."

They had reached the captain's quarters, which was nearest, and Chuck turned in at that door. Kris didn't object. It was nearer than the crew quarters. In his condition she doubted he could get into the lowest of the three-tiered bunks without cracking his skull.

The captain's bed was also wider and she steered him toward it. He flopped down but was sitting up so fast that they cracked skulls.

"Ohhhh," he groaned. "Can't . . . get . . . boots . . . off."

She did that service for him with fingers that had trouble opening the closures. The next thing she knew, he had locked his arms about her and tumbled her into the bed along with him. By the time his head was down, he was snoringly asleep. She waited a few moments, wanting to get horizontal herself because suddenly the Mayock that she'd been sipping for hours was catching up with her. But he had some sort of a death grip on her and she couldn't disengage herself.

Well, she was as nearly horizontal as he was, though she still had her boots on. She inched her way into a more comfortable position, put her head on his chest and went to sleep.

SHE WOKE FIRST THE NEXT MORNING. CHUCK was no longer snoring but he had his head resting on her bare shoulder. She'd had the most remarkably vivid, almost pornographic dreams, and gasped in dismay.

"And I'm bare?" Chuck also was—clothing strewn about the cabin. "Oh, my god, that Mayock did it again."

She swallowed. "That's unfair. I don't remember anything about it. At least I hope that dream wasn't what we *did*!" She stared at the relaxed, sleeping face of Chuck Mitford and slowly shook her head. She could not, would not believe he, and she, had done *that*! Such behavior, even in their super-drunken conditions, was as uncharacteristic as it was unlikely. Even impossible. She shook her head, infuriated and irritated.

Then she tried to remember when she'd last had a period and couldn't. Between Botany days and the elapse of time on the Catteni trip, she couldn't figure out if she was in a fertile period or not. She glanced over at Chuck. Well, if she was pregnant by him, at least she'd spared both of them any embarrassment over actually going to bed for that purpose. But she did wish she'd remember *something* both logical and in character. That was unfair.

A buzzing penetrated her ruminations. The com unit on the bridge was announcing a message coming in.

Mitford was so relaxed—well, she'd done that for him at least—that she was able to withdraw from his side. She covered him with a blanket, hoping that he was so far gone in sleep he wouldn't rouse as she went to answer the buzz. She did grab up her clothing as she left the room. Let him think he slept alone.

She didn't waste time dressing—she'd just leave the visual off but she wanted to stop the buzz. She managed the correct response in her guttural disguised tone.

"Venlik here. All repairs finished?"

"Yes, Emassi."

"All cargo aboard?"

"Yes, Emassi."

"Prepare the ship for immediate takeoff."

"Yes, Emassi."

He didn't even ask why she didn't turn on the visuals.

Did she have time for a quick shower? Well, she was going to have one anyway. She'd have to take care of that detail, or some of the other Humans might notice a certain other reek about her. And her eyes hurt. Oh, Lord, the contacts. She slipped hers out, and they were the first things she cleansed. Then she remembered that Chuck's would surely still be in so she knelt beside his bed, and delicately stroking the eyelids, managed to slip the contacts out. His eyes might be sore, too, but maybe seeing the lenses in a cup of water might make him think he'd had the sense to do it for himself.

She washed quickly, dried herself off, and remembered to check her color before she dressed. She was still gray enough. Oh, Lord, how glad she'd be to be Human again. She used some eyewash to soothe the irritation, hoping it would ease before she had to use her eyes for something important. The way Chuck was sleeping, her eyes would be normal by the time he woke. Should she wake him before Zainal returned? No, she'd say she'd just relieved him on watch.

"You caught me in the shower, Zainal," she rehearsed aloud as she dressed if he asked about the delay in response.

Damn, he hadn't indicated how long before he'd be there. No, he'd said he wanted the ship ready for immediate takeoff. Had he run into trouble?

She started the pre-flight check, having watched Zainal, Gino, and Raisha do it often enough to know the drill. She then checked each cargo deck to be sure everything was locked down there for takeoff and left the empty deck ready. When she returned to the bridge, she noticed a dust cloud appearing at the edge of the forestry. The truck, and it was a good-sized one, did not, as she half-expected, come directly to the ship but paused in front of the command post. Whatever transpired there was very brief for the vehicle did not stop long. And, as it turned toward the ship, she noticed it headed toward the cargo hatch so she made her way as fast as she could down the companionway, rather pleased with being able to move with some speed in the heavy gravity. One really did get used to it. She unfastened the hatch so all was ready for a speedy loading as the truck backed up, almost but not quite banging against the freshly repainted hull.

Coo and Pess emerged first, lifting the accordion back-door of the truck. They hurried on board with a large and heavy-looking carton. It made a heavy thud as they let it down. Behind them Ninety, Mack, and Gino each struggled to bring in more crates and containers. Zainal appeared with satchels that he deposited with more care on the bow end of the cargo space. He grinned at her, his eyes sparkling with success but he immediately turned to bring yet more crates on board.

"Where's Chuck?" Zainal asked on his next trip back, and he was speaking English again.

"He had a busy night as the Emassi's guest," she said and stepped forward to help unload in Chuck's absence but Zainal shook his head and tapped the control panel for her to be ready to close the hatch at his command.

It didn't take all that long to unload with Pess, Coo, and Zainal all more used to Catteni gravity than the Humans who handled the lighter objects. This deck was almost as full as the others and Kris was obsessed with curiosity.

"Pess," Zainal said, pointing to the truck and indicating that the Rugarian was to take it back to the command post. They had to wait until Pess came back, covering the distance quickly with his oddly jointed long legs.

"That's all?" Kris asked, her hands on the cargo controls.

"Yes. You didn't happen to do a pre-flight check, did you?" Zainal asked as she closed the cargo hatch. She nodded an affirmative. He and Coo were netting the cargo down, fastening the ropes tight to the deck cleats.

Gino had already gone forward. Mack and Ninety looked about done in as they leaned against the bulkhead.

"Had a good time, lads?" she asked blandly.

"It'll take the entire trip back to fill you in," Ninety said with a ghost of his usual impudent grin. "Lenny will never believe what I've seen and done."

"Yes, he will. I'll vouch for it."

"C'mon, let's get strapped in for takeoff," Zainal said, urgently pointing forward.

"Is anyone after us?" Kris asked anxiously.

"Not exactly," Zainal said with a grin, "but they're not above following us back to where we left all that high-grade ore."

"How can they find an asteroid that doesn't exist?" Kris asked, answering his grin.

"Ah," and he put his hand under her elbow to speed her along the companionway, "but that is exactly what we must find before we can go home to Botany."

They were almost to the bridge compartment when Kris remembered that Chuck wasn't strapped in. "I'll have to net Chuck down."

"Don't waste any time," Zainal said, turning sideways to squeeze past her. He smelled of something acrid which she couldn't identify.

"Zay's also got to be gone for at least a full Catteni day," Mack muttered to her as she strapped in beside him.

Kris rolled her eyes. "You can't leave that man out of your sight but he gets into trouble."

Fortunately Zainal was far too busy laying in the course with Gino, making the necessary com calls to hear their soft remarks.

"Tell you one thing, Kris, he's not a man I'd tangle with anywhere or anytime, and even in my own gravity," Ninety said, impressed.

Mack chuckled. Having received clearance from Emassi Kivel himself, they proceeded to take off at a sedate vertical ascent.

"Kivel tried to get Chuck drunk enough last night to interrogate him," Kris said. "I don't know what they use for such purposes here on Catten, but it was a miracle Chuck made it back this morning."

Kris severely berated herself for her adjustments to the exact truth but no one would be hurt by her version, and she might not even have any reason to explain anything to anyone.

After enduring the Catten homeworld gravity, the take-off pressure was minimal. As they rounded Catten on the outward-bound orbit, Kris once again found the beauty of the planet almost breath-stopping.

The space station hove in sight and this time, one of the dreadnoughts was maneuvering out of its dock. By noticing some of the H-class ships nearby, Kris got a better idea of just how ginormous the dreadnoughts actually were. It was comparable to being in a Tomahawk with a 747 looming behind you. And these ships had *not* been able to penetrate the Bubble?

The com unit blurped, and Gino answered in a totally expressionless Catteni voice.

"Your destination?"

"This is Emassi Venlik. Eosi Ba is responsible for our destination," Zainal said.

"Understood."

Maybe Kris only imagined it, but there was even a note of awe in that response. Zainal grinned at Gino who chuckled softly when the com line was off.

The KDL executed a course alteration and then showed its stern to the space station. Zainal poured on the speed as the ship headed out to where thousands of stars gleamed in the black of space.

"Did he beat someone up?" Kris asked when she felt they were safely away.

"To a faretheewell," grinned Gino, and then he rolled his eyes. "Some nerd sycophant of an Eosi. I don't think the ones we met were that anxious for trouble. At least not the ones that Worry and Leon saw. Now the guys I met . . . One was humongously wide and I made myself as small as possible against the nearest wall. But the ones in an ugly mood were worse than anything Hollywood ever dreamed up, including the aliens in *Aliens*."

Zainal now leaned back in the command chair and stretched until every joint and tendon seemed to crack.

"Let's hope Duxie can get us some more of that high-grade ore and we'll be the toast of the capitol," Gino added, "in and out as often as we choose."

"Gino, are you okay?" Zainal asked, rising.

"I'm great, Zay, you need the rest."

"Chuck's in your bed," Kris said.

"Where is immaterial so long as I am horizontal," Zainal said and, pointing to Mack and Ninety, "and you're off duty, too. It should be all clear ahead, Gino, but wake me if something you don't understand comes up."

"Get some rest, Zay," Gino said and made shooing motions with his right hand. "You, too."

Kris looked around for Pess and Coo. Surely they'd need some rest as much as the others, but neither Deski was there.

"They zonked out as soon as we made orbit," Gino said. "Move up here, Kris, and I'll give you a rundown of all we did and what Zainal managed, smooth as a baby's butt."

A DRASSI CLERK NOTICED THE EXCESSIVE charges and ill-assorted cargo registered against this particular vessel. When he checked through to administration, holding the com line open for nearly an hour, he was told that the ship had sufficient credit to cover the expenses. There was no problem. He was to return to his duties. Being a Drassi, he did so, but felt more abused by his superiors than ever. There were no rewards for being diligent on behalf of his Emassi. But what choice had he?

Chapter Five

"I HAVE TO TELL YOU, KRIS," GINO BEGAN, "I wasn't all that keen on seeing a Catteni there on Botany, but . . ." and Gino whistled expertly and shrilly through his teeth, "when you see how that guy operates, I'd walk through fire for him now."

"He does have a way about him," Kris admitted with a grin, "so how did he operate?"

"Blizte was a boondock of a berg, all Rassi in godawful hovels, just staring at us. Or to be more precise, staring at nothing really. Two Catteni vets—one had both legs missing and the other was minus an arm—managed the one— get it—the one eatery in Blizte. They were sitting on a bench as we went past. Zainal got a wave. A few klicks on and we came to a surfaced road. Don't know with what but there were few ruts in it and that old banger could move when you put your pedal to the metal." Gino executed a joint cracking stretch, and Kris wondered if she couldn't possibly manage the bridge and let him sleep, too. "No, I'm fine," he told her, hands back on the armrests. "I can sleep anywhere and be fresh with half an hour's catnap. I slept on the way back from the city.

"And that was an eye-opener." Again that distinctive whistle of respectful awe. "Like something from future worlds 'n' stuff. Beautiful layout and even the important buildings weren't squared-off in plate glass but . . ." he mimicked a commercial voice-over, " 'ecologically situated so as not to mar the natural beauty and making good use of flora and fauna.' Nothing higher than one story. Mostly because the buildings are built down rather than up. Zainal says some of them go down a good hundred plegs."

"What do the Eosi live in?" Her curiosity got the better of her dislike of the overlords.

Gino raised his eyebrows. "Only for Zainal pointing them out, I wouldn't have guessed. Though they do enclose their properties with high walls and force screens. Saw a bird-like thing get fried trying to land on one. So we didn't get to see anything inside the compounds. They're also scattered all over Cattena—which is what they have so imaginatively named the city. Still, if it weren't for the neighbors, it'd be better than Beverly Hills. Or even Carmel.

"Zainal showed us where his family home was, and it's spread out over quite a hunk of real estate. Zay says it's because so many Eosi hosts have come from his lineage, or pedigree or whatever you want càll it."

"Did you see an Eosi?"

Gino's shudder was not faked. "Four of 'em. Big bastards, even when you know the poor damned Catteni that got stuck with being subsumed was big to start with. Crazy eyes! Scare the shit out of me . . . begging your pardon." Again his whistle. "Sure was glad Zay got out of that living death. Worse than a zombie in my opinion.

"However, he stops at a place where there're public

com units and made a half dozen calls, while we ambled over to the eatery." This time Gino grimaced. "They don't know a damned thing about good eating. Cram anything into their mouths, but Zay had told us what to order and we did and that was pretty good. Almost as good as what we regularly eat on Botany." He said that with an air of condescension.

"He couldn't reach all the guys he wanted to see, but he said that these four were the best and he was just lucky to find any one of them at Cattena. We did the secret hand signs and passwords and stuff and met at what passes for a service station here. Sort of Catteni-style garage sales." He grinned impishly at her for his witticism. "We made as if we were trying to sell the transport so much of the conversation between Zainal and the others appeared to be discussing the condition of the truck and the engine it uses. That engine is stuck above one of the ground level panels. Zay had parked obliquely to the station so no one could see anyone coming or going. One of us was there to keep the mechanics or whatever they were from closing in when inconvenient. There were two or three other vehicles being inspected so it was a good cover to use."

He paused, rubbed the side of his nose.

"And?" Kris prompted him.

He chuckled a smug "he he he he" of satisfaction. "There seem to be a lot of Catteni Emassi fed up to here," and he levelled his hand with his nose, "with Eosi domination. Especially . . ." and he paused again for emphasis, "since Mentat Ix—that's the one Zay's brother's lugging around—and Co and Se have been agitating every one of the other Eosi about demolishing Botany, diverting all naval forces to that end."

Gino looked worried. "No one has ever seen the Mentats—they're the leaders among the Eosi—going so ballistic. They've *got* to penetrate or burst or explode or implode the Bubble—because it's there, I think, and has them stumped. And stumped, they don't like to be."

"Anything said about Earth?"

"Yeah, and it's not good. They haven't stopped mind-wiping specialists so those who were lucky enough to escape being caught have had to go into hiding. And hiding places are getting filled up and harder to find . . . especially as we have no air transport at all. And very few working trucks or cars. The Eosi have found another use for petroleum products—all theirs. It's not as if they can burn the Bubble away—no oxygen in space, thank God.

"And the Emassi Zay talked to are not the only ones beginning to get ideas from the rebellion on Earth." Gino nodded in satisfaction. "Evidently we've really got 'em going, Catteni and Eosi. Never had so much opposition before. We might not be as technically advanced as Eosi, but I'll tell you, there're not enough Emassi to deal with what we're giving 'em back on Earth."

"So we could actually rebel enough to get Earth back?" Kris felt a surge of triumph flow through her.

"I didn't say that," Gino replied cautiously, tilting his head to show his skepticism. "In the first place," he held up one finger, "Emassi and Drassi like Earth and want to keep it—just get rid of the troublesome population. Meanwhile they're looting everything that isn't cemented into the ground and sometimes they jackhammer loose what they fancy. In the second place, they have stopped ruining manufacturing complexes and keep some of the specialized companies working nonstop . . . which means until the workers drop from exhaustion. I mean, shift work was never like that. Nor those sweatshops in India and Asia we were hearing so much about. We do have some items high on the list of acquisition and they're being turned out in bulk. While there might not be enough *good* Emassi to help a worldwide coup, I'll tell you one thing: the Eosi invasion sure stopped all the petty squabbles and got all Earth working toward one real good goal—getting rid of the invaders."

"I always did think a really bad extraterrestrial menace would unite the world," Kris said.

"It sure has. Palestinians join Israelis; the Northern Irish have allied with the Brits in covert actions against any Catteni on the British Isles. Even North and South Korea are cooperating against the mutual enemy. The African nations got some real rough treatment—because they're black fer Gods' sake and the Catteni tried to make Rassi out of them." Gino snorted. "That didn't work. In fact, I think the African nations have wracked up more fatalities among the Drassi and Emassi than any other race. Turnabout's fair play. Now, if that will hold when we've thrown out the invaders, it'll be the first wonder of the twentieth century."

Kris sighed in a hopeful breath. "I suppose it *could* happen."

"Might not until the twenty-first but we'll see. We've a few years to spare."

"So, where does that leave us?"

"Well, I'm not quite sure, since this is going to take a lot of planning and under difficult circumstances. We've got to wait until Baby and the KDM make it back. Then we'll have to somehow get some of the Emassi sympathizers to Botany so we can correlate plans and stuff."

"Lord, how'll we do that?"

Gino laughed. "Zay's started the process and, as long as we can keep bringing in the high-grade ore, no one's going to wonder where he's getting it. So he can check in as much as he needs to to mobilize dissidents."

"What did he mean about being followed? By the friends of the Catteni he beat up?"

"Oh, him. He didn't have friends smart enough to follow us. But there are others, Eosi, in particular who might try," Gino said with a laugh. "Probably will. But one of his Emassi friends gave him a chart of an asteroid belt so dense you could hide the entire Catteni fleet in it and they wouldn't be able to spot each other unless they knew exactly where the other ship is. There're so much heavy elements in the belt, supposedly, that it jams all signals. We can slip in and out of there neat as a whistle. In fact, that's where we're headed right now."

Reacting subconsciously to being followed, Kris turned about in her seat but Gino laughed.

"Don't worry, Kris," and Gino patted her knee. "Zay and I spotted them. Way back. We took off before they expected us to so they were late leaving the space station. They'll try to track us by the ion trail and let's hope another ship crosses ours and confuses them. Any way, we'll be in the asteroid belt long before they make it. You wait, Kris, you'll see."

"See if this so-called friend of Zainal's is setting us up?"

Gino shook his head. "Not Kamiton. You know how reserved Catteni are? Well, this guy all but kissed Zay he was so glad to see him. Not that he knew who he was at first . . . and in fact, damned suspicious because he had known Venlik, the Emassi Zay's pretending to be, and hated the man. So there was a bit of an impasse at first. Until Zay removed the cheek pieces and reminded Kamiton of a few details only the real Zainal could have known. You should have seen Kamiton's face when he realized who Zainal really was. And I like Kamiton. He can smile, and he's got that same wacky sense of humor Zay has." When Gino noticed how dubious she was, he laughed. "Look, hon, I've been a good judge of people all my life and there's not that damned much difference between us and Catteni when you get down to basics."

Then unaccountably Gino blushed.

"Well, if you say so, Gino," Kris said, ignoring the blush since she had a good idea what caused Gino Marrucci's sudden embarrassment. There was indeed one very notable difference between Human and Catteni that she happened to enjoy exceedingly. And Gino had suddenly remembered that. "I'll reserve my opinion until I meet him. If I ever do."

"I think you will," the pilot said, recovering his composure quickly. "He's the first one Zay wants to bring through the Bubble."

"Really?"

"Yup, because if they had a Missouri on Catten, Kamiton'd be from there. We gotta show him the Farmers' part of Botany and what we've managed to do on our continent before he'll really believe what we told him. Humans speaking Catteni are not that uncommon these days, but Humans living beyond Eosi control need to be seen to be believed."

Kris nodded. "Sometimes I don't believe it myself."

"Hell, kid, you were making it happen before I got transported."

"That doesn't change the fantastical aspects of it, Gino."

They were silent for a long while, watching the stars, then Gino pointed out some of the anomalous primary colors, and even one double star. They were so far away as to resemble opaque marbles rather than suns. Gino crossed his arms on this chest, a slight grin on his face, and shook his head ever so slightly.

"Never thought you'd be this far from our solar system, huh?"

"You got it."

"Hungry?"

"Something hot would go down well, food and drink, if you don't mind, Kris."

"Drassi hear, Drassi obey," she said with mock humility and made her way back to the companionway. She had become so accustomed to the heavy gravity that a normal one had her bouncing along.

Snores from the various sleeping accommodations indicated that the others were well and truly asleep. She had the galley to herself and prepared enough food for them both. Then she remembered she didn't need to wear the lenses anymore so she took hers out, cleansed them once more before putting them back in the little container. She got an extra cup of water for Gino to get rid of his.

As she handed him his tray of food, he gave her a puzzled glance and then chuckled. "Excuse me, while I get my own eyes back." He put his lenses in the cup and put that to one side. "I'll clean 'em later. I'm hungry enough I might eat 'em as hors d'oeuvres."

"Naw, they don't taste at all like oysters," she retorted facetiously and started in on the stew she'd reheated for them.

SEVERAL HOURS LATER SHE DECIDED THAT there was nothing to do and she would certainly know which lights indicated trouble in any section of the ship.

"Go get some rest, Gino. I can sit here and look at the telltales just as sensibly as you can."

"Not quite yet," and he pointed ahead, without taking his eyes from the sensitive scope he was using. "The pulsar I've been looking for. We make a course correction when we line up with that. Then I'll go get some sleep. And wake Zainal up. He said to."

WHEN ZAINAL TOOK OVER THE BRIDGE, HE first pressed his cheek against hers and kept one arm about her shoulders even after he had seated himself.

"Did Gino bring you . . . how does he put it? Up to speed?"

"Including your brush with another Catteni."

"He asked for it. But he's a mere nothing," and Zainal gave a contemptuous flick of his hand. "Getting Kamiton on our side was more than I expected. Tubelin, Kasturi, and Nitin can be valuable to us, but they don't have the connections that Kamiton has. Or the family prestige."

"And?" she prompted.

He ruffled her short hair, tipped her face toward him so he saw she had removed the lenses. "You look much better with your own eyes. You did make a convincing Drassi."

"Noble Emassi, you are too kind."

Zainal chuckled in that bass rumble that made her grin. "Don't let that get around just yet. However, all four are due to go back to Earth for various tasks. If we could somehow get them in touch with our Humans there, we could begin to make the Catteni regret what they've been doing to your planet."

Kris thought that over. "But you're Catteni. And you said 'our' Humans."

"I like the way Humans think better than I like the way Catteni don't ever think."

"Some of them must. You do."

"Luck."

"What are our chances of doing what you want? Getting rid of the Eosi, with or without the help of the Farmers?"

"I heard something I have never heard about an Eosi Mentat before," he said, his tone very somber and thoughtful. "The one who subsumed my brother went totally out of control and his juniors had a very difficult time reducing his . . . wildness. He's the one that wants to burst our Bubble no matter how long it takes."

"Eosi can have nervous breakdowns?" She was astonished.

"I don't know about nervous, but Ix was dangerously out of control."

"What does it take to kill an Eosi?"

He gave her a quick look and a humph. "I've never heard that one has ever been killed. Though . . ." and he paused reflectively, "killing one has never been tried. They are well protected, by the fear of them that is instilled from the time we understand anything outside childish needs. We don't even know how long an individual Eosi lives. Except that it needs to change hosts."

"Poison it?"

Zainal shook his head, drawing the corners of his mouth down. He gave her a sideways look. "You Humans say you do not like to take Human lives. It is against your laws."

"The Eosi are not Human," she said tartly.

"The Farmers would not like it."

"You haven't given up then, on gaining their assistance?"

"No," he replied.

"What if Humans managed to kill an Eosi . . ."

Zainal waved both hands in a cutting negative gesture. "The numbers they would kill in retaliation would decimate your population."

"The Eosi are already doing that, aren't they?"

"They are, on a small scale, but if an Eosi was known to have been killed by some Human agency, they are just as likely to destroy the entire planet."

"Well, there goes another good idea. We have to kill them all then."

"What is it Ninety says? Bloodtirsty?"

"Bloodthirsty," she corrected him. "I just want my planet free of them."

"As I want my planet free of them. We've had them longer. We get the first chance."

"Not without us right there beside you, Zainal. You Catteni can't have all the fun." Then a yawn overtook her.

"Get some sleep, Kris. You've served a double watch already."

She tried to argue but with one hand, he lifted her out of the chair.

"Get some sleep. I can hear the sergeant moving around." He reached into one of his thigh pockets. "Tell him to take this powder in water. It'll help."

She took the packet he handed her.

"Didn't know Catteni ever needed hangover remedies," she said, amused.

"Headaches are caused by other things than too much Mayock."

Kris left before he could see the guilty expression on her face. She found Chuck, looking more green than gray, just coming out of the head, one hand clutching the door frame. He was definitely in need of whatever remedy Zainal had given her for him if it had taken him this long to sleep off the hangover. She cleared her throat, and her mind, of other details.

"Zainal said this will help."

His eyes weren't really focusing, but she'd got the lenses out before they could have irritated the eyelids. Mind you, his eyes were pretty bloodshot in spite of having no lens aggravation. She took his other hand and—sternly forgetting what her erotic dreams reminded her his hands had been doing—slapped the packet into the palm.

"All in the line of duty, sarge," she said brightly. "Take it immediately in water. I'll even get the water . . ."

"I'll get my own water, Bjornsen," he said with great dignity and straightened himself out and walked, however slowly and carefully, back to the galley.

Chapter Six

IT TOOK NEARLY TWO WEEKS TO REACH
the coordinates Kamiton had given Zainal. Kris said
nothing about it, but she hadn't realized she'd be so long
away from Zane. She thought a lot about him and there
was plenty of time to think as they hurtled at top speed
toward their destination. "Top speed" was somewhat
dampened by a device which Zainal had attached to the
propulsion unit just before they shifted to a new heading,
and before they left what would have been a well-
traveled area of Catteni-controlled space.

"It alters the ion emissions slightly," he explained. "We
may not be as easy to follow. Certainly it will delay pursuit. Kamiton knows where to meet us."

"He's *meeting* us?" Chuck exclaimed.

"Didn't Gino tell you?" Zainal asked.

"He told me that Kamiton would have to see before
he'd join wholeheartedly," Kris said.

"Oh," for once Mitford was taken aback. He rubbed his
forehead. "I seem to be missing a lot."

"There are alcoholic drinks even I wouldn't take,"

Zainal said reassuringly. "I think Kivel probably did his best to get information from you."

"Fraggit, I thought I could hold anything and not spill any beans," Chuck said. "I did hear you mention Kamiton but I didn't know you intended to take him back to Botany."

"Him and how many others?" was Ninety's query.

"Only Kamiton," Zainal said. "He is a scout explorer, which is why he knows about this asteroid belt where we will meet him, and then return to Botany. Spatially we are traveling in a triangle so we won't be long getting home once we contact him."

"Do we have to be Catteni with him?" Gino asked, rubbing at the stubble over his gray skin.

"No, because it will give us the . . . the upper hand," and Zainal grinned, "to show him how well we can fool Catteni, even on their own world."

Kris was not the only one who took in the significance of his last phrase. Ninety nodded slowly, and Gino grinned more broadly than ever. Coo and Pess nodded. Mack Dargle made a comical grimace.

"What did I say?" asked Zainal who was becoming more and more sensitive to Human nuances.

"Their own world," Kris said, enunciating the three words slowly.

"I would give my eyeteeth to hear other Emassi speak that way of Catteni," Mack said.

The asteroid field was a spectacular vision as they passed the heavy Uranus-type planet well away from the slowly orbiting mass of space detritus. Chunks large enough to be small moons were interspersed with smaller, uneven hunks following eccentric orbits about each other as well as the big planet, which, like some interstellar miser, seemed unwilling to release any of its satellites. The cosmic do-si-do dance was almost mesmerizing. Gino wondered just how many of the original inner worlds and moons had been involved in a collision of such magnitude. And how it had occurred. Two charred and dead planets, pockmarked by impacts centuries old, wobbled on erratic Mercury- and Venus-type orbits, each with more small moons of spatial debris attracted by the gravity of the planets they now orbited but not large enough to head for final dissolution in the primary. The star was dying, according to the spectroscope analysis Gino had done: the readings suggested that the star was doing its damnedest to continue to live. Yes, all this space junk wasn't really an asteroid belt . . . a field of planetary and lunar fragments hugging the one thing that gave it some stability—the heavy Uranus planet. The area would take days to circumnavigate. To wend a way through it would require not only a very, very experienced pilot but a ship with heavy shielding and good gunners to explode those bits and pieces that were too small for them to avoid and too big to bounce harmlessly off the shielding.

"Only someone like Kamiton would find a . . . a curiosity like this." Zainal shrugged and settled himself more firmly in the pilot's chair, hands poised over the control panel.

"How'll we ever find the one we want with that mess churning around like that?" Gino asked, his hands tense as he readied himself to use the thrusters on Zainal's command. "It's damned near a light year across."

"No," Zainal replied prosaically, "but certainly it covers an enormous area."

They'd rehearsed the maneuvering tactics all the previous day, using the diagram that Kamiton had given Zainal. They were to approach from coordinates at the ecliptic and weave a course that, in itself, would have thrown any pursuer off. Not that the ship's detectors had spotted anything following them. Kris wondered how anyone could rely on the diagram since every rock, boulder, mountain, and small moon seemed to be on a totally erratic orbit.

"I SEE WHAT YOU MEANT ABOUT BEING ABLE to hide . . ." Chuck murmured respectfully.

"Right thruster two seconds . . ." Zainal interrupted Chuck's remark.

Gino responded, and they seemed to be heading directly at a cluster spinning end on end when Zainal asked for three seconds right thruster and they broke into the clear . . . briefly.

No one dared say another word to risk breaking the concentration of the two pilots. They sat, occasionally with an inadvertent gasp at the terrifying proximity to a space obstacle large enough to crush them, clinging to the armrests of their seats, and grateful for the safety belts that held them in place. Zainal had insisted they don protective helmets and emergency oxygen tanks, and these precautions, pitiful though they seemed as the ship wove a torturous way through the maze, irrationally gave them a sense of security.

It seemed like hours, and possibly it was, before they finally saw empty space again. Then Zainal ordered a left thruster for five seconds, which swung the ship right back at the belt. The second course change, just before they would have reentered the asteroid belt, brought them parallel to it.

A sparkle caught Kris' eye and she pointed. "Look! Three-fifteen!"

Zainal gave a nod of his head and slowed the KDL almost to a complete halt. The ship drifted toward a ginormous asteroid, which turned ever so slightly to display an obvious cavern, which had been punched into it at some point. Zainal now slowly moved the KDL toward the dark hole, and they caught sight again of a glint where no light should be. He activated an exterior light, and they all reacted to the sight of an EVA-suited figure making for their hatch.

"Light the air lock," Zainal said, "and prepare to accept boarder."

Kamiton was as much a surprise to Kris as he was to the rest of the Botany group. He acted, Kris thought, much as Zainal had on their first meeting: dismissive, even contemptuous, until he realized that each and every one of them understood what he said to Zainal.

"I did not expect you to arrive so promptly, Zainal. I have only just arrived myself."

"With no pursuit?"

Kamiton shrugged shoulders as broad as Zainal's and began to strip off the rest of his space suit, looking around with a frown as no one seemed to immediately assist him.

"You're closest, Chuck," Zainal said in Catten, "give him a hand. These are awkward even with plenty of space." He took the helmet from Kamiton and the harness of the one-man thruster pack.

"Your cabin has the most room," Chuck said as Zainal opened a compartment where the helmet and thruster could be stored. "This way, Kamiton, in case you are unfamiliar with this class of ship." By tone, gesture, and courtesy, Sergeant Chuck Mitford was establishing his equality with the new arrival.

"They all speak Catten?" Kamiton asked, surprised as Gino and Mack pressed tight against the bulkhead to give him room to move aft.

"All of them," Zainal said.

Kris, too, had made as much space in the companionway as she could to allow Kamiton to pass her, but he stopped and stared hard at her. She merely raised an eyebrow in askance. He was a touch taller than she.

"Is it a female?" he asked Zainal, not taking his eyes off her.

Anne McCaffrey

Kris was glad that her gray skin did not show the flush of blood to her face at being referred to as an "it."

"Female and of command rank," she said in a cold hard voice, almost spitting out the Catteni syllables. "A fact you will remember."

"One of the Terrans, though, is she not?" He looked forward at Zainal.

"Do not speak *of* me, Kamiton," she said, thoroughly incensed and determined to be certain he answered her directly, "speak *to* me as you would to any other of equal rank."

"I would, were I you," Zainal remarked in a mild tone to Kamiton. "She's dangerous in a fight. Gino," and he paused at his cabin, "set course for Botany, top speed." Then, as soon as Kamiton and Chuck had entered the cabin, he winked at Kris and closed the door.

Whatever might have been said during the short interval in which Kamiton was assisted out of his EVA apparel, he did not again refer to her as an "it" or "she" but addressed her directly, as he did the rest of the crew. Since he asked a great many questions, glancing about the cramped table in the crew mess, he did seem to accept her answers if she gave them. Once or twice, he rephrased the question later on, looking at Gino for an answer.

"Kris would know that, and I think she's already given you the answer," Gino said blandly.

Kamiton was quick enough never to use that ploy again.

"Which of you were first on Botany?" Kamiton asked.

Chuck held up his hand first followed by all, including the two Deski and Zainal, except Gino. Kamiton had the same habit of raising one eyebrow as Zainal would, in the manner of requesting explanation.

"I am space pilot, too," Gino said with a shrug. "Third Drop."

"The rest of us," Chuck said, "were what the Eosi picked up in the initial invasion."

"So you have learned Barevi as well?" Kamiton asked.

"Well enough to barter in the markets," Kris said.

"And other places," Chuck added in a droll tone.

Kamiton started to cross his arms, but there were too many wide bodies to permit that so he put his elbows on the table. Gino got up and started to clear the remnants of the meal, which provoked a startled reaction from Kamiton. Gino grinned.

"We all take turns," he said. "You do know, Kamiton, that there are many minerals in the asteroid belt. Read traces as we wandered through."

Kamiton gave a curt nod of his head. "I picked it so."

Coo and Pess, evidently having had enough of the social scene, rose and left the room.

"Now," Kamiton asked in a patient tone of voice, "I wish to see the spatial photographs of this refuge of yours. And especially of this Bubble that has our leaders . . ." his tone was contemptuous, "so aggravated."

At least that was what Kris thought the word meant. Most of the language Kamiton had used could be understood in context if he used words that she wasn't familiar with. At least he did them the courtesy of not speaking in pidgin Catteni.

Mack Dargle came in then: he'd been standing the watch. "Nothing around here but us, Zay," he said, nodding to Kamiton. "Pess has taken over the watch."

Zainal nodded, then asked Mack to collect the hand viewer and the file that had been compiled as what they facetiously called the "travel guide." Kamiton went through the file several times, first very quickly, grunting now and then. The second round was more selective as he magnified certain scenes, like the enclosed valleys, which caught his attention. Zainal had had Baxter take shots of the new Farmer equipment in the garage and then in action. There were also shots of the units, which the settlers had made of the original equipment.

Kris noticed it about the time that Chuck must have because the sergeant's eyes made contact with her. In no shot did Zainal actually show the geographical location of either the original installations or the current ones. Nor any details that might have given their positions away. Kris wondered if this was intentional. Zainal had said that he trusted Kamiton. How far? That was when Kris began to fret over the possibility that Kamiton was actually a spy for the Eosians.

Then Chuck tapped her on the arm. "Your shift, Kris." He also gave her a nod to reassure her that he would remain. And that he was still assessing this new recruit.

Kris glanced at the timepiece on the wall. "The time has just flown, hasn't it?" she said inanely. Then pushed herself around the table, which also meant momentarily displacing Kamiton from his position.

"I think the Cat's okay," Gino said when he came forward an hour later. He'd brought her a cup of herbal tea. He had one as well as he slipped in the pilot's seat and absently ran his eyes over the panel lights. "So do Coo and Pess, and they'd have more to go by than any of us. 'Sides which, I can't imagine Zainal risking any chance of aborting phase three." Then he wriggled his fingers in a characteristic stretch of his hands over the control panel. "Got a course correction to make soon." He leaned slightly to the left to peer at the rearview screen. "Nary a sign of pursuit either. Hope the others are okay." And doubt crept into the pilot's voice.

"So far Zainal's been right . . ." Kris said loyally.

"You only need to be wrong once," Gino said.

"For Pete's sweet sake, you sound like Balenquah."

Gino sat up straighter in the chair. "Kindly keep your insults to yourself, young woman," he said. "To begin with I'm a much better pilot than that idiot ever was."

"Sorry," Kris said, feigning meekness.

Gino had his eyes on the timepiece now and, toggling up the course correction made it with swift movements of his agile fingers. "There now. We should be home in next to no time."

"Really?"

"As the man said, that asteroid jumble wasn't all that far from where Botany is after all."

GINO'S WORDS WERE TRUE ENOUGH FOR THEY made it home just as the watch changed. Before that, however, Zainal and Gino had done the computation to find which window was the best one to take, avoiding the thirty-hour satellite. They had three and Zainal decided to use the one that would bring them in just "beyond" the range of the geo-synchronous, older one while the thirty-hour sat was on the other side of the Bubble.

By mutual consent, Kamiton was allowed to take the second seat so he could have the best view of the Bubble and the insertion. He sat, arms folded across his chest in best Catteni mode, and watched, his keen yellow eyes missing nothing. Zainal had indicated that Kris and Gino should remain in the cabin. The others were detailed to rig the ship for landing and check the cargo restraints. There was always some buffeting as they entered the atmospheric envelope of Botany.

Zainal altered one view screen to show Kamiton the Eosian arrays still stuck in the Bubble at that point of exit. Kamiton snorted, then peremptorily gestured for Zainal to turn all screens on the Bubble. He seemed surprised when Zainal slowed to penetration speed. They almost popped through like a pea coming out of a pod, Kris thought. She gave a nostalgic sniff. Peas were so good, fresh out of the pod. Maybe someone would have thought to bring back some Earth-type seeds to experiment on Botanic soil. She hoped so, and that peas were among them.

They slipped easily through the Bubble's skin, and Kamiton rumbled a request for a rear screen view. Of course, there was absolutely no indication that a large ship, with arrays of all the same sorts that had been ripped off the Eosian vessel, had passed through it.

Then Kamiton saw Botany, the largest of the continents in full view, though clouds were obscuring the seas and the other landmasses. His eyes opened wide. He said nothing but the crisp nod of his head was approval enough for Gino and Kris who grinned at each other.

Zainal did the necessary orbits, pointing out the original continent they had inhabited, also the half-desert one they had partially explored, barely visible under cloud cover. Then at a much lower altitude, he did a flyby of the command post, magnifying the screen sufficiently so that Kamiton could identify that this was an alien structure.

They flew on, low enough over the neatly cultivated fields to show Kamiton a few Farmer mechs at work, spraying in one case, harvesting in another. Again that sharp Catteni nod to indicate Kamiton had noticed.

Almost at a glide—conserving fuel had become second nature to all the pilots—Zainal took the KDL across the narrow sea and up to the landing field.

"God in heaven, what's happened?" Gino cried.

Zainal snapped on the intercom. "Scott? Beverly? Someone. Landing instructions."

"Five, I count five," Kris said, her voice rising in a squeak. "We've been invaded?"

"Welcome back, Zainal," and Scott's voice was far too vibrantly triumphant for the extra three ships to be menaces.

Suddenly Zainal began to swear in Catteni, only a little of which Kris understood but it had to do with boiling and eating and other usually fatal applications. Kamiton was roaring his head off, laughing and whooping in such uncharacteristically Catteni behavior that Kris and Gino were both grinning, too. Kris couldn't quite understand his angry reaction: after all, he was the one who proposed the acquisition of Catteni spaceships.

Zainal was definitely not amused and continued to growl out his fury all through the landing procedures. As soon as he put the KDL down, to one side of the now crowded field, he jerked his head at Gino to power the ship down. He brushed past Kris who was considering what options she had of cooling him off before he did something that would really put the cat among the pigeons. She slipped in ahead of Kamiton who was nearly staggering with laughter down the companionway to the hatch. Zainal didn't wait for the landing ramp. He jumped to the ground and started looking about for someone to holler at.

The other ships could not have been there very long, because two were still unloading groggy passengers or cargo or both. The passengers were enough of a surprise all on their own because Kris recognized the unmistakable lanky figures of black Maasai, with their long hair and distinctive garb. She missed the customary spears and shields that she'd seen them carry in the documentaries and news reports during the African famine.

Cargo was being unloaded, boxes and crates and larger items that required the use of a quickly constructed hoist told her that the mission, however increased, had been very successful.

"AH! SCOTT!" And Zainal had seen his victim and turned in that direction.

Halfway up the field, Ray Scott acknowledged that shout with a wave and the most cheerful expression Kris had ever seen on the ex-admiral's face. She groaned at the thought of that dissipating when Zainal confronted him. Standing in the now fully open cargo hatch of the KDL, she began to semaphore her arms, trying to catch Ray's attention. Just warning him might help.

There was nothing wrong with the ex-admiral's eyesight, and he caught her frenzied signal. His smile began to fade as Zainal closed the distance between them. Even Zainal's back looked angry, Kris thought. He was in a towering rage and even Kris could understand why other species were afraid of Catteni. What she couldn't understand was why he'd be so angry at what seemed to be a very successful undertaking.

He was confronting Scott, waving arms and fists about, pointing from one of the newly captured ships to the other. Two were as big as the H-class, which had kidnapped her from Denver ages ago. The other was another new K-class. One way or another, Botany was assembling a substantial space fleet. So why was Zainal so put out?

Kamiton had disembarked the KDL, Chuck Mitford and Gino Marrucci acting as guides as well as sponsors. Mack was following at a more leisurely pace, taking in all the activity and the new arrivals, Human as well as material. The busy stevedores didn't even give Kamiton a second look. Kris ran to catch up with Zainal and caught the last of Zainal's diatribe, so well interspersed with more Catteni curses and allegations, that Ray looked so stunned Kris could almost feel sorry for him.

Abruptly Ray Scott began to chuckle. "You taught us how, Zainal. Don't bitch at me when we had a chance to improve on your tactics and save a lot of people the Eosi want badly."

"One ship at a time would not be missed," Zainal began again, his voice harsh, his manner so belligerent he looked more Drassi than Emassi.

"These all went unnoticed, too, Zainal," Ray said,

calmly, suavely defusing the unexpected anger Zainal displayed. "And who is this you have brought?"

If there was an edge that approximated disapproval in Ray's voice, Kris could hardly blame him as he now caught the approach of Kamiton and his guides.

But evidently Zainal had spent most of his anger. With a definite effort, he contained himself, taking a deep breath. Looking over his shoulder, he saw how close Kamiton and the others were. He also turned his head just far enough to take in the anxious expression on Kris' face. Suddenly, the gray of his skin lightened and, with a massive shake to his whole body, he relaxed, gesturing for Kamiton to approach.

"Admiral Ray Scott, this is Emassi Kamiton, a friend for many years and one as committed to removing the Eosi domination as I am." Zainal let the two men shake hands—he'd mentioned that custom to Kamiton since Catteni rarely touched in cordiality—and Ray did not wince at the grip Kamiton produced.

"You are welcome, Emassi," Scott said in Catteni, with a slight grin when he noticed Kamiton's surprise. "Most of us can speak a little Catten . . . these days. Come, join us, you, too, Kris, Chuck, Gino. We can debrief in turns." He added the last in English. "Report, I meant to say," he put in, remembering the Catteni words.

Kamiton was looking around with great interest, especially at some of the unusual people who were being helped out of one big H-class.

"We've almost doubled our population again," Ray said, gesturing for them all to go up to the hangar and his office. "Later, Emassi Kamiton, it will be my pleasure to introduce you to the leaders of our colony."

As they entered the hanger, Kris saw Baby already ensconced, her hatch wide open. How had they managed to get pilots enough for three more ships? The KDM had had Laughrey as a second pilot and Boris with Raisha on

Baby, and Ricky Farmer, maybe that's how they did it. She shook her head. But none of them, except Laughrey who'd captained Concordes, would have any experience with such big vessels, which would also require a minimum crew.

"Kris . . ." and obviously Ray Scott was calling for her attention a second time, "there's coffee over there," he said with a broad grin. "And even some reasonably fresh milk."

"WHAT?"

That shook her out of her introspection.

"COFFEE?"

Gino and Chuck reached the serving table almost as soon as she did. Chuck inhaled the aroma, eyes closed in ecstasy.

"I'll take a fresh cup, Kris," Scott said as he gestured the two Catteni to the chairs around the long table.

"Maybe a cup of coffee'll help settle Zainal, too," Chuck murmured to her as she poured for them all. His eyes were twinkling but his expression was sober. "I don't ever want him to get that mad at me, and I've been chewed out by experts."

"You?" Gino said, trying to ease the tension he felt in the atmosphere.

"Sugar as well, Ray?" Kris called out, noticing the large package of it open on the table.

"Two," Scott answered and she wondered just how much sugar had been acquired.

Without even an apologetic look on his face, Chuck used three spoonfuls but no milk. Kris was still deliberating what to add to the two cups destined for the Catteni when Chuck splashed in both sugar and milk, stirring vigorously.

"They can always try it pure later," he said. "This is *real* army coffee."

He took three cups as deftly as Kris did while Gino,

eyes glinting with amusement, carried his and Scott's over to the table.

"See if you like it, Zainal," Chuck said at his most affable in trying to placate Zainal's still visible anger. He spoke in Catteni but when he went on, he had to use the English words where there were no equivalents even in Barevi. "Army can't move without coffee, nor the navy."

"It is a pleasure for us all," Scott said, also in Catteni. Then he blew on the surface of his coffee before sipping judiciously. As the other Humans were following that example, so did Zainal and Kamiton. Then Scott dropped into English. "First thing Sandy Areson off-loaded was a huge pot of brew and doled it out. I got that pitcher and two refills. I think she'll be brewing for the rest of the day, we're all so eager for the taste of it. Boxes of tea as well, so Ainger's happy."

"How much coffee did she bring in?" Chuck asked hopefully.

"Sacks full, though not all may be as fresh as this," Ray said before he switched to Catten. "I don't think the Catteni," and he nodded graciously at Kamiton, "realized . . ." and he made gestures of grinding with his two hands, "that the beans have to be ground to be useful."

"Sort of like potatoes when Sir Walter gave them to Queen Elizabeth," Kris said, slipping in the remark to allow Zainal more time to regain his usual dignity.

"Now, let me explain to you, Zainal, Kamiton, about the three ships," Ray said, sitting forward but keeping both hands on his coffee cup.

"I listen," Zainal said in a firm voice and sipped again at his coffee. Kamiton did, too, rolling the liquid in his mouth and savoring it.

"Neither of the two ships we sent on this reconnaissance of Earth had any trouble with their ID's or traveling. As you said, Zainal, Catteni ships are moving about without any restrictions at all. All right, all right, that might change because of what happened next," Ray intercepted Zainal's objections. "But considering how easy it all was to take over three more, I doubt they will be missed."

"They will not be missed," Kamiton said, having followed Ray's somewhat basic Catteni even with the ex-admiral's atrocious accent. He grinned broadly. "Everyone is too busy taking valuables and loading cargo drones. Those who are assigned to the Eosi do not have the same freedom, but those, as you know, Zainal, are the chosen few!" Kamiton's smile was a mixture of contempt and condescension.

"Matt Su and Vic Yowell managed to find an unused channel on the communications band and kept in contact with our scout ship." Then Ray rubbed his forehead and, with an apologetic nod at Kamiton, asked Zainal to translate to Kamiton while he resorted to English. "That proved extremely useful because once Raisha and Boris saw what had been done to St. Petersburg, they were so shattered it took hours for Bull Fetterman and Lenny to talk them back into action." Ray paused briefly. "I'll say this for them, once they got over their initial shock, they really showed the stuff they're made of. By then, the KDM had realized how easy it was to get in and out of any major Catteni landing field and were reconnoitering." He sighed heavily. "Not much is left of the major world capitol cities, except the ones that don't look big enough to be important. After the KDM dropped off Basil Whitby and Leila in England, they let Sandy off in what had been the Boston-Cambridge area, and Joe Latore in upper New Jersey. Then the KDM proceeded, as planned, to Houston and the big Catteni/Eosi installation there.

"That's when they had the chance to take over the two H-class ships. The H's had just been loaded with more folks and were headed to one of the mining planets. Matt Su pretended to be in command and reassigned Bert Put and John Beverly as the new Drassi officers in charge of the newly acquired HTS. It was loaded but had only two crewmen on board so they were easily fooled into believing a change in command . . ."

Zainal actually grinned. "Perhaps it wasn't a bad idea, after all."

"No, because John Beverly knew where some air force personnel might have gone into hiding. And they were. So that didn't leave just two fake Catteni to manage that big mother. They aren't that difficult to operate but some crew had to be used. Beverly got to the hideout—but he had a bit of a problem, dressed as a Catteni until he wiped off part of the makeup and recognized one or two officers he knew. After that, they had enough to crew half a dozen more ships." Ray chuckled at the startled look on Zainal's face. Kamiton grinned, shaking his head at the audacity.

"We also now have NASA ground crew personnel who'll know how to service the ships," and Ray was obviously relieved about that aspect. "Beverly brought Laughrey and two more experienced Hercules pilots back with him to the Houston facility in the H's shuttle and enough men to crew a second H-ship." Ray paused, noticed that his cup was empty. Chuck rose, took it, and went to fill both. "That's when we got the African contingent. Even the Hutus and Tutsies resented Catteni interference with their little war and joined forces against the Gray Men. We've Maasai, Luo, and Kikuyo and evidently a smattering of Tuareg and Zulu. The Catteni took savage reprisals all across Africa."

"So I also heard," Kamiton put in.

Over at the coffee table, Chuck murmured to Kris: "He's laughed once. Relax." As he poured coffee from the large bottle, he inhaled the aroma with a look of pure pleasure on his face that Kris had recently seen, but in much different circumstances. Fortunately he didn't see her blushing.

"And the K-class? Three spaceships disappearing from the same area would arouse suspicion," Zainal said bluntly.

"No, the K was Joe Latore's contribution to our growing navy," Ray said. "He found a lot of people hiding out in the forests in New Jersey, and they told him about all the ships they'd seen coming and going from what's left of New York City. He organized a bunch to go have a look. Had enough volunteers to make an army but kept it to a sensible force. Lots of people have rifles and small arms, you see. Have to hunt to live. They got to the city via the Lincoln Tunnel."

"The tunnel?" Chuck asked, exchanging surprised looks with Kris and Gino.

"Well, all the bridges were gone, and the Holland, but debris from the old Port Authority hid the entrance to the Lincoln and evidently the Catteni hadn't noticed the New Jersey entry. Can't get vehicles through the ones already stuck there. Some folks are using them to camp out in: those who got stuck there when the Catteni hit the city. Joe said they nearly caused a landslide getting through the debris on Fortieth Street and that didn't make them popular with the refugees. But . . ." and Scott shrugged off that complaint. "According to the tunnel people, Central Park was a prime landing and loading area. So Joe and his group started up Eleventh Avenue toward the park. When Joe saw the K-class parked on top of the Cunard building at Fifty-fourth Street, he decided to take a closer look. It was fully loaded and the crew drunk out of its tiny minds on champagne." Ray grinned. "By the way, Catteni do not know how to swim."

When Zainal translated that, Kamiton gave another of his bursts of laughter. Even Zainal had a grin on his face.

"So no one's going to miss that K right away. It was only a matter of getting in touch with the KDL. General

Beverly sent his shuttle with a couple of air force Hercules pilots and enough crew to handle her. Joe brought as many folks back as possible and promised to lift more when he could." Scott sighed.

Not, Kris thought, that he didn't blame Joe for promising, but because it might be difficult to honor it.

"Were proper precautions taken to avoid the thirty-hour satellite?" Zainal asked in English.

"Hid behind the moons until they got the olley-olley-in-free," Ray Scott said with a boyish grin in keeping with the hide-and-seek password.

"The what?" Zainal glanced at Kris for explanation. She was relieved to see that his eyes were back to a normal shade of yellow and that the tension in his face muscles had dispersed.

"A children's game word. Quite appropriate."

"But how did the new vessels pass the Bubble?" Zainal asked, frowning.

Ray gave a flick of one hand to indicate the ease of that operation. "Baby brought one H-class in, using the same trick you did, Zainal, with a magnetic linkage. Then the KDL piggybacked the other two the same way when the coast looked clear of surveillance."

Zainal blinked. "Piggybacked? *More* children's games?" he asked, with a weary but tolerant sigh.

"As far as we know, before they got through the Bubble," Ray went on, filled cup raised in both hands, "no alarms were heard on any of the Catteni channels. If they haven't missed the ships in nearly three weeks, will they ever?" Then he took a long drink of coffee.

Zainal repeated that in Catteni to Kamiton, then stood up with his empty cup in his hand, and silently held out the other for Kamiton's.

"It is refreshing to drink," Kamiton said, handing the cup over but he followed Zainal's progress to the service table to refill their cups while answering Ray in Catteni.

"I doubt even the Eosi know how many ships they have in the fleet. The shipyards keep building them," and Kamiton shrugged his heavy shoulders diffidently. "The ships not to touch are those used only by the Eosi. They are distinctively marked and no one enters who does not have to."

"I can easily understand that," Ray said with a grin. Then, as Zainal returned with the refilled cups, he leaned across the table toward them. "But would not *they* be the very ships we'd need to hijack if you," and he pointed at both Zainal and Kamiton, "want to be rid of Eosian domination?"

Chuck grinned, though Gino, for a moment, looked apprehensive.

"There are at least one hundred Eosi," Kamiton said. "That is one hundred ships to destroy and you have . . . how many now? Six?"

"It's a start," Ray said, grinning slightly. "Are you also with us in our fight against Eosian domination?" When Kamiton nodded slowly, he added, "Are there any more at home like you?"

"There are," Kamiton said firmly and soberly. Now he leaned forward across the table. "We must plan. It will not be easy."

"What is worth having never is," Ray Scott said. "Now, it's your turn, Zainal," and he continued in Catteni, "tikso."

ZAINAL "REPORTED" IN THE SAME LANGUAGE, although occasionally Ray had to ask for a translation. He chuckled over the asteroid belt deception.

"Well done, well done," Ray said, rubbing his hands together.

"We cannot make mistakes, Ray," Zainal said as if he could see Scott planning all kinds of hijacking missions that would eventually be noticed: perhaps even traced to Botany.

"There is one Mentat, the Ix," Kamiton said, glancing at Zainal with a significant nod, "who is certain you all," and his large finger circled the table, "are responsible for every disaster that has occurred recently. You realize that a moon base is being constructed to keep watch over you."

Ray nodded. "We know, which is one reason why we are using the south polar windows."

"Good." Kamiton hitched his chair forward, the wood creaking under his weight. He glanced down at it, shifted experimentally, and then ignored the occasional noises.

Kris really did hope that the chair, though made of lodge-pole wood, was sturdy enough for the heavily built Catten.

"The Mentat Ix has had one seizure . . ."

"Seizure?" Zainal came alert.

Kamiton nodded, grinning. "Interesting, isn't it? The Immortals have flaws. We must discover how we can use them to *our* benefit."

"Tactically," Ray said, showing appreciation for that information, "it is always smart to get your enemy to destroy himself . . . if you possibly can."

"No species' injury," Chuck said with great satisfaction. "Only how the hell do we do it? One of them losing his cool doesn't mean we'd be able to blow the minds of the others." He cocked his forefinger and clicked his thumb, making his hand into an imaginary weapon.

"A seizure in a Mentat has never happened before," Kamiton said in Catteni, sitting back and folding his arms across his chest.

"No, it has not," Zainal said, then switched to English, addressing the others. "The significance of such an occurrence wouldn't mean as much to you as it does to us," and he turned back to Kamiton. "I would like to know more since I heard nothing of that on Catten," he added in Catteni.

"Nor would you," Kamiton said in a droll tone. "But I know of it and several others as well. The Bubble frustrates Mentat Ix. Total annihilation of this planet is required as retaliation for the humiliation suffered by Ix."

"But this Ix fellow can't get past the Bubble and we know he, it, whatever, has tried," Ray Scott said smugly.

"Necessity is the mother of invention," Gino reminded them pointedly.

Zainal translated to Kamiton.

"Have you heard if their brain-wiping of Human specialists has given them any help?" Ray asked.

"We know that it was done," Kamiton said. "We are trying to find out if any worthwhile information was discovered. More importantly, if any new projects have been started. Not so far as I know." And Kamiton's attitude was that if anyone would know, he would.

"I think that the Eosi," Ray said slowly but with a glint of satisfaction in his eyes, "have underestimated Humans."

Kamiton smiled. "They have and it gives us," and his thick thumb touched his chest, signifying his group of dissidents, "immense satisfaction. And hope. How best may I serve you, Emassi?" Kamiton bent his head toward Ray in an unexpected gesture of compliance.

"My rank *was* admiral, Emassi Kamiton," Ray said, with a grin. "And it looks likely that I may resume it. We'll have to consider how best to use your services. Welcome aboard." Then he stood up and turned to Zainal. "I think that perhaps it would be wise if you all," and he gestured to include Gino and Chuck, "escort Kamiton up to the hall and make sure everyone knows he's on our side. I'll see how soon we can schedule a tactical conference, but right now, unloading and the disposition of our latest arrivals takes precedence."

Kris was on her feet. "And I have a son to see." Clearly it was safe for her to leave now that Zainal was himself again. And she was suddenly overcome with the urge to see Zane.

"Take my runabout, Kris," Ray said expansively. "I've got reports to write while all this is fresh in my mind."

Chapter Seven

ZANE WAS SO INVOLVED, PLAYING WITH others his age, giggling outrageously over something they found funny that she stood and watched, drinking in the sight of him.

Suddenly they went dead quiet, eyes wide open and staring. One of the little girls whimpered in fright but was instantly comforted by Sarah McDouall, one of the carers on duty at the crèche.

"Great heavens, where did they come from?" she said, her voice part surprise and part reassurance.

Kris turned and saw a line of the tall thin Maasai men and women striding up the hill. They had not been outfitted with the customary Catteni coveralls, possibly because the Catteni hadn't made any that size before, so they wore the tatters of their traditional garb. And were as proud and dignified as she remembered seeing them in occasional news broadcasts when there had been that awful drought in Africa and Bob Geldof had started Band Aid.

The size of the Maasai would intimidate more than two- and three-year-olds.

"How come you're leading the Maasai, Bart?" Kris asked, noticing him in the front, almost lost among the tall folk.

"They seem to trust me. Now a few smiles wouldn't go amiss right now," Bart Tomi said firmly and immediately everyone complied, waving as well. "Hassan says 'Jambo' is a greeting. Can we have a chorus from you all?"

Everyone obediently repeated the greeting. The Maasai beside Bart looked surprised, eyebrows ascending up his wrinkled forehead but he stopped. So did the others behind him.

Abruptly Sarah brought the child she was holding closer, waving its arm as she did so. The transformation of the Maasai from surprise to delight was amazing. They all smiled now, at the children, rather than the adults.

The leader came right up to the playground, the picket fencing not as high as his knees, grinning broadly and saying something that Kris heard as "kasserianingera?"

Sarah held out the little girl's hand to the man. Smiling with very white teeth and bending his tall frame down to her level, he very gently touched her fingers, so gently that the child, wide-eyed though she was, did not withdraw. The Maasai nodded and stepped back, then smiled at all the children. Behind him, the rest of his tribe, if that's who they were, nodded and smiled and murmured their response of "jambo."

"Good, good," Bart said. "That's the first any of them have reacted at all."

"I'd heard," Sarah said, "that they love children. And cattle. Our loo-cows are going to give them quite a shock."

The little girl had a grin hovering on her lips, but she

burrowed her head into Sarah's shoulder, peeking coyly at the tall man. But the breakthrough had occurred and a ripple of soft words went down the line. The Maasai all had smiles now and strode forward more cheerfully.

Bart pointed toward the hall. Then, looking down at a strip of paper in his hand added in Swahili, "Hapa chakula kizuri! Get me?"

"Ndio, ndio," the leader said, nodding and looking around to gesture for the progress to continue. "Hapa chakula kizuri!" He repeated the same words Bart had used but with the proper inflections, and the Maasai behind grinned and nodded.

"So much for Hassan's instant Swahili lessons," Bart said, grinning as he stuffed his paper back into a thigh pocket.

At that moment, Zane came running towards Kris, arms outstretched to be picked up. "Mommy, mommy, mommy."

She was only too glad to collect him and hug him tightly and kiss him all over. Then she took his arm, turned, and had him waving at the Maasai as they flowed by in their long striding gait.

"Mommy?" Zane whispered in her ear, his eyes wide.

"These are good people, Zane."

"Not Deski, not Rugars . . ."

"No, Maasai."

"Massssi."

"Maas—ai," she corrected him and he got it right.

"Has a quick ear, this one," Sarah said. "Have a good trip?"

Kris chuckled, thinking of some of the elements she was not going to mention. "Mind you, all we brought back was a dissident Catteni which isn't much against the increase in Botany's fleet . . ."

"Dissident Catteni?" Sarah made round eyes at that. "Do tell!"

"Didn't you see him go up to the hall with Zainal a few minutes back?"

"Can't say as I did. But then, I can't say as I knew of any Catteni dissidents either." Sarah grinned. "Nice to know we might have inside help, though. Will we?"

"Tell you later."

"Over lunch perhaps?" Sarah said, her eyes sparkling with curiosity.

"If you share what you've heard that I haven't had time to find out."

"Good. It's nearly lunchtime and sandwiches are all made. LUNCHTIME," Sarah called.

Out the window of the crèche dining room, they saw the procession of what Sarah called the "repossessed," mainly Africans, but some whites, and their nationality not so obvious as they had been given Catteni coveralls.

"Not so many injured either," Kris remarked.

"*We* did the unloading," Sarah said, "and wait 'til you see what else we got."

"Zainal came back with equipment as well," Kris said. "But it got loaded in such a hurry I don't know what all he acquired."

"Did you see much of the planet?" Sarah asked, as others joined their table, eager to hear of Kris' adventures.

Kris shook her head, breaking a piece off her own sandwich, which Zane evidently preferred to what was on his plate. "The gravity damned near wore me out. I stayed on board and answered the com unit. My Catteni's good enough for that but I don't look the part. And I sure couldn't operate in that gravity! Chuck did all the fronting for us. I'll tell you one thing for sure, I was awful glad to lift off safely." Then she laughed. "We ended up in an asteroid belt and whatever created it must have been one helluvan explosion."

She told them the ruse they'd used so that the space station hadn't wanted them to land there, which would

have meant handling more formalities than was wise. So
they'd got to land on the surface of the planet, far enough
away from any settlement so that their "faulty" systems
would cause no damage. "And we sure were sent to the
boondocks. I did see the Rassi and they are . . ." she gave
a shudder, "really little more than animals. You can't call
them morons or retarded because they don't have much
intelligence at all. They copy what they are shown to do
and even that has to be repeated over and over. But Zainal
and the others got into the main city and made contact
with Kamiton."

She could relate the deception about having to off-load
an extremely valuable ore cargo, which is why they came
back via the asteroid belt, and how they could get back to
Catten if they wished.

"So what's this Kamiton doing here?" Sarah wanted to
know.

"Seeing's believing, isn't it?" Kris replied.

"And if he likes what he sees, he brings in more dissidents?" asked another woman. Belatedly Kris recognised
her as Jane O'Hanlan, the TV reporter who'd been one of
those rescued from Barevi in a mindless state.

"You've recovered!" Kris exclaimed.

Jane gave a rueful smile. "I'm improving. Many are.
Dorothy Dwardie's been marvelous."

"Indeed she has," Sally Stoffer said, as she wiped cereal off a baby's face. "I'm practically out of my job
there."

"Really?"

"Seventy-five percent have recovered enough to function on their own now, to talk and help out. We've been
busy while you were gone."

"I don't doubt that for a moment," Kris said. "But boy-
oh-boy, am I glad to be home."

"Daddy, daddy," Zane cried excitedly just then, and
Kris looked up to see Zainal and Kamiton in the doorway.

" 'Scuse," Zane said in Sarah's direction and ran up to his father, squealing in excitement when Zainal swung him up.

"Watch out, Zainal, he's just had lunch," Kris cried.

Obediently, Zainal positioned Zane on his back while Kamiton looked on in amused condescension at the sight of a paternally occupied Zainal.

LATER KRIS HEARD ALL ABOUT THE RESETTLE-ment of the Maasai from Sarah at dinner in the hall. Zainal had taken Zane off for an evening walk and talk. Zainal was also teaching Zane Catteni, and if Kris was there, he preferred to jabber away in English, which defeated the purpose.

"Well, I did do some work in the outback with Aborigines, so they guessed I, and Joe, might be able to help," Sarah said in her matter-of-fact way. "Problem is that the Maasai're used to a totally different lifestyle, which was getting ruined in Africa even before the Cat . . . Eosi hit Earth."

"I remember the famine there in the eighties," Kris said.

"So they won't be happy up here but Chuck thinks that the southern end of this continent might do, where we found semi-desert."

"Why not the desert continent?"

"Maybe, in time, but right now, that'll keep them in a more or less familiar terrain. Oh, and you should have seen their faces when we showed them the loo-cows!" Sarah laughed. "They couldn't believe 'em and they wouldn't believe that the critters don't give milk until one was captured for inspection."

"What about night crawlers? As I recall it, the Maasai are nomadic, looking for grazing for their . . . cattle. Will loo-cows *do* for them? And they have huts or kraals . . . or something like 'em to live in."

"Well, tonight's the big demo on night crawlers and all the newbies are going to have to attend," Sarah said with a certain amount of grimness. "We gotta get that lesson across."

"What about using some of the closed valleys?" Kris asked.

"That's another solution but nothing to hunt and they don't like fish. But you should have seen them looking at all the plants, grass, and stuff we wouldn't think twice about. Hassan was damned near tongue-tied translating for my Joe and the other herbalists . . ."

"It'd be helpful if there just happened to be a book on Swahili in that latest shipment . . ." Kris thought, remembering the crates of books she'd seen being transported to Retreat's library.

Sarah gave a snort. "They're rummaging through 'em right now. Hassan's running out of useful vocabulary."

"That'll be a first," Kris said with a grin. The former Israeli spy was the chatty sort at any time.

"Let's see what they got in. I'd love a good juicy murder mystery to read," Sarah said.

"With this new lot in, how'll you find time?"

"I'll make it," was Sarah's firm reply. Then she sighed again. "I have missed reading, I really have."

"That's because you weren't rescued from two college survey courses with required reading lists this long," and held her hand out at about four feet above the flagstones of the hall.

"So this," and Sarah gestured ironically around, "is a much better way to spend your time." Before Kris could open her mouth to answer, Sarah added, "Actually, college would be pretty dull in comparison."

"Prof, do I get an A in this survival course?"

"Too right," Sarah said and they both rose, taking their dishes back to the window that led to the KP section of the dining hall.

• • •

WHEN THEY REACHED THE STRUCTURE, THEY found only Dorothy Dwardie unpacking and shelving books.

"Oh, good, some help. I've found the most astonishingly eclectic . . . texts here. I can't imagine how all these books got in the same case together," and she showed them the ones in her hand.

"Post-Renaissance Painters?" Sarah said, reading one title.

"How the Grinch Stole Christmas?" Kris read the second title and took it from Dorothy, leafing through the colorful illustrated pages. "We may not have Christmas here, but I'm sure glad to see some good children's books. Can we help?"

"Yes, please," Dorothy said and pointed over behind her.

Cases had been stacked three and four high all the way back to the tarpaulin that covered the end of the present library and the addition under construction. Aisles allowed access to the cases.

"Marian, the librarian," Sarah began in a sing-song voice, "where's the mystery section?"

"Now that's a mystery to me," Dorothy replied, rising to her feet with an effort. "Have at it. I can't promise there will be any. I'm cataloging as I go along and thank God for more computers. Otherwise we'll never know how much we've got."

"You're not doing it all yourself, are you?"

"Well, I'm supposed to get some help shelving," she said. "We had some Victims in here this morning and I think it's helping them remember some of the basic skills they once had."

"What're you looking for?"

"Anything, everything. Dr. Seuss for the children ranks in my eyes as a far greater treasure than anything Post-Renaissance. Though I've nothing against painters at all."

"Actually, light classics that we can read to the Victims: even Westerns or a good mystery story."

"Gotcha," Sarah said and closing her eyes, she turned herself around and pointed. When she opened them, her finger directed her to one of the side aisles. "C'mon, Kris."

Kris was still chuckling at Sarah's whimsical manner of choosing when they heaved a crate to the ground and opened it.

"Lord love us, how're we going to sort this mess out?" she said looking at the tumbled collection: books with spines bent and pages crumbled, all heaped together. A few loose pages only added to the tribulations of transfer.

"By starting at the top and working down. I'll get a few of those shelves over here," Kris suggested, going over to one side where she'd seen the empty shelving, "and separate as we go."

"Good thinking," and Sarah sat herself down and started pulling out books.

However, they had "unerringly," as Sarah remarked, migrated to a whole case full of mysteries and romances. Their conscientious efforts to perform their assigned task were interrupted by seeing books they either recognized or titles that looked interesting.

"A new Hillerman," Sarah crowed and settled against the back of the crate, shamelessly reading her find. "I'll just read a few pages . . ."

Kris worked more diligently but not much longer because she found an Elizabeth Peters' Amelia yarn and she, too, couldn't resist reading "just a few pages . . ."

"Ah, Doctor Hessian, have you come to help shelve books?" they both heard Dorothy say.

When Kris would have moved guiltily back to unpacking, Sarah grabbed her arm and whispered at her.

"No, let's just listen," Sarah said in a very low voice. "Dorothy's been trying to pin him down since he got his mind back. He wants all the Victims to undergo proper Freudian sessions. He feels that he should be in charge of the treatment team, not Dorothy."

"Are you Miss Dwardie . . ."

"Doctor Dwardie, Doctor Hessian," Dorothy replied calmly but there was a slight edge to her voice that alerted both Kris and Sarah. Kris would have risen but Sarah grabbed her by the arm, pressing her back against the crate.

"You've made a remarkable recovery," said Dorothy with apparent pleasure.

Sounds like "grumph grumph" and an audible "be that as it may" seemed to indicate that this Dr. Hessian was not in complete accord. His raspy baritone gave Kris a mental image of a portly man of advanced years, probably balding, overweight, and overbearing.

"I was told that there had been new additions to the library and wished to avail myself of some suitable reading material."

"Oh? Were you not also told that your help in cataloging our new shipment would be sincerely appreciated?"

"Shelving? Books?" was the pompous and astonished reply. Kris thought he sounded remarkably like Lady Bracknell in *The Importance of Being Earnest*, declaiming: "Handbag? Station?"

"Doctor Hessian, we all do community work . . ."

"He's from the Freudian school of psychology," Sarah whispered to Kris. "Dorothy's a social learning psychologist . . . completely opposite to him."

"The community work," Dr. Hessian went on inexorably, "for which I am eminently qualified is to help those Victims still in severe mental distress. I am quite willing to allot all the time necessary with some of the more prestigious Victims whom I have recognized, despite their appalling ordeals. I can certainly provide blueprints of the underlying psychodynamic conflicts of their conditions."

"We *know* what happened to them, Doctor Hessian. As it happened to you, and it is quite a triumph to see you walking about and conversing with everyone. Quite normal again."

"Normal? Normal?" the second repetition was louder than the first. "What *is* normal . . . ah . . ."

"Doctor Dwardie," Dorothy put in gently. "Shall we take a walk, Doctor Hessian? I think the shelving of the books can wait."

Kris looked chagrined and Sarah evidently felt the same way for they were obviously not supposed to know what Dorothy needed to tell Hessian. Books in hand, they crept quietly out by way of the tarpaulin.

Although Dorothy had seen the slight ripple of the tarpaulin, she wanted to continue this discussion outside, where there was no danger of them being overheard. Hessian, responding to a tug on his arm, followed her out of the library, saying as they went, "My normal self scarcely compares with anyone else's so-called 'normal state,' " and "certainly anyone here" lingered in the air as if the doctor had spoken aloud. "I have only just begun to recall how exceptional *my* normal self is. You cannot *expect . . . me . . .* to shelve books?"

"If I can do it, why should it be beneath your capabilities, Dr. Hessian?"

"Now, just a moment, young woman," and his voice dripped with opprobrium.

"Doctor Dwardie, Doctor Hessian," Dorothy said firmly but kindly. "This colony survives because everyone . . . everyone . . . is willing to do the basic tasks as well as the application of their *previous* profession, whatever that might have been. My entire team looks forward to your helping us with the psychological treatment of the remaining Victims. Treating trauma response has been such an overwhelming task that even I have been doing this, as a much needed change of pace. There are so many more Victims," and her voice was not exactly imploring him to be reasonable, as encouraging him, "than we can effectively treat with so few psychologists, psychiatrists, and nurses. Will you join our treatment team, Doctor Hessian?"

."Arumph. Be part of a *team*?" and his voice and manner reminded Dorothy of the English actor Robert Morley at his most pompous and petulant. "You're not serious? I hardly think so. Not with my exemplary qualifications."

Fortunately, there were few people around as dusk settled over Retreat so she steered him to the flagstone path that would eventually lead to his current residence.

"Yes, they certainly are, Doctor Hessian," Dorothy said warmly. "I am quite familiar with your professional background. However, the psychological team here is under my direction and we have designed a multi-modal treatment program, which has indeed healed the trauma of many of the Victims. While your work within the psychoanalytic community is a valuable asset to the field, we have employed a social learning framework here because of its efficacy with psychological trauma."

"And I would, I opine, have to *use* . . ." and once again Dorothy was treated to the magnificent disdain he could inject into such a small word, "this . . . this multi-modal treatment?"

"Yes, you would, since we have found it to be so effective. I worked with trauma units before I was . . . dropped here. But undoubtedly you would not be aware of my professional work in that area."

"No, I am not," he said in a flat discounting of any expertise she might have. "Especially since you now have someone of my stature in the field. Surely you realize that a change of treatment models would benefit those still in the grip of what appears to be catatonia. When the main troops arrive, as it were," and his supercilious tone suggested that he was smiling condescendingly at Dorothy. ". . . the reserves are no longer needed."

Dorothy was undaunted. "Let's take a stab at this situation from the viewpoint of research, and see what happens. I understand that it is probably a shock for you to discover that there are other treatment models with empirical efficacy greater than the one you are most familiar with and have evidently spent most of your life studying. I know, for example, that your résumé includes eight books on the life and work of Freud in theory and psychoanalysis. I really do believe that you will be a tremendous asset to the Victims."

There was no immediate response by Dr. Hessian.

"Doctor Hessian, please don't misunderstand me. I am not implying any undervaluing of Sigmund Freud or the power of his work. I think that Freud was one of the greatest thinkers of all time in the study of nervous disorders. It's just that we are using a model with proven efficacy, and the model your work is based in is most applicable to a different treatment problem—neurosis. We're dealing with deep mental trauma, not neuroses."

His earlier long stride, as if he had intended to outwalk her, had shortened. Now he stood, head down, pulling at his lips.

"I doubt that you and I, Doctor Dwardie, can ever work together with any degree of mutual respect, much less find a basis for a *proper* course of treatment for these unfortunate Victims."

"I can accept that, although with great regret, Doctor Hessian. No, please don't go yet. There is one trauma case I'd like a chance to discuss with you. It was one that baffled all of us."

"Oh?"

"Yes, now do sit down, Doctor Hessian," and she indicated a strategically placed stone bench that had a magnificent view of the Bay, "this might take a little time."

"I should imagine so."

"Well," and Dorothy seemed to be taking a breath before plunging into this case. "There is a professional woman, Doctor K—a psychologist of exceptional brilliance—whose case, though successful, was very difficult. She experienced the mind-wipe shortly after a series of Victim deaths, or so one observer tells us. These had resulted from the effects of the modulated electrical current level. Some of the early deaths were those who had been trained as neuropsychologists although leading professionals of all branches of sciences also were among the dead."

"Yes, I had heard that," Dr. Hessian was willing to admit, "from talks with Doctor Seissmann. Evidently Doctor Stanley Kessler was one. Tragic loss to the field."

"I agree," Dorothy said. "From various sources, we did learn that the Eosi reduced the current to prevent additional deaths due to central nervous system overload. Unfortunately the reason was less humanitarian than selfish. The Eosi were killing before they could complete the retrieval process that would extract the information they wanted. To be useful, the subject had to remain in a state of altered consciousness, therefore alive, during the probe."

"What could be their interest in neuropsychology?" Dr. Hessian asked.

"This is theory, of course, because they mind-wiped leading professionals and state officials on a random basis but it might have to do with increasing the compliance level of the races they have dominated. They have had an unusual amount of resistance from Earth's races and they may well have been trying to find a way to disempower their ability to resist. Just 'turn them off,' so to speak, by inhibiting or altering the synaptic receptor response. It would have the same effect as removing the drive unit from a computer—you can punch the keys but nothing will happen. For some reason, and fortunately for the rest of those subjected to the mind-wipe, the Eosi went off on another tact of mental exploration entirely. Or the percentage of death was discouraging."

"What happened to those who were so examined?"

"Some experienced organic damage to both frontal lobes from experimental current levels. Still others were left with the effects of psychological trauma and some had both. In addition, many have had survivor guilt, as they were aware of the eminence of many that died. They have, quite naturally, questioned their own worth at having remained alive. Others grieved. Actually, in the case of Doctor K, there was some of both."

"Tell me more," said Dr. Hessian.

"Our patient, Doctor K, heard of the deaths of several such scientists, colleagues at the university, and prior to her own ordeal under Eosian instrument. And, while the mind-wipe current level had been reduced and no further deaths resulted, she was severely traumatized. Having the power of her mind stolen by ruthless aliens who had strapped her into a chair and assaulted her with a searing blue beam of bright, laser-fine light was devastating. She had flashbacks of the blue beam following her, aimed directly at the forebrain, entering her head while she was physically and psychologically paralyzed, unable to escape."

"Hmmm. Could cause severe neuroses, indeed." He cleared his throat. "You have told me about the trauma Doctor K experienced. Now I'd like to know something about her development history, psychological defenses, and pre-morbid adjustment level."

Dorothy took a deep breath as she was coming to the difficult part. "Pre-morbid adjustment level is not a very useful concept in the treatment of post-traumatic stress disorder of highly functioning individuals. The focus is more closely conceptualized as helping them gain self-efficacy and self-control over their symptoms at the conscious level."

"Well," and Dr. Hessian's tone was pompous, "if you don't take pre-morbid treatment into account, you are not offering comprehensive treatment."

"In your theory that is true: in mine, technically, it's not," she replied. "Imagine a nearly new automobile that is totally destroyed in a head-on collision. We would seldom ask how well it ran prior to the accident or expect it to return to its nearly new form after a visit to the body shop. In fact, such wrecks are discarded. But, with people, the nature of the human spirit often allows them to achieve an amazing level of functioning so that they can transcend the level of the trauma. Teaching how to do that by employing techniques from cognitive psychology, behavior therapy, and multi-modal treatment has proven efficacious."

Another pause. "Well, then, tell me," Dr. Hessian said again with that hint of gracious condescension, "what were the symptoms of post-traumatic stress that were most difficult to treat?" he asked.

Dorothy decided that he was trying to buy time to revise his strategy.

"Doctor K had temporary post-trauma amnesia and flashbacks of the blue light. She could not sleep or remain awake without recurrent images of the blue light attacking her forehead. Everywhere she went, it haunted her. In dreams as well as in waking life, she was trailed by this nasty flashback that impeded every aspect of her recovery."

Dr. Hessian straightened himself, a smug gleam in his eye and Dorothy wondered what hole he would try to pick in her method. He was making eye contact now while he assumed his characteristic condescending expression.

"This is why pre-morbid adjustment is so important to know," he said. "I would guess there was some unresolved conflict in this woman's background that made her more prone to the flashback. Do you know if there was some unresolved guilt toward a parent or unresolved shame in the area of sexuality, for example, that showed itself in this way?"

By now the sun was disappearing behind the mountains. They could hear others hurrying home but no one used this path. She didn't want to rush the man but they would soon have to leave, to avoid the night crawlers. However, she had to make an end of this power struggle between the two opposing camps of psychological treatment. The base of their current discussion, she reasoned, is power, not just theory. There are two ends to this rope: he is pulling one end and I have hold of the other in this psychological tug-of-war. I will decide not to play and see what happens.

"Well," Dorothy said out loud, "while I would continue our discussion, we must make it back to our respective residences before full dark. I had wanted to tell you that the way we treated Doctor K's flashbacks was to bring under stimulus control using a fading procedure combined with deep muscle relaxation. We also provided her with an imagery intervention which was highly effective."

Dr. Hessian looked at her, unimpressed. He was probably not inspired by the a-theoretical even if it was effective.

"We'd best call it a night," she said, standing up and his deep-rooted courtesy made him get to his feet, too. "I hope you decide to join us. Would you sleep on it? We could use your clinical help and perhaps you could summarize Doctor Kessler's work and present it to the treatment staff. It might be a fitting tribute since you knew him. Anyway, let me know what you decide."

She took the few steps back to the safety of the flagstone path but turned back, assuming a humble expression. "Oh," she said, "Doctor Hessian, before I leave, I do need to apologize to you." She even managed the slightest hint of chagrin.

"Apologize to me?" he repeated, obviously pleased that she was seeing the mistake of her own ways.

"Yes, you see, presenting the case of Doctor K was my way of attempting to share with you the power of the treatment model. I guess I was not successful in helping you see that."

"Well," he said, with an almost gracious wave of his hand, "you tried."

"The irony," she responded gently, "was that while most of the case data was accurate, one part was not. I changed the gender of the doctor involved."

"Well, I hardly think that is significant."

"Not when Doctor K is you. We used social learning techniques to revive your fine mind, Doctor Hessian, and they worked."

She saw his gaping mouth and hurried away, leaving him to digest that final thrust.

KRIS AND SARAH HAD RUN AS FAST AS THEY could to leave the scene of their eavesdropping.

"Should we apologize to Dorothy?" Kris asked, her expression repentant.

"How were we to know Hessian would come in, all ruffled and precipitate a set-down? I hope he got it from her, too," Sarah replied, not the least bit repentant. Then she shuddered. "I hadn't heard her theory about what the Eosi might have been trying to do. Make zombies out of all of us."

Kris had a sick feeling in her guts. She shook her head

slowly in denial. "No, Zainal is certain that the Eosi were trying to search for possible new scientific theories . . ."

"And what, pray tell, was that?" Sarah asked acidly.

"A point, but it wasn't just psychologists and psychiatrists that got the treatment. There were heads of state and government departments and whatever NASA personnel they could find. All kinds of specialists." Kris realized she was talking more to reassure herself than Sarah. And she wasn't sure she was convincing. "Well, with all the information that's come back, the High Command," and she managed a grin, "are sure to come to some conclusions. I'm sure Dorothy would have told Leon Dane, at least, since he's still more or less chief medic."

"Well, it's not something we just *ask* about, is it?"

"Nope, but that doesn't mean we can't find out if it's been discussed." Kris muttered under her breath. "That's the downside of being away from here. You can't keep up with what's happening."

Sarah raised her eyebrows and regarded Kris with a wry grin. "Look who's talking? You've been traveling the galaxy and I'm stuck at home . . . Oops!" She caught Kris' arm, then pointed to the cluster of torches at the dark edge of the settlement. "Demonstration!"

They were not so far away they didn't hear the gasp as the latest arrivals witnessed the emergence of night crawlers. They could hear male shouts of surprise and alarm and female cries of terror. They saw plainly the shadows of a milling throng, wanting to put distance between themselves and the wet, slimy denizens of the night ground. A chant began, and from the depth of the voices, the two friends decided that was a Maasai response to danger.

"I'm glad they're on our side," Kris said.

"Me, too, and Joe won't be on mine if I don't get home," Sarah said and turned off toward her own home on the flagstone path where their way parted.

• • •

WHEN KRIS REACHED THEIR HOUSE, ZANE WAS asleep and Zainal busy with papers on the table, so she slipped in to check on her son. He'd grown inches in the weeks she'd been away. What else had she missed of his development?

Zainal grinned at her. "He walks well now."

She pulled up another chair to sit beside him, their bodies barely touching at shoulder and thigh. She had worked herself into a nervous wreck on the walk home, thinking about Dorothy's theory. Well, eavesdroppers never heard anything good, about themselves or other matters: as just demonstrated. But maybe Zainal could reassure her. She was certain to have nightmares tonight, remembering the blank looks of the Victims as they had been led off the two K-ships.

"Zainal?" she began and then noticed he was dealing with figures and time slots, and entry windows through the Bubble. "What's being planned now?"

Zainal leaned back, tossing the pencil to the table and stretching until his tendons cracked which made her shudder. The sound made her wince, thinking of bodies on a rack.

"Kamiton met some of the other leaders, and I must agree with some of their ideas." Zainal linked his fingers together across the back of his broad head. Which reminded Kris of the burning question.

She put her hand on his upper arm in brief apology. "The Eosi couldn't come up with a means to turn off all our minds, could they?"

Zainal tipped his head back, roaring with laughter, and she had to hush him. Zane would sleep through a great deal of noise but not a bellow like that.

He slipped an arm around her shoulders and gave her a reassuring squeeze, his face against her cheek.

"They've only one of those mental helmets. They

could scarcely cope with the millions of you Humans, and that's what they'd have to do. Though Ray asked Kamiton, too, if it was possible. It isn't! It would be better if we could put the Eosi under that device." He made a grimace, a new trait of his which made him seem all the more Human. She'd caught the surprise in Kamiton's eyes over Zainal's facial reactions. Very un-Catteni, probably. "Of course, their enlarged heads wouldn't fit so we can't use that as a way of cutting them down to size."

She grinned back at him. "So?"

"So, since Kamiton needs to get back, we are going to see what other mischief . . . is that the right word," and his yellow eyes twinkled at her, "we can get into. Actually," and he retrieved the pencil to tap it on the various sheets that she realized were now laid out in a semi-circle on the table, "Beverly wants to dazzle them with surprises everywhere. Everyone who went back to Earth is all for it." His expression was solemn. "Your planet had taken a terrible beating and still won't succumb to practices the Eosi have always found effective. If not being able to get through the Bubble has been frustrating Mentat Ix, why not prod them elsewhere! Frustrate them more! Confuse them! Harry—I thought that was a man's name—harry them until they don't know how to deal with the various strikes we'll make."

"Well, there're ways to totally confuse a computer," Kris said, "and make it blow up. *Could* there be a way to do that to the Eosi?"

"Kamiton thinks it's a good way to go," Zainal said, with a sly grin. "He says it might be the right way, too."

"So?" and she pulled one of the sheets toward her which Zainal then deftly shifted back.

"So, since Kamiton can get access to all the recognition codes, *and* find out which ships of which class have been destroyed or believed lost, we can make our fleet into a much larger one."

"By changing the code name?"

"And where it appears. For instance, as Emassi Venlik, I need to bring back all the metals I had to off-load in the asteroid belt. First, as Emassi Kulak, I will go to a mining planet and acquire a load . . ." He interrupted himself. "Walter Duxie says he can't mine enough to make a full load of interesting stuff, so we go where they are mining it. Then, we take that load back to Catten." He stopped and took a deep breath. "I wish to bring my sons to safety here," and he looked her squarely in her eyes.

"Of course," Kris said quickly. "They would be at risk if the Eosi found out you're still alive."

"There is one who is sure I am," Zainal said in a heavy voice.

"Your brother?" And when he nodded, she went on, "But where are your sons now?"

Zainal clenched his teeth a moment before he answered. "With my sire."

"Aren't they . . ." and she stopped because it was obvious from the pain in his eyes and the tension in his body that they were not safe. "Kamiton's seen them?"

Zainal nodded.

"Well, it's an easy way for me to increase my family," she said in an airy tone.

"I will be their father but you will not be able to mother them," he said, surprising her. He held up his hand. "They are now too old to be mothered. But if you can be their friend, that will help integrate them."

"We've managed to integrate everything from Deski to Maasai, there should be no problem with integrating two Catteni boys."

Zainal gave an odd snort. "They will be safer here than on Catteni and Kamiton wants to bring his. Though he would prefer to bring his woman and set her and them in one of the closed valleys. We may have to assume responsibility for any other young who might be used as hostages by the Eosi against the activities of their sires."

"I'd think . . ." but she stopped when he put his hand over hers. "Okay, it's your call. So are we all going back to Catten with you?" She really didn't want to: that heavy gravity had been a killer, but she wouldn't desert him for such a specious reason.

"Drassi Kulak proved very useful," he said with a grin.

"So, once we've delivered all this ore, what else is on the agenda?"

Zainal smiled. "Kamiton can find out the other places where Humans have been dropped. Some of them are very bad places, where many deliveries of workers have to be made, and we may not find any Humans left. But we will make the effort."

"Oh."

"Three of the ships, with a change of ID, will go back to Earth and see what else they can . . . what does Chuck call it . . . liber—"

"Liberate," and Kris grinned.

"Liberate any poorly guarded ships. If they are loaded with loot, we will just take off. Otherwise, we will have what Leon calls a 'shopping' list."

"Well, you guys didn't lose much time planning, did you?"

"Kamiton thinks we must strike as often and as hard as possible to prove to the others in our group that we have ways to annoy and hamper the Eosi domination. To make them helpless to counterattack."

"Lord help us if that Bubble bursts," she said. "But it must be so very satisfying to you, and Kamiton, to make the Eosi helpless."

Zainal kept nodding his head but his smile altered from anticipation to immense satisfaction. "We also do no species injury."

"Oh, Lord, that's a good thing. I wouldn't want to lose

the good opinion of the Farmers. That Bubble is essential to making any of these plans of yours work."

"I do not think the Farmers will find fault with what we do. They are, I think, flexible entities." And when Kris nodded in agreement, he added with a droll smile: "What impresses Kamiton most about Humans is your flexibility. We Catteni do not possess that."

"Ha! You're as flexible as anyone on this planet."

He stroked her short, blond hair, running his fingers through it. She'd had to wash it nearly fifteen times to get the awful dye completely out.

"I have learned."

"The more remarkable when all your lifetime before you had to operate on a need-to-know basis."

Zainal turned his head away, looking out into the darkness around them. "I want my sons to know all they *want* to know."

"I think sometimes we forget what a gift free thought is."

Chapter Eight

THE NEXT DAY, HASSAN FLEW SEVERAL LEAD-
ers of the Maasai, for the remnants of five separate tribes
needed to be consulted and shown, down to the southern
end of the continent. Mpeti Ole Surum, Caleb Materu,
and Sikai Ole Sereb spoke some English, understood
more, and calmed the other two leaders, Pakai Olonyoke
and Tepilit Ole Saitoti, who had excellent Swahili. Bart,
who had boned up most of the long night on Swahili
words and phrases, came along on the trip in the KDL, as
did Yuri Palit, who was nominally in charge of resettle-
ments. Baby would have been more practical. The Tub
would have taken a lot longer but the tall Maasai would
have been cramped on the one and experienced some
claustrophobia on the other, so Hassan said he'd just
make altitude and glide as much as he could on the way,
to save fuel.

"I see . . . planes . . . often," Caleb said, pointing sky-
ward. He was sitting with great dignity on one of the
command chairs of the bridge. Overnight he and many of
the older men had managed to equip themselves with

lodge-pole spears. The straightness of the wood had fascinated them and Geoff, who did a lot of the iron fabrication around Retreat, had fashioned spear tips. "Never think I fly in one." He grinned all around the bridge cabin.

Mpeti Ole Surum stood directly behind Hassan as the Israeli sat at the control panel, his eyes not quite wide with any readable expression but he missed nothing Hassan did.

Sikai Ole Sereb was the most relaxed of the three English speakers, more like a curious kid having a special outing than the most senior of the Maasai leaders.

"I think they were all so busy setting examples to each other, they didn't have time to be afraid," Hassan told the Head Council that evening when he reported the day's outing. Kris, Zainal, and Kamiton were among the group—so that Kamiton could be shown how the colony governed itself. Zainal translated in low tones, which did not disturb the others in the big hangar office. "They *do* understand about the night crawlers. Last night's demonstration certainly was dramatic and frightening enough. They do want their own loo-cows, even if the creatures are ungrateful enough not to give milk. You know, we could import some cattle, or goats and sheep. They'd be useful for us to have."

"If you can find any," Beverly remarked.

"True but we can look. A lot of Terran animals would do well here."

"Now, wait a minute," Beverly said, raising a big hand in caution, "we have rocksquats which serve as good protein and supply us with quite a few byproducts. I can't promise we can do a Noah's ark bit."

"We wouldn't know until too late," Leon Dane said, "if Terran grazers or browsers would survive on Botany . . . not with night crawlers and those avian terrors."

"I agree. We've got to go slowly. We've got a lot here

163

going for us without wanting what might not be ecologically feasible," Beverly said.

"The Maasai will be grateful, I think," Yuri Palit said, "to be allowed to live in their own ways on their own land, which was taken from them back on Earth, and make the best of things as we've done, as they've always had to do. We did discuss the need to have shelters, built either on stone—which isn't their way—or on platforms set high enough above the ground and the reach of night crawlers, using steel plates on the underside. I wouldn't trust night crawlers not to eat wood if something edible got spilled on it. I think they'll opt for the platforms. It's a good even climate down there, edging into really hot but Africa's like that, too. Each tribe will have its own com unit and I think they've mastered calling in and taking messages. But I think we better check on a regular basis."

"Once we know all the women are in good health. Some of them are expecting," Beverly said. "There are only that gaggle of young boys and five or six girls in their early teens who survived."

"Ah, and those boys bring up a minor problem which I think we'd better solve as soon as possible," Hassan said. "Five of the teenagers are about to go into training as warriors. They are going to require some of the ritual drugs. Olkiloriti," and Hassan stumbled over the unfamiliar word, "is one of them. Joe Marley said that's only Acacia nilotica, which is taken as a digestive excitant and to prevent hunger and thirst on raids. It's also said to prevent fatigue and fear."

"Were they looking for it here?" Chuck asked. "They seem to be examining every single bush, shrub, and blade of grass."

Hassan grinned. "They're big on knowing the flora around them. It's how they've survived as long as they have—knowing what to take for sickness and fever and how to keep wounds clean."

"Well, I suppose that we could import some of the acacia for them . . ." Bull Fetterman began. "If we can find any in their part of east Africa."

"The roots must be clean," Leon Dane spoke up. "Let's not import Terran dirt or we might just import something we don't want growing wild on Botany." As an Australian, Leon knew something of the problems vegetation could cause when transplanted to a different ecology.

"Good point."

"I've been showing them what we've been growing for medicinal use," Leon went on with a wide grin. "And the old guy kept telling me everything was good for some ailment and patted me on the back as if I'd done something spectacular to have everything growing in one place."

"You have," Bull said with one of his deep rumbling laughs.

"Indeed," Hassan said. "They would have to travel many miles to get to where certain bushes grow."

Just then Dick Aarens came rushing in, Pete Snyder trying to keep up with the long-legged mechanic's stride and also reason with him.

"But I've got it! I've got it," Dick said, beaming with self-satisfaction. He shrugged off Pete's final attempt to control him and spread his arms wide in apology to those at the conference table.

"Hold it, Aarens, we're discussing another problem right now," Ray said.

"Can anything be more important than being able to *see* and *hear* outside the Bubble?" Aarens demanded, head thrown back and chin high in challenge.

Ducking her head and putting her hand to her brows, Kris shook her head slowly at this latest display of Aarens' egotism.

"See and hear?" Ray repeated, glaring at Aarens.

"I don't know how such a simple thing could be missed." And Aarens was contemptuous.

"Then just how did you miss such a simple thing, Aarens?" asked Ray Scott, leaning back in his chair, an absolutely blank expression on his face.

Aarens frowned, knowing he was being ragged.

"You do leave yourself wide open, Dick," Pete said, shaking his head. He leaned his hands on the table opposite Ray and explained. "The Eosi ship left all its com arrays stuck into the Bubble. They haven't moved in months. I doubt they can, even if I don't know why the material holds them in place. But it does. If Zainal or one of the NASA guys can do an EVA, we can probably make connections on this side of the Bubble and get to use the Eosi equipment to intercept messages and check on who's visiting us. We've got the spare parts we'd need, thanks to Zainal. We can actually put a com sat up there on our side of the Bubble."

"You see," Aarens said, his lip lifted in a sort of supercilious superiority. "Simple thing and you missed it."

"We all missed it," Pete Snyder said, patiently but with an irritable glance at Aarens. "I'm not all that sure we'd get much filtered through the Bubble, but certainly it's worth a try."

"It is," Zainal said. Then he grinned. "I like it. Using *their* arrays to do *our* looking and listening."

"Save us a lot of fuel, too, as we wouldn't have to go make a check before departure," Beverly said, chuckling. "Which we will be doing a lot of soon enough."

"Do I ever get a chance to come along?" Aarens said, his jaw still stuck out in belligerence.

Ray regarded him. "Only if you can lose about five inches, Dick," he said in a deceptively genial tone. "You're taller than either Zainal and Kamiton, and they say they're tall for Catteni."

"You've let Bert Put go, and he's nearly my height," Aarens went on, angry and frustrated.

"He's a pilot, who stays on board and seated so no one

checks his height," Ray said. "But if you want to go back to Earth—so long as you remain on board the ship—it could be arranged. We'll talk about it again. After . . . we've got eyes and ears upstairs."

"Something for something, just like we were back on Earth," Aarens muttered.

"Oh, come off it, Dick," Pete Snyder said, putting a hand on the tall mechanic's back and gently urging him out of the hangar.

"That's a great idea, Aarens," Beverly said and, taking their cue from the ex-air force general, others murmured appropriate phrases. "Sometimes it just takes the right eyes to see what can so easily be missed."

"It may not work," Aarens said as he slowly let himself be eased out of the hangar. "I mean, we may not be able to get through the Bubble from this side."

"The idea remains a smart one even if it doesn't prove feasible," Ray said and then the door closed behind the two men. Ray cleared his throat.

"It certainly would be a help," John Beverly said.

"He's a damned good mechanic—a genius at some things," Ray Scott said.

"But he's not a team player," was Bull Fetterman's assessment.

"Exactly," and Ray sat forward at the table, shuffling notes. "I wouldn't trust him not to jump ship at the first chance. Where were we?"

"I think we just settled the Maasai for the time being," Yuri Palit said and settled back in his chair.

"I suggest we see how fast Aarens can fix a connection to the array," Zainal said. "I will help. And so will Kami-ton."

"When we have that, the rest of what we were going to discuss tonight will be easy enough. So let's see if Aarens' idea works. I think this'll be all for tonight," Ray said and, placing his hands on the table, pushed himself to his feet. "Thank you, gentlemen, for your reports and attention."

A LOT OF JURY-RIGGING WAS NEEDED ON THE Bubble side of the Eosi array, with both Zainal and Kamiton working in space suits. One of the NASA communications personnel—uneasy at doing an EVA—finally solved the problem of the connections. They pulled and tugged at the material of the Bubble until it was as thin as they could make it. Then they rammed into those frail holes the connecting linkages. Dick Aarens had wheedled himself on board with the communications crew and made such obnoxious comments about how ineffective, stupid, fumble-fingered everyone else was that Zainal shoved him into the spare space suit—Aarens had to crouch to fit and complained that the helmet was wearing grooves in his skull—and closed the air lock behind them. There were those who wished that Zainal had not securely attached the safety line.

Aarens had known that he didn't like heights. He'd screamed enough when they had to haul him up to the command post to see what he could make of the control panels. He'd been so damned keen to say he'd been in space in an EVA suit that he didn't realize that his height phobia would also include vast, black open spaces where, in every direction, there was nothing. The other space walker had to push the rigid man back into the air lock.

"Take him inside. He's useless."

But that incident happened early on. The completed connections were initially attached to the Baby's com array to see if they could actually use the Eosi equipment through the thinned skin of the Bubble. They could. And great cheering and congratulations resounded between Botany and Baby. The next step might take longer since a com sat had to be built but Kamiton sampled the messages that were audible through the link and smiled with great satisfaction at what he learned.

"We can proceed with our plan," he told Zainal in Catteni. Then, in thickly accented English, he added to the rest of the group on board who did not know much Catteni, "Is good. Works. Hear good."

"I told you it would work," Dick Aarens said, clinging to the door frame, and still very pale from his disastrous EVA. "So how soon can you get this crate back down to Retreat?"

"Soon," Zainal said and turned back to Kamiton, speaking in rapid Catteni. "We will leave on the KDL as soon as we return. I want to get back to Catten as fast as possible."

"Understood."

WHEN KRIS' NAME APPEARED ON THE LIST FOR KDL and a return to Catten, she did some counting on her fingers. Well, if they didn't have any delays, she'd be back in time for Zane's first Botanical year birthday. Zainal did not anticipate any delays with the plan he had filed with Ray Scott. He had been amused by the request from the ex-admiral but, with the other ships also departing in opposite directions, he filled in the data.

"Did I do it right?" he asked Kris, shoving the paper toward her across the table in their main room.

"You'd better have," Kris said with mock threat, "or you're no advertisement for my teaching."

He printed in bold letters, using both capitals and lower case as required. But he spelled properly and, even if he used short sentences, they were correctly phrased.

"You get an A."

"Just an A?" he said, pretending to be disappointed.

"Oh, that's the best you can do."

"Oh?" and he leaned across the table and neatly lifted

her out of her chair and high enough so that, when she bent her knees, she cleared the surface. "I must lesson you, too, to see if you can achieve the A."

Zane was long since asleep, so they could indulge in the intimacies that would be impossible for the duration of the trip.

"I hope to bring out my sons," Zainal said, when they lay side by side, mutually satisfied. "You must not treat them—at first—as you would a Human child."

"How old are they?"

"They are nine and seven."

"Same mother?"

"No. Good Catteni blood in each."

"They will have a lot to learn, won't they?" And, while in one sense Kris felt able to accept the challenge, she hoped she would be able to meet it. Another aspect of it was that Zainal would trust her with his own children. How badly would they have been treated because Zainal had failed to accept the family's obligation to present himself as Eosi "chosen"?

"We all have a lot to *learn*," Zainal said and, pressing his face against hers, turned her over so they could sleep, spoon fashion, his heavy arm warmly against her.

"NOW COMES THE FUN PART," ZAINAL SAID TO the crew of the KDL, all assembled on the bridge. They were orbiting into one of the most desolate-looking planets: how could anything, or anyone, live down there?

They had first let Kamiton off at the asteroid belt and lingered long enough to hear him report that the spy sats he had released in the belt confirmed the fact that there had been quite a few ships poking around the field: more likely, for traces of where Zainal/Venlik might have stored the remainder of his cargo.

Kamiton would then proceed back to Catten with the report that he had found no suitable planets in the three systems he was supposedly exploring. He would have the opportunity to get in touch with any of the other dissidents and assure them that Zainal's refuge was invulnerable. He would also visit Perizec, Zainal's father, and, hopefully, locate the whereabouts of Zainal's two sons. Since the family had supplied so many "chosen," they had acquired many assets on the planet. The two young males could be anywhere.

With a purloined cargo, Zainal would arrive. This time they would have to dock at the space station.

"It will be easier for you as the station is not on full Catten gravity," he had told Kris, who had not been looking forward to a second period of feeling more like a piece of compressed stone than a human being. "But you may not leave the ship. You are not Catten enough," and he had tousled her cropped re-dyed hair.

The rest of the crew was the same. Gino, Ninety, and Mack Dargle had learned to speak, and understand, much more Catteni. Kamiton even taught them a few so-called Catteni jokes which, when translated, left the audience wondering what possibly could be funny about them.

"Old slap-stick routines is what they remind me of," Kris said. "Sort of Marx brothers without any of the same class. More like the Three Stooges."

"They were never as good as the Marx brothers," Ninety said.

"Speak Catteni," Zainal said, scowling at all of them.

"Does not translate," Kris said with mock obedience in a very deep rasping Catteni voice.

WITH THE KDL BEARING THE ID OF A SHIP Kamiton had found, its forward section embedded in an asteroid it hadn't been able to avoid, they orbited the desolate planet and made contact with the mining station. This was a huge, scarred globule planted like a ravaged blister on one of the main raised areas. This particular station had been chosen because it had no processing plant in which to refine the ore. So their purloined cargo would match Zainal's story of finding such ores in an asteroid belt. Once this planet had evidently had oceans that some unimaginable catastrophe had drained or boiled away. There were other, smaller blisters set in deep ranges of what had once been ocean trenches. As they were given clearance and descended, they could see heavy vehicles drawing numerous, and immense, carts of ore toward the main depot, for that was what Kris decided it must be.

Several such vehicles were already drawing into parallel lines by the facility, which Zainal said was where the cargo levels would automatically be loaded.

"By what?" Ninety said. "We don't have enough space suits . . ."

Zainal grinned and held up his hands. "That is why there are space locks between the main compartments of the ship and the cargo area. The K-class is a versatile carrier, cargo, slaves, whatever."

There was a bit of a scene when the station Drassi wanted Zainal to take on board three Catteni who had been so seriously injured they were no longer any use to him. All this while the ramps from the loading platform were being extended through the KDL's open cargo bay, and while Ninety, suited up, handled the controls.

"As soon as the decks are full, Ninety, we're taking off," Zainal told Ninety. "So be sure to hang on to something the moment we're full."

"I hear and obey, Drassi," Doyle said, slapping one fist to his chest in a Catteni salute.

"Won't you get into trouble?" Gino asked nervously.

"Just plot a rapid ascent. This station has no weapons," Zainal assured him.

"But can you just refuse to take injured men aboard?" Gino asked.

"Not for a two-week journey back to Catteni with them

on board," Zainal said. "This station has frequent cargo ships in. The next one can take them. I won't."

So, when Ninety signaled that all four cargo levels were full, Zainal gave Gino the nod to lift just as three space-suited figures, two helping the third who did not seem to have legs, exited from the surface loading facility.

Zainal reached over and shut off the com board, silencing the threats of the infuriated Emassi in charge of the mining operations.

"We couldn't afford the risk," Zainal said, aware of the shocked look on the faces of his crew.

WHEN THEY WERE AGAIN IN SPACE, ZAINAL AND Ninety, who had come to enjoy such EVA outings, changed the ID symbols on the KDL's hull to match those used in their first trip to Catten. Once more in communication with the immense Catteni Space Station, Zainal became Drassi Venlik again, cheerfully (for a Catteni) back with the ore he had to leave behind in the asteroid belt.

There were some scary moments for Kris, however, when the space station sent officials on board to see if the KDL's cargo should be unloaded into drones for transport to the surface or allow the ship to land at the manufactories needing the ore. The rest of this trip depended on Zainal being ordered to make planetary delivery. One of the officials seemed determined to figure out the site of this rich load.

"It is my site. By right," Drassi Venlik said, standing with legs parted in a fighting stance, hands at his sides. This semi-belligerent posture was not lost on the officials, even if they were Emassi.

Finally they admitted that they had orders for his ship to land on the surface at the refining plant awaiting these very fine metals. Zainal and his crew saluted the officials off the KDL and received immediate clearance from the facility and the location of the refinery.

"Couldn't have been better if I'd cut the orders myself," Zainal said in English, grinning at his success.

"Yeah," Ninety began skeptically, "but would you really have laid into the Emassi?"

Zainal laughed. "There are many Drassi who are Emassi who did not pass Eosi standards to be chosen. They have family who would come to their assistance. Those station Emassi know only what they need to know," and he dismissed them with a contemptuous flick of his fingers.

Kris decided that Zainal became more Cattenish the nearer he got to his natal planet. She wasn't sure she liked that change in him. Then they landed and the weight of Catten gravity pulled her down, until she felt her belly would end up near her knees. And ordinarily her stomach was as flat as Zainal's. It had a decided bulge to it right now.

She spent the hours the KDL was being unloaded on her bunk, on Zainal's order, being "off-duty" as the corridors swarmed with Rassi and Drassi. Zainal, with Chuck and Ninety in full Catteni dress, eyes, and hair, went to the refinery office to complete the forms required and get the credit voucher for the ore.

It was evidently most unusual for a cargo vessel to require a credit voucher, but Zainal had a story ready for that. They needed special equipment to mine the ores on this asteroid and had been given permission to make such purchases, but would have to show a current voucher to verify that the ship's account would stand the expense.

"THAT DEPOT'S LIKE ALI BABA'S CAVE," NINETY said, returning after the first day's scrounging through the supply warehouse. "Mind you, a lot of the stuff was made on Earth," he added in a sour tone. "But I located most of what the com sat boys ordered."

With great determination, Kris had made a huge stew of the meat Coo and Pess had gone out to the nearest marketplace to get for her. It had taken almost all the energy she could muster with the constant pull of gravity on her muscles and bones. She was sure she'd shrink: she certainly felt compressed.

Zainal did not return that first night. The Catteni diurnal cycle was only an hour longer than Earth's but, to Kris' intense relief, he was back just past dawn the next morning with Kamiton and two other Catteni making a surreptitious dart up the ramp of the open cargo bay.

The men were introduced as Nitin and Tubelin. Bolemb could not leave as yet and Kasturi was going to bring Zainal's two boys as soon as the ship was ready to take off again. For Catteni they exuded enthusiasm for the chance to relieve their world of Eosian domination. To believe that Zainal's crew was really Human, every one, including Kris, had to take out their yellow lenses and show the natural shade of skin on their upper arms and legs. Kris was on watch at that moment and thus did not have to reveal her subtly different limbs.

Nitin looked older than Tubelin but later Zainal told her it was the other way round. Nitin had had harder duties than Tubelin, and so looked his years of service to ungrateful Eosi. Nitin said little but Kamiton's exuberance made up for his silence.

The next day the three real Catteni assumed other identities and went about acquiring more of the material that was on the shopping list. Nor, to the Humans' surprise, did they question that they had to buy such odd items in unusual quantities: like the huge iron kettles (which were used by the Rassi to cook their mashes in— about the only thing, Nitin said, that they could manage to do without constant supervision). The kettles were destined for the Maasai who were much, much smarter than most of the Drassi Kris had encountered. She stood her shifts on the com desk and had to deal with the calls of merchants who wished to check on the ship's account and its current position. She had also managed not to reveal her femininity to new members of the Catteni. If Zainal did not think to mention it, she would not.

The KDL had been parked to the side of the refinery's double-ballpark of a landing site to allow other vessels to unload. Zainal had neatly maneuvered them close to one of the refinery's secondary gates, to allow access for his "equipment" to arrive without upsetting the regular traffic in and out.

"It's a good place to be," Zainal had said in explanation. "Many ships come and go. It is also the last place where any Emassis would be found."

With their cargo levels full, they waited for word from Kasturi. Kamiton fretted more than Zainal did and paced up and down the corridors, cursing at the com unit which did not utter so much as a burp. They waited two full days, until Zainal, too, showed signs of stress.

Both men were on the bridge when a low, sputtering ground vehicle came through the gates and trundled around behind the KDL.

"It has stopped," Chuck said, swiveling around in his seat at the com board. He flicked on the exterior camera. "Three, two smallish, one not so small."

Instantly Zainal and Kamiton were on their feet and pounding down the passageway to the cargo air lock.

"Prepare to take off," Zainal called over his shoulder, and Gino hastily started the pre-flight checks as he had done from time to time as something to occupy them during the long wait. "And turn the ship slightly to starboard to incinerate the vehicle." That came through over the intercom from the cargo level.

"Right ch'are, captain," Gino muttered, fingers busy tapping in the necessary code and engaging the rear thrusters to be certain the object was reduced to an unrecognizable lump.

As they were at the refinery, their leaving would go relatively unnoticed. They lifted and were well above the atmospheric envelope of Catteni before Zainal and Kamiton came forward, both grinning broadly.

"We got them," Kamiton said as Zainal motioned for Gino to move out of the pilot's chair. Kamiton, oddly enough dressed in a space suit, and carrying his helmet, positioned himself against the bulwark.

So as not to be seen, Kris thought, when Zainal had to make visual contact with the space station for clearance out of Catteni space. But why was he suited up?

"I'm parked right by net four," Kamiton said as if he had heard her mental query. "Head slightly in that direction now."

Contact was made, clearance was given, and Zainal said that he was going back for another load of the fine ores he had carved out of the space debris.

"Of course, they'll come after you again," Kamiton said. "See you back on Botany," he added before he put on his helmet and stumped down to the air lock. "Can you read me?" he asked a few moments later.

Kris stuck her finger harder than she needed to on the pad—her body didn't realize she was out of Catteni's depressing gravity—and gave him an affirmative.

Zainal made a small adjustment to his direction, seeming to head directly for the center of net four—large Catteni glyphs had been plastered on the net fabric—one could not miss "4" unless one was totally blind. He also slowed so that when the air lock lights came on, he was almost stationary. He allowed the KDL to drift a count of two hundred, because Kris was counting right along with him, before he gently reengaged the thrusters and pulled away. Then he made a drastic course alteration and signaled to Gino to pour on the power.

There was a little time for Kasturi to meet the Human crew and for Bazil and Peran to get accustomed to the idea of Humans, and Humans who could speak their language and were not slaves. Kris almost wept at the condition of the two boys: they had come on board filthy, in clothing that was a shred away from being indecent, with many bruises on their limbs and visible through the remaining scraps of their tunics. Their ribs were showing and their faces had the gaunt look of the starved. What they asked Zainal for first—once they had recognized their father—was water.

"They wouldn't take anything from me," Kasturi explained. "They did not show fright, Zainal. They have your blood and courage. In my opinion, many cruel and vicious things have been done to them."

Zainal himself bathed the boys, carefully tending their hurts and seeming to count every healed scar. Kris handed him Botanical medications, and they had flinched, even from their father's very gentle touch. She was close to tears for how they had been treated . . . worse than even the Rassi she had seen so casually whipped to work.

All the time Zainal spoke softly to them, not gently, not as he would speak to Zane, but as an adult would speak firmly and reassuringly to a frightened animal.

Tubelin put his head around the door and both boys stiffened, their yellow eyes dark and wide with the fright of surprise, which his unexpected appearance provoked before they could conceal their reaction. Once they recognized Kamiton, they relaxed a little.

"I have clean clothes, Zainal. I'll space those rags if you'll hand them to me, Kris." She did, holding the mess by the tips of her fingers and letting them all fall into the receptacle Kamiton offered.

"Have you any clear soup to give them, and perhaps some journey bread," Zainal said as he gently pushed the boys ahead of him toward the galley. Coo and Pess were alone at the table but the boys merely glanced through them, as if the two Deski did not exist.

Well, Kris told herself sternly, they've probably been taught that Deski are little better than Rassi.

When Coo and Pess made to rise, Zainal gestured for them to remain where they were. Someone had already put some clear soup in the heater so all she had to do was pour it in cups and get out the travel bread. Zainal raised one finger to show he'd have some, too. Lord, those kids were messed up bad, Kris thought. How will we ever get through what they have been conditioned to expect? Or, having been roughed up so much, would they rough up her son?

Zainal sat opposite the boys, beside Pess, and dipped the bread into the soup, blowing on it to cool it. The boys did nothing, though Kris saw the tongue of the older boy, Bazil, protrude slightly between his cracked lips. Then Zainal put his bread first in Bazil's cup and then Peran's before he ate it as if to prove it was not only edible, but harmless.

"Eat. You need food. This is good."

Peran, being the younger, could not contain his hunger at that invitation and nearly burned his tongue to get the bread into his mouth. Bazil gave him an almost contemptuous sneer, but he was no less quick to take his first bite.

When they had finished their meal, although their eyes darted back to the heater unit, which they knew still had soup in it, they waited. Peran's lids wearily descended over his eyes, but he shot bolt upright again as soon as Bazil pinched him.

"No more now, Bazil," Zainal said in a neutral tone. "You need sleep, too. There will be more soup when you awaken. That I promise!" Zainal rose and, still not offering them his hands as he would certainly have offered one to Zane, he pointed the way for them to go.

Coo leaned across the table and patted Kris' hands; Pess offered a square of fabric when she started to sniff and then to cry.

"Being Emassi not easy," Coo said.

When Pess' thin arm came about her shoulders, Kris just leaned into the embrace and let the tears flow. She didn't even care if one of the other Catteni came in and saw her weeping.

So, by the time Zainal returned, she was over the worst of it. He knew she had been crying because her eyes always turned red.

"They have suffered much," Zainal said. "That shall be considered when this is ended." He reached for the Hooch bottle and poured himself a large tumbler full, taking a big gulp of it.

"Tubelin is a good Emassi but even he did not like what he saw when he visited the farm where they had been made to work like Rassi."

"Is that why they were so dirty?" Kris heard herself asking with great indignation. "But why were they beaten? They're seven and nine? They've been starved, too."

Zainal took the hand she was waving about in consternation and clasped it firmly.

"I had not thought Perizec capable but it may have been the idea of my brother's mate. She is such a good Catteni mate," and his emphasis on "good" was sarcastic. "It will take longer than it should but they will learn much on Botany and want to know more."

THEY FOLLOWED THE TORTUOUS COURSE INTO the maze of their infamous and rich asteroid belt and once again, while Nitin, Kasturi, Tubelin, and Zainal's two sons watched with varying degrees of consternation during the twisting route, made contact with Kamiton at his hollowed-out asteroid.

Then Zainal poured on all the power at the KDL's disposal on the way back to Botany.

The two boys did not speak unless spoken to, and Tubelin, whom they knew almost better than their father, would tell them stories in a decidedly avuncular and uncharacteristic manner. Zainal put them on a feeding schedule of every two and a half hours, each time little meals until their cheeks began to fill out and flesh appeared over their ribs. He also taught them how to print their names in Catteni glyphs and then in English letters. What astonished Kris was their absolute obedience.

"It's been beaten into them to obey without questions, Kris," Ninety said when she voiced her distress to the Humans. "We'll just be sure they never hear another discouraging word on Botany, that's all."

Chuck tilted his head sideways. "I've seen whipped puppies a time or two. It's going to take a lot of patience to make that a happy pair again."

"If they ever were," Kris said glumly. "I don't think Catteni have happy childhoods. Or expect to."

"Now, Bjornsen," and Chuck Mitford patted her shoulder, "we'll all help."

And so he contrived to make a checkerboard from a bit of stiff packing casing, coloring it in, and then neatly scissoring out the counters from another piece.

"What makes you think Catteni kids play games?" Gino asked when he saw the finished product.

"Ah, a zemgo board," Kamiton exclaimed in surprise as he entered the mess room.

"What makes you think there wouldn't be something similar in such a warlike culture, Gino?" Chuck demanded, grinning at Kamiton. "Will Bazil and Peran know how to play . . . zemgo?" he asked in Catteni.

"Hmm. I shall soon find out. Or will you teach them since you made the board?"

"It might be good if I teach, and you tell them the moves at first," Chuck said. "I wouldn't know the right words and they should learn the proper words."

"I will return with them. A good idea, Sshuk," Kamiton said and went to find the boys.

"They were on the bridge, standing watch with their father," Kamiton said when he returned with them. He pointed at Bazil to sit at one side of the table next to Chuck and Peran to sit on the other. Then he sat beside Peran and asked if the boys knew the game.

Bazil managed the barest of negative head shakes. Peran just stared at the bright colors of the board and the round white counters on his side.

"This is a good game for Catteni to know," Kamiton explained. "It teaches how to form your troops for battle and how to win against an equally matched opponent. You are white, Peran, you must start first."

Peran kept his hands in his lap, his little body stiff with indecision.

"Why don't *we* play, Kamiton?" Chuck suggested.

"He is Emassi," muttered Bazil, glaring up at Chuck.

"So he is," Chuck said, amiably. "And so am I."

Bazil darted a surprised look at Kamiton and received a confirmatory nod. Bazil sank in on himself in dismay.

"All on this ship are Emassi," Kamiton said.

"Even the little one?" Bazil asked, his dull yellow eyes flickering with doubt. But his tone was more courteous.

"All," Kamiton said.

"So we shall play, Emassi Kamiton?" Chuck asked as demurely as only a sergeant of marines could.

"Yes, let us show Bazil and Peran how this ancient game is played, Emassi Sshuk."

• • •

THE TWO BOYS WATCHED CHUCK AND KAMITON play four games (ending in two wins each), every time explaining the moves and discussing the game so the boys would know why. Then Gino played Chuck and won, but when he played Kamiton, the Catteni won. The boys showed the first spark of interest. It wasn't until Zainal entered the room and saw that the boys only watched, making no move to play at all, that he pointed to the board and said in a hard voice: "Play! Need to know!"

He left the room and Kris followed, furious with his so-Catteni manner that she almost couldn't speak as she dragged him into the captain's quarters. She slid the panel shut and told him off, madder than she had ever thought she could be with him.

"Those boys have been so mistreated," she railed at him, "could you not show a little give?

He listened, with his Catteni face.

"I've never seen such bruises, nor such constant brutality on boys so young. What were your folk doing to them? Systemically brutalizing them as punishment for what *you* did?"

"Yes." And his quiet reply, and the sad look in his eyes, silenced her.

"Then why aren't *you*, their father, from whom they can expect some affection . . ."

He held up one hand. "Catteni fathers are not affectionate."

"But you are with Zane!" She was flabbergasted. "How can you differentiate like that? All three are children and need love and kindness and care . . ." And when he opened his mouth to speak, she advanced on him so infuriated that he recoiled slightly, not trying to evade the hard finger she poked into his chest as emphasis to her words. "And don't tell me Catteni children cannot expect such treatment, too."

"From their mothers, not from their fathers."

"And, I suppose, now you'll tell me that Bazil and Peran are too old to be with their mothers." When he nodded, she made a sound of total disgust and frustration. She was so mad she couldn't think of what to say next. "If you ever . . . ever . . . take a Catteni line with Zane, I'll . . . I'll kill you!"

"Or Pete Easley will," Zainal replied calmly. Mad as she was, she could see the shadows in his eyes. He might have expected the treatment his sons had received, but that didn't mean he liked it.

"Oh, God, Zainal, why am I angry at *you*?" And she put her arms around him in apology and returned affection.

Hesitantly, she felt, with great relief, his big hands gripping her shoulders, pressing a response to her expression of regret.

"We must treat them—for now—as Catteni boys are reared, and gradually, when they have settled, teach them that there are other ways, and that they may learn whatever they want, not just what they 'need to know.' I want them to be more Human, too."

"Well, that's better," she said, sniffing back the tears that pricked her eyes: tears of frustration and relief. "I couldn't stand it if you turned all Catteni on me suddenly. And if you ever . . ." She raised her finger threateningly.

"Zane is Human. He is your son and I will always treat him as I see Human children treated."

"When in Rome . . . huh?"

He repeated the phrase without comprehension.

"Oh, I'll explain later, Zainal." And she cupped a hand on his head. "Must we all be hard with the boys?"

"For now. We must give them the orders they need to know . . ." And a ghost of a smile pulled at his finely shaped lips. "To make them sure of how to act and what to do. But we will be fair, where others have not. And, if we can get them to play zemgo, it will help. And if you are not as firm as we are, they will not respect you. And they must for they will find out that you are a woman and therefore, now that they are becoming adult, they will need to see you as a being who commands respect, too."

She leaned against him, accepting the burden of such an uncharacteristic manner for her.

"Am I not a warrior already, being on this ship?"

"Reinforce that as often as possible, for when we reach Botany, they will see that you are also a woman and a mother. And wonder."

"They'll have an awful lot to learn on Botany," she said, ruefully.

"They will have the need to know," Zainal answered, a lilt of rueful laughter in his voice.

"So, if I preface remarks with 'you need to know this,' it will be all right?"

"They'll . . . how do you say it . . . catch on quickly. Neither is stupid."

"Of course. They're your sons."

CHUCK HAD CAUGHT ON TO ZAINAL'S METHOD of treating his sons. Which must have been easiest for Mitford, Kris thought, having had to train recruits in the marines. Gino, whose Italian background was totally at odds with Catteni child rearing, had to be talked into playing it Zainal's way. Coo and Pess had no problem, and Mack Dargle taught them how to carve things out of pieces of wood and how to assemble useful equipment. They knew how to handle knives but returned the blade immediately after they had finished their turn with it. They liked the assembling best, though, and their fingers were quick once they'd been shown how the first time.

The other Catteni ignored them, save for Kamiton who

kept trying to get Bazil to make moves against his counters on the board.

When they were within the Botany system, all stations were on the alert for any possible Eosi presence.

"The work on the moon base has stopped," Zainal observed.

"They were sent the useless materials," Nitin said with a wry expression. "My contribution. They will be stopped for some time as the regular shipments have also been diverted. They may even run out of oxygen and water."

Kris' sense of fair play was assaulted by such doings, and she had to keep her mouth shut. Catteni could deal with Catteni as they wished . . . just so long as Botany was safe from their methods and ethics.

THEY ENTERED THE BUBBLE ON THE EQUATORial line, just out of the range of the geo-sync satellite. Prior to that they had spotted a distant "V" formation of Catteni ships headed directly toward Botany.

"See if we can get through to Retreat," Zainal asked Gino who was sitting at the com controls.

"Oh, you're back, are you?" said a female voice. The visual was not clear so only a hazy picture came through the thinned Bubble material. The voice sounded slightly filtered but intelligible.

"Who's this?" Gino asked.

"Jane O'Hanlon, here. Now we can use the array, someone has to man the com desk all the time. Or woman it as the case is today. Gino Marrucci, right?"

"Right."

Fortunately only Kamiton, of the five Catteni on the bridge just then, had enough English to catch some of the words he knew. But the other four exchanged surprised looks that a female had answered.

"Did you get what you went after?"

"We did but there are some boogies . . ."

"We're expecting them. Baby returned last week with her piggyback G-class ship to warn us of the traffic to come. She may have to go back and lead some through the Bubble. You may be needed, too, as the other K's are still wandering around."

"How many ships were hijacked this time?" Zainal asked, frowning slightly. He was still nervous, despite assurances from Kamiton, Nitin, Tubelin, and Kasturi that, with due care, the disappearance of the ships would not be immediately noticed.

"Catteni ships are all over the galaxy and some never come back," Kamiton had said repeatedly, waving his hand indifferently at such losses. "It works to our advantage. We must have enough to be able to strike at Eosi before they know that death approaches."

Since that was not the strategy which Ray and the other head council members were advocating, no one on board contradicted Kamiton, not even Zainal.

"There are three G-class coming back from one of the other colonies where Terrans were dropped. The K's are coming back with supplies and equipment and only a few refugees."

"If the G-class are full," Zainal said, "we will be very busy."

"Preparations are being made," Jane said, "and Ray Scott is thinking of the closed valleys as safe interim sites. With the K's coming back with food and equipment, what we have won't be spread so thin."

Zainal nodded, occupied with slowing the forward speed of the KDL so that it could gently nudge its way through the Bubble. Immediately the picture of Jane's duty station cleared up.

"That's better," she said, smiling and then caught sight of the four Catteni just visible behind Zainal. "Ah, we have guests," and she added in good Catteni, "welcome to Botany, Emassi."

"How does she know we are Emassi?" Nitin asked, as if slightly offended by being addressed as an equal by a woman.

"Why would I inflict Drassi on Botany?" Zainal asked. "The ones we have are more than enough."

"The ones you have?" asked Nitin, surprised.

"The crews of the ships we have captured have been placed in an isolated area."

"You did not kill them?" Nitin frowned.

"And ruin Catteni uniforms when we needed them?" Gino asked, though there was an edge to his question.

"Those who disobeyed died," Zainal said in a tone that did not leave any need for further questions.

Chapter Nine

BIG AS THE FARMERS' HANGAR WAS, IT could no longer accommodate the "fleet" Botanists were assembling. Jane informed them that they could unload there, but might have to take some of their supplies to other locations, thus cutting down on the transportation problems.

"We need more ground vehicles with heavy load capacities. Doesn't do any good to steal trucks from Earth because we have no gasoline or diesel here. So you'll have to do the transporting. You don't happen to have a list of your cargo, do you? Then we can figure out where else to send you."

"It's in Catteni," Zainal said with a chuckle.

"Okay, then Sally Stoffers will be supercargo," Jane replied. "Send it down and safe landing."

And it was. Immediately the stevedore contingent and several of the large flatbeds, plus a forklift which had been "acquired," surrounded the KDL. There was only so much gasoline available for it so the engineers would have to convert it to solar power. Aarens and Pete Snyder were there since Zainal had indeed brought back some of the elements needed by the engineering group. Sally Stoffers was acting as supercargo with two assistants to check off what was to be off-loaded as she translated the manifests from Catteni.

She smiled a greeting at the three new Catteni and added Kamiton's name to her general welcome. Then she saw the two boys, looking in much better condition landing than they had in boarding. But Kamiton signaled to her to ignore them: a signal she obeyed.

"Zainal says medic for these. We walk."

Ray Scott came hurrying out of his office and took charge of Nitin, Tubelin, and Kasturi.

"Whose are those?" Sally asked when Kris made her way down the gangplank, avoiding those carrying some of the lighter cargo.

"Zainal's," Kris said, "and we have to treat them as Catteni *boys* are treated." She gave Sally a sour grimace.

"What? On Botany? Bring up another generation like the one we're trying to educate in new ways?" Sally was indignant.

"To begin with at least," Kris said with a sigh. "You should have seen the state they were in when Kasturi brought them aboard!"

" 'The sins of the father' sort of stuff?" Sally asked, perceptive as ever.

"In spades," and she broke off, hearing Zainal's familiar step on the cargo ramp.

Zainal looked around and spotted Kamiton, on his way to the infirmary with the boys following a discreet two steps behind him, and nodded. He gave Kris a squeeze on the arm but one that subtly suggested that she should not accompany him, and went to join Ray Scott and the new Catteni recruits.

She struggled with an uneasy resentment and won.

"D'you have any questions, Sally? Chuck and Mack

marked much of the stuff with English subtitles, as it were, during the return. I can help if you need me," she said.

"Nonsense, girl, go soak somewhere and come back looking completely Human. Here," and she handed over a com unit, "I've a spare. If I need you, I'll contact you."

All the Humans on the KDL had removed their yellow lenses as soon as they were safely out of Catteni space: that had been surprise enough for the newcomers. As the supply of water was limited, no one was able to wash the Catteni gray off from more than their hands.

KRIS WOULD HAVE RATHER GONE WITH Kamiton and the two boys to see what their general physical condition was but Zainal had vetoed that. There didn't happen to be any children the ages of Bazil and Peran on Botany, so Kris wondered how on earth the two could be integrated with a peer group.

Zainal solved the problem and took his sons down to the Maasai encampment.

"They are warriors. They have boys the right ages. They will learn Terran ways."

"Not in a Maasai camp," Kris objected vehemently.

"Why not?" Zainal was surprised, believing he had made a good decision.

"Because they treat their women the same way Catteni do. I mean, they practically starve a pregnant woman so she'll have a small baby and no problem delivering."

That part of the Maasai culture had been a shock to most of the medical staff for several of the Maasai women were in the last trimester of pregnancy. How the embryos had survived the trip was a matter of considerable speculation at the infirmary. All the women tested had been anemic and undernourished. With some skilful diplomacy on Hassan's part, he managed to get the Maasai leaders to allow the women normal pregnancy multivitamins on the grounds that they would not have the usual herbal digestive medications. These would replace what the women were used to using. Hassan insisted that the tablets contained no milk, which was a taboo for Maasai pregnant women. That the multi-vitamin contained calcium as well as trace elements was not mentioned.

Kris canceled a half-formed mention of the other extreme racial differences. There *were* boys the right ages. The Maasai were warriors, even if they used only spears, and their height would ensure the boys respected them.

"But they won't learn English," was the only other protest she could summon.

"Not now. That will come. When there are males their ages here in Botany."

They were his children. She had no right to tell him where to send them or how to raise them. The Maasai at least would be fair to the poor waifs. Which was a distinct improvement.

The boys were kept overnight at the infirmary in a separate room. They both had intestinal parasites, which could not be spread on Botany.

"Considering they have been half-starved for a number of months, they're sturdy boys," Leon reported to Zainal. "At least the Maasai are also eating well now and that can only improve the general health."

If Leon did not concur with Zainal's disposition of his sons to the Maasai, he said nothing to that point. He did mention that word had reached him from one of the incoming ships that Joe Marley had managed to secure a fair number of the plants the Maasai considered essential, including the olkiloriti though he could give no reassurance that they would survive on Botany. The boys could go on the transport with the plants when they arrived.

"I will go with them, too," Zainal said.

As such matters sometimes work out, it was Kasturi

who took them as Zainal was needed to pilot Baby which, with the two K-class ships that had already been "accepted" by the Bubble, was needed to get the G-class ships past it. But Zainal delayed his flight long enough to give instructions to his sons.

"You are going to a warrior camp to train with your age group as befits your rank," he told them in Catteni. "They are different folk but known for courage and (a word which Kris did not recognize.) But you will consider them Emassi as I am, and you are. You will learn from them as you need to know their ways, too."

Small bruised fists hit cleanly clothed chests in the Catteni farewell gesture and, without a backward glance, Bazil and Peran boarded the float and sat among the various bushes, shrubs, grasses, and two saplings in their plastic-covered cans of hydroponic solutions. They each wore a replica of Zainal's Catteni face.

One day, Kris promised herself, they would learn to smile and use expressions instead of those awful alien deadpans.

GETTING THE G-SHIPS THROUGH TOOK ALL THE available Botany fleet to bring them into Botany space.

"We sandwiched them in," Gino said when he returned. "Even then, we had to push the stuffing well back of the bread. That Bubble doesn't fool easy."

"What happens when we want to get them out again?" Bert Put asked. He'd been piloting one of the G's and privately confessed that he thought he'd never get home. It was his ship which had brought back the Maasai plants as well as others: roots steam cleaned and tested to be certain they brought in no Terran parasites. Seed as well had been irradiated to ensure purity as a much more varied diet was needed, especially the complex proteins. Rocksquats bred fast but not as fast as the population of Botany was growing. Loo-cows produced one calf at the height of the Botanical summer. The actual birth took place in a tight, deep circle of other loo-cows, all tramping round and round the female to deter nightcrawlers reaching the newborn, attracted by the bodily fluids also exuded by the birthing female. The wonder was that the newborn was not inadvertently stamped to death before it could get to its six wobbly legs.

Not so many refugees had been accommodated on the G-ships, but some families of those of the First Drop had been located and there were happy reunions, as well as tearful ones for those relations who had not been found.

There was a celebration for the placement of the permanent Botany com sat when it was connected to the inner arrays. The NASA folk had managed to jury-rig one to serve in the interim.

The infirmary, which now had satellite clinics dotting the continent, had received much needed diagnostic equipment, an ex-ray machine, and generators large enough to power them. And sufficient oil and gasoline to run them. (Empty barrels were then recycled as anti-night crawler defenses and the bases for stilt homes.)

Nitin, Tubelin, and Kasturi began to learn enough English to respond to greetings. They would not conduct meetings with the Head Council in anything but Catteni. Kris often sat in as translator, so did Chuck Mitford, Mack, and Ninety. Their trips had at least improved vocabulary and usage. Though there were a few phrases which none of the men would translate for Kris. She decided they must be so pejorative and anti-female that she'd rather *not* know.

Nitin was agitating for speedy returns, to acquire more spaceships—and missiles. He wanted to see the total destruction of all Eosi on Catten. He dismissed the problem of getting armed ships past the space station that guarded the planet from attack, even a sneak one, by units of its own space force. The ships used in attack missions were based in another system. He pointed out that he knew all the code words to gain access to naval ordnance: there was even a high-ranking officer who was a member of their covert group. But he had been an administrator until he had been dismissed from his post and a much younger junior with excellent blood and Eosian connections had taken his place. That had been sufficient for Nitin to wish to retaliate against a hierarchy that had not rewarded his many years of devoted service.

"Almost Human of him," Hassan Moussa said with a chuckle. "Happens often in Israel."

"But does that attitude assure us of *his* loyalty?" Ray bluntly asked Zainal.

"Considering that his family bloodlines date back to the Original Hundred, yes, it does. He needs to wipe that dismissal from his family's history," Zainal replied.

The latest news from Earth was both good and bad— the good being that the Eosi had given up their mind-wipe program. The bad was that they were now concentrating on razing cities, towns, settlements of any size, to the ground.

ZAINAL SEEMED TO HAVE NO TROUBLE PLAYING with Zane in the affectionate way he had always used with the child who was walking without assistance. If he fell down, he got himself up. If he bruised himself in doing so and started to cry, Zainal would cock his head and the tears would dry up.

Kris didn't approve of Zainal's attitude toward perfectly reasonable tears. They had another fight over that.

"If he is badly hurt, he may cry," Zainal said. "But, on Botany, he must learn to take tumbles and get up and walk on," he added. "As you did on our initial treks."

"I was an adult, not a baby." She was also stung that he would bring up those incidents, so long ago she'd forgotten them.

"If Zane walks, he is no longer a baby."

"He's my child and I'll dictate what he may or may not do."

"Tell him not to bother me then."

"Bother you?"

"He seeks my company."

"And you never push him away."

"No, but I will if you do not like the way I treat the son of my mate."

Zainal's face had assumed the cold Catteni look that devastated her, and she caved in.

"I want you to be fatherly toward Zane. He couldn't understand you changing," she said more meekly than she meant to sound.

"I do as I see other fathers here do, Kris," he replied in a quiet, kinder tone. Then he caressed her cheek. "And when my sons learn that you are really Emassi in spite of being female, I would like you to be elder mother to them."

"Truce?" she said, holding out her hand.

"Truce? Yes, truce. We two should not be angry at each other over nothing."

"Nothing?" That was enough to get her back up all over again but Zainal stopped the incipient quarrel by kissing her so thoroughly that she had to cling to him to keep upright.

He was learning some other tricks of Human males, too, she thought as he carried her to their bed. It was nearly midday but neither was due for duty for another hour or so. Zane was already in the crèche. They had not been together often enough recently, she thought. No wonder they were fighting.

When they had finished a very satisfactory passage in arms, Kris asked Zainal how plans were going for the next series of "raids." Despite the inconveniences of masquerading and enduring the heavier gravity of Catten, she realized there must be a piratical—certainly a Viking— streak from her ancestry that gave her such enjoyment in these forays. It was so very satisfying to sneak in under Catteni noses and get away with such good plunder. Though she gave a little shudder thinking what might happen if they didn't get away with their deceptions. She quickly gave up thinking about *that*.

"The Council thinks hard about the next step. We," and Zainal turned his thumb in on himself so that Kris knew he meant the other Catteni, "must make additional contact with those who can help with our challenge to Eosi domination."

"Will that mean only you go?" she asked. After being with him again, she hated to be separated. Not that they could indulge in intimacies aboard even the larger KDL, but she would miss him acutely no matter how short a separation.

BY THE FALL OF NIGHT THAT DAY, THE RESIdents had another problem. Some of those brought in on the last G-class ship were young folks, aged between five and twelve: children who had grown up knowing nothing but the Catteni domination. Most of them were either orphaned or had been separated from their parents, and three could not even remember their names. Dorothy Dwardie turned the most violent over to Dr. Hessian since his Freudian training would be valuable in these instances. *Their* childhoods, if one could use the word, had been so traumatic that, unless therapy was used, they would be neurotic by their teens.

"Children can survive the most appalling circumstances," Dorothy said as she addressed those who had volunteered to house the orphans, "but the one thing they have, which adults often lack, is resilience. Shown kindness, especially fair play, will do much to show them what we, here on Botany at least, consider 'normal' behavior."

Some of the wildest had had to be sedated throughout the trip. Laughrey, who had been captain of the purloined ship, said his crew had been totally unable to cope with this group.

"We did find out that, when we brought them to the ship . . . the first time," and he grimaced, "we were Human quislings and were taking them to work to death as slaves. When we rounded them up again, we had to sedate them. Most were covered with infected sores— well, you've seen their scars—and wounds. In my opinion, they're worse off than the Victims. And they're just as much Victims of the Eosi as the mind-wiped."

Every attempt was made over the next few weeks to integrate the children. The placements were not universally successful, though Sarah and Joe lucked out with a five-year-old girl. Once she realized that she was safe, she refused to be separated from her foster parents and either Sarah or Joe had to have her in tow. She also didn't speak, but Dorothy Dwardie felt that, once she felt really, truly safe, she would talk.

"Children pick up speech patterns from their carers. If they've had no carers, of any kind," and Dorothy shrugged. "There's certainly no impediment in her vocal equipment."

The psychologist grinned, reminding the foster parents of the screams the child had uttered when she was given her three-in-one injection. Two of the children on board the G-ship had had measles so preventative shots were essential.

Maizie, the name Sarah and Joe had given their waif, was derived from her constant look of amazement at food—all she wanted to eat—and clean covers on a bed that only she occupied. She did take to carrying the fluff-filled pillow with her everywhere. That was a useful habit, not only reinforcing her sense of security, but because she was inclined to take unexpected naps, both hands clutching the pillow.

"I don't think she ever slept on Earth," Sarah told Kris. "At this rate, you won't have to have a second child," and she cocked her head at Kris. "Especially now Zainal's got his two sons here."

"Kasturi hid his family away before he defected, and he wants to bring them in. He has daughters. I just hope he doesn't do a Maasai on them," Kris said in a jaundiced tone of voice.

"If you ask me, it wouldn't hurt some of our latest drop-ins to be sent down to Chief Caleb Materu," Sarah said.

"I believe that's also occurred to our noble leaders. Dorothy's against it," and Kris paused.

"So are you," and Sarah snorted. "But I catch any of them bullying some of the littler boys again, I'm going to thump 'em."

There was a hard-core group of eighteen who had banded together: six black, eight white, two Japanese, one Chinese girl, and one French lad: ranging from seven to the eighteen-year-old black lad, Clune, who was their acknowledged leader. They had actually been rounded up by the Catteni, as they were old enough to survive the drugged journey. Laughrey freed them from the DC-area holding pens where they awaited transportation.

They had become a unit, fourteen males and four females, calling themselves the Diplomatic Corp. They were still a unit, despite being assigned to foster parents. They refused to work but managed to acquire food whenever they wanted it. Several sessions in the stocks for Clune, and his two "consuls," Ferris and Ditsy, failed to correct their attitude. Twice their unit disappeared from Retreat and had to be tracked down by Rugarians and

Deski, with Chuck Mitford in command. The second time, he marched them back without a single rest break.

Not even demonstrations of what night crawlers could do seemed to deter them from defecting from Retreat. The supplies they had acquired on both occasions showed that they could access anything they chose to have: including com units. And they were clever enough to have opened secure premises to get the weapons they wanted. Oddly enough, among the goods they took from infirmary supplies were condoms. One of the group, the seventeen-year-old who called herself Floss, had insisted that none of the girls should get pregnant: an unexpected display of common sense.

It became clear within the first two weeks that they had no intention of integrating. They were not, in Leon's medical opinion, physically well enough—after four or five years of eating whatever they could scrounge for the unit—to look after themselves in one of the closed valleys. Which had been suggested as one remedy to their recalcitrant behavior. Floss had been acting as their medic, since she had taken a first-aid course before the invasion, but she would not be capable of dealing with the serious wounds nor the various infections, external and internal, which plagued the young folk.

"We can't let them go half-healed, and that Floss needs a D and C," Leon reported. "Mary said it's not urgent . . . yet. But fibroid growths have a tendency to keep growing unless there's a curettage."

"Why don't we see if Chief Materu would take them in for a spell," was Laughrey's suggestion. "Let's make it really basic for them."

"Haven't they endured enough 'basic'?" Dorothy asked, though she could come up with no other suggestions. Almost all the other children that had been rescued were settling in or responding to trauma therapy.

"Not a structured basic," Ray Scott said. "I'd rather

they had enough training to survive on their own, if that's the course we have to take with such a hard-nosed bunch. I'll give Chief Materu a call."

Chief Materu accepted the challenge. It didn't surprise Kris, though, that Zainal decided to go along with those marching the Diplomatic Corp down to the southern settlement of the Maasai. She chuckled, thinking of the pace that Zainal would set. Chuck, the two Doyle brothers, Joe Latore, Coo, and Slav came along "for the exercise."

When Chuck met Kris on his return, he said that the trip had been instructive for all concerned. "Chief Caleb's segregating the girls who certainly don't like that part of it. Nor working with only women. But work they will. Good thing those Maasai are *so* tall." He grinned with satisfaction of an assignment suitably fulfilled.

"Ah . . . how are Zainal's two fitting in?"

Chuck eyed her. "They are. Even manage to chatter some in Maasai. Zainal allowed a smile for each of them, and you'd've thought they'd been turned loose in a candy store. They've picked up some sort of skin problem but the Maasai now have the medical plants they need to cope with almost every ailment."

That reassurance gave Kris enormous relief.

"Were our renegades similarly impressed by seven-foot chiefs?" she asked.

Chuck laughed. "What's that word that Ninety uses? Oh, yes, gobsmacked. They were that in spades. Turns out that two of the black kids were Africans from their countries' respective embassies. They knew the Maasai, certainly by reputation, and enough Swahili to understand basic orders." Chuck took a long pull on his beer and then folded his hands across his stomach. "Yup, that was a good idea Laughrey had."

THREE DAYS LATER THERE WAS AN URGENT com call for Zainal and Leon from Chief Materu. The skin problem for the two Catteni boys had not responded to Maasai cures and the boys had developed fevers that could not be reduced. Kris offered to come, too, and Zainal was worried enough to want her company. Leon brought what he felt would be the appropriate equipment, carefully strapping the microscope box into a travel net on Baby, as well as a variety of medications.

"It's unusual for Catteni to have skin infections," he murmured to Kris as Zainal drove Baby at its best speed. "Or fevers. Zainal's never shown any toxic reaction to anything here on Botany. That I heard of?" the Australian looked inquiringly at Kris. She shook her head. "Well, we'll just have to wait and see. Not that, with this speed, we'll be long waiting."

ZAINAL LANDED BABY AS NEAR TO THE CHIEF'S high-set platform as he could. Materu had heard the noise of the approaching ship and beckoned them to follow him to where the boys were being cared for.

The fevers were high, even when Leon adjusted the thermometer reading to Catteni levels. The sores exuded yellow pus that had a nose-shriveling odor to it. Leon quickly made slides and, taking his microscope out in the light, did a quick investigation. He was shaking his head when he returned.

"I've never seen anything like it. It's some sort of . . . allergic reaction that's causing the skin to erupt like this."

"Will antihistamines work on Catteni systems?" Kris asked, hands clenched into fists with anxiety. Zainal wore his worst Catteni face, and she was sure he thought the boys were dying. So did Chief Materu and his medicine man, or whatever they were called in Swahili.

"It's the one thing I can try. The only Human equivalent to those sores is pyoderma gangrenosum," Leon said. "And that may be the result of a colitis. Neither lad had any sign of that sort of problem when I checked them over." Then he asked what the boys had been eating, but he shook his head when the listing was complete. "Nothing they didn't have on board the KDL except for fresh rocksquats and fish, and they haven't bothered Zainal. Nothing else, Chief Caleb?"

It was the medicine man, introduced as Parmitoro Kassiora, who said something in Maasai to the chief.

"He says he gave them a very, very small dose of olk-iloriti because they ate too much and had bellyaches. Much less than he would use with our boys because they are different."

"Isn't that from the acacia plants that were just brought back?" Leon asked.

Parmitoro added something else.

"He says that some of the Catteni who rounded them up took ill like this, with sores, and died," the chief translated, looking exceedingly pleased.

"Hey, you could be right about allergy, Kris." He checked through the medications he had brought with him and found several, looking from one bottle to another. "Their metabolism runs at a different level despite other similarities to our own body mechanisms. Give me your arm, Zay," he said.

When Zainal had bared his arm, he did a quick reaction test of all three possible medications. Leon whistled under his breath as he timed the testing. Behind him the boys muttered in their fevers, tossing and almost, but not quite, crying with the pain incurred by moving.

"Not a damned thing," Leon muttered after the required reaction time was up. "At least you're not allergic to antihistamines." Then he looked Zainal straight in the eye. "Do I have your permission to try, Zainal? At least I believe they will take no further harm from the shots."

Zainal nodded. Leon bowed slightly to the Maasai medic, who had been observing with close interest but no reaction to what Leon had been doing. Chief Materu had murmured some explanations in Maasai.

"Do I offend your Parmitoro Kassiora by using our medicines?"

Caleb Materu gave them a wide smile of very white and even teeth. "Not at all. The boys have been good boys, and they are *not* Maasai so perhaps Maasai medicine could not work on them." Materu turned to Zainal. "For that he apologizes."

"None needed." Zainal nodded once to Parmitoro in acceptance.

"That takes care of the medical ethics," Leon said in a wry tone. "I'll give one to Bazil here, and another to Peran. Then we've one spare . . ."

He made the injections.

And they waited. Some of the women, and that included a rebellious and surly Floss, brought food and cool water. The hut was not only stuffy but also reeked of the suppurations. Kris did edge toward the opening of the hut.

"I want out of here, bitch," Floss muttered as she and an older Maasai woman returned with a fresh bucket of cold water.

"Only when you're no longer one, dear," Kris replied in a low tone.

"D'you know what they do to women here?" Floss said, and there was a certain desperation in her eyes now.

"All the more reason for you to reform your outlook on life on Botany," she said, for she had heard about the female genital mutilation practiced by some African tribes. Were the Maasai one? She couldn't remember.

Floss made a sudden movement toward Kris, which, in retrospect, Kris decided she deserved for the taunt, and immediately the tall Maasai woman grabbed hold of Floss and threw her from the hut. Kris could hear the thud of the girl hitting the hard ground. She thought she'd better make certain that the girls of the Diplomatic Corp were not required, during this reeducation period, to adhere to *all* Maasai customs. They should have brought along one of the Swahili speakers. How the hell was she going to explain this one?

They waited. They could and did try to ease the boys' fevers with the cool water, laying fresh cloths carefully over the sore-covered bodies.

It was dark before Leon extracted a thermometer from Bazil's armpit and exclaimed, "The fever's coming down."

Kris was in the process of changing a cool cloth when she noticed that the sores were no longer oozing. In fact, the smell was lessening, too.

"Hey, look!" And she pointed to the nearest sore. "It's drying up."

Zainal immediately stripped the coverings from Peran, and the younger boy also seemed to be responding to the medication.

"It's four hours. Time to give them another shot."

During the next four hours, the sores seemed to dry up in waves, starting from the chest working downward to the limbs. The boys' temperatures dropped to normal, and they each fell into a deep sleep.

"Empirical but you Catteni are not impervious to the minor ailments to which Human flesh is heir," Leon said as they all left the hut and stood in the fresh night air.

"This acacia? They swallowed it?" Zainal asked.

Materu said, "It is ground fine and a small amount taken with water."

"Do I know what you're thinking, Zainal?" Leon asked, eyebrows twitching and the gleam of a smile on his face.

"The problem would be 'how.' "

"Yes, it would, wouldn't it," Leon said.

Kris had no trouble following their line of thought but

she also couldn't figure out how the olkiloriti could be administered to the Eosi. How could they possibly get Eosi to swallow sufficient to kill them? Or at least give them an awful allergic reaction?

"Were the boys in real danger from just an allergic reaction?" she asked Leon. She'd never even had a bad case of poison ivy.

He cocked his head. "If the antihistamines hadn't taken effect, I don't think they'd've survived the night." He looked back at the hut. "They'll still need a lot of care . . . and no further herbal medications. I hope Parmitoro won't take offense."

"He would take more offense if you had come and the boys had died," Caleb Materu said with an amused snort.

"I do have some salve I used on Catteni wounds," Leon said, dragging his medical bag out into the cool night air. "To heal the sores. I know it doesn't react on Catteni. The sea, too, will help. Can they swim, Zainal?"

"They do now," Caleb said in his deep voice, and in the torchlight, his eyes sparkled.

"When the sores are closed, have them swim in the sea. Salt's still a superb cure-all."

"You wish them to remain in my care?" the chief asked Zainal.

"I do," Zainal said firmly.

"How are the others doing, chief?" Leon asked and his eyes danced with mischief.

"They learn."

Kris pulled at Leon's sleeve, to get him to listen to her whisper. "Floss is terrified that the Maasai will do something . . . down there," and she pointed to the correct spot.

Leon covered a burst of laughter. "I imagine she would be. Don't worry. Hassan made it plain that the females must return in the same physical condition in which they arrived. He also said that Chief Materu is one of the more modern leaders."

Kris let her breath out with a whoosh.

"Don't reassure her, though," Leon went on. "Being real scared is effective conditioning as negative conditioning. Dorothy and I did discuss an aversion state, like intense fear, to be used to cancel out a lesser, unpleasant state . . . like choosing to be cooperative if you're angry. If there is something that does terrify that hard-boiled little minx, let's let it stand. Right?"

"Right."

LEON GAVE THE BOYS A THIRD INJECTION. HE measured out tablets, which he put in a jar for Parmitoro to give the boys orally during the next ten days. Then the two medical men shook hands.

By common consent the three retired to Baby to sleep for the Botanic night wasn't even half over when the boys began to improve. In the morning, when Leon had gone over to check on his patients, Kris heard an odd noise, small but definitely not a regular sound.

She caught Zainal's attention and pointed to the passageway. Two of the Diplomatic Corp girls, and one of them was Floss, were attempting to squeeze into one of the storage compartments. It was the opening of the panel that Kris had heard.

Zainal had no sooner made it to the doorway with Floss under one arm—and Kris behind him with an arm lock on the other, younger girl—than four Maasai women arrived.

"If you behave, Floss," Kris said sternly as the Maasai women took firm charge of the would-be stowaways, "you'll come back in the same physical condition you arrived here. But if you continue to misbehave . . . well," and Kris spread her hands wide to indicate the outcome would be out of her control.

Floss turned dead white under the tan she was acquiring. Then she gathered herself up to snarl back and, before she could utter a word, she was pinched so painfully by the headwoman that whatever invective she had been about to spit out at Kris was lost in her yelp. Zainal drew Kris back in the ship. He was grinning.

"Doesn't like you, does she?"

"I can't blame her, but tough love works."

"Love?" Zainal queried.

"Well, discipline meted out fairly for failure to obey." And she pointed to the tableau of Floss. Balancing a big basket on her head with both hands, she was bracketed between two tall Maasai women who moved with a grace Floss had yet to achieve. The younger girl was sobbing softly, her arm in the grasp of the headwoman.

Kris didn't at all like the sexism practiced by the Maasai but, if it taught Floss discipline and respect, she might even become a useful colonist when she returned to Retreat.

THE CIRCUMSTANCES OF THIS MEDICAL ALERT were immediately reported to Ray Scott and the other Catteni were hastily gathered together. When Zainal had explained what he hoped to achieve, Nitin and Kasturi both started shaking their heads.

"Eosi are well aware that even the Emassi who surround them might seize an opportunity to use a poison. Anything they consume is first tested by a Catteni," Nitin said gloomily.

"Perhaps it is effective only on young bodies which have not matured enough to deal with dangerous substances," Kamiton said.

"Care to try it?" Leon said, taking out a vial containing some of the powdered olkiloriti. The Australian had an odd sense of humor.

Zainal held out his hand for it but Kamiton snatched it first. He pulled out the cork top and sniffed deeply.

"See? There is no danger . . ." His yellow eyes turned

up in his skull and he started to have such severe convulsions that he jerked off the chair he was sitting in.

Leon sprang into action. Fortunately he still had his medical kit handy and, muttering under his breath about what dose would be sufficient to counter the reaction, he filled a syringe. Zainal and Kasturi were trying to keep Kamiton from hurting himself with the severity of the spasms that beset him but, strong as they were, they were having difficulty holding him. Leon tried twice to pierce the tough Catteni hide with his hypodermic needle, cursing about elephant hides and crocodile scales, but managed to plunge the medication in.

The convulsions did not immediately cease, though Kris—watching anxiously, for she had come to like Kamiton—thought they were not as violent. Leon readied a second syringe from a different bottle with the longest needle Kris had ever seen.

"Let's hope your hearts can take this kind of convulsion," he said as Kamiton's spine arched grotesquely. "Here, hold this, Kris. Hold it up."

He gave her the hypodermic and got his stethoscope out.

"Keep his arms out of my way, can you Zainal, Kasturi?" he asked in Catteni. Over Kamiton's inarticulate cries, whatever he managed to hear worried him. "I don't like the sounds in his lungs. Inhalation was a damned foolish idea. Cardiac arrest is possible. Kris, call the infirmary and send the team down here fast as possible."

"I've already called in a medical emergency," Ray said, com unit in his hand as he stared down at the writhing body of the Catteni. "I think that shot is beginning to work."

"It is?" Leon said, surveying the contortions. "You're right. The spasms are reducing in intensity."

"Eosi must breathe, mustn't they?" Kasturi remarked

in Catteni to Nitin, their eyes still on the slowly relaxing body of their colleague.

"Yes, even Eosi breathe," Nitin observed. "But their living quarters are so carefully guarded . . ."

"Crop dusting might do," Leon observed with the fingers of one hand on Kamiton's neck. "Pulse still racing. Damned fool thing to do with a drug he knew was dangerous."

"A very Catteni thing to do," was Kris' rejoinder, her pulse racing as well from fear of the consequences of Kamiton's rash impulse. "Do I need to keep this?" she asked, meaning the syringe she still held.

"We might. I'd rather have conducted a controlled experiment but the empirical test was certainly conclusive," Leon added in an admiring tone.

Kamiton's body twitched only slightly now but his breathing was still labored, and he had not regained consciousness.

"Crop dusting?" Zainal asked, looking up at her, not having understood Leon's remark.

"A term for an aerial application of fertilizer or insecticides over large areas. Airplanes are used," and she made a sweeping gesture with her free hand.

"What has she said?" Nitin asked, his English being almost nonexistent.

When Zainal explained, Nitin once again shook his head. "No aerial traffic is allowed over Eosi compounds."

"There's more than one way to kill a cat without choking him with butter," Kris said.

"Say again?" asked Zainal, blinking with a lack of comprehension.

" 'There are nine and sixty ways of singing tribal lays,' " Leon chanted, " 'and every single one of them is right.' "

Ray Scott laughed. Kris wouldn't have thought he'd know Kipling that well. But they needed a spot of relief after the anxiety over Kamiton.

"I'm sure we'll think of some way," Scott said.

Just then the cardiac arrest team arrived.

"There *has* to be some way," Kris said.

"We will find it," Zainal said, stepping away from Kamiton as the emergency team moved in on him.

Leon was explaining what had happened and what precautions he wanted taken when they got Kamiton to the infirmary. Almost as an afterthought, he took the syringe from Kris' hand as he followed the team, with Kamiton carried on a stretcher out the door.

"Are there any dissidents on board an Eosi vessel?"

"If this stuff is spread through the air circulation, it would kill everyone on board," Ray said, putting the stopper back in the vial and placing it well away from the remaining Catteni.

"More will be needed, too," Zainal said, regarding the little container with considerable respect.

"Why?" asked Nitin, returning to his seat. "There is no way it can be spread for Eosi to inhale."

"There must be," Zainal said, giving the table a pound with his fist that rattled the vial of olkiloriti. Ray immediately steadied it.

"We will somehow contrive," Kasturi said, giving Nitin a dire look for his pessimism.

"Meanwhile, we have other problems," Ray said, "and, while I am relieved that your sons survived their ordeal, Zainal, we've a meeting later today to decide how to cope with the growing destruction of our own planet."

With a nod of dismissal, he pulled his keyboard to him and began to call up a program to consider.

Zainal, Kris, Kasturi, and Nitin left the hangar office in thoughtful silence.

"WHAT'S THIS I HEAR ABOUT A LETHAL DRUG for the Eosi?" Raisha asked when Kris came to collect Zane from the crèche.

Kris paused in lifting her jubilant, and heavy, son into her arms. "Boy, the grapevine works faster than light."

Raisha grinned broadly. "Well, we did see the cardiac arrest team speeding down to the hangar and then back . . . so naturally, we had to find out the details. And thank goodness, Zainal's sons are all right."

"Yes, that was pretty tricky for a while. So who's spreading the word? You or Sarah?"

"Actually, Mavis rushed down. She was collecting her daughter after her shift." When Kris, busy with her son, was not forthcoming, Raisha added more curtly than her usual manner, "Wellll?" and she raised the elegant curve of her fine brows in query.

"Yes, there is a substance that produces a violent allergic response in Catteni, young and old. But whether it can be got to the target area is the point. Don't get your hopes up."

"I will try not to, but it will be hard," the pilot said. "There simply *has* to be a way . . ."

"We'll find it. Maybe we'll hear from the Farmers. It's been long enough," Kris said, hoping to distract the woman.

"Huh! I have come to believe more in your Yankee ingen-oo-ity," and Raisha grinned, parodying Zainal's use of the word.

"See you, later. Say good-bye, Zane and thank you to Raisha."

"Goo-by, t'ank," the obedient child managed.

"You should have another before he is much older," Raisha said.

"Ha! Won't need to if we import more kids."

"Has that wild group settled in with the Maasai?"

Kris chuckled. "They've had no choice."

Raisha nodded with satisfaction.

"I think Zane'll have to spend the night here . . . a big meeting this evening. I'll feed and bathe him first."

"This good boy's always welcome."

ZAINAL WAS NOT IN THEIR COTTAGE SO KRIS let Zane wander about the place while she cleaned up from their hurried departure the previous day. All the time her mind kept working through possibilities, but any bright ideas that occurred required more knowledge than she had of Eosian habits and habitats, information she did not have on hand. Even if Nitin was so pessimistic, she had the feeling that Zainal and Kasturi were not.

Her com unit buzzed, and Beggs informed her in his prosaic manner that her presence was requested for twenty hundred hours at the hangar for an emergency session of the complete Council. She opened her mouth to thank him when he closed the connection. She didn't like him and he knew it, but Beggs was the sort who would do his duty though it choked him. And he was efficient. With the com unit in hand, she called the infirmary to ask how Kamiton was.

"He's left," was the report from the agitated receptionist. "Dr. Dane tried to keep him in for observation, but he just walked out."

"He's all right then," Kris said, chuckling. No Catteni worth the rank of Emassi would let a thing like a near brush with death keep him abed. So he'd be there at the meeting. That meant that Tubelin would probably side with Zainal, so it would be three Catteni for and one against.

No, she shook her head, correcting herself. The meeting was about other matters entirely. While wiping out the Eosi would be the answer to many problems, that wasn't the panacea for all the woes that currently beset Humanity.

That was the subject of the meeting.

John Beverly addressed those who crowded into the hangar. When the numbers attending exceeded space available, a com system was hurriedly set up to allow those outside to hear what was being said. Kris noted with approval that the four Maasai chiefs were there, with Hassan Moussa whispering translations.

"Our last trip to Earth showed us what the Eosi are doing to our planet . . . stripping it of anything valuable and destroying what they do not understand. They are also systematically shipping Humans out as slave labor. The old, the very young, the infirm, the injured or sick are being left to fend for themselves and many will die. We cannot, here on Botany, continue to provide succor to those, much as we would like to. There is a finite limit to what Botany can provide.

"However, Kamiton has been able to supply us with the information of the other planets—some of them as habitable as Botany—where Humans have been dropped, as we were, to make the best of what was available. We want to check on these. If necessary, support them with tools, medicines, and other supplies. That will mean healthy people to take back to Earth when it's ours again. I'd like volunteers to go with *our*"—and he paused to emphasize the recent acquisitions—"G-ships to show them how. There are five other drop"—and he grinned to use the term—"planets that we know of and we want to visit each. We also know of four installations where, according to Kasturi, Humans are being used as slave labor in appalling conditions. Some of our Maasai were sent to an ice planet. We want to free those we can. Right under Catteni noses, so to speak." And Beverly flashed a smile when someone demanded to know how. "Pretend we're Catteni shifting work forces. We've inside help now besides Zainal." And he turned to indicate the four dissident

Catteni seated to one side of the table. "We can't emancipate—" and again that roguish grin on the air force general's face "—all the slaves but we can try."

"Why?" someone roared. "They'll be half-dead. I don't mind helping now and then, but all the time?"

There was considerable support to that complaint.

"I know, I know," John said. "Altruism can go too far. And if we can, we will disperse these folk on some of the other planets we know about.

"Don't lose sight of the fact that the reason for these forays is to spread confusion among the Eosi and the Emassi in charge by a series of totally unexpected shifts of personnel and material which will disappear completely. The Eosi don't like mysteries."

"Yeah, but won't they just retaliate by killing more of us back on Earth?"

"They might, if they could see the connection," John Beverly said. "We'll be using Catteni ships they haven't yet realized we have. How can they hold Earth responsible when Catteni are the only ones involved?

"Meanwhile, Catteni dissidents will be mobilized—and there are many Catteni who want to be free of Eosian domination just as much as we do."

"You going to use that dust to kill those bastards?" someone shouted.

John Beverly paused a moment, smiling. "Doesn't take long for rumor to circulate Retreat, does it?"

There were good-natured chuckles.

"We now have a means, but we don't have a way."

"Set up a Ways and Means Committee then," some wit shouted and laughter greeted that suggestion.

"We have. Any ideas are cheerfully received. Now," and John looked down at his notes, "we're making another foray to Earth, to collect supplies, visit the other planets where Humans have been dropped, so I'm asking for some of the First Drop to come along in case we can help. Zainal's making another run to contact other dissidents."

Suddenly Gino Marrucci, who had been in the bridge on com link watch, came rushing up the steps to the platform and whispered something in Ray's ear.

He rose. "We may not be able to implement those plans just yet," he said. "Gino says there's a massive attack force approaching. We may just have annoyed the Eosi too much."

"What do we do now?" a woman wailed in the silence that followed the announcement.

Kris had no trouble identifying the wailer as Anna Bollinger.

"I think we go out the back door NOW," Zainal said, gesturing for John Beverly to nominate his crews.

"What if the Bubble bursts?" Anna screamed.

"Don't be so stupid, woman." And Aarens was on his feet and faced her. "The Farmers design much better than the Eosi do."

Kris smothered her laugh. Anna's panic did spread. Those at the head table rose to try and restore calm. Beverly didn't waste any time, but pointed out those he wanted as crews for his ships. He took them off with him, gathering other men and women as he went. The hangar was emptying rapidly, with many running outside to look up in the darkening sky to check on the Bubble's distant nebulosity.

Many watched the barrage all night long. In some places, the force of the repeated assault turned the Bubble a glowing orange. There is no noise in space, of course, but there was plenty on the com sat link. Those who gathered in the bridge rooms of Baby and the two K-class in the hangar listened to the sharp exchange of Catteni and Eosi commands. Kris had joined Zainal and the other Catteni at the bridge installed in Ray's office where the ex-admiral and the rest of the Council followed what they could of the attack.

"Mentat Ix seems to be in charge," Ray said, looking at Zainal. "All the orders seem to be issued in his name."

Zainal only nodded as he reached for paper and pencil and, with Kamiton's help, listed the force trying to batter down the Bubble.

"Both the new AA-ships," Kamiton said, "and five of the big H's that have been refitted with missiles."

"Ah," and Nitin was cheered up slightly. "I hear Niassen is commander of one of the H's. He's useless."

"All he has to do is follow orders," Kasturi said, grinning.

"Isn't Redinit on that H?" asked Tubelin.

"Yes, I believe he is," Nitin said. He had supplied Zainal with the captain and crew complements of most of the ships the Eosi had been using against the Bubble.

"Don't we have three on the HHT?" Kasturi asked.

"Not in command posts, unfortunately," Kamiton said with a sigh.

"Can you give me some idea of how large a dissident group you're talking about?" Ray asked.

"Roughly three thousand, spread throughout Eosi-dominated space," Kamiton said.

Nitin regarded Kamiton with some apprehension, but the Catteni shrugged the implied reprimand away.

"Only three thousand?" Ray said, having hoped for a much larger subversive element.

Zainal laughed. "It is the nature of our group that's far more important than the number. Most of them are in strategic positions. Quality counts more than quantity."

"I suspect it could," Ray admitted.

"Oops," and even Gino recoiled when the Bubble above the com sat area turned a livid shade of red. "They're obviously hoping the fabric of the Bubble is weaker around the array."

"Is it holding?" Ray demanded with a hint of anxiety in his voice.

"It'll hold," Gino said, "but it's taking a beating."

At some point during that long vigil, Ainger arrived, much annoyed, with a folded note from John Beverly.

"I resent being used as a messenger simply because I happened to be on hand," he grumbled as he handed over the paper.

"John's taking all the G's out the back door," Ray said, frowning a bit.

"Isn't he exceeding his prerogatives?" Ainger said with an expression of deep censure. "Unless, of course, you intended him to attack the Eosian?"

"With G-ships carrying a minimum of weapons?" Zainal asked, surprised. "No, he's going to provide further distractions, as was planned."

"He's away," Gino said, grinning.

"He broadcast?" Ainger was livid.

"In Morse," Gino said, laughing. "I just caught it. Thought it was only static at first, but he's got it on repeat. I'd best tell him his message was received." He manipulated some toggles on the com board and then, listening intently to the chaotic Catteni messages, finally nodded. "Yeah, he got it."

THE BARRAGE OF THE BUBBLE WENT ON ALL the long Catteni night and into morning, but the fabric of the sphere did not collapse. The sun blotted out the colors the bombardment made but Bert Put, working the dawn shift as com officer, said he could hear the orders for continued barrage.

"This should infuriate the Mentat Ix," Zainal said, a smile of intense satisfaction on his face.

"Too bad there's no way to use that anger to our benefit," Ray said.

"Ah, but there is," and Zainal held up one finger, his smile deepening.

"How?" Nitin said. "There's no way to get that dust . . ." and Kamiton gave an uncharacteristic shudder.

"Having failed, the Mentat will have to explain its defeat to its peer group," Kamiton said, rubbing his hands together. "And such a convocation *can* be of benefit to us."

"How? We have the dust but not how to disperse it to kill 'em all off, even if they are in one place together?" asked Ray.

There was a long and thoughtful pause, which Jim Rastancil finally broke.

"Where are they likely to assemble?" he asked.

"Ah, now that is something we should find out," Zainal said, "and as soon as possible." He jerked his head at the other dissenters. "Nitin, what's your best guess?"

"My guess?" And Nitin seemed surprised to be asked such a question.

"Where they seem safest, of course," Kamiton said, flicking his fingers.

"Where?" Jim asked, looking at Zainal for a translation.

"Catten itself," Zainal replied.

"Most likely," Kasturi agreed, nodding.

"No," Nitin corrected him, frowning. "The space station where everyone can be searched and monitored. Security will be very, very thorough," and Nitin looked more pessimistic than ever. "You won't be able to get in."

"They will, however, need missiles to replace what they have wasted against the Bubble," Zainal said with a satisfied grin. "Emassi Venlik and a cargo of very useful ores would be made welcome."

"You don't have more than a few immature bushes of the olkiloriti down south," Kris felt obliged to point out.

"Baby could sneak in and out without being noticed, couldn't she?" Ray asked. "To get more from East Africa?"

"You'd better take someone along who knows where to find enough bushes," Kris added.

"It only took one sniff to disable me," Kamiton said with a grin.

"You must have more than a sniff to get all the Eosi," Nitin grumbled.

"It will take some time for all the Eosi to assemble, you know," Kasturi said. "If this requires a full inquiry."

"Oh, it will," Nitin said, once again sunk in his usual gloom.

"I'm counting on the full inquiry and the time it will take to assemble a sufficient number of Mentats," Zainal said, addressing Nitin. Then he turned to the others. "As for gathering the substance, I think Parmitoro Kassiaro, or even Chief Materu, might assist."

"Don't the women do the actual work?" Kris asked for she couldn't construct a mental picture of Chief Materu pulverizing leaves in a mortar with a pestle.

Zainal shrugged. "We use it as a weapon. That may alter his mind."

"The Maasai have declared war on the Catteni, you know," Ray Scott said with a wry grin. "I don't believe you'll have any trouble getting the stuff."

"That is," Jim added in a cautious note, "if there's still enough available. The mission report had trouble finding what they did bring back."

"Then we must send for what can be found immediately," Zainal said. "I will go myself to ask the chief's help."

And, Kris thought to herself, to make sure that Bazil and Peran are fully recovered. In his own Catteni way, he did care for them.

Chapter Ten

RETREAT BUZZED WITH A BARELY CONTAINED excitement when Kris brought Zane up to the crèche before reporting to her shift on the com watch in the hangar. Some of the buzz sounded ominous but then there had been a lot of criticism about taking on more problem groups: like sick and disabled ex-slaves. The Victims could not have been left on Barevi: everyone admitted that. Now! Especially since all but thirty of the original group had responded to the trauma therapy. The remainder, Dorothy sadly reported, had been too damaged to reach. But the psychologist felt that the ratio of recoveries was very good indeed. Even Dr. Hessian had had to admit that her program had been the proper one . . . in this instance. He was happily at work helping the disturbed children in a blend, Dorothy had said with a perfectly straight face, of both traditional therapies.

Kris always allowed ample time to walk Zane up to the crèche so she had some to spare and stopped in the main mess hall to sample the general temper.

"Are they still trying to burst our Bubble?" asked Fred

Gambino, who was serving coffee. "Only one cup allowed, you know."

"That's better than none. I've really missed my caffeine hits," she said. "And no, the Bubble's holding."

Fred leaned across the counter. "I got a place picked out where I'll never be found."

"You do?" Kris managed to imbue her tone with surprise and amusement. "I doubt you'll need it."

"You sure?"

"Sure as I can be about anything apart from death and taxes, and we don't pay taxes here, now do we?"

"Hmm. Well, it may come to that . . . taxes, I mean."

"Weren't you among those who met the Farmers, Fred?"

He gave her a long look. "Yeah . . ."

"Haven't they done what they promised? Kept us safe here on Botany?"

"Yeah . . ."

"Well, hold that thought because that Bubble's there to stay."

"Yeah, but where are the Farmers if we need them? They don't have any satellites buzzing about us like the Catt—'scuse me—Eosi do."

"Who's to say they haven't?"

That brought his eyebrows up but she put one finger to her lips and winked. A harmless enough white lie if it helped reduce panic.

"Thought the Farmers were sent a message?"

"They were. I suspect that they have a lot of other planets and systems to manage, too. If we really get into trouble, they'll be back. They don't approve of injuring any species."

"I know one I'd like to take apart, bit by bit," Fred said, making tearing motions with his hands.

Kris merely smiled at him, took her coffee and a hunk of fresh bread, and found a table at the side where she had a good view of those eating. Fred had probably expressed what many were thinking or fretting about. And he had a hidey-hole picked out? Interesting.

Fragments of arguments, some of them heated, reached her. Most concerned the possibility that the Bubble would be breached. She heard snatches of complaint about being saddled with more groups who wouldn't pull their own weight. Community service hours were long enough as it was and why did they have to keep on increasing the population. There were already enough here. Some were earnestly discussing the deplorable conditions on Earth and would they have to go back and help rebuild, just when Botany was beginning to have at least some amenities. Where would coffee grow on this planet? All right, rationing at least gave everyone a cup a day but when you were used to having as much as you wanted, a cup barely got you started. How much more food crops would they have to plant to feed more new arrivals? What would happen if a Catteni warship did manage to sneak through the Bubble? Or one of the ships that left so precipitously got captured and was used to penetrate the Bubble with all the Eosi ships right after it? That could happen, couldn't it? There were Humans who were vile enough to collaborate with the Catteni, weren't there? Shocking to turn against your own kind like that. One of the nearer tables composed of women only were discussing how best to cope with the outrageous behavior of their foster children. The waifs had initially seemed so happy to have the basic essentials instead of having to scrounge whatever they could, you'd think they'd be more grateful to be well fed, well housed and not complain about the chores they were assigned. Everyone worked on Botany. This colony didn't tolerate freeloaders. Didn't hurt anyone to sweat? Making bricks wasn't that hard. Or weeding.

Then Kris realized she'd better make tracks for the hangar and her shift.

• • •

BABY WASN'T THERE, BUT THEN, THE PLAN HAD been for it to be used for a fast round-trip to obtain sufficient olkiloriti. One of the K's was gone but not the KDL, which she had crewed on so often with Zainal. She took over the com watch from Matt Su.

"They're still pounding away," he told her as he rose from the station. "My ears burn from some of the stuff they're saying about us and . . . what they'll do when they get in."

"Well, they can't and they won't," Kris said because there was just the hint in the Chinese's dark eyes that he was worried. "They have tried the heaviest stuff they have, haven't they?"

"Then why haven't they just left?" Matt asked, dubious.

"Well, the shan will hit the fit if they fail. More likely, they just don't know when to give up."

"That Mentat Ix is some mule," Matt said. "It's roaring more and more, and I think it axed some of the captains. I'm hearing new names."

"Maybe it'll have another fit and die," Kris said, very much wishing that was possible. Though how Lenvec's subsumed personality could have had any effect on his host Eosi, she didn't know. She'd ask Zainal. The Ix was certainly the bête noire—wanting Zainal's hide for sure.

SHE STOOD HER WATCH, COLLECTED ZANE, AND took a turn at playing with other children: some of the five-year-olds who had been rescued. Most of them had to be taught games that children seemed to know instinctively.

"Well, none of them *had* a childhood, did they?" Anna Bollinger said, treating Kris in a very stiff and almost insulting manner, as if somehow this were Kris' fault. "Some of their personal habits are revolting."

Ah, thought Kris, she doesn't want her little darlings corrupted, does she?

"At least they have good role models now," Kris said mildly, pointing to Anna's well-grown youngster, nattering away to two boys, so undernourished at five that her three-year-old appeared older.

"I'd prefer that Jackie had proper children his own age to play with."

"Jackie seems to feel that it is his job to rectify their ignorance," Kris said. Chattering away, Jackie was showing the others how to build a little cabin out of the small logs that had been whittled as toys. They watched, their faces expressionless, even if their faces were now clean and their cheeks rounder and tanned.

One of them sent a foot into the log cabin and scattered the blocks. Anna gave an exclamation of concern but Kris caught her arm. "Let's see how Jackie handles it first."

"Really, Kris, you exceed your authority. I'm in charge of the . . ." Her voice trailed off as Jackie's reached the two women.

"Now that was very naughty of you," he said, hands on his hips and sounding exactly like his mother. "You collect them, and we'll start over. On Botany, we make things. We don't break them. That's what the Catteni do and you don't want to be Catteni, do you?"

The boys glanced over at the two women watching: Anna's expression was stern enough to frighten anyone. Kris grinned and made a gesture that suggested that it was wiser to obey. After a little more hesitation, possibly to show that they were making up their own minds about this, they bent to gather up the logs.

A little girl caught her finger on something sharp and she came rushing over to them, sobbing. Anna's whole countenance altered to one of concern and sympathy.

Kris let her handle the consolation and first aid. For all her other faults, Anna was a very good mother and the children—at least the Botany-born—trusted her.

ZAINAL WAS IN THEIR CABIN WHEN SHE RE-turned with Zane and their evening rations from the main mess hall. He was busy with lists and diagrams and a curious gadget on the table, which, when she picked it up, Kris recognized as an inhaler bulb. The sort she'd seen asthmatics on earth use to forestall an attack.

"Think you can get close enough to a Mentat to give him a dose of this?" she asked.

Zainal looked up, saw the bulb, and took it from her. He squeezed it.

"There's nothing in it," he said as she instinctively swatted it away from his face.

Her heart pounding, she exhaled. "Don't scare me like that."

Zainal chuckled.

"Baby got off all right? The Ix was still at it when I finished my shift."

"They must have ordnance—that's the English word, isn't it—"

"Right on." Kris grinned.

"Resupply vessels. Only a Mentat would continue like this," he said.

"The Mentat, who once was your brother," she said and when he nodded, she continued. "Is there any connection? I mean, would . . . the Lenvec personality have any influence on the Mentat?"

Zainal leaned back, idly sliding a pencil through his fingers, up and down on the surface of the table.

"It could, but I'm not certain how. The subsumation takes in the entire personality and then the dominant Mentat is in total control . . ." He paused. "Although it was the Mentat Ix, once my brother, who investigated

226

Ayres Rock and then seemed to be searching over the sea we were safely under . . . possibly for me."

Kris began to assemble dishes and utensils to serve their meal. Zane was playing with his goes-inters—the shapes that Zainal had made for him to fit together. These afforded the child hours of pleasure. As she leaned over to put a glass before Zainal, she got a better look at the diagrams.

"Isn't that the space station?"

He nodded.

"When is the brave captain Venlik and his crew likely to set out for another mining expedition?"

Zainal gave a shrug. "First Baby has to return. Then we have to wait to see what Beverly finds out about the other drop planets."

"There's a good deal of feeling that Botany's population is large enough right now," she said.

"We know," he said and jotted down something else in a combination of Catteni and English. He gave her a wry smile as she chuckled at the mish-mash. "It is difficult for me now to remember which language to think in for the words I need."

The barrage of the Bubble continued but in nowhere near the force that had been first launched against it. All four Catteni found that amusing as well as reassuring.

"It takes time to call in sufficient Mentats and senior Eosi to deal with an obsession like the Ix's," Zainal explained. "I will worry more when it stops."

OVER THE NEXT FEW WEEKS, CERTAINLY while Baby was on her mission, Kris sensed that Zainal was hiding something. She couldn't think what because they had had no previous secrets from each other, and he was as willing as ever to talk about any subject: especially the upcoming forays. Several times Zainal was dragged out of bed in the middle of their sleep period to race to the hangar to speak to some of the Catteni dissidents on the com link. He used a code that had proved successful. At least none of their group had been arrested by Eosi, or suspected by High Emassi supervisors.

The bombardment turned sporadic and occasionally a force tried to penetrate another point on the Bubble, or several at once, since they had failed to pierce it with all their might.

Kasturi, Tubelin, and Kamiton—not so much Nitin, though the older man, for all his pessimism, seemed to be a vital key in the subversive actions—were able, by means of careful codes, to be in contact with many of their adherents. What was being set up, Zainal did not say, or if even something was. Contact had to be made, though, especially with those dissidents in command positions on other Catteni-dominated planets.

"We have to be sure our people are warned, and ready, to take over. They must take control," Zainal did tell her. "We could lose one or two but more would be disastrous. We've worked so long and hard to get our men where they are right now."

"A good point. Have you someone on all the Eosi-controlled planets and installations?"

He shook his head. "Hardly. There are a great many more than we have personnel to cover but the most critical positions are."

BABY RETURNED WITH THE HARVEST OF OLK-iloriti leaves. Raisha had reminded Chief Materu that this dust was a weapon of significant power so he helped to make it on that condition. Parmitoro had shown them how he preferred to prepare the powder and taken his turn at the mortar, working alongside the other Humans of the crew.

Although the back of the job had been broken on the way home, Leon had off-duty personnel from the infirmary helping to complete the manufacturing process.

There was also a small, very dirty, and scraped box of inhalers among the supplies Baby had had time to collect, but the bulbs had not been broken.

"We went all over the place," Raisha said, presenting it with due ceremony to Leon. "I thought we'd have to scavenge from drugstores, where we could find any not already cleaned out. But we got in touch with the underground, and they found us these. Are they enough?"

Leon rubbed away enough of the mud to check the quantity. "Three dozen ought to be enough."

"Enough for what?" Kris asked.

"For the job to be done."

"There are a hundred Eosi," she said.

"Catch 'em all in the same spot and that'll do it."

"And here, we got the nose plugs in a scuba diving place Bert Put suggested." And Raisha handed over a smaller rectangular box.

"For them who shouldn't breathe deeply," Kris said, quite relieved to know that Zainal and his friends weren't going on some sort of a suicide mission, sacrificing themselves to get all the Eosi.

JOHN BEVERLY RETURNED WITH CHEERING news, having left behind some volunteers to help. And bad news, because two of the planets were inimical to Humans. Remnants of the usual Catteni crates and supplies had been found, bits and pieces of gnawed leather but no sign of a Human, even when they had done a low-altitude search for life signs. Nor any Deski, Rugarians, Turs, or other known "slave" species. On the other three planets that had been used as experimental colonies, people had made the best of what was available. Although on one, even the Human groups had widely separated and wished no contact with others, especially the other species. The other two had not turned to any form of anarchy or lawlessness but formed communities not unlike Botany's.

"Common sense prevailed," John Beverly told those who assembled in the open hangar to hear him, "although they were very grateful indeed for some of the supplies we brought."

"Did they give you any shopping lists?" Sandy Areson called out.

"Oh, yes," John agreed. "Our compatriots on Dystopia . . ." some of the audience groaned, others laughed, "offered the most amazing amount of metals, gemstones, gold, silver, and stuff to purchase any spare ship we'd give them."

"Do 'em no good unless they have an Emassi," someone else said, and Kris smiled appreciatively at this oblique salute to Zainal.

Since Kris was privy to so many of the Head Council meetings, she knew that Dorado's attitude toward alien species made it low on the list of help. Dystopia and NoName (so called because no one had come up with a name that a majority could approve) were at the top for whatever could be spared of medical instruments and medicines that would supplement what the colonists had found useful and effective by the same sort of trial-and-error method the colonists on Botany had used. That meeting concluded that basic medications, part of the results of their raids on Catteni-held Earth, and what extra medical equipment could be spared should be delivered as soon as feasible.

"When we explained, they did say that they'd even consider working with an Emassi, if this is what resulted," and he waved over at the G-ship. "So we got friendly neighbors, establishing the banners of Humankind. Kinda good to know."

NATHAN BAXTER HAD BEEN ONE OF JOHN'S crew in his professional capacity as photographer. He had brought back pictures of the other planets, both from space and on the surface, including some group photos of inhabitants and examples of how they had settled in. When these were developed, there were lines of those waiting to see the pictures up on the bulletin board outside the mess hall.

The infirmary actually treated more work injuries than diseases so, between what Kris had got on Barevi and others had found on Earth, they had enough to share. A second trip, and three cargo holds of wheat and dried rocksquat and loo-cow flesh, was planned. Microscopes, surgical tools, and other basic supplies were packed. Dystopia had only Humans while both NoName and Dorado had mixed populations. So some plursaw was sent along for the Deski inhabitants. The Turs had killed each other off in some sort of a bloody battle that had also taken many Human lives.

There had been no official census taken on any of the other planets but, during his flyby of the surfaces, John Beverly estimated that all three had more inhabitants than Botany.

"Basically, we're way ahead on the amenities," he told the Council. "I'd suggest we try to set up some sort of a com link . . ."

"Not with the Catteni ships likely to make more drops," Rastancil said.

"Which reminds me, John," Ray began, "did you see much Catteni traffic in space?"

"We kept our com open all the time and there was a lot of chatter on the various channels, but I'd no really fluent Catteni speaker aboard. There was a lot of interference, too. Jamming, I think."

"Possibly high-security messages," Zainal said, after asking Kamiton a quick question in Catteni. To which Kamiton nodded. "Many?"

"Com officers logged them if you want to check the records," John said.

Kasturi leaned forward eagerly. "Ask if they kept voice records?"

"Oh yes," Beverly grinned toothily. "We figured you guys might be able to understand them."

"You have them?" Kasturi stood up, eagerly holding out his hand.

The ex-air force general laughed as he reached for the sack that he had deposited on the floor at the beginning of the meeting and handed it over. "Every last one we caught."

"We leave. We listen. Where?" Kamiton asked Ray.

Ray glanced at Kris, jerking his thumb toward his private office, and she pushed back her chair to lead the way. She stayed to help because while Kamiton had been learning English with almost the same speed that Zainal had, neither could write English without a lot of false starts. So Kasturi made the initial transcriptions and then she and Kamiton translated them.

"They *are* convening the Mentats," Kamiton said suddenly, when they had gone through about half the recordings. He raised both arms, waving his fists with great satisfaction. He and Kasturi exchanged broad and gratified smiles.

"So how are you going to dust them?" Kris said, leaning back to rub the taut muscles of her neck and shoulders.

"Dust?" Kamiton asked.

She pantomimed inhaling and then fell to one side, twitching, as Kamiton had done.

"Ah, plant dust. Yes, we are thinking."

That was the same answer that Zainal gave her later that night when they finally returned home. Once again she had had to leave Zane to sleep over in the crèche but instinctively her head had turned to where his crib was when they entered the door.

"He is safe," Zainal said gently, circling her shoulders with one arm and drawing her toward the bedroom.

"I know that," she said, almost peevishly. "Sorry," she added instantly, rubbing at her neck again. "All that thinking in one language and writing down in another gave me a headache."

His strong fingers pushed hers out of the way and he began a restorative massage, all the time easing her toward their room. She chuckled. But she was not at all unwilling. Especially when the fingers of his other hand began to massage elsewhere.

WHEN SHE WOKE THE NEXT MORNING, AND IT was morning, not dawn, so she had been very tired indeed, his space in the bed was empty. She allowed herself the luxury of a leisurely awakening. She needed a shower so she took that, since the solar panel would have warmed the cistern water by now. Her hair was growing out from its last crop but she'd have to endure that again for the KDL's next spurious trip back to Catten. It was while she was soaping herself that she noticed a bulge in her abdomen and felt it. Firm and . . . She stopped and didn't move until the water turned cold once the tank had emptied. Her mind rapidly did a series of figuring, taking into account the length of the Botany day, the number of days since her last period and when she had had it. Could she have been fertile on Catten? Could she be pregnant by Chuck Mitford? He'd been too drunk to . . . hadn't he?

But when she began to fasten the belt to her overall, she realized that she was buckling it two holes up from the usual one. She sat down heavily, as much because she needed to sit to put on her boots as to gather her stunned wits. Not that she would really mind having Chuck's child. But she hadn't been nauseated or had any morning sickness and her breasts weren't that tender—yes, they were a tad sore, but last night could account for that.

"Stop fooling yourself, Kris Bjornsen," she said out loud.

Well, it could be worse. But she couldn't tell Zainal. At least not yet. He wouldn't let her crew the KDL, not if it was going back to the heavy gravity of Catten. Though gravity oughtn't to interfere with her pregnancy, not if she wasn't even showing the usual discomforts. She figured again. She was well into the first trimester. But she didn't want to have to admit a pregnancy, just when things were getting so interesting. And Zainal would need her help, wouldn't he?

She looked at the time. She did a swift deduction for the longer Botany day, reset the watch to what would be the local hour and figured she had time to see Zane, take him along to the mess hall and get her cup of coffee and something to eat while she played with her son. Boy, there'd be some explaining later on when each separately sired child wanted to know why. No, why should they know why? That was the Botany way of doing things, not the Terran one. And even if they did manage to get Earth back—*no,* Kris Bjornsen, not if but *when* Earth was returned to its proper owners and governments—she intended to stay here on Botany. Catteni, even erstwhile heroes like Zainal, might not be appreciated on Earth for some time to come.

TODAY SHE HAD TO COMPLY WITH BOTANY ethics, which required everyone to do some "dirty work." She had drawn KP but that happened so infrequently that she could almost consider it a vacation day. Well, a change *was* as good as a rest.

She had her breakfast with Zane who was a vacuum cleaner at breakfast time the way he gobbled his cereal.

Sarah joined her with her three children and offered to take Zane to the crèche.

"Maizie's getting to be quite a help," Sarah said, smiling at the much-too-sober-faced orphan she was fostering. "Will you hold Zane's hand?"

Maizie nodded after a quick, too-mature evaluation of Zane. Then, with what was for this five-year-old an almost daring action, she picked another piece of toast from the plate in the center of the table. In an absent fashion, Sarah passed her the jar of sweet berry jam. Sighing with relief, Maizie slathered the jam over her piece.

"Yes, I saw that," Sarah said without turning toward Maizie. "She is improving. Now if we can get her to talk. I know she understands every word I say. Maybe I should have made her ask for the toast," and Sarah made a grimace, then sighed. "It's hard to know."

"What does Dorothy say?"

Sarah made a second, self-accusing grimace, "That I shouldn't just give her what I know she wants but make her ask for it." Then she laughed in a self-deprecating way. "When I think how firm I was with Tony here . . ." and she broke off with a weak laugh.

"She may just start talking all on her own once she knows she's really, truly, genuinely safe, won't you, Maizie dear?" Kris said, smiling as she leaned toward the girl.

"Yes," Maizie said quite distinctly and continued licking the jam off her mouth with a pink tongue.

Kris and Sarah exchanged stunned glances.

"Would you like another piece of toast, Maizie?"

"Yes." She reached toward the last one on the plate.

Sarah immediately snatched it out of reach, and Maizie sort of crouched in surprised terror. Quickly Sarah shoved the plate back in reach but Kris intercepted.

"First, it's good manners to say, 'yes, thank you.' Can you manage that after 'yes'?"

Maizie, her face recovering its color, looked from Kris to the plate Sarah still held.

"Thank you," came the almost inaudible reply.

"You're quite welcome," Kris said formally and removed her hand.

Still watching her, Maizie took the piece of toast but she didn't pick up the spoon to spread the jam.

"Would you like more jam with your toast?" Sarah asked.

"Yes . . . thank you." This time it was more audible.

"You may have jam with your tea, too," Kris said, as proud of Maizie's little step forward as Sarah was.

As it was time for Kris to start her day's work, she hunkered down by her son.

"Maizie's going to take you with her to the crèche, Zane. Give me a hug and be a good boy."

Zane threw his arms about her neck and she could tell she had jam there for she had missed a patch earlier in wiping his mouth. Then she put his hand into Maizie's and watched, with a deep sigh, as the two small people followed Sarah who was carrying her youngest.

BABY REACHED THE HOLLOW ASTEROID WHERE Kamiton had stashed his spaceship. They could take no chances with a ship of dubious identity. Nitin, ever the pessimist, had voiced a serious concern that, especially with a convocation of Mentats requiring extra security measures, a vessel that had supposedly been destroyed or lost could not suddenly appear. Security checks could be extremely thorough. They must cover every contingency, including the two non-Catteni crew members. Chuck Mitford at least passed, and his knowledge of both Catten and Barevi was an asset. Lean and tall, the Australian Bert Put, who might have to pilot Kamiton's ship, would never pass as a Catteni. A hide must be constructed for him.

It was Bert who suggested it. The lower crew bunk in each bank had three drawers for the personal belongings. That meant just enough space under the lower bunk to accommodate Bert if the drawers were left ajar. As the general mess in any crew quarters, short of an inspection by a High Emassi, was never very tidy, half-open drawers, with contents half-in and half-out would be unexceptional. The credentials which Nitin had supplied for the unquestionably Catteni members had been genuine with support documentation on the files of the administration. There were even a few more that would pass the most rigorous inspection.

It was as well that such attention to detail had been observed for Kamiton's vessel had to pass five separate full inspections to be passed to land on Catten. There would have been more had the conspirators tried to land on the station.

There had, however, been a very tense moment when an Emassi captain who knew Kamiton quite well was the inspecting officer. He had given the vessel and the documentation only a cursory inspection but settled himself in the mess for an update on Kamiton's latest exploration.

Kamiton had played out his part with laudable indolence, ordering Chuck and Nitin to provide food for their guest.

Bert, sweating in his hiding hole, worried about Zainal, Tubelin, and Kasturi on the KDL. But it was laden with ores—all in the useful platinum groups—that would make it so welcome any suspicion of its genuineness would be overlooked. Nitin had also supplied the non-Catteni members of the crew with equally authentic documentation. Since their destination was the refinery area of the planet, well away from the main city, they ought not to be in any danger.

Nitin had so picked at that first part of the overall scheme that even he had come to be satisfied with its high chance of success. About the rest he was only certain that *he* had done all he could to ensure the possibility of success: not, he was quick to add, the *probability*.

"Too many things could go wrong. Our group could have been infiltrated and our plans known . . ."

"Only so much of the plan," Kamiton interjected. *"When,"* Kamiton stressed the conjunction, "we get down on Catten and when we have contacted the rest of us, I think you will raise the odds in favor of probability."

Kamiton turned his head ever so slightly to see Zainal taking a few more sips of water, all that he was allowing himself since he had designated his role in their plan. He hoped that Zainal would not overdo the starvation he had deemed necessary to the success of their stratagem. One did not underestimate an Emassi of Zainal's proven ability.

He was however glad to change into his own ship and let others do what was necessary to improve on Zainal's disguise.

Well, as soon as this niggit left, Kamiton thought, they could proceed. This appeared to be the last of the space inspections. He had never seen so many security shuttles and craft zipping around the planet before. Ah, well, there hadn't *been* a full convocation of Mentats during his lifetime. And, with any luck, this would be the last. The most that ever had assembled since he had taken up his adult duties had been ten. He rather doubted that some of those farthest from Catten would make the journey but whoever came would receive a lasting reward for their trouble. He did spare a thought for those on the KDL. He really wanted to get the dependents away to the safety of Botany. Good idea of Zainal's on several counts: one of them being that Kasturi had a girl child and so did Tubelin: mates for Bazil and Peran. That way some of their families would survive the blood bath that would be certain to follow a failure. But this time, they would *not* fail. Kamiton grinned and fortunately his smile coincided with some fatuous remark of the security Emassi, and Kamiton rose, able to signal that they really had best end their conversation.

They landed on the field they had been directed by security to use. Then proceeded, as planned, in a ground vehicle to Kamiton's quarters in a secluded area of the city where many Emassi kept temporary units. As Kamiton disarmed the alarm system, it blinked its message that persons still within the apartment had recently deactivated it. Kamiton warned the others by silently pointing at the message and took out his stun weapon, setting it on medium.

"Kamiton?" and, as that was Zainal's voice, Kamiton reholstered the weapon with relief.

He stopped in the doorway to his main room, shocked at Zainal's altered appearance, and quickly looked beyond the haggard man to the other members of the KDL group and ignored Zainal's battered and nerve-whip lashed body.

ZAINAL REMAINED IN SECLUSION WHEN THE others went out on their individual errands of contacting other dissidents and setting in motion the next step of the scheme. If some of the dependents objected to being forced to leave their comfortable homes in the middle of the night, carrying only basic necessities, they were silenced by the dire consequences of ignoble deaths or futures if they chose to stay behind. By dawn, the empty ore carrier, the KDL was aloft and received only the most cursory of queries by security patrol ships as it proceeded at a leisurely speed out of Catteni space. As soon as it was in relatively empty space, the KDL would run at maximum speed, red-lining if necessary to be sure the dependents were safely at Botany before the last of the Mentats arrived, and more were assembling in their fast and comfortable ships every time period.

Anne McCaffrey

• • •

ON THE FIFTH DAY AFTER THE KDL HAD DE-
parted, Kamiton received the short burst of code from
their space station colleague.

"Ugred," said Kamiton when he had translated the
message, "says that there are only two more Mentats and
four juniors scheduled to arrive. All should be in place by
morning."

"Everything else is ready?" Zainal asked. He spent a
lot of time on his belly buffered by the softest material
Kamiton's quarters contained since his back had been
lashed by nerve whips. He rather thought Kasturi had enjoyed that exercise a little too much, but the disguise had
to pass any close inspection. He wasn't sure, at this point,
which annoyed him most—the necessary wounds or the
equally necessary starvation.

The medic among their secret group had injections
ready to sustain him—but these would only last so long
and would have to be administered in the last safe moment on the space station. If they made it that far.

"Everything essential to the operation is in place, or so
Ugred said in his last message. The presence of so many
Mentats has everyone nervous, agreed, but one more security vessel is not likely to cause any unnecessary attention. And Ugred will have issued a special clearance to
the duty officer in case he cannot himself be there."

"Waiting is always hard," Kasturi remarked to no one
in particular.

No one had an answer for such a truism.

"Any message from Chuck and Bert?" Zainal broke
the silence to ask.

Kamiton shook his head. "No message is good."

Zainal fell into a light doze, which he did more often
than he liked, but it helped him to conserve energy. He
went over and over the plan, fretting that Chuck and Bert

who had remained aboard Kamiton's ship might be discovered. He reassured himself that the ex-marine sergeant, with his knowledge of both Barevi and Catteni, could handle any eventuality. He would be able to move about the huge field, would be able to listen to any rumor in the mess on the field where other Drassi were awaiting the return of their captains. Most of the talk was about the Mentats coming to Catten and everyone wondering what it was all about.

The variety of speculations amused Chuck, but he added a few little tweaks to find out just how popular Eosi rule was. It was not. No one said so in so many words, for that was dangerous, but many lowly Drassi were unhappy with their lot, with their Emassi, and the crazy planet that was resisting unexpectedly. Some Drassi boasted of the loot they and their officer had come back with, though a lot of the stuff that wasn't edible or potable hadn't seemed worth the fuel to transport it back to Catten.

As it was normal for a ship to be securely locked when empty, Chuck did so, which meant Bert had some freedom of movement. Chuck had arranged a code remark so that Bert would know to resume hiding if someone might be snooping about the scout ship. And Bert was also there in case they received emergency messages and had to hightail it back to Botany. The package containing the new ID decals had arrived by special messenger on the first day, a fact that they confirmed to Kamiton in an innocuous report by his Drassi that the ship had been serviced and was awaiting his convenience.

Chuck never found waiting easy, and it was almost twice as bad in the heavier gravity of Catten. At least, when he and Bert were safely alone on the ship, they could play poker. Right now, Bert owed him a small fortune and had suggested bezique as a change of game. Chuck had learned that game from an English commando and, though he didn't win as often, he didn't lose much either.

Anne McCaffrey

• • •

WORKING KITCHEN DUTY ON BOTANY HAD A few rewards, like first samplings of the day's baking and first servings of lunch, before the crowds started in. There were always options: sandwiches which people could take to eat elsewhere, or a quick snack of soup and bread at a table, or a more leisurely meal. On a fair summer's day like today, many chose to take their food outside and enjoy the fine weather. That meant less washing up to be done. Paper plates had once been discussed but paper was too valuable for other necessities to be wasted when pottery was available. Pottery and some finer china as well, now that Sandy had a full kiln again, bigger than her first ones at Ayres Rock on the Farmers' continent. Those who had bartered for a fine china plate did not use it to eat off of—especially the hand-painted ones, which were hung as wall decorations or displayed on the mantelpiece.

Since this sort of mechanical work required no great mental effort, Kris occupied her thoughts with whether or not she should say anything about her pregnancy. She had imaginary discussions with Mavis, who did a lot of the midwifery, about the effects of heavier gravity on an unborn child. She ran several scenarios on telling Chuck that he was going to be a father—even if both of them had been too drunk to know what they were doing. That was almost a pity, in a way, but in another, a relief. Chuck might well be mortified to think he had abused her—but, hell, she hadn't resisted and she could have—since he seemed to be seeing a lot of Dorothy Dwardie. Kris rather hoped her having Chuck's child wouldn't complicate *that* arrangement. She'd be quite willing to explain the circumstances to Dorothy. It certainly hadn't been premeditated . . . not in that gravity! She shook her head because she kept trying to imagine how they had managed, both of them damned near wrecked with the heaviness and alcohol. But not completely wrecked, Kris told herself. Let's face that fact squarely. I'll simply have to give up drinking any more than a glass of hooch unless Zainal is with me.

About then, she realized that she had seen none of the Council eating in the mess hall. She'd been out in the main hall often enough, making sure that surfaces were clean for the next diners or picking up stray cups and glasses. There were still folks who did not know to clear their tables off.

She had an hour's rest before she was expected to help with the supper. So, though she had half an urge to go spend it with Zane, her feet and legs were aching and, if she wished to be efficient this evening, she'd better put them up now.

She almost fell asleep but someone dropping a kettle in the kitchen roused her, and she jumped to her feet and went back in to her duties.

She was tired enough when she got home to shower with Zane, who loved mommy showers, before stowing him in bed. Then she stretched out her weary legs and aching feet up on the bed and arranged the pillows behind her. In broad daylight, she thought in self-deprecation, but she'd just take a short nap.

She was roused, in the dark, wondering what had awakened her. Zainal wasn't back yet from wherever he'd been working that day. He'd been on the duty roster in the hangar with the other Catteni. Probably kept late at a session of the infamous Ways and Means Committee. That thought amused her as she turned over on her side, the one that would face Zainal when he came to bed, and she went back to sleep.

She had the next morning off, but was due on shift at the com unit for the afternoon. But when she and Zane reached the mess hall for breakfast, the place was full of the exciting news that, sometime during the night, the Eosi ships had given up their attack and left.

She was as excited as everyone else and wondered where Zainal and the other Catteni were. Everyone was as dizzy with relief as she was. But that didn't mean she'd have the shift off. For all anyone knew, the Eosi had only taken a breather to reload or something.

She did look around for Chuck, but didn't spot him. She should inform him of his imminent fatherhood. She should also, she told herself sternly, make an appointment for a prenatal checkup at the infirmary. And find out, if she could, about the effects of gravity on the unborn. What had that title been: "The Effects of Moonlight on Man in the Moon Marigolds"? No, no, no. So she bored around in her memory for the exact title. She'd read the book—oh so very long ago now. In another life entirely. "The Man in the Moon Marigolds . . ." no, that wasn't it, either.

Suddenly Mavis rushed up to her. "Kris, can you help us? We have a concussion patient. Needs someone with him, and we're short of staff since John took a bunch off on his run to Dystopia and the other two."

"I'm due on com watch," she said, and Mavis waved that aside.

"Beth can take that. She's got enough Catteni. It's Bart, and I know you like him and he likes you."

"Bart?" Kris was instantly on her feet. "What happened?" she asked as she and Mavis made their way out of the hall. "I'll just drop Zane off. How'd Bart get a concussion?"

"Fell off his ladder putting slates on the roof. Nearly splattered his brains on the flagstones. He should pull round but we need someone to monitor him in case there's a significant change."

"That's me."

Maizie was at the gate into the fenced area, and she blinked in pleasure at the sight of Zane in Kris' arms.

"One day that child will surprise herself and smile," Mavis said.

"Maizie, Maizie, Maizie," Zane chanted, reaching for her and Kris lifted him over the pickets.

"Yes, thank you," Maizie said very distinctly.

"You're quite welcome," and to Sally Stoffer, "I'll be at the infirmary."

BY THE FIFTH HOUR, KRIS WOULD HAVE changed duties with anyone. Glad as she was to sit after yesterday's kitchen duty, enough was enough. Bart was on one of the cardiac monitors but that didn't give much indication of what was happening in his cranium. His color, generally a dark creamed-coffee, was not tinged with any lividity. The wound had been sutured and sealed with nu-skin, another of the items "liberated" from hospital stores on Earth. She'd seen enough of Mayock's neat handiwork to recognize it. Nine stitches from just above the hairline, skewed to the right brow. Quite a gash but it would be the fracture under the skin that would be worrying. Whatever X-ray had been taken was at the nurses' duty station. Did no one notice that a state-of-the-art X-ray unit had gone missing on Earth?

IN HIS AIR-CONDITIONED OFFICE ON EARTH, Emassi Plovine, struggling with the printouts of ship IDs registered as landing in Catteni fields across the globe, was puzzled by some anomalies in the records. He had received a stern reprimand from the Mentat who had ordered the use of three G-class ships for the bombardment of that wretched enclosed planet, and Plovine had been unable to locate them. He had had interviews with four indignant Emassi who had reported, as ordered, to the bays where the G-ships should have been awaiting them, to find them gone. Two from the main Catteni landing site, once named Houston, and one from the eastern continent. Reports of the departure of these ships seemed perfectly normal and the ships had taken off with no untoward problems. Except that the duty officers had been told that the crew assignments had been altered. Since that happened frequently enough these days, with the Mentats being more erratic than ever, no one had questioned the changes. Until the Ix Mentat had demanded, not requested, the Mentat in charge of subduing the Terran rebellions to deliver all G-and-over-class ships available to help bombard the planet, which was defying Eosi control.

Plovine's search had been thorough but the results mystifying. Indeed, one cargo vessel full of slaves, due to be sent to one of the cold planets that had far too many slave deaths, had taken off with them on schedule but never arrived at its destination. The Emassi governor of that planet was now demanding more slaves or he would have to close down operations. Even Rassi could do this sort of work. Probably better. But, by edict of the Eosi, no Rassi was ever taken from Catten.

There was also the matter of huge charges made against the accounts of three K-class ships which he finally discovered have been written off as no longer in service: one had blown up in space, with suitable debris to make a positive identification of the KDL. Another had disappeared on a routine voyage. The third had taken off from Barevi with a full cargo but never arrived at its destination, and it had been in the company of a KDI of which there seemed to be two by that designation.

Not to mention the duplication of cargo vessels, both sent to a mining planet to collect ores. The cargo had been duly loaded onto a carrier, and later the ore had been logged into the refinery on Catteni, but a second ship had arrived at the mining planet two days after the first, expecting to load up immediately. The captain had lodged a formal complaint since he had had to wait until the mine superintendent had been able—by increasing the hours of his workforce—to extract enough ore to fill the second ship, as the Emassi of the cargo ship had no wish to return empty of goods and receive reprimands from his superiors.

"Very irregular, very irregular," Emassi Plovine said as he wrote up his findings. At least he had concrete proof that what he had discovered could be verified. Only where had so many ships disappeared? And did it matter?

WHEN ORDERS HAD COME FROM NINETEEN Mentats that the Mentat Ix was to cease and desist its attempt to penetrate the Bubble, the juniors expected it to have a second seizure. The Mentat Ix could not, however, disobey such an order. It had to issue the commands to cease the barrage, despite the fact that resupply ships were on their way to this quadrant.

The Ix replied to that desist order by issuing a demand for a general meeting of Mentats to discuss an alarming and dangerous situation: one that must be countered as quickly and efficiently as possible.

As the Mentat Ix had the power to call such a meeting, and most of the others of its age and service were as desirous of a meeting to find out why the Mentat Ix was wasting so much in its attempt to penetrate an obviously impenetrable barrier, the summons were sent out in coded bursts to those who would comprise such an assembly. Such a convocation of Mentats occurred rarely enough to provoke considerable speculation among the Emassi who zealously guarded their Mentats. For some, it meant a rare chance to visit the home world and families unseen in the decades of their service to a Mentat. For others, it meant giving up comfortable quarters to squeeze into whatever accommodations might be available on the space station. Of course, the Mentats would be safe on the station. Safer than they would be in the luxurious homes they kept on the surface of the planet.

Many other Emassi, not in personal service to the Eosi, decided to take the chance of arranging for personal interviews with Mentats about this favor or that new condition. So, many ships converged on Catten over the next few weeks while the Mentats returned from their far-flung dominions. Codes had been set and, if the incoming ships properly answered these, the guardian ships protecting the space station allowed them to pass. A few could not and were immediately taken to one of Catten's moons until the Mentat convocation had ended.

Had Emassi Plovine been recalled from Earth, some of the anomalies he was searching for might have been solved: two vessels, a K-class and an exploratory scout, both listed as lost in space, would have been of particular interest to him. But he had forwarded his report to the Mentat Governor of Earth.

Ships that left Catten outward-bound were neither stopped nor searched by the patrols, though their departures were noted on the duty sheets.

BY THE TIME THE KDL RETURNED TO BOTANY with the mates and families of fifty Emassi, Kris had already discovered that Zainal with his Catteni colleagues had left Botany and that the Ways and Means Committee had been disbanded. A lot of her usual friends, who had never been used as crew, were also missing. She finally cornered Coo who gave her a big Deski smile and said, "All gone. Fix valley."

"Fix? Fix for what, Coo?" Although images of Eosi trapped in an enclosed valley for the rest of their unnatural lives had a certain appeal to her, she did not think those were the intended "guests."

"I go help fix. Good idea."

No one else seemed to know, even Bart, who usually heard rumors other people didn't. He was on light duties since he was still on the sick list from the skull fracture.

"I don't know, and I gotta tell you, Kris, I *hate* like hell not knowing."

She agreed completely with Bart. Leon Dane was missing from the infirmary, and all Mavis could say, and she was telling the truth, was that he had taken off for a few days' rest.

She had Zane and, when she discovered that Sarah and Joe had gone off as well, leaving Maizie and Tony in the crèche, she opted for a change of duty and worked in the crèche instead of hangar duty. Maizie seemed to like her and, because Zane was learning to speak, it seemed a good idea to include Maizie in her informal lessons.

Ray Scott didn't avoid her and she could almost believe him when he said he didn't know where Zainal was, but that they'd gone off to make personal contact with other crucially situated dissidents.

"Every important position has to be covered by an Emassi who can be trusted, you know."

"Why?"

"That I don't know. Zainal got very reticent about his strategy," Ray said, and he seemed a bit annoyed with such reticence.

Bull Fetterman didn't know. Jim Rastancil was wherever everyone else had gone. Ainger was so annoyed that she wouldn't have asked him if he'd been the only person who did know.

Maizie learned to say "please," "thank you," "may I have . . ." and some other useful words and enunciated them more clearly than Zane did. Clearly Maizie felt safer with him and Tony than with any of the other children, even those who had taken her into their orphan group.

Then one morning at the crèche, Kris' com unit bleeped. It was Beggs. "Admiral Scott requests that you proceed immediately to the hangar, and be prepared to stay at your destination for several days."

"How several? Can I bring Zane with me?"

"I have given you the information I have, and no, the child would not be an asset."

Just like Beggs to consider Zane an "asset" but she gave him a long smacking kiss and told Maizie that she would be back soon and left Maizie clinging to Zane as if he were the elder of the two. That didn't do her mood any good but she borrowed a runabout, slammed into her cabin and, as she was throwing a change and other needs into a pack, realized she had liquid dribbles drying all down the front of her. Fortunately she did have a recent issue of clothing and changed, cursing under her breath as she hauled the belt tight and then had to let it out over her expanding middle. As she stormed out, she got madder and madder—with Beggs and Scott. She was only halfway to the hangar when she heard the familiar sound of a spaceship coming in to land. Her heart beating faster, she threw the speed bar as far across as it would go and had the pleasure of being on the landing field when the KDL landed.

"Now, Emassi Zainal," she murmured, "you've some explaining to do."

"Kris, come on. It's only touching down to pick us up," Scott called over the loud noise of the idling ship engine, beckoning her to hurry. He looked her up and down with a very admiralish stare that made her realize that he was sharply dressed, too.

"If you don't tell me what's going on, Admiral Scott . . ." she began as the ramp extruded partway: enough to jump up to the personnel hatch open in the cargo door.

"I'll explain it when we get where we're going. Climb aboard."

She did because he was hauling away at her arms, and she refused to be manhandled even by Admiral Ray Scott.

She caught just a glimpse of a lot of people sitting or lying on the cargo level, and then he was guiding her toward the bridge, past Ninety who seemed to be standing guard. Which he well might have been because she realized that all the faces had been Catteni.

"What the hell . . ."

"They're the women and children of the dissidents who were based on Catten and therefore at risk," Ray said, briskly urging her toward the bridge.

Well, she could understand the wisdom of getting dependants safely away from Eosian retaliation. The abuse that Zainal's two sons had suffered certainly made that a priority.

"Zainal got them out?"

"Ah, more or less. We're installing them in the largest of the enclosed valleys. They'll be safe there."

That made sense because not all of the Headquarters valley's buildings had been taken down, so expanding that facility was a perfect solution. Then there was another aspect of a shipload of Catteni arriving at Retreat. One Catteni, even four, wouldn't raise much resentment at Retreat, but an influx of mates and children could be a source of irritation.

Gino waved a backhanded "hi" in her direction, and Raisha shot a quick look around as the two pilots lifted the ship from the hangar field. Everyone else on the bridge gave her a nod or a smile. They were all, Kris noticed, those who had a fair knowledge of Catten.

"Kris," Gino began in an odd voice and paused to clear his throat, "the plan is that you'll act Emassi to our . . . guests. Zainal said you'd had practice. He said them knowing there was someone in charge of them might help in the long run."

"What long run?" Kris asked casually.

There was a long pause.

"Oh, it's just a contingency idea."

"Gino, you don't lie very well," Kris said, folding her arms across her chest and glaring around, her gaze ending at Ray Scott.

"It *is* a contingency," Ray said, but he stopped right there, without specifying for what. "We agreed to give sanctuary to relatives of Kasturi, Tubelin, Kamiton, and several other key dissidents. A precaution. When the dust settles, they can return."

"I've a letter from Zainal explaining . . ." Gino paused again. "It's in my cabin. Just let me land, and help us get these people settled. It explains everything. Ah, see, we're nearly there."

"I'm not a fool." And Kris swept the entire bridge complement with a stare.

"No one has ever accused you of that," Ray said. "But you're tall, imposing, you speak good Catteni, and you act Emassi without half-trying. It'll make settling the dependants easier. I will pretend," and Ray accorded her a smile and a little bow, "to be under your command. Now assume it!"

His last three words were tantamount to an order that he intended she would obey. She looked him in the eyes long and hard, and he did not flinch. He did, however, steady her when they landed with a little thump.

Wheeling, she looked out to the quiet scene of the HQ valley. The main hall, only half-finished when she had last been here, was completed. There was even smoke coming out of the chimney. Several large houses, with half dormers for sleeping lofts, were interspersed with small accommodations, scattered throughout the lodgepole forestry. It was certainly a lot better housing than the First Drop had had. She took a deep breath.

"Ninety," she called, turning again on one heel and moving back down the corridor.

"Yo!" was Ninety's unexpectedly army response.

"Prepare to unload," she said in Catteni, having no trouble at all sounding harsh. "Is there a list of who's who?" she asked in English over her shoulder.

Ray offered her a clipboard, presenting it to her with a smart bow, thus showing the women that Kris was the superior officer. Kris looked down at the board. All the names were in Catteni glyphs, which she couldn't read, but also in English and she recognized the English script was written in the bold, forceful style Zainal used. Unexpectedly her eyes filled with tears. She blinked them away, pretending that the sun was glaring in her eyes and shielding them as she took a position at the head of the ramp.

Ninety had opened the cargo hatch and the loading ramp was down.

"Just this level, Drassi?" she asked in Catteni.

"Yes, Emassi Khriss," he said, staring straight ahead.

Emassi Khriss turned to the passengers, the sunlight streaming in. The women were all standing now: the children, the youngest showing some fright, the others very silent and wary, grouped around them.

"As your name is called, come forward and leave the ship. Follow the Drassi who will lead you to your quarters." She noticed that each name had a number after it, indicating the number in the party. Flipping the top sheets, she noticed that each family had already been assigned quarters. She had only to call them out. She had no trouble remembering Catteni counting. She also remembered enough of what Zainal had told her about Catteni women: that they were almost as subservient as Drassi or Tudo and would have to be shown what to do. "You will be safe here."

One woman stepped forward and cleared her throat, bowing her head for addressing an Emassi without first being spoken to.

"We were told that no Eosi can come here. Is that true?"

"You are . . ." and Emassi Khriss impassively awaited an answer.

"Sibbo, Kasturi's mate. These are his sons and his child." She bowed again.

Well, at least one of them had some guts, Kris thought with relief.

"Ah, I know Kasturi well. He has been here," Kris said. "Eosi have not been able to penetrate the shield that surrounds this planet," she added with as smug a smile as she had ever seen on any Catteni face. "You are safe. We have *made* you safe. Go with this Drassi to the quarters prepared, Sibbo. Place twelve."

Sibbo and her children picked up their bundles and they started down the ramp after Ninety. Crew members stepped forward to escort each group called.

It took a while to work her way down the list. She had one interruption, an older woman, who bowed.

"Drassi Khriss," and she bowed an almost embarrassing depth, "are there no Rassi or slaves to assist us?"

Kris was so surprised that she blinked, her mind racing to find an answer. She pretended to consult her list. This was the oldest of the women . . . ah, Nitin's wife. How like him to have a critical mate!

"Rassi do not leave Catten, as you know, Milista. There are no slaves on this planet. You will do what is necessary yourselves."

"But," and there was real consternation on the woman's lined face as she spread out her hands in a helpless appeal, "we have never been without slaves."

"Oh, my God," Gino muttered behind Kris. "Never thought of that."

"Well, by God," was Scott's equally low but quite firm addition, "they're going to damned well learn how to cope without them."

"All the food is Catteni, with pictures on the sacks or boxes," Ninety said. "We did that special."

"With recipes?" Gino put in hopefully.

"I dunno. Can't read that much Catteni," Ninety added.

"Bummer," was Gino's final remark.

"Any ration bars?" Kris asked.

"Yeah, lots of those."

"Let them eat rations, then," Kris said, startled to find

herself paraphrasing Marie Antoinette. She turned back to Milista. "It is enough that you are safe and have food to eat and shelter. You will take what is provided and be grateful."

Kris didn't have any trouble acting Catteni just then. She was thoroughly annoyed. Surely Kasturi or even Tubelin would have thought to tell Zainal, or someone, that the women were accustomed to servants. Not that she'd ask anyone to serve Catteni women. They could bloody well learn how to do for themselves as the colonists had.

"All work will be shared, Milista. Learn that now." She gave a curt dismissal to the woman who backed away before she turned. Indignation and fury were obvious in the way she stalked down the ramp, carrying a very small bundle, which she kept hitching or changing from hand to hand. Briefly Kris wondered what Milista had brought with her that could be heavy. She didn't know if Catteni women had jewelry, and if that was all Milista had brought, instead of clothing, she was going to get very tired of the one wrap she was wearing.

With mixed emotions of chagrin and irritation—and the latter was stronger—Kris crisply called out the next name. The gall of the woman, wanting servants as well as safety. Maybe once she'd had a taste of—Shut up, Kris, it's not Milista's fault.

She got through the rest of the unexpected and generally unhappy guests. She'd been so busy ushering them out, she hadn't seen that there were Humans boarding the KDL on the far side of the ramp. Some carried just tools while others humped excess building materials aboard.

The last few arrived as the final Catteni family of seven was led off to cabin thirty-five. So Kris nearly gasped when Sarah passed her with a wink. Joe was right behind her, carrying carpentry tools. Sandy stalked up the ramp last.

"They wanted servants," Kris muttered savagely to Sandy, who burst out laughing.

"That'll be the day. Did you hear what Kris just said?" And Sandy was spreading the remark, causing both chuckles and exclamations of surprise.

Kris was about to turn away, to retract the landing ramp, to get away from her before she lost her cool entirely. Then she paused, looking out at the tranquil valley. The scene was all wrong, even disturbing. Not a soul was in sight and the mess hall and quarters looked as empty as when they had landed.

"Kris?" Sandy came to stand beside her. "What the hey?" And she frowned. "What's wrong with them? Sulking?"

Kris listened intently, but apart from an odd mechanical creak or a hiss from a vent, she didn't even hear crying or angry voices.

"Hell, any normal kid would have been out and snooping about by now."

"Maybe when we leave," Kris said. "They've had a bit of a shock."

"Ha! About time!" Sandy took Kris' arm and drew her inside. "D'you know how to close this?"

Almost absentmindedly, Kris depressed the right switch and the ramp slid up and inside, and the cargo hatch made a low, well-oiled rumble as it slid shut.

Kris strode along the corridor to the bridge.

"We're ready then?" Raisha asked, looking up from her pre-flight check.

"Can I have a rear-view screen as we take off, Raisha, and do a slow ascent, huh?"

"Sure, Emassi Khriss, whatever you say, Emassi Khriss," and Kris managed a little smile for Raisha's teasing.

"You do a swell Emassi act," Gino said, entering from the captain's ready room. He had an envelope in his hand

and his expression was carefully neutral as he gave it to her.

"Positions, please, for takeoff," Raisha said in warning. Not that strapping in was needed with the smooth vertical lift she achieved.

Kris watched the rearview screen as long as she could but the valley might have been uninhabited for all she could see. Then the KDL was over the enclosing wall and beginning to level out for the flight back to Retreat.

"Well done, Kris," Ray said, clapping one hand lightly on her shoulder. Then silently he gestured toward the captain's room Gino had just vacated.

Kris looked down at the envelope in her hand as she walked toward the privacy the room would offer. She had an awful feeling about what the letter would say to her. Sliding the panel shut behind her, she sat on the nearest surface and looked down at the message. It was upside down and Zainal's distinctive script made an interesting pattern of her name from that angle.

She turned it around. "Kris." She spoke her name aloud.

"Well, waiting's not going to change a single word inside," she said and, with a decisive nail, opened the edge of the sealed flap and then ran her finger up, spreading the paper. She also tore the corner out of the envelope with the force of her action.

There were two sheets. Well, he tended to sprawl his words across a page, even if the sentences were exceedingly straight . . . as if he'd followed a ruled line.

Kris, love,
Don't look back in anger or be angry with anyone if
I do not come back to you. It was my plan.

She stopped reading, her eyes filling with tears, terrified of what he would say next.

There is only one way to get into the Mentat meeting, and we shall take it.

"We," he had written. He had specified "we," not just himself. But which we? Had the old pessimist Nitin been included in that plural noun?

You will understand why the mates and children must be sent to safety. The Ways and Means Committee agreed as Scott will tell you.

We . . .

Somehow Kris couldn't really believe in that plurality. Zainal *led* the others. He would lead them into whatever it was he had decided to do. But that didn't mean "he" would be safe.

We know that, should things not turn out as we have carefully planned,

You leave him alone, now, you hear, Murphy? Your damned Law doesn't operate in Catteni space, d'you hear me, Murphy?

you and the rest of the Botany colonists will allow them to live in peace. The Council has promised us that and you will understand why Humans must learn to live with Catteni for the good that really is in us as a species, misguided by those who have controlled us for so long.

If we fail, and I do not (she gave a sob when she saw that fierce underlining) *return to Botany, this letter authorizes you and Chuck Mitford to be guardians of my sons, to rear them as near as your hearts will let you to be good Catteni but better Botanists. They will need to know all they can learn from you and Chuck. He will teach them what young men need to know. Chuck and Bert will be able to get home in Baby. We have every intention of being in that ship on its way back to Botany.*

I did not like keeping the plan from you who have invaded my heart and spirit. I never expected the wealth of love would be mine. And I have been so very happy with you that even this Catteni can ache with longing for you. You would have insisted on coming. I could not allow you to be in such jeopardy.

You have been my only love.

And the final letter was the bold crossed "Z" that he liked using.

"Well, you were right, weren't you, Kris, m'girl," she murmured aloud, her voice sounding scratchy in the quiet cabin. "He was planning something dire. And he really doesn't expect to survive."

She folded the two pages with very careful motions and replaced the precious letter in the envelope, smoothing the ragged edges down, over and over, until they remained flat.

She opened the door and, although everyone was studiously looking elsewhere, she flagged Ray Scott and beckoned him into the room.

"Okay, I've had my Dear John letter. *What* are he and those other madmen planning to do?"

Ray exhaled and gave her a long look. "I don't know either," he said slowly. "Unless I was sure of its success, he knew I'd try to talk him out of it. Therefore, he's taking unacceptable risks." Ray sighed again. "They left before they could be stopped." Another pause as Ray looked down at his hands and dug something from under one fingernail before he made eye contact again. "I didn't think I'd ever say it of a Catteni, but I admire that man. I will always admire that man. And I hope to hell he gets away with whatever it is he went to do."

"I'm glad you're rooting for him, too, Ray. More than you would have done when you first got here, but better late than never," Kris said wryly. "Is there any of Mayock's brew on board this ship?"

Ray took one step to the wall units and pulled out a drawer. She heard the click of glassware as he extracted two glasses and a bottle of the somewhat ale-pale alcohol.

Solemnly he filled the glasses and handed her one.

"Down the hatch!" Ray said, lifting his in a toast.

"Murphy," Kris said raising her glass, "stay the hell away from my man!"

They both knocked back the toast and turned as one to symbolically smash the glasses against the outer wall.

Chapter Eleven

"WE HAVE THE PRISONER," SAID THE EMASSI commander, dressed in security uniform. He jerked his head back at the limp figure, which had been dragged on the knees between two members of the rather strong detail. The slimed skin of the naked captive showed a crisscross of angrily red, raised welts from frequent lashings with a nerve whip, and his legs and arms were bloodied from other wounds.

"Prisoner?" asked the duty Drassi. "I have no knowledge of a prisoner summoned by any Mentat. The convocation is in session," he added as if this was a sacred occasion.

"Mentat Ix has been searching for this man," and the Emassi stepped back, lifting the drooping head to display a gaunt, half-starved face, "for months. The name, I believe, is Zainal." A smug smile suggested that the name was enough to secure admittance.

"Zai*nal?*" The name was certainly familiar to the Drassi guard and produced an instant conference between him and the other door guard.

"I will inform the Junior Pe. It is just inside."

The door was opened just wide enough to admit the guard. It remained slightly ajar in his haste to deliver his news.

The security Emassi tapped his foot impatiently, sighing. Then he stepped closer to the second guard, raising his right hand as if to muffle his words and the guard leaned closer. A slight breeze crossed his nostrils and he gave a reflexive sniff.

"How much longer is the security going to be . . ." the security Emassi began conversationally. Then he caught the suddenly convulsing body of the door guard as he fell to the ground. Instantly two of his detail slipped out of line; one dragged the guard off down the corridor while the second stood in his place at the door just as it was thrown open.

The grotesque body of the Junior Pe came out and went straight to the prisoner. It pulled up the head and stared into the grimed and bloodied face.

"Revive him. When he is conscious, tap on the door and bring him in immediately." The Junior Pe's face shone with an awesome light and it washed its hands vigorously in anticipation of the delightful culmination of a long search. It reentered the room. As soon as the panel had closed, the limp prisoner got to his feet unaided, though his breath hissed from stretching muscles and flesh made extremely sensitive by the nerve whip. His dirt- and blood-grimed hands, restrained by Catteni manacles, were oddly cupped together.

"Long enough?" the Emassi asked softly.

"The rest have been deployed?" the prisoner asked as softly.

"Yes."

"Then let us proceed," and he stepped back and, as the two guards took hold of his elbows again, he nodded once.

The security Emassi tapped and the door swung outward smoothly, giving the detail a good view of the many Eosi within the long narrow chamber where Eosi faced Eosi. A quick glance showed that there were very few vacant seats. If he experienced relief at the numbers within the room, he gave no hint of the elation he felt. Indeed, his expression was studiously impassive.

"BRING HIM TO ME!" And the Mentat Ix, halfway down one side of the rectangular room, rose to his feet and pointed to the floor in front of it.

The security Emassi beckoned to those holding the prisoner to follow him forward while the rest of his squad stopped at intervals on both sides, trotting beyond the Ix to complete a security cordon, formally protecting the Eosi. The Emassi then stepped ahead and turned to gesture dramatically at his prisoner.

"As you have commanded, Mentat Ix, the chosen who chose not to serve is here. His physical records confirm that he is indeed the Zainal you have searched for."

The Mentat Ix looked down at the figure in front of him, head bowed as if in submission. The Ix towered above the captive, and the triumph of this moment seemed to expand the huge Eosian head.

"Look at me, Zainal," the Ix commanded, its voice rich with an anger that had grown moment by moment over the years since the subsumation of Lenvec.

"At you, Lenvec? Or at the Ix?" Zainal said calmly, as he looked up, not at all the submissive and cowed prisoner. "Do you envy me any longer, brother, that it was I who was chosen? For you have succeeded."

Then he raised his hands in what appeared to be supplication. The Ix inhaled at such a reaction just as a puff of mist issued through Zainal's fingers, curling up to the Mentat's nostrils. He turned to the Mentat beside the Ix and repeated the puffing of mist.

"What is this?"

The restraints fell away from Zainal's hands. Then, with an energy surprising for one who was rib-gaunt and had been savagely beaten, the former prisoner began squeezing his bulb at the next Eosi who had jumped to its feet and opened its mouth to protest. The other soldiers of the detail, following Zainal's example, were vigorously making use of their bulbs and the startled Eosi, never expecting to be attacked in this sanctum on the security-protected space station, inhaled the deadly mist in their surprise. Indeed, the long room was soon filled with particles, shining in the brilliant illumination of the room, as they slowly sank to the floor.

The Ix was the first within the room to collapse, its body writhing and arching in agony as the dust it had inadvertently inhaled reached its lungs . . . reached and filled them with lethal allergens. Others were catching at their throats with despairing hands and reacting with the convulsions that the substance produced in Catteni bodies.

"What is happening?" cried a voice from one of the screens at the end of the room. Not all the Eosi were in the long room but the fourteen who had been unable to attend in person had been viewing the proceedings on a visual com link. "Ix! Pe! Co! Se! Answer, one of you."

In the long chamber filled with Catteni bodies skewed in the rigors of death, Zainal strode forward and, hands on his bare hips, answered the impatient query.

"These Eosi are dying. We, Emassi Catteni, have executed them for the twenty-five hundred years of exploitation and enslavement, for the heinous crimes you, and they, have forced us to commit against helpless planets. You had better find a new sanctuary for we, the Catteni," and he brought his fist to his chest, "will hunt down and destroy you as we have destroyed these. There will be nowhere safe for you in this galaxy. Leave it."

He turned his back on the Eosi whose horrified expressions were probably the first honest reactions they had shown in centuries. He heard several gasps at what was an insult to their dignities.

"Are they all dead yet?" Zainal asked, padding down the line of the Eosi who looked more like collapsed bags of shuddering and putrid flesh to the one that had been his brother. The Eosi host that had subsumed Lenvec still retained some of its genuinely youthful, and recognizable, facial appearance. This was fast turning to a viscous mess and to the size of the original host before subsumation. There was so little of Lenvec left even after the short time the Eosi had inhabited it. But enough to have waged a stupid and futile war against the planet which sheltered Zainal.

"I think that does it," the Emassi security officer said, tipping back a helmet to reveal Kamiton, a mightily relieved Kamiton. "I didn't think we'd bring it off. I really didn't."

"I always knew it was the only feasible way of eliminating them all," Nitin said, stepping around a slow-moving rivulet of varicolored fluids.

"We didn't," Tubelin remarked, pointing toward the screens, some already blank.

"Those fourteen will be scrambling to leave. They do not have enough power to regain command," Zainal said. "Now, all we have to do is get out of this level. The sooner the better."

· He moved toward the door—staggered would be more accurate since his emaciation and the nerve whip welts were real, if the wounds were somewhat exaggerated by dramatic additions of blood and excrement. Leaning against the wall, he shook the bulb that had been secreted between his "force" bracelets.

"Who has the stuff?" He looked around, one shoulder resting against the wall.

"I do," and Kasturi came forward, holding out the flask and the little tundish with which he carefully added the lethal dust to Zainal's innocuous-looking device.

"Better do it all round," Kamiton said, "while we're where we can't be observed."

Tubelin shook his head. "Even with nose plugs, the stench is awful. Will the doors keep it out long enough?"

"Call the other guard in," Zainal suggested.

Nitin was nearest and, opening the door enough to see the real guard, beckoned him in. The smell wrinkled the man's nostrils but he was too well trained to show either revulsion or hesitation. He had time to take in the scene of the mass execution. In fact, he caught his breath in astonishment and terror. And that was sufficient to inhale enough of the free dust particles in the air of the long room to ensure his demise.

Quickly, the detail assembled outside again.

"You did it? I can smell you did it," their bogus guard said, touching his nostrils to make sure his nose plugs were in place.

"Anyone passed by?" Zainal asked, and their colleague shook his head, looking relieved.

"Then let's get out of here," Kamiton said, settling his helmet correctly on his brow. He looked about as the security detail formed up and nodded as Zainal resumed his inert posture between his "guards." He had no trouble at all assuming an expression of intense and smugly self-congratulatory pride as he led his detail back the way they had come.

The dissidents were by no means in the clear yet. Anyone with some urgent message for a Mentat could arrive in that corridor. The absence of guards at the door would be the first thing noticed and then, undoubtedly, the presence of an incredible putrefying stench would seep into the corridor. Since this was a space station, there were devices all over that should detect unusual alterations in air circulation.

On the space station, down on the planet and across Catteni-occupied space, other dissidents awaited news that the execution had been successful. There had been enough to secure the most important Eosi installations. Once deprived of orders, many other Catteni would be so totally confused that they would not protest Emassi rulers. They had been trained too well to operate on orders and not on their own initiatives. As Zainal had said, there might not be that many Emassi dissidents but most of them were in critical positions, or could assume them. One of their number ranked high in the security section, and he had deftly changed assignments on the station to include more rebels, as well as preparing himself to take control of the space station if the executions were successful. He could do only so much until he knew the coup achieved its prime objective.

It was Ugred, in the central communications and security section of the station, who could then send the coded message to those waiting to hear, and act upon it. On receipt, those who had waited almost a lifetime would go into action and initiate actions that would forever end Eosian domination.

First, they had to escape the station before loyal Catteni discovered the deaths and, in turn, eliminated the perpetrators. The Emassi in control could do only so much to assist the dissidents. And it would take time for the others to complete their takeover.

THE FIRST SIGNAL WAS THE RETURN OF THE prisoner detail.

"Was the Ix finally satisfied?" a High Emassi fleet officer asked, pausing to watch the prisoner dragged by, leaving a trail of blood.

"The Ix went into spasms again," Kamiton said smugly. He had to swallow against the nervous laughter inside him at the so accurate remark.

"What'll happen to him?" The Emassi nodded down at the prisoner.

Kamiton barked an unpleasant laugh. "You know the games Eosi will play with those who displease them. I am glad I can hand him over," and Kamiton pointed to the floor, "to the cells. He's got until the convocation ends."

With a suitable bow to an Emassi of superior rank, Kamiton curtly gestured for the detail to move forward again, across the main corridor of the space station.

If his glance took in the high-security window of space station control overlooking this space, it was more part of a general survey than a signal. He did settle his helmet more securely on his head as he crossed to the grav shaft that would take his detail and its prisoner to the lower levels.

Reaching the appropriate level, the detail marched along, still dragging its prisoner, down the corridor and to the ship bays that ringed this level of the station, and the security Emassi paid no attention to others going about their duties.

They reached their destination. Kamiton tapped in the security code for the locked room, and he curtly beckoned to the two carrying Zainal to bring him through first. The others hastily filed in. As soon as the panel closed, Zainal was swung up on his feet. Kamiton passed him moist towels to clean off the blood, grime, and also the slime, which was actually an antihistimine cream to protect him from the lethal dust. Kasturi peeled off some of the multiple nerve whip welts—carefully—since the first layer was genuine. Tubelin washed down his legs, while Zainal did his own arms: both used some degree of care for the gouges and slices that were visible were also genuine, if realistically enlarged. Nitin was opening a cabinet and taking out the Drassi security uniform and passed the helmet to Zainal. The erstwhile prisoner quickly inserted into his now clean cheeks the pads, which Sandy Areson had made for his first impersonation. He pulled off the unkempt wig, wincing as the glue stuck to the skin of his forehead a moment, revealing a properly trim Drassi hairstyle underneath. He put his legs through the trousers, his arms through the tunic, stood first on one leg while a boot was pushed on and tied and then on the other for the second boot to be shoved on his foot.

The change had been achieved in seconds. No one would have suspected a delay of any kind as a detail marched out of that antechamber and toward the shuttle on which they had arrived.

"You got a reward?" asked the Emassi in charge of that section of the hangar deck, intercepting their path to the officially marked security shuttle.

"I expect to be honored at the next official ceremony," Kamiton said, swelling his chest. This was quite truthful, as Kamiton's reward was the command of the planet.

"You did well, Emassi."

Kamiton merely nodded as Zainal, posing as an alert Drassi, opened the shuttle door so his officer could enter. The rest of the detail—and the hangar section Emassi didn't think to count or he would have come up with the wrong number for patrol strength—filed in. The hatch slid closed and was locked on the inside and the hangar Drassi waved them off, opening his com link with hangar control to assure the security guards that all was in order for the departure of this shuttle.

KRIS MANAGED TO KEEP GOING THOUGH THE days seemed even longer and the nights were even more dangerous with her longings for him. Until she began to do silly things in her assigned duties, like garbling messages on the com unit. Or weeping over Zane when he had only a scratched knee, not a broken leg, and Sarah had to pinch her sharply to end the incipient hysterics.

Dorothy Dwardie suggested a mild sedative. Even in the daze, which seemed to surround her during the long weeks, she did notice that someone was nearby: Sandy, Sarah, Dorothy, and occasionally Peggy and Marge. The presence of ex-Victims among her watchers afforded her a little private amusement: the carer being cared for. But she hadn't the energy to smile over the irony. Dorothy's presence was soothing, especially after Kris surfaced out of her self-absorption sufficiently to realize that Dorothy was probably suffering, too. Chuck had been seeing a lot of the psychologist but, as Dorothy was somewhat of a private person, Kris wasn't at all sure if the "seeing" went both ways.

"I apologize, Dorothy," she screwed up enough courage to say one afternoon when she was assigned to help Dorothy teach the orphans some basic R's.

"Why? You're doing a very good job, you know."

"Not of handling my emotions."

"Oh?" Dorothy smiled kindly at her. "You're very Human, Kris, and this is a very trying time for you."

"And you, too?"

"Me?"

Kris thought for a moment she had exceeded propriety, but then Dorothy flushed and turned her face away.

"You have the right to be worried about Chuck. I am, too, when I stop being selfish enough to realize that he's in jeopardy as well."

Dorothy looked down at her hands, which picked at a frayed seam in her coverall. "There's nothing been said . . . I mean, I do like his company. In fact, he's a surprising fellow. All that ruggedness, and he's not bad-looking either, though not the sort of man I'd *say* was my type . . ."

Kris managed a wry smile. "Chuck's not what he appears to be."

"No," and Dorothy gave a wistful sigh, "he's not. Yes,

Dick?" And her tone abruptly altered to her professional manner as one of the orphans held out his slate for her to correct.

That ended that exchange of confidence but it was Zane who pulled her out of her depression. It upset him terribly to see Mommy in tears when he asked where Daddy was. So he stopped asking and that made her heart ache even more. When she realized that he had stopped asking, she began to tell him tales about Zainal every evening as she put him to bed. He liked those stories a lot more than the ones she read to him. Relating their first explorations together helped Kris get a grip on herself. It also made the missing man not half as "missing." The discreet observation tapered off and people were nice to her in whatever jobs she was assigned to do. Not too nice, for she would not have tolerated condescension from Janet or Anna Bollinger. Those two must be secretly delighted with her situation: "only what she deserves, carrying on like that with a . . . Catteni male."

So as the days dragged into a week and the weeks to the month, and then days beyond that elapse of time, she became almost inured to his absence and refused to believe that his absence would be permanent. Zainal would survive as he had survived so much: such as the flitter crash he had walked away from the day she first met him. She clung, also, to the rationalization that because they had been so close emotionally as well as physically, she was certain that a lover's prescience would have subconsciously known he had died. She really didn't think she was assigned most frequently to com desk duty in the bridge because she could translate Catteni messages. She decided even Ray Scott had a heart after all. She might even be the first to hear his voice. But there was little enough chatter via the com sat. Amazingly little. But this was as close as she could get to Zainal, wherever he was and whatever he was doing.

She was asked to sit in on all the Council meetings, so she forced herself to listen to what John Beverly could report. Dystopia had been very grateful for the supplies and so had NoName. Beverly had brought back a delegation from each planet, and they had been welcomed. If there were ironic comments from some who envied Botany its advantages, that was the luck of the draw. Of course, they wanted to know every detail about the Farmers, saw their machinery in action on the big continent, saw what had been contrived of the parts, and envied the Botanists their Bubble which awed them, one and all.

None of them spoke Catteni or even Barevi, and some of those on NoName eyed the Deski and Rugarians with suspicion. (John said very little in those meetings about the inhabitants of Dorado—at least until the KDM took the visitors back with more supplies and equipment, which Botany felt it could spare.) When Laughrey and his crew set off to return the visitors to their respective planets, he told the Council that Dorado was off his list. He had been proudly told how all the ET's had been killed, generally as soon as possible after they had been dropped.

"Seems that the 'aliens' had been killed because they were 'different' and not mentioned as God's creatures anywhere in the Bible," John said. "And I won't say I got the courtesies my rank can expect. In fact, they ignored me whenever they could, but my crew wouldn't let 'em, thank God."

"Let's cancel them out of consideration then, shall we?" Jim Rastancil said and tore up the sheet headed DORADO. Others did the same and Kris felt a small twinge of satisfaction break through the numbness that she carried around with her.

She had to, in her capacity as Emassi in charge of the refugees, visit them in their valley. Mostly she listened to complaints about their lack of amenities, the need for additional clothing since none had brought sufficient with them. She supplied them with Catteni ship suits, which appalled Milista. She also supplied them with needles and thread as most of the women, and certainly the children, would swim in the standardized garment. Sarah made her include some lengths of fabric since the last "shopping" trip had brought back great rolls and bales found in a warehouse. Sarah had included a child's sewing book with sufficient illustrations to give even the Catteni women useful instructions.

Sandy Areson had done an inventory on supplies in the mess hall and came back, looking both exasperated and amused.

"They've been living off the ration bars of which there are none left." Sandy shook her head. "As useless a bunch as I've ever seen."

"I could cook for them," Bart said who'd volunteered to come along on this "light duty."

All three women pounced on him.

"No way, José!" Emassi Khriss said. "But who knows enough Catteni to teach them how to cook? And it has to be female. I'm not going to let them know that Human males *can* and *do* cook."

"Zainal makes a mean grilled rocksquat," Sarah said and then flushed, having inadvertently reminded Kris. "Sorry, luv."

"I wish you would all stop pussyfooting around the subject of . . . Zainal. But we can't return starved women."

"Ha! None of them are starved, and the kids at least are playing," Sandy said.

"Only the younger ones," Kris pointed out.

"Maybe we should send the older ones down to keep Bazil and Peran company in the Maasai camp," Bart suggested.

Kris considered that. She had even considered bringing the boys up to the valley. But . . . she didn't have that authority yet . . . and hoped she really wouldn't have to deal with that pair. Well, Chuck would be handling them as "males"—if Chuck got back. She found her hand halfway to her belly and drew it back. No sense in giving anyone any more to talk about.

"What about making Janet teach 'em?" Bart said, his eyes twinkling. "It'd be her Christian duty."

Kris burst out laughing and almost went into the weeps because she'd let go of the rigid command she'd been exercising on herself. Sniffing and wiping at her filled eyes, she plastered the grin on her face after the initial and genuine outburst of laughter. The others looked so pleased with her reaction.

"Now that was plain mean of you, Bart Tomi," she said. "I just wish I had the nerve to order it."

"I think," and Sandy cocked her head at Kris, "you could just about order Ray Scott to jump rope with those kids and he'd do it."

"Beth Isbell cooks—does a lot of the pastry in the hall, at least—and she's a Catteni speaker," Sarah said. "Let's check in and see if she'd take the duty on. I think we'd better leave Bart and a couple of other men here to be sure she's safe."

"Why should we fuss over them, if they're so stupid they even let the fire go out," Raisha asked, pointing to the chimney. She'd come aft from the bridge with Joe Marley to find out how long they'd be on the ground.

"Zainal," and Kris didn't hesitate on his name, "promised to keep them safe and that means keeping them fed, too, so they don't have a real complaint to lodge against our hospitality. And clothed. Some of us had to learn to do basic things when we got here. I'll go check in and ask."

"None of us were lords, or ladies, of all we surveyed either," Raisha said, and then sighed. "But you're right.

Why should we fault them for ignorance when all of us are ignorant of something or other that we've never had to do before."

Sally Stoffer agreed to accompany Beth who was a good friend. Sally liked to sew, was teaching some of the older orphans, and her Catteni was excellent. Lenny Doyle, Dowdall, Bart, three ex-soldiers from the last drop, and Patti Sue returned and set up tents for themselves and the three female instructors.

And that minor hiccup was smoothed over. Not that the Catteni women were pleased to be forced to do slave work. The three soldiers instructed the older boys on how to catch fish from the stream. They'd been sitting around doing nothing since they were old enough to have started some sort of training for their life's work. They were happy enough to form a small detail and marched up and down. Their mothers also seemed happier to have them occupied.

"I don't say I'd ever want to eat what they cook," Beth said when they returned, "but at least they can now build a fire, open a can or unscrew a jar, make what they call 'bread,' fry fresh fish which they do like, by the way. One of them will make a good seamstress. At least she figured out how to take in the ship suits. The rest were happy enough to wear something new even if they did have to learn how to sew up the edges to keep the lengths from fraying. Who would have suspected that Catteni women would wear sarongs?"

"Makes most of them look like boxes," Sally said, grinning. "Even the ship suits have more shape."

"The Catteni women sure don't," Lenny remarked with a wry grin.

THE SHUTTLE REACHED CATTEN'S ATMOSPHERE and dropped speed quickly, homing in on the main government buildings. It hovered over the roof, though a surveillance guard ship instantly appeared to inspect it, recognized the security markings on the shuttle, and retired without questioning its presence.

"There is something to be said for protocol," Kamiton said with a grin. He was now attired in a fresh Emassi uniform, smartened with tabs of the highest rank available to Emassi. "Have Tiboud and Valicon reported in yet?"

"Just got their signals now," Tubelin said from the com desk. "They're in position."

"Tell them to proceed," Kamiton said coolly, knowing that several more unsuspecting Catteni who were dedicated to their Eosian masters would shortly be dead. He turned to the others, checking to see that his former security detail were now all clad in uniforms similar to his. It amused him that all members of the prisoner detail had been rewarded with major steps in rank. "We all know how to proceed." He checked the nose plugs once more and then indicated to Zainal, in the pilot's position, to land.

He gestured for the others to precede him before he turned once more to the pilot.

"Good luck, Zainal. I'll keep you informed."

"You had better. I need to return your families. They will undoubtedly tell you how mistreated they were on Botany."

"Of that I have little doubt for they have been accustomed to luxuries not available on your home planet."

Zainal answered Kamiton's rueful smile with one of his own.

"Go finish the business, Kam."

Kamiton stiffened then and gave Zainal not only a salute but also the low bow that indicated great respect. He jumped off the ramp and Zainal shut the hatch.

Zainal swung the shuttle away then and flicked on the

com unit to wide range so he could hear what was going on . . . and know when the shock hit the sleeping planet.

Nitin might be a pessimist but he was also a realist and they would be following his plan of reconstructing their world, and the worlds the Eosi had once dominated.

They had not been able to get a dissident into a prestigious position on Earth, but he rather thought that once the news was out, the Terrans would double their efforts to regain control of their own planet. Nor were there sufficient colleagues on the various fleet elements to take control of the AA's or some of the great H-class, but Catteni were so accustomed to being told what to do and how, that Kamiton's forceful manner, the backing they did have, should eventually result in capitulation. Surely no Catteni had *enjoyed* the Eosian domination even if many, singly or in family groupings, had benefited by their loyalty to entities they had never before attempted to supplant.

Often enough during Zainal's flight to the main security landing field did he have to shield his eyes from the spotlights of other guardian vessels. But the purloined ship did have the right markings and permission to be aloft in night hours. Zainal put the vehicle down at the edge of the force-field-protected landing area.

He rose, stiffly, hissing against twinges from the nerve whip. That had been a necessary ordeal, as had his starvation on the way to Catteni, but he had to *look* the part and whole-skinned and fat would not have been credible. His knees hurt from all the dragging but at least that posture had allowed him to keep his head down and his eyes closed as he faked unconsciousness.

Now, all he had to do was find Baby, which should now bear the security markings of yet another authorized vehicle. He had to stride out purposefully and each heel jarred the various tormented parts of his body, from the scratches to the long welts of the nerve whip. Kasturi had not struck as hard as he might have done to a real offender but hard enough. Whippings endured from his father had been lighter. His stomach ached with hunger and, by the time he passed the first rank of unlit ships on the pavement, his mouth and throat were parched. He took time to drink from the flask he had brought with him from the ship, first swirling the water about his mouth and letting it trickle down his throat. Then he took the stimulant from his pocket and, with a big swallow of water, let that go to work in his empty belly. He'd have food soon enough. Fourth rank east, Chuck had said, second ship. Chuck had managed that discreet parking but it was a long way from first rank west.

He walked inward now, shielded from casual notice from the parked vehicles, made it past a wide turning circle and on toward the distant fence and fourth rank. He had to lean against the side of the scout to catch his breath. At least there was a light on inside it to reassure him that this was right. He tapped out the code on the door to alert them to his arrival.

The hatch opened immediately.

"Keep back, dammit, Bert," Chuck said and the Australian vanished from the brightly lit hatch. Chuck was down the steps, instantly supporting the sagging body, his eyes wide and then closing in relief as Zainal's nod as well as his presence told Chuck that, so far, all had gone smoothly.

"We've got to get out of here, and fast," Zainal said.

"Yeah," Chuck said, his voice unsteady with relief as he helped Zainal up the short flight to the hatch, "it ain't over 'til the fat lady sings."

"What fat lady?" Zainal asked, realizing that the sergeant had answered him in English as he made his way forward. "Why a fat lady?"

"Explain later." Chuck closed the hatch with a clank.

"You got 'em? All of 'em?" Chuck persisted with his questions as Zainal made a slow way to the pilot's compartment. Bert was now in the other chair, having let Chuck help Zainal.

They'd had the harder job, Zainal knew, waiting without being able to use the com unit for fear the position of the scout ship might be discovered.

"We got all but the fourteen who were not present," Zainal said, noting that a course had already been laid in, preparatory to his arrival. He nodded approval at Bert, who was completing the last of the pre-flight checks. "They are unlikely to remain where they are. They're too scattered to unite. In any event, once the news gets out, they may decide to leave the galaxy as we suggested. Coded messages should have gone out from the space station to our other colleagues who are waiting for our signal. Kamiton got to the center before the execution could be broadcast . . ." He shrugged and grimaced at such an unwary and painful action. "If it has. Or Ugred has managed to give us more time by deferring an announcement. Otherwise we couldn't have landed at the building. But we were able to. Kamiton gave the word and those who could not be trusted have been eliminated by now. But let's get out of here. Just in case."

"Too right," Bert Put said. "Strapped in, Chuck?"

"Only after Zay gets something into his belly," Chuck said, thrusting a ration bar over Zainal's shoulder.

"I need that," Zainal said and tore off the wrapping, taking a huge bite. "Clear us from the field, will you, Chuck?"

And the sergeant leaned across to the com board. They had to wait for a reply.

"They're all bored," Chuck said while Zainal impassively chewed.

Bert was chewing, too, but on his lip as they waited until the line was opened.

"Schkelk," Chuck said in his hoarse Catteni voice, "Emassi has called. I go. Clearance?"

"Given," was the bored response and the line went dead.

The ship lifted carefully out of the crowded parking area and turned away from the city.

Having finished his slowly consumed meal, Zainal opened the com link, pausing at the various channels to check on the tone of exchanged messages. They were, in fact, in space and heading obliquely away from the vicinity of the space station before the first report was aired.

"This is the Supreme Emassi Kamiton, informing you of a change of government on Catten and the execution of eighty-six Mentats and Juniors on the space station which is now under my control. High Emassi Ugred is now commander of the space station . . ."

"Supreme Emassi?" Chuck asked, wide-eyed and grinning.

"That is the title he picked."

"What'd Nitin get?"

"Oh, he's speaker for Parliament . . ."

"Speaker?" Bert said in astonishment.

"You guys don't have a parliament," Chuck protested.

"We will soon enough."

"You learned a lot we didn't know about on Botany, didn't you?" Chuck replied but his tone was admiring. "Uh-oh, look! Bogies at three o'clock and coming in awful fast. Can't we pile on some speed? We might be able to miss 'em."

KRIS WAS ON COM DUTY: SHE HAD REQUESTED the assignment and, except for those weekly visits to the closed valley and the Catteni guests, that had been her duty. Now she didn't even answer Catteni complaints but impassively saw that supplies were unloaded near enough to be easily carried to the mess hall for storage.

So, she just happened to have the duty in Scott's office that evening when Ray Scott and Jim Rastancil rushed in.

"What's going on up there, Kris?"

"Up where?"

"Up near the Bubble."

Kris gave her head a little shake, reset the earpiece. "Nothing. Nothing that I can hear since all those coded messages stopped shooting back and forth."

"Well, there's something coming down. Gino says there's some sort of shooting stars. And there aren't any of them in this sector of space, especially not with the Bubble . . ."

Ray stopped mid-sentence and rushed outside, Rastancil right behind him.

Kris didn't know whether to stay on duty or join their exodus to see what had made Ray and Jim move that fast. She heard startled cries, some panicky, others, loud and incoherent cheers. Her curiosity roused her from apathy. She abandoned duty and joined the others outside the hangar on the landing field. It wasn't full dark, but the bursts of flame or brilliant light were obvious to the naked eye. The shower—of whatever it was that Gino now said was burning up in upper atmosphere—didn't last very long even with several tiny late flashes. What was obvious was that the Bubble was gone. The sky above them was as clear as it had been before the Bubble had been woven into place. One of the moons was even visible, the one on which the Catteni had tried to build a base. Kris gulped, frozen to the spot. Unable to grasp the significance. There hadn't been any more bombardments. Those had ended just before the surreptitious departure of Baby and the KDL. She strained her eyes, trying to locate any glitter that would be their com sat or even the roving spy satellite the Catteni had placed in the thirty-hour orbit.

Why had the Bubble come down? Were the Farmers

about to visit them? But surely they didn't need to re-move the Bubble to get in. Or did they?

Ray gave her a little shake. "Back to your post, Kris. Tell us what you can hear?"

"But there's nothing up there. The Bubble's down. How could the Eosi dissolve it . . ."

Now Ray gave her a shove toward the hangar. "Tell us what you can hear. We need to know if the com sat's still operating."

Kris didn't ask how she could tell from just listening to static. Or maybe that, in itself, was proof the com sat was still operating? But it had been connected to the Eosi array that had been sheered off their ship in its attempt to exit. Surely, if what they'd seen burning up in the atmosphere were the bits and pieces dropping now that the Bubble no longer held them in place, everything would come down. No, no, that wasn't quite right. Pete Snyder had told them that the com sat was independent, with vanes trapping solar power so that it functioned all by it-self. But, what about what it had been attached to? She had this vivid image of an umbrella with a crooked han-dle, the rain shield pointing downward and the crooked handle pointing out toward empty space.

Ray now hauled her with him back to the office and then took up the earpiece himself, frowning as he lis-tened. Jim Rastancil, Gino Marrucci, and the others who had been in the hangar office stood about, anxiously waiting for his report.

"All I get is static," Ray said, handing the earpiece to Kris who put it on and sat down, listening to the same sort of static, which might be very faint messages. "So it is still up and functioning. Nevertheless, Gino, get a skeleton crew and the KDL up to check."

"With the Bubble gone?" And Gino's normally swarthy skin paled.

"Yes, damn it. To see if it's gone. We've got to know

what action to take if it is. That is, unless the Farmers vouchsafe to give us some indication that we don't need it anymore."

Kris held up her hand. "I'm getting something . . ."

"Look!" And Jim was pointing to the bridge screen, which showed the moon that was coming up, and a small sparkle that couldn't be debris since it moved with astonishing speed on a steady, inward-bound direction.

"Oh, my God," and Ray's voice was an awed whisper. "Have they been watching all along?"

"Does it mean that Zainal succeeded?" Jim Rastancil asked.

For the first time in her life, Kris fainted.

SHE CAME TO, LYING ON THE COT IN RAY'S spartan accommodation at the hangar, with a folded towel on her forehead. She could hear male voices beyond the open door. Carefully, hoping the attack of vertigo had passed, she sat up, holding the towel in place as it felt good on her forehead, and swung her legs over the side of the cot. However did Ray get a decent night's sleep on this thing? Then memory flooded back, and she whimpered.

An anxious Ray Scott was instantly beside her. "Sorry, Kris."

That was when they both felt the almost electrical tingle that they had experienced before.

"We need more than *that*," Ray shouted, raising a fist above his head in challenge.

But that was all they got, and everyone they checked with over the next half hour confirmed the sensation. The Council called a meeting of its main members in the hangar as soon as they could get there. Fortunately a good deal of Retreat's population was asleep and might even have been oblivious to the mild shock. Others called in, having seen what they thought were "shooting stars."

Blandly, Gino had agreed that that's what they were. Few realized that the Bubble was gone, and Ray thought a general announcement could wait until the Council could figure out what to do.

Dorothy Dwardie took the chair next to Kris at the end of the table. The psychologist had been studying notes on her day's clinical sessions with some of the more unresponsive orphans when she'd felt the tingle. Unusual enough a sensation to make her want to find out if anyone else had experienced this phenomenon. She wasn't far from the infirmary so she opened a com link to the duty officer at the infirmary who had just been told to inform Leon Dane of a special meeting at the hangar. Dr. Dwardie ought to go, too. She was Council, wasn't she? And, yes, she'd felt the tingle, too. It had happened once before that she knew of. Then she excused herself to answer another message. No sooner had Dorothy closed the link than she was buzzed, and hurriedly informed that she was needed at the hangar.

Walking down from her cabin, it took Dorothy a few hundred yards to realize that she could see the stars. Then the moon came shining through a gap in the lodge-pole trees. She ran the rest of the way to the hangar. She arrived breathless and took the first available seat, which was beside Kris.

"The Bubble's down?" she murmured, and Kris nodded without looking directly at Dorothy.

Then everyone heard the unmistakable sound of a ship taking off, and the brilliance of the propulsion units in the darkness of the landing field made them cover their eyes.

"Who's going where?" Dorothy softly asked, trying to squelch a feeling of anxiety.

"Checking on the com sat. Everything else up there came down in a shower," Kris said.

"I felt the oddest tingle, like an electric current running through me," Dorothy added.

"The Farmers do that now and then. Counting noses," Kris replied.

"The Farmers? Have we had a message from them after all?" She leaned toward Kris, having just realized that Kris sounded very subdued. "You look awfully pale." She paused a moment, blinked as she came to a logical conclusion. "How would the Farmers know we don't need the Bubble anymore? If that is the case, then your Zainal succeeded?"

Just then Ray Scott's characteristic calm deserted him, and he banged his fist on the table.

"How the hell can we construe a reassuring message from one goddamned short tingle!" he said in a loud, frustrated voice to Judge Iri Bempechat beside him. "Are they so goddamned busy monitoring the rest of the universe that we don't qualify for an explanation?"

Judge Iri Bempechat raised a gentling hand. "The message, I would think, is clear. We no longer require the protection of the Bubble. They've done a planet-wide search and counted noses again. It is my opinion that we should be grateful for what they have done, instead of—if I may be allowed to use the vulgar expression—bitching about it."

"The Judge is right." And Kris rose to her feet, having heard all the wrangling and speculation she could stand. Not even the calm Dorothy had been oozing in her direction had helped. "And it took the Bubble away because Zainal and the others succeeded in . . . doing whatever they planned to the Eosi."

"JUST . . ." Ray raised his voice above the immediate babble of comment, "in case, I want the crews of all the other ships standing by and ready."

"Why?" Dorothy asked, almost amused. Obviously

that was what an ex-admiral immediately thought of as appropriate. "There're too many of us now to be evacuated and where would we go?"

"Earth, of course," Geoffrey Ainger said, disgusted with her obtuseness.

"I dropped. I stay," Kris said and walked out of the meeting.

Chapter Twelve

AFTER THAT SCARE WITH THE THREE bogies looking as if they were coming straight at them, the ships had not so much as hailed the scout, so they had proceeded on their return to the asteroid belt.

"I don't see why we need to pick up Baby now," Chuck said since that would lengthen the journey home.

Bert nudged him in the small of his back and held up one finger, making a grimace, and two, altering his expression of a beatific smile. Then he gestured to his whole body and winced.

Chuck Mitford had never considered himself slow in comprehension but the fright of that squadron bearing down on them—and then passing by, close but no cigar—made him interested in getting back to Botany as fast as possible. So Zainal wanted Baby back. Hell, why would Kamiton want this ship returned? He had a massive navy to pick from. But Bert's other point—that Zainal wanted to be as fully recovered as possible from his "disguise"—made more sense. Although Chuck had been there when the first layer of the "disguise" was laid on, so to speak, he had been shocked when he'd seen Zainal in the cabin light.

They hadn't dared bring any Botany foods on Kamiton's vessel but there were some on board Baby. Chuck had some fresh goods in the galley, having enjoyed the daily haggle with the scruffy providers who brought their carts and baskets around to the occupied vehicles. A lot wasn't very fresh, probably rejected from the main markets in the city, but it was better than what was served in the mess where Chuck was permitted to eat as a Drassi crewman. Years of eating marine chow had inured him to practically anything remotely edible. Some of the messes served to the crewmen were definitely remotely edible. But he pretended the same lip-smacking enjoyment the others did, even if he didn't eat as many servings as the others did. He ate more slowly, though, so as they slopped food into their mouths, he seemed to be keeping pace with them.

He made a stew of the vegetables, then whipped it into submission as a puree which Zainal's abused intestines should be able to manage. He served the meal in small portions and often.

Then they encountered a squadron of mining vessels, and Bert had to scramble for his hiding place as the larger ship informed them that they were sending over a pinnace.

"We could outrun them," Chuck said, thinking that their luck must have run out. The bogies hadn't bothered them but mining ships could only be searching for the precious metals that had been found by Emassi Venlik. There were times when one could get too clever by half, Chuck thought.

"No. They have missile launchers and tractor beams. We're a sitting duck for the one and too close to avoid the other," Zainal said and opened a line to the DMV, the leading ship, jovially awaiting the arrival of the pinnace and any news they might have.

The news was, indeed, that the Eosi had all been executed and every captain was free to do what he wished from now on.

Captain Kabas was half drunk when he arrived, and he and his pilot, Wenger, who was completely sober, brought the same nauseating stuff which Chuck remembered all too well from his stay at the boondock field they'd first landed on at Catten.

It was in character for Zainal to demand all the details.

If some of them didn't quite jibe with the facts as both Chuck and Zainal knew them, that was all to the good. They did hear, which was excellent news and their cheers were genuine, that most of the High Emassi who had not been part of the coup now backed the Supreme Emassi Kamiton to the last male of the line.

When finally the conversation got around to Zainal's presence in this area, he replied that he had been exploring in a distant quadrant, had seen the asteroid belt, and wondered if he should report it when he got back. Some of the bigger rocks looked as if they might contain useful ores.

"Well, now," Captain Kabas said, "you can leave that to us. We're all our own masters now, you know. I wouldn't stop you going your own way."

"Good of you." Zainal turned to Chuck in a semi-confidential air. "We saw a place we'd rather like to be masters of, come to that."

He lifted his mug, its opacity hiding the fact that Zainal's apparently hearty use of the contents had been faked, in a toast. "May you find what you deserve, captain," he said.

The captain who had continued to sip while he gave details of the momentous news had now gone through most of a new bottle. He laughed raucously at Zainal's toast and tipped back the last of his current glass. Gave a huge burp and, bloodshot yellow eyes turning up into his head, slumped slowly over the table.

"Help Wenger get him into the pinnace, Drassi," Zainal said, slurring his words as if he had had more than enough, too. He waved them to remove the unconscious man.

"Were I you," the pilot said, "I'd get out of this area as fast as you can fly this thing. Captain ain't the only one is worried about you being nosing around this belt."

"Agreed," Chuck said as he carried the captain's feet and helped the pilot arrange him in a seat.

When he returned, Zainal was already in the pilot's chair. "Fasten up, Chuck, we're making all due speed out of here."

"The pilot suggested that, too."

WHEN THEY FELT THEY HAD PUT ENOUGH distance between them, Zainal did insist on turning back, to collect Baby, despite Bert taking Chuck's part in trying to dissuade him.

They used a huge rock to hide their return, but their encounter with the miners had also skewed them far from the course that would bring them to the hollow asteroid. There had been a specific way in and through the belt to reach their destination. So they were forced to prowl counter to the spin of the belt until, just about the time they would have been in danger of being spotted by the miners, they found it.

Chuck insisted on remaining with Zainal.

"You need feeding. I'm not going to answer to Kris if you return like a goddamned scarecrow."

"Scarecrow?"

Chuck explained. "Maybe even, you'll get a chance now to see one on Earth. Boy, while I was glad to be in the thick of it on Botany, I wouldn't mind seeing a scarecrow again, or having a rock in the porch hammock. If it's still there."

Piloting Baby, Bert kept on their port side, as escort, so that when Chuck noticed Zainal was having trouble keeping awake, he suggested putting on the auto-pilot and having something to eat. In the spicy rocksquat stew he'd heated up, he mixed into Zainal's plate a few dollops of a sedative that Leon had included in the first-aid supplies as a painkiller.

It did take some maneuvering to hoist the inert Catten from behind the table and into his bunk. Chuck took off the boots, loosened the belt, and covered the snoring man. He caught himself wondering if Zainal always snored and how Kris . . . he censored the rest of that and went forward to inform Bert what he'd done.

"Good idea, sarge, even if he will give you hell when he wakes. Okay, now here's how I pilot both ships," Bert said and gave Chuck detailed instructions. "We've some days to go on this leg so let's arrange a schedule for each of us to get some shut-eye. I know Zainal was going to do one with me. We're unlikely to run into another thing in this zone. Nothing but planet-less primaries. No good to anyone."

"I got enough sleep at the field," Chuck said. "I'll take first watch for us both. Okay?"

"Right."

And that is how they managed during the twenty-two hours Zainal remained asleep.

He was mad as hell at Chuck for dosing him but he calmed down when he realized that his energy had improved, as had his appetite. And that each of the pilots had also had some sleep.

Chuck's much vaunted six-hour requirement had him up and ready to take over from Zainal who tried, but not too hard, to continue for a full eight hours. Bert was asleep in Kamiton's ship but Chuck insisted he could handle anything, and besides, he'd wake Zainal if there were any alarms.

THE FIRST THAT THE COLONISTS AT RETREAT knew of the success of the mission was when a cruiser of the Catteni navy contacted them via the com sat, requesting permission to land on Botany.

"RAY!" Matt Su roared and grinned at the scowl on the ex-admiral's face as Scott careened into the bridge room. "We got a cruiser of the Catteni navy asking permission to land."

Ray ran to com desk. "Identify," he snapped in Catteni."

"Can't you clear up the visual, Ray?" asked Matt.

"Tikso," Ray ordered.

"We . . . kum . . . frum . . . Catten. Su-preme Emassi Kamiton. We . . . coleckt Catteni feee-males and male young."

Ray and Matt exchanged startled glances. A Catten was addressing them in English . . . or trying to.

The visual flowed clearly on the screen. "This is High Emassi Captain Tiboud," and there was relief in the Catten's voice for being able to speak in his own language. The man beside him had a sheet from which he had obviously been reading phonetic English. "All Eosi dead or gone. Catteni now own Catten . . . and all previously owned planets and installations . . ."

"He's making sure we got that . . ." Matt muttered sotto voce.

"With the exception of the Human planet, Earth and, of course, the impregnable Botany. Earth is gratefully returned to its rightful owners and inhabitants in view of the help given by Humans to end Eosi domination. Botany's extraordinary defense against the might of the

Eosian navy has been admired—if silently—by many. We Catteni honor bravery."

"Damned white of them," Matt added sotto voice, avoiding the kick that Ray directed at his shins to shut him up.

"That is very good news, captain," Ray said with great poise and solemnity. "Has my home world learned of its freedom from Eosi domination?"

"The news was relayed by Supreme Emassi in person over a special com link." Tiboud bowed respectfully. "Good news to you, I am certain."

"Indeed it is, and thank you for relaying the message."

"Is it possible to have speech with the Excellent Emassi Zainal?"

"He's not here," Ray said, and his elation at the news of Earth's liberation evaporated. Matt looked shocked.

"Not there?" Then the short Drassi who had read the English message spoke a quick word into his superior's ear. "Ah, the Excellent Emassi Zainal was aboard the scout which does not have the speed this vessel has. He will doubtless arrive very soon now."

"Then he . . . he is alive and well?"

"That is our understanding," Tiboud said, again with a respectful bow. "We . . . all Catteni . . . owe our freedom to the Excellent Emassi Zainal."

"We here on Botany owe him as much," Ray said, returning the bow. Then added, out of the side of his mouth, "For God's sake, go tell Kris Zainal's alive while I deal with this."

Matt nodded once, eyes round in his face, and departed at speed. Ray heard him shouting at someone in the hangar and then heard the tools dropping and the cheering as the good news was absorbed.

"We have the honor to collect the mates and offspring

of those to whom you gave sanctuary," the High Emassi Captain continued.

There were shouts at the door now, which Ray turned to silence. This planet was run properly and wild demands for details would have to wait until he'd finished the interview with the incoming ship.

"Cool it, guys, I'm doing the diplomatic but tell the Council to get their asses down here on the double." He turned back to the screen. "Do you need the coordinates of the landing field?"

"They would be welcome. We understand that the continent on which the original shipments were made is no longer available."

"That is correct," Ray replied with a wry twist to his lips and then supplied the landing field's coordinates. The appropriate protocols were being scrupulously observed.

"Received," the captain said with another bow, "and course laid in. We anticipate touchdown in two of your local hours."

The contact was broken. Ray felt the need to seat himself at the desk, wondering why success always weakened you whereas imminent defeat caused you to stiffen in protest. So Zainal's crazy plan had worked, whatever it had been. And Kamiton had snatched away the leadership. Well, perhaps Zainal hadn't wanted it. Not with a woman like Kris to come home to. But maybe he'd take her back to Catten. No, not with that sort of gravity to combat on a daily basis. Mitford had mentioned how she had coped, but only just. Mitford hadn't been too happy with the problem but marines could handle anything.

Just where in the new power structure, Ray Scott wondered, did an Excellent Emassi fit, if there was now a Supreme Emassi? He wondered what plums had gone to Kasturi, Nitin, and Tubelin. As Catteni went, they'd been pretty straight guys.

He had only those few moments before people once

again plagued him for details. He gave them what he knew and warned them of the impending arrival of a "friendly." Beverly and Judge Iri arrived together, Rastancil close behind them, and the four had decided that first there would have to be some sort of honor guard. Now that Botany was liberated, it had the right to its own protocols.

"Why didn't you just tell them where those bitches were and just get them away from here?" Beverly said, his brows knitting with displeasure. "When I think what a rough time they've given Kris . . . ah, Kris," for she was standing in the doorway, looking white as a sheet. Behind her, Matt was making all kinds of incomprehensible gestures at him. Warnings, Ray realized, and noticed that Kris was dressed in her Emassi uniform. But the look on her face . . . He strode over to her.

"He's all right, Kris. He survived. He's on his way back. The cruiser that's going to land here was just faster and came on a direct line . . ."

Her hands, when he took them, were freezing.

"Kris, he's all right," he repeated and, without thinking what he was doing, he embraced her, patting her shoulders and stroking her hair as she burst into tears. Ordinarily tears were enough to drive Ray Scott as far away as he could take himself, but this was Kris. The long and difficult wait was over. "He did it, Kris. He did it and Earth is free. Botany, too." He held her off. "Do you understand? Earth is ours again as well as Botany."

"Botany, too?" She'd taken a deep breath as he started to cajole her.

"Botany, too. And they asked . . . *asked*. . . for permission to land, which is damned well the first time they've done that." He wondered if Zainal had traded rank in the new government for the freedom of the human colonized planets.

"That's a change," she replied with a crooked smile. And burying her face in her hands started to weep again.

"Come, Kris, my dear." Dorothy Dwardie took her off to one side, giving Ray Scott the dirtiest look he had received since he got his junior grade bars.

SO THERE WAS TIME TO PLAN A PROPER CERE-mony when the cruiser landed. Drums, pipes, and two bugles were assembled, and the Council put on their best clothes since they now had some from the same shipment of purloined materials that had gone to clothe the Catteni exiles. Kris decided to keep on her Catteni uniform since she would officially hand over that duty to Captain Tiboud. And relieved to do so.

The cruiser was so new that there was not so much as meteor gashes on its side, and it bore a much different design on its prow than vessels had displayed under Eosi management.

Not very artistic, Kris thought, but probably the Eosi hadn't encouraged the arts and at least the runes used were in different, bold colors. She just ached to be able to ask Zainal what they meant.

When the crew, Captain Tiboud leading the formation, drew up in front of the Botany deputation, Ray embarrassed her somewhat by introducing her first. High Emassi Captain Tiboud startled her when he bowed with unexpectedly deep respect to the female introduced as Zainal's life companion.

"Excellent Lady Emassi," Captain Tiboud said, his eyes keenly inspecting her. Then, with an unexpected show of Catten amusement, he pointed to her shoulder tabs. "These are incorrect." He snapped his fingers, rattled a command to the aide who jumped to his side and then bounded off to the cruiser, almost hitting the top of the hatch he had so misjudged his stride. "Zainal is on his way here or so the Supreme Kamiton himself told me when he dispatched his fastest ship to retrieve all those you were good enough to protect."

Kris couldn't stifle her reaction but hoped Tiboud would not see that relief was the main one. "We secluded them in the safest place on Botany but I fear that the accommodations could not meet what they are used to."

The aide was back, bowing as he opened and presented a large box with many pairs of fancy rank tabs. But the pair he selected was the most lavish in terms of the use of platinum, gold, and a fine dazzling diamond.

"I was ordered by the Supreme Emassi as well as High Emassis Nitin, Kasturi, and Tubelin that you, Kris Buyorzen (which was near enough for a Catteni trying to enunciate a Scandinavian name) be the first to receive the honors which I have brought."

With a quizzical look for permission, he stepped forward and made a quick job of replacing her shoulder tabs. The new ones sparkled with the diamonds that capped the platinum half-spheres. She saluted, feeling that was an acceptable gesture. He bowed very low and she followed suit though did not bow as low. After all, she figured, an Excellent was higher in rank than a High Emassi.

Then he stepped to Ray and frowned slightly as he realized that Ray was not wearing a uniform-type tunic on which it would be easy to affix the rank tabs. But Ray held up one hand before the Captain could start any presentation speech.

"One small matter, Captain Tiboud," Ray said, clearing his throat. "You mentioned that Earth has been returned to its rightful owners and governments and that Botany has independence. There are three other Human settled worlds that we know of. What disposition has been made of them?"

High Emassi Captain Tiboud managed an expression of amused understanding.

"Your altruism is only to be expected of a Human, Ray Scott. It is not in my authority to deal with that issue but, since so much is owed to Humans in general, I would anticipate a similar courtesy of independence may well be granted those three."

"Thank you," Ray said, barely heard above the cheers and shouts and whistles from the crowd of settlers.

"You are welcome. But to the matter at hand, Admiral Scott, for your assistance to the Supreme and High Emassi in their bid to overthrow Eosian domination, please accept these and the honorary title of Highest Emassi." The Captain then handed Ray a splendid set of tabs, crowned by rubies that flashed in the sun.

The rest of the presentations went all the way from High Emassi Leon Dane for saving Kamiton's life down to Emassis Sally Stoffers and Beth Isbell for their translations and to Emassis Dick Aarens and Peter Snyder for jury-rigging the com sat on the wreckage of the Catteni array.

By then, everyone welcomed the drinks and other refreshments, which the cooks had managed to make and serve on the two hours' notice.

"They don't seem in a very great hurry to get those bitches and leave, do they?" John Beverly said in Kris' ear.

"Do I have to do the bloody honors there, too?" she asked.

Beverly grinned down at her. "Oh, I think you should, Excellent Lady Emassi. Duty before pleasure." Then his grin faded, and he gripped her shoulder firmly, his expression reassuring. "If everyone says Zainal lived through it and even got promoted, he'll be here soon now."

"How soon is soon? Damn it."

KRIS WAS NOT GIVEN AN OPTION, EXCEPT THAT she was escorted on board the cruiser with Leon Dane, Ninety, Ray Scott, Dorothy, and Judge Iri Bempechat who would make the journey with her. Raisha followed in the KDL, using a quickly assembled skeleton crew to take the Botanists back to Retreat. Captain Tiboud had requested permission to launch on his return flight once he had the refugees safely aboard.

"I trust you have suitable accommodations for the Emassi ladies," Kris couldn't resist asking.

The Captain's yellow eyes glittered. "They will be made comfortable, I assure you. They will find their new quarters on Catten all, or even more than, their fondest dreams."

"Have you a mate, Captain Tiboud?"

"I have," and there was that in his eyes that suggested to Kris that perhaps all Catteni women were like those he was required to restore to their men.

They, especially Sibbo and Milista, did not wish to be collected, even after repeated assurances, and handwritten rune messages from their respective male partners. They were terrified that it was some kind of Eosian trick.

"Is your com link strong enough for direct contact with Catten?" Kris asked, thoroughly fed up with these antics. "Then call . . . High Emassi Nitin and have him confirm your orders to Milista. She's the one who has to be convinced."

Milista said nothing when High Emassi Nitin, annoyed at being interrupted and taken out of an important government meeting to reassure his mate, gave her what had to be a tongue-lashing. She blanched almost ecru and began to bow apologetically, her bows getting lower and lower to exhibit her willingness to comply. She said several short, sharp, low-voiced phrases to the other women which Kris thought she must have misinterpreted. Did Catteni women know such language?

As soon as they were boarded and being led to their quarters by obsequious junior ranks, Kris signalled to her companions that their duty was done. Perhaps Zainal had made it home while she'd had to dally here with the wretched ungracious Catteni females.

The captain, however, paused, looking out over the valley, once again tranquil, despite bits and pieces dropped or discarded en route to the cruiser ramp.

"I do not think the females will have appreciated the beauty of this valley," he surprised her by saying. He sighed. "But I would. Good-bye, Excellent Lady Emassi Kris."

They exchanged bows, she keeping hers to the shallow dip that indicated the difference in their ranks. Then she went down the ramp. Maybe the Farmers had used the valleys as vacation spots for corporeal enjoyments. That wasn't such a wild notion. Raisha was circling above in the KDL because there wasn't room enough for two ships to land without knocking down either the houses or the lodge-pole groves. The cruiser lifted over the retaining wall and discreetly sped up, allowing the other ship to land. That was when Kris noticed that someone had painted new ID letters on its prow: BSS 2. Was Baby to be BSS 1? And where was Baby? Her momentary lapse into amusement at the newly styled ship quickly dissipated.

Once aboard the BSS 2, Kris sought refuge on the bridge while those who had come with her stopped at the mess hall for coffee and to unwind.

"He'll be here soon, Kris."

"Oh, yes," she said in a weary voice. Half of her did not believe she would ever see him again. The other half wondered what his rank of Excellent meant in terms of the work he'd now have to do. Would he take Bazil and Peran back to Catten with him, to be raised properly as young Catteni males were? "Nice touch, renaming the ship," she said after a moment and because she knew that she ought to make some reference to the alteration.

• • •

AS RAISHA PILOTED THE B S S 2 OVER THE HILL above the landing field, she had a clear view. No Baby perched there.

"When you get your hands on him, eh?" Raisha said, cocking her head at Kris, as if she'd known how much Kris hoped to find them there.

"You'd better believe it!" Now she was angry with Zainal for this unconscionably long delay. How could he keep her in such unending suspense? Did he have any idea of how she had suffered during his absence? Especially since the moment she had figured out that he was going to be the sacrificial lamb? That he would deliberately put himself in the ultimate danger as the only way of gaining admittance to the Mentat Ix?

Raisha landed the ship and did all the after-flight checks.

"It can stay out tonight: the visible confirmation of our change of status. Frankly, Kris, I'm exhausted after so much good news and emotion and all that wearying ceremony. Aren't you, Excellent Lady Emassi?" She turned one of the shoulder tabs on Kris's shoulder. "Those are really fine diamonds."

Kris was as tired, too, weary beyond belief. Raisha had gone down the passageway and seemed to be gathering up the others for their voices drifted away.

She heard steps. Someone was coming to get her so she ought to go. Zane would be waiting for her to take him home. If she hadn't had him . . . She pushed herself out of the chair and had reached the passageway when she realized it was filled with a large . . . and familiar figure.

"I thought you'd never come out," Zainal said, "so I came in to get you. You can tell me off in privacy."

"Tell you off?" Kris inanely repeated his words, because she had to be sure that it was really him.

"Raisha said you were waiting to get your hands on me . . ."

"I am," and she threw them and her arms around his neck. "But if you ever go away like that again, I . . . I . . ." He closed her mouth with his, and they spent a long time like that. Until she had to come up for air, patting his face, his shoulders until she felt his muscles tense.

"You did, didn't you? You went as sacrifice, didn't you?" She pulled him into the better light of the cabin and saw the marks of suffering and starvation on his face: marks that only a keen and loving eye would now notice.

"It did the trick," and he smiled a little, his hands touching her hair, her face, brushing away the tears on her cheeks, "and that's all behind me. Behind us." Then he held her away from him, noticing the thickening of her body. He raised one eyebrow. "You gave me up for lost?"

"No, never! It's Chuck's, just like you wanted."

"On Catten?" He was astonished but smiling with pleasure. "Well, well."

"We were both legless, between hooch and whatever Chuck was given to drink by that field keeper. Promise me you won't ever be away again when I get drunk?" she pleaded.

"I promise," he said solemnly, crossing his chest before he reached for her again.

"Just a moment." And she pushed away his hands, standing up very straight and tall, her expression suspicious. "Where do you fit into the new hierarchy of Catten, Excellent High Emassi Zainal?"

"Oh, Excellent is the title they decided to give useful foreigners. I dropped. I stay." And his yellow Catteni eyes glittered as he folded her into his arms. "How about you, Kris Bjornsen? Will you return to Earth?"

She shook her head. "I dropped. I stay."

* * *

IN FACT, ONLY A FEW RETURNED TO EARTH: some of the specialists stayed to help reconstruct their damaged home world. Most of those who went back did so to find what relatives remained alive and brought them back to Botany. Chuck Mitford brought back two cousins, a scarecrow, and the repaired hammock that had been on his front porch the day the Catteni arrived.

Afterword

THE NEXT TIME A FARMER UNIT SCANNED Botany, it reported that the population had increased five-fold. A decision was reached since these newest, and un-expected, protégés had proved so innovative and independent. When the maintenance vehicle reached the planet, it lifted not only the food that had been harvested on its cultivated continents but also all the equipment, vacating their premises to allow the indigenous population to expand as populations had a habit of doing.

An unusual species had done well, and they could devote their attentions where similar discreet and carefully limited assistance was required.

DENISE VITOLA

MANJINN MOON   0-441-00521-7/$5.99

Ty is a twenty-first-century detective on an Earth choked with corruption, violence and greed. When she investigates the deaths of three intelligence agents, she uncovers an assassin with strange powers and deadly cunning: the Manjinn.

Now she must rescue the man she loves from the grip of an enemy more dangerous and terrifying than any she has met.

OPALITE MOON   0-441-00465-2/$5.99

Winter grips District One like a steel fist. Even the most basic resources are stretched to the breaking point. And Ty Merrick, weathering the psychological ravages of her lycanthropy, is busy. Three members of a secret sect—known as the Opalite—have been murdered.

Now, under the suspicious eyes of the government, Ty must venture into the frozen fringes of a bankrupt society where the Opalite keeps its secrets. Where the natural and supernatural collide. Where only a lycanthrope would feel at home...

QUANTUM MOON   0-441-00357-5/$5.99

In the mid-twenty-first-century, the world as we know it no longer exists. The United World Government—with its endless rules and regulations—holds an iron fist over the planet's diminished natural resources. But some things never change. Like greed. Corruption. And murder.